Behind The Mask

BEE DECLAN

BEE DECLAN

Behind the Mask

To the Bellamy's of the world: You are worthy of love.
To the Cyr's of the world: You are capable of being loved.

Contents

Foreword

Preface

My Lovely Readers:

Please note this novel contains explicit content that may not be suitable for people triggered by the abovementioned topics. The purpose of the explicit content is to shed light on the trauma some people face who feel the only way to cope is to lock it away. This book goes out to everyone who needs a gentle reminder that it's okay to not always be okay. Take care of your mental health first and foremost. Be easy on yourself, and don't be afraid to speak up. You're never alone.

National Suicide Prevention Lifeline:
  Dial 1-800-273-8255 or Dial 988

Crisis Text Line:
  Text HOME to 741741

SAMHSA (Substance Abuse and Mental Health Services Administration):
  Dial 1-800-626-4357

In cases of an emergency - call 911

Acknowledgement

To Elise and Brianna: Thank you for being such guiding lights for me over the years. For keeping me sane and always letting me know I have friends to turn to when I need it most. I love you both with all my heart.

To Holly: This book never would have reached this point if it weren't for you and your constant love and support. Your guidance is unmatched and I'm eternally thankful for you. I can't wait for all the stories we'll write together to become real.

To Jake: Your love and encouragement helped bring this book to life at every step of this process. To explain my gratitude to you would be longer than this book, so, in short, I appreciate the fuck out of you, forever and always.

To my parents: I'm grateful every single day for your unyielding support and couldn't be more thankful to have parents as wonderful and loving as you both. For the countless hours I spent hiding away writing this book, I've been striving to make you as proud as I am proud to be your daughter.

1

The Beginning

When I imagined moving to Boston, Massachusetts with two suitcases and a duffle bag strapped to my sides, I expected a warm welcome as I stepped off the train. But in comparison to the warm, welcoming breeze of my home back in Santa Fe, the chill wind of Boston is a harsh slap in the face. It bites through my thin cardigan and denim shorts painfully enough to bring regret to the forefront of my mind for not deciding to cover up more. September in New England, I quickly realized, already hit near-freezing temperatures, and I wasn't in New Mexico anymore, Toto.

By the time my flight touches down in Boston, I swear to myself that will be my first and last time flying on a plane, at least by myself. Being launched 30,000 feet into the air strapped inside a tin can reminded me of putting Mentos in a Coke bottle for fun as a child. The suspense, until the inevitable explosion, was humorous when I was 10, but the similar feeling of suspense while waiting for that tin can to finally combust created the longest four hours and twelve minutes of my life.

As I stand at the platform to the train station, it dawns on me that I have no idea what I'm doing as I have never ridden a train before either. Being a nineteen, soon-to-be twenty-year-old with no self-awareness on how to use public transport is quickly becoming overwhelmingly pathetic. Growing up a sheltered child had its pros, but certainly had its cons as well. Stepping out of my little bubble of bliss and naivety and out into a world very much unlike the one I'd grown accustomed to left me feeling inept. Like teaching a toddler how to rebuild a carburetor; unheard of and damn near impossible.

Further proof of my inexperience in life comes swiftly when attempting to navigate from Boston-Logan Airport to the Blue Line, then to the Green Line to board the C train then hop over to the B train which finally drops me off at the campus. After repeating the train order in my head for a solid fifteen minutes to make sure I didn't forget it, it might as well be tattooed on me. It's a never-ending hellscape, to say the least, and a good indicator that once I reach my dorm, I'm never leaving it for the sake of myself and everyone else in my immediate vicinity.

Between missing trains, hopping on the wrong train which sent me backtracking in the wrong direction, and achieving the grueling task of managing to have someone talk to me in hopes of receiving helpful directions was like pulling teeth. That particular voyage, which should take approximately twenty-five minutes, took the better part of 2 hours. At last, the sight of the campus in front of me tugs tears from my eyes and spills down my cheek, but that could also be the bitter wind making my eyes water.

The trees surrounding the campus are all beautiful shades of lingering greens transforming into oranges, reds, and yellows.

I have only ever seen trees like these in movies and paintings which I only hoped I would be able to capture on a canvas immediately. As I wander my way along through the courtyard, I can't help but take in every ounce of the mesmerizing scenery. However, I have to pull my attention away from the beckoning call of the trees and nature surrounding me to gaze at the map of the campus I had picked up from the administration building upon my arrival. My only lifeline in navigating the endless maze of buildings and pathways is tightly pinched between my fingers, turning my digits nearly white, as I roam from building to building, and hall to hall in all attempts to locate my dorm.

After an hour of navigating, which I determine will be utterly fruitless, I finally manage to find my way to the dorms of Upper Campus. I officially couldn't feel my shoulder from the thirty-pound duffle bag I swore was filled with bricks by mistake. Or my forearms, for that matter, from lugging my suitcases around Hell's half acre and back. When I see *#113* on the door ahead of me to my left, I sigh in relief.

"Fucking. Finally," I utter under my breath.

I sidestep and scooch myself along through the throng of other first-year students all moving into their dorms throughout the hall. The white-tiled floor below me absorbs the sound of hundreds of footsteps as students, friends, and parents all maneuver their way through the dormitory.

Seeing a handful of parents dropping boxes and suitcases off with their children tugs on my heart. I wished my parents could have been here to help me unpack and enjoy this branching-off moment with them, but it was an easier goodbye from the airport at home.

Pulling out my key card from my back pocket, I tap it against the lock and hear the door unlock with a soft *click*. Using my weight, mainly from the duffle bag, I shoulder the door open. As the door swings open, my eyes catch sight of a petite figure making her bed across the room. The girl turns toward me with a gorgeous smile that could make even the holiest of nuns perform the greatest of sins.

"Need a hand?"

To match that smile, an equally beautiful English accent leaves those glossy light pink lips.

It takes a few moments for me to realize my mouth is gaping open like a God's damned dog begging for a treat. Before I can snap my mouth shut, the girl laughs softly and approaches me to take the duffle bag from my shoulder.

"You're not mute are you?" The beautiful blonde questions, walking over and placing my bag on top of what will now be my bed for the foreseeable future. The way the blonde's hips sway like an ocean wave, and her ass- *Fucking hell. Use your words, Bellamy, for the love of the Gods.*

"N-no." Is all I could force out of my mouth, internally punching myself in the face, "And no, I don't have a stutter. It's just been a…" I exhale a long breath, "Long day."

The curvy blonde stands before me, and I try my damnedest not to look her over, fixating my gaze on the girl's shining hazel eyes.

"My name is Bellamy. Bellamy Tyler."

The girl smiles once again, the dimples appearing in both of her freckle-lined cheeks making my knees wobble, but I recover before I tumble to the ground.

"Jamie. It's a pleasure, Bellamy."

Holy shit.

I want nothing more than to have my name on Jamie's lips in multiple different positions and scream aloud in a few different octaves.

***

After a few hours of unpacking, Jamie and I sit on our respective beds, plates of Chinese food on each of our laps. After my day of traveling and unloading my bags, doing absolutely nothing but munching on food definitely outside of my diet is completely worth the impending heartburn. I pop another piece of sweet and sour chicken into my mouth with a pair of chopsticks, then glance in the direction of Jamie across the room.

"So, why the United States? Of all places, Boston in particular?" I question the blonde sitting across from me who is currently slurping up lo mein like she hasn't eaten in days. A small part of me feels insanely weirded out by myself realizing I could watch her for hours and never grow tired of it. Watching the way her lips move and-

Yeah, Bellamy, not fucking creepy at all.

"After living everywhere, you find the places you've traveled the least the most intriguing." She sets down her chopsticks and plate to the right of her atop her pastel floral bedspread. Jamie grabs her phone, and fluidly slips off of her bed, "Care to go on an adventure?" Jamie's bright hazel eyes glimmer and I can't say no even if this 'adventure' meant jumping off a bridge. I nod, also grabbing my phone and room key before chasing Jamie out into the hall.

We walk side by side through the hallways of our dormitory. I casually glance from door to door down the long corridor as students continue to unpack. As per college traditions, it's common for first-year students to leave their doors open on the first day to introduce themselves to their dorm neighbors. Orientations begin the next day and even though this building is for art students, art takes on many forms and occupations. Therefore, many new people to meet along the way.

We pause occasionally as Jamie pops her head into a few dorms we pass to introduce herself to the other students. I've never been one to usually initiate first conversations, so I smile and wave as Jamie introduces me on my behalf. My eyes find themselves more invested in everything the blonde has to say than paying any heed to the new dorm neighbors I should be investing my attention into getting to know. But I couldn't look away from her no matter how hard I tried. Granted, I'm not trying overly hard, but there's something entrancing about the way she speaks and the kindness that emanates from her body like the effortless ebb and flow of ocean waves. As she says her goodbyes to our new friends and neighbors, we continue down the hall of dorms to an unknown destination.

"May I inquire as to where our adventure is taking us?"

"I'm thirsty and didn't want to walk to the mess hall on my own," Jamie replies, flashing me a friendly smile. I'm thirsty too and could think of a few ways Jamie could help me quench it.

Gods, you horny bitch, snap out of it!

Jamie gives her shoulders an innocent shrug, and we share a laugh. While my eyes are preoccupied with watching Jamie, my body collides and recoils against a body that shamelessly runs into me. After what felt like running into a brick wall, the boulder of a person sends me tumbling backward onto my ass in the middle of the hallway. A mumbled apology floats my way as fleeting as the person I ran into; more like who ran into *me*, rather. When I finally pull my feet back underneath me, Jamie's attention is drawn to the back of the brunette man's head who is currently walking in the opposite direction toward the stairwell.

"Now, *that* is why I moved to America," Jamie says exasperated as if the temperature of the building skyrocketed. I frown with a slight huff at Jamie's reply, looking back as he rounds the corner to head up the dormitory stairs. I didn't catch sight of his face, but for the brief moment he stood in front of me, he had towered over me by almost a foot, which wasn't hard with me barely reaching 5'5". As I bent down to brush some invisible dirt off my shorts, Jamie leans close to my ear as she softly says, "Men aren't the only reason why I came to the United States."

Jamie takes off in a sprint down the corridor toward the mess hall, shooting me a wink over her shoulder. With that realization, I attempt, with every ounce of my willpower, to not have my jaw hit the marbled tile floor below me. Summoning an ounce of courage and the will to finally chase after a new life, my feet take off carrying me down the hall toward the blonde, a wicked smile on my lips.

2

The Girl

SPRING

This girl is going to be the fucking death of me. This statement I know for a fact. Over the past seven months, I spend damn near every waking hour with Jamie. The girl never stops moving whether it be rollerskating around campus, or being the first to jump into a mosh pit at a concert. Don't get me wrong, I admire the girl's ambition and sense of adventure, but as to how she manages to stay this alive all the time is exhausting. I have never really found interest in much other than my easel and paint, yet Jamie pulls me by the collar out of my anti-social bubble; something that I would never be able to repay her for. But all the while, attempting to match her energetic nature has been damn near impossible without the use of multiple energy drinks over the course of an hour.

Thursday's are always dull for humanity, consisting solely of my art history class with a professor older than the history of time. Most people in the class are surprised the old man still knows how to function, let alone teach. As I exit the hall after class, heading back toward Upper Campus, I'm greeted by a smiling face and wavy blonde hair fluttering in the late spring breeze. There was never a time when the sight of Jamie didn't bring those somersaulting butterflies in my stomach up to my throat. She's an absolute vision to behold and it took me pinching myself from time to time to believe this wasn't all just in my head.

"I didn't think the old man would ever shut up," I call out sarcastically as my feet shuffle down the steps of the main building toward Jamie. The sound of her laugh sends goosebumps racing over my body.

"I told you not to take his class, but nope, you had to be as headstrong as ever." Jamie's accent floats across the courtyard toward me. I roll my eyes with a brief shake of my head in retort.

"I don't believe I asked for your opinion, lovebug." I shoot back as I walk up to Jamie and give her a peck on the cheek. Jamie pokes along the side of my ribs as I walk past the blonde. The two of us walk shoulder to shoulder, and I bump hips with Jamie, jostling her off-kilter for a step. Her playful expression from a moment before lessens into what shifts to sorrow. My smile turns to worry, and I take Jamie's hand, tugging her with me toward the shade of a nearby tree in the courtyard.

"Jamie? What's wrong?" Her fingertips graze the back of my hand resting over her cheek. My free hand brushing a strand of hair back and Jamie sniffles in an attempt to hold back tears.

"My parents…they won't let-" She pauses, a tear silently falling from her cheek and into my hand. I know the rest of what Jamie attempts to tell me, eliciting a sigh from my lips, dropping my hand from Jamie's cheek.

"They won't let me come home with you for Spring Break."

Jamie looks down, nods, and sniffles again in answer. A slight frown adorns my face, but I step toward Jamie and envelop the petite blonde in my arms. Jamie returns the embrace, wrapping her arms around my torso as she cries, staining my red and black flannel with tiny teardrops.

"It's alright, lovebug. I'll be right here waiting for you when you get back," I coo softly to Jamie, gently playing with her hair, and rubbing small circles into her lower back in consolation.

Jamie pulls back from my chest, wiping at her tear-streaked face, and shakes her head. "I just know they would love you if they gave you the chance…just like I do." Her voice breaks as she speaks, and my heart cracks open at the words.

The two of us have never been exclusive throughout the several months we have spent together, even though she's been the only one in my bed since I arrived, but Jamie stole every piece of my heart from the moment I walked into our dorm room. We never agreed to officially date out of fear from Jamie's parents being not too keen on same-sex relationships. I was content with that, but it still didn't stop me from falling for her with my heart, body, and soul. I was well aware that her parents weren't as progressive as my own, so their rejection of me on the spot wasn't too out of the blue, but the blow still stung nonetheless.

"I know. We just have to take the hard days as they come. Maybe one day they'll see the love we share." I flash Jamie a soft smile, leaning forward to plant a kiss on her forehead, "How about you and I partake in some day drinking?" Jamie smiles with a soft laugh, nodding to me happily.

"I'd love that. I have to make a quick stop first, but I'll meet you in the dorm in an hour." And with that said, Jamie reaches up to peck a quick kiss on my cheek before exiting the courtyard.

I stand beneath the tree which has only just begun to bloom again after a harsh winter and I find myself feeling one with the tree looming above me. A strong force attempted to knock it down and at the end of the battle, it still remains strong and willing to repeat the cycle without breaking.

***

I know two things and two things only at this exact moment: One, I'm beyond drunk for comprehensive thoughts, and two, the taste of Jamie's arousal on my lips sends me into a permanent state of euphoria. The gorgeous blonde with curves that put Aphrodite herself to shame drive me into the depths of insanity. Jamie's hips rock back and forth across my mouth in rhythmic bliss.

"Gods above, Bellamy."

Fuck. Yes.

The woman mounted above me could scream my name until all the stars in the universe turn to ash and I will never tire of hearing it. Jamie's thighs begin to quiver and I know she's close. Gods allow me to have this beautiful woman come all over my lips until my dying breath. I slowly drag my tongue through her rosy center, circling over her clit in tantalizing swirls. Jamie's moans and whimpers of pleasure drive me into sweet ecstasy. Just as I can feel Jamie's release coating my tongue, a weight lifts off of me, pulling me into a state of shock at the sudden shift.

Jamie swings her leg back off of me and crawls down the bed toward my waist. Before I can open my mouth to attempt a cohesive sentence, still in a dazed state that only this woman's body could do to me, Jamie cut in first.

"My turn, darling."

I couldn't find it in me to object as Jamie's sinful English lilt sends my head falling back onto the pillow beneath me. With an encouraging pat on my hips, I lift them up for Jamie to slip off my sweatpants and lacy black thong. The feeling of Jamie's lips grazing their way up my inner thighs nearly sends my eyes rolling into the back of my head. The sinful nips of Jamie's teeth against my skin have my body rocking in anticipation. Goosebumps spread across my skin at Jamie's wandering touch as her lips and fingers find the slick spot at the apex of my thighs. The blonde traces her fingertip around the most sensitive spot of my core before claiming the area with her mouth. A gasp leaves my lips at the bliss consuming my body with the movement. My hands make their way down to entangle themselves in the unruly blonde hair in front of me and give it the slightest of pulls. The moan that leaves Jamie rumbles across my clit, nearly sending me tumbling off the edge of sanity.

"Jamie...I-"

I'm cut off as she plunges two fingers inside my warm center, causing my grip on the blonde's hair to tighten. Her fingers twirl and prod inside of me, sending my body into a frenzy. Every single touch strikes a new heightened sense within me, and I swear my soul leaves my own body to observe the view from above us. Jamie's fingers pull out of me as I'm mere seconds away from combusting from the pleasure ripping through me. My dazed chocolate eyes meet hers which are dripping with sensuality and lust as my hand tangled in her hair drops back to my side.

Jamie smirks down at me as her body lifts from the bed, and the blonde positions herself above me to straddle my waist sideways. She holds my leg upright in the air for support as our bodies connect at our heated centers. My hand grips tightly onto Jamie's hip as she begins to rock her body against mine. The moan escaping Jamie's beautiful pink lips has me guiding her harder against our joined centers. Her grip on my leg tightens as the friction between the two of us continues to grow and grow. Our breathing becomes labored and quickens as the goddess above me finds her pace grinding against me. Jamie's release erupts from her in a series of moans and gasps, sending me over the edge soon after. Her exhausted body topples over on top of mine a few moments later, collapsing into a pile of entangled limbs and exasperated breathing.

Once our minds, bodies, and lungs return to normal, we slowly untangle our limbs from each other. Jamie's petite frame curls beside me with her head atop my chest. My fingers gently comb through her blonde waves, coaxing us both down from our highs. Her breaths are even once again as they match my own, her chest softly bobbing up and down. Jamie's soft snores bring a smile to my lips as I lean over to kiss the blonde's temple.

"Gods, I love you."

Even though I know Jamie is soundly asleep, I can't help but imagine feeling Jamie smile against my chest.

3

The Vacation

SUMMER

Finals flew by in a whirlwind of all-nighters studying, lots of sex, and enough booze to supply an entire battalion of soldiers. I sent a silent prayer to the Gods for giving me strength through all of it but especially thanked Jamie for sticking by my side through all the tears and emotional havoc. As a surprise for completing the year, my parents paid for a trip for both of us to fly to Santa Fe for the summer. Jamie was ecstatic upon hearing the news, one because she'd never been to New Mexico before and two, it warmed my heart that she'd also been so excited to meet my parents. It made my mind, body, and soul soar to bring the love of my life home to meet my parents as Jamie's parents still denied our relationship could be anything more than platonic.

After touching down in Santa Fe, my parents met us at the airport to take us back to their house. I sat in the backseat of my parent's car with Jamie's hand held in mine. My parents have been as supportive as any child could wish their parents to be when being Bisexual was an internal battle for so long.

***

"Bellamy! I've never seen anything so beautiful." Jamie gasped as she took in the scenery surrounding her at my favorite place in the whole world. Well, other than in between her legs. Bandelier Park was my place to escape when the world seemed too small and, with one look around, I felt like the whole world was in my hands. Nothing was impossible and there was so much in this world for me. All I had to do was reach out and take it.

"I have," I reply softly, coiling my arm around her lower back to snugly fit her hip against mine. Jamie's blush rises up her cheeks and she slaps my chest playfully. She wraps her arms around my torso while keeping her gaze fixated on the mountains surrounding us. The feeling of her warm body against mine with the summer winds whirling around us was a moment of bliss I wish would never end.

As the hours passed, we watched the sun turn from yellow to orange and red as if Michelangelo painted it himself across the horizon. We hiked through the mountains and as the sun finally fell below the peaks, we returned back to my parent's house for the night.

***

"Dinner's in the fridge for you both if you're hungry. Just pop it in the nuker when you're ready." My mother softly called from the living room without lifting her gaze from her small, heavily worn paperback book of Sudoku puzzles.

"Thanks, momma. We're going to take a quick shower first." I call to her as we head down the hall towards my bedroom.

"I put some fresh towels on your bed. Holler if you need anything else, sweetheart." My mothers sentiments always warmed my heart and I didn't know what I would do without her. I'd probably lose my head if it weren't for my mother to keep it screwed onto my shoulders.

Jamie walked into my bedroom, picked up one of the two towels, and handed it over to me, "I'll warm you up some food while you shower."

A slight frown graces my lips, "You're not joining me?" I ask quietly with a soft whine. Jamie laughs softly, shaking her head.

"With your parents down the hall? You must be mad." She squeals as I reach out and yank her to me by her hips. I dip my head down, and my lips graze over the sensitive part of her neck. She let out a soft moan as I gently suck on that skin, the sound of her pleasure sending me into euphoria.

"Mad as a fucking hatter, lovebug."

***

Over the course of an hour, I ravage her on the sink of the bathroom counter, again in the shower, and once more in my bedroom. I'm an addict and Jamie will forever be the drug I can't get enough of. Our bodies lay entangled, sprawled across my bed in a heap of jelly-like limbs and sweat-slicked hair.

"I hate to break it to you, lovebug…" My words float silently into the air as I glance down at the beautiful blonde lying atop my chest. Her green eyes flick up to me in curiosity, "We're going to have to shower again."

Jamie dramatically rolls her eyes.

"I'm going first this time."

***

Those three months of summer flew by in a flash. We spent the days hiking in the park, introducing Jamie to the beauty of Frito pie, and copious amounts of life-altering sex. I painted Jamie at least one hundred times and none of them justly captured her perfection.

From the time we landed in Santa Fe, it only felt like hours before my parents were dropping us back off at the airport to return to Boston. The goodbyes were bittersweet, but we promised we'd both be back for Thanksgiving in a few months time. After checking in our luggage, we boarded the plane for the short flight back home to Boston.

Home.

My true home is Santa Fe, but home was also where my heart is and my heart was sitting peacefully beside me with her head on my shoulder.

My home.

4

The Note

As the weeks turned into months, and months into a year, I couldn't complain about a single thing in my life. The classes are terrific, my professors are brilliant, and I've made some incredible friends along the way. And one smoking hot friend in particular who was previously curled up beside me only an hour ago. The beautiful blonde I couldn't take my eyes off of since the moment Jamie stepped into my life.

Were we dating?

Unfortunately not due to Jamie's parents' being extremely disapproving of their daughter having sex with another woman. I couldn't convince Jamie to let me speak personally to her parents about believing the two of us would make a great couple. She told me it would be a fruitless endeavor and to not waste my breath. My efforts were extensive to have her let me explain to them our relationship, but every time it was an instant and resounding no. So, I would be content with the fact that fuck buddies would be all I could have with the beautiful human who shared my bed.

Occasionally Jamie would have an extra period class, which was what pulled her from my grasp early this morning. My body protested against her shifting and wriggling out from under my arm at a time far too early to be awake. Jamie had been gone for about 2 hours and I knew her lecture would be over within the next hour, so now was the time for me to pop over to the grocery store. I promised Jamie we'd have a peaceful dinner tonight with just the two of us, a movie, and a bottle of wine since both of us had been stressed with finals before the break. We have rarely seen each other except for late at night when one of us comes home from a lecture or study session in the library. More times than not the night ends with a rough round of sex and then promptly passing the fuck out due to heavy exhaustion.

With a little extra effort this morning, I shimmy my way into my favorite skinny jeans and button up my red and black flannel over my sports bra. My hair is quickly yanked into a high ponytail and slip on my Chuck Taylor's before grabbing my keys, and heading out the door.

The trek back to the dorm is serene as I walk through the beautiful breezeway of the Upper Campus courtyard. Leaves from the trees across campus have mainly fallen from their branches, leaving them bare to the approaching winter elements. To prove a successful shopping excursion, I tightly hold the grocery bags of goodies and a bouquet of colorful flowers with my free hand. Surprisingly, I haven't heard from Jamie, so I can only assume she found her way to the library for a study session. The two of us will be leaving for my parent's house in two days, so every waking hour has been spent cramming for all our work until the last moment we can manage. I struggle to balance the grocery bags and flowers in one hand while pulling my room key from my back pocket to scan it against the door. After the familiar 'click' of the door opening, I shoulder lightly into the door. Before the door can open all the way, I have a brief feeling of panic that I can't place. Something is wrong. I can feel it.

Time stops. Frozen in space.

The world slows to a trickle. The bags of groceries slip from my fingers and the items tumble across the tiled floor. The bouquet drops a moment later; the petals break from their stems and litter the floor in a kaleidoscope of colors. All I can process at that moment is the pale, limp, and lifeless body in the middle of the dorm room floor. My legs refused to function as I slowly wobbled my way further into the dorm room. I fall to the ground beside the body, reaching toward that beautiful wavy blonde hair with a trembling hand. My mouth drops open to say her name…to call out for help…but nothing leaves my dried-out lips and cotton mouth. Those same lips I kissed just this morning, now purple and slightly gaped, and her skin bloodless and ghostly white. I couldn't breathe anymore. My lungs excruciatingly cave into my chest with each heartbeat.

My person.

My lover.

My best friend…gone.

I run a hand over Jamie's soft hair, shuddering a breath as I gaze into those lifeless once-hazel eyes which now are clouded in a milky shade of white. The sobs rush out of my lips all at once, but I can't hear any of it. The blood pounding through my ears clouds every thought as it eddies in and back out of my mind. It's blank. My whole world grows empty and silent. I've been gone only a few hours.

What went wrong?
What happened?
What had I done?
With no goodbye...

Out of the corner of my eye, a folded white note lay tucked into Jamie's cold hand. I tried to reach out to take the note but instead collapsed atop Jamie's chest, clutching onto the girl's light green blouse. As my trembling hand grazes over Jamie's hand containing the note, my blood boils and curdles then crashes into me like a fucking tidal wave. All at once, a scream rips through my throat loud enough to cleave the world in half.

5

The Breakdown

The world ceases to exist in my mind and nothing makes sense to me anymore. In an hour, my whole world came crumbling down like the walls of the Parthenon. The only thing I know for sure in this life is the love I shared with Jamie and that was all I needed. But now? Nothing was certain anymore.

Could I be certain this pain would pass?
Could I be certain Jamie leaving this world was my fault?
Could I be certain I would survive this heartbreak?
No.

Nothing in this world was written in the stars. Even though I swore my world would begin and eventually end with Jamie at my side. But that wouldn't be the case anymore. It ended with voice-shattering screams, blurred vision, and a note.

One. Single. Fucking. Note.

That's all she left me. After all that the two of us had gone through and done together over that year. Jamie summed up everything her final words wished to convey in one page. The number of words I wanted to tell Jamie right now would be longer than one of my final dissertations. However, I couldn't bring myself to open that one page. It sat in the top drawer of my nightstand back home in Santa Fe.

I traveled back home to New Mexico for Thanksgiving as planned, only without my plus one. I couldn't stand to be in that dorm room any longer as the police continued their investigation into what happened. I snatched the note before the cops could get their hands on it, and didn't tell anyone there was a note. It was left for me and only me, as I told myself. Even Jamie's parents reached out to me in hopes of finding some sort of information about what happened to their daughter.

I have yet to respond.

They didn't deserve to know what happened to Jamie. Was it selfish of me?

Yes.

Did I care?

Not at all.

Hell, they could be part of the reason why Jamie took her life. They denied their daughter to live the life she wanted with the woman she loved, and the pressure of it all could have been too much for Jamie. I only wished she could have been open and honest with me that she was struggling so much as to think that taking her own life was the only option.

It broke me. I couldn't understand no matter how many times I attempted to justify the situation to myself, but no. It would never be explained. I missed my best friend, my lover, and my confidant. But clearly, I wasn't the confidant to Jamie as I presumed I was. Was I not there for Jamie as much as I thought? Was this all my fault? I wouldn't know until I read the damned note, but I couldn't. Not right now. Maybe tomorrow? Next week? Next year? Only time would tell.

***

In the spirit of Thanksgiving, I spent the week mulling about anything and everything that had possibly gone wrong in my life. Stealing a candy bar from a classmate in first grade. Punching a bully in the nose for picking on me in fifth grade. Failing my first math test in my Sophomore year of high school. Being told I deserved what came to me for dressing like a slut my Senior year in high school. Letting myself believe I was the reason that Jamie…

Stop it, Bellamy. Just stop with the fucking pity party.

I would be catching my flight back to Boston tomorrow, and I didn't think I would be ready to look at Jamie's things in our dorm room. I wondered if it had all been cleared out. If her parents had already come and taken all of her belongings back to England along with their daughter's body.

The police reached out to me yesterday and released the information on Jamie's cause of death as the coroner was permitted by Jamie's parents. They wouldn't allow Jamie to be happy and live her life with me, but they would allow me to know how my lover killed herself. What a cruel fucking world this was. It was revealed to be an overdose of Jamie's over-the-counter medications and excessive amounts of alcohol in her system. She passed out from the medication and the mix of the alcohol levels in her bloodstream sent her off into a state of permanent sleep.

The results sent me into a frenzy and I wanted to rip the note to shreds. I stared at the folded letter in my hands, shaking with the rage that consumed my entire mind, body, and soul.

Why did you leave me? What the fuck did I do to deserve this, Jamie?

The weight of it all dropped me to my knees, curling into

myself, and I let the screams and sobs tear through me like a tornado. Within the span of a few breaths, the arms of my mother wrapped around me.

"Breathe, sweetheart, breathe."

That was the last thing I could physically do. My mother saw the note clutched in my hand and pulled it away to set it on the nightstand beside my bed. I sat up and looked into the light chocolate brown eyes of my mother, the eyes I also possessed, which were as glossy with tears as my own.

"Momma…why?" My broken voice whispered to my mother, and she only held my cheeks tighter in her hands. She wiped away my tears with a gentle caress of my cheeks.

"Love does questionable things to people, even if we don't understand their reasons," My mother coos into my ear and lovingly runs her hand through my hair reassuringly. Sobs continue to wrack my body as I attempt to think of any reason why Jamie leaving me makes any sense. Thankfully my mother rushes to the rescue in time before I spiral too far into my own thoughts, cradling, and rocking me like a toddler for the next several hours.

***

I abruptly woke from my fitful slumber laying in my bed, still wearing the clothes from the day before, and drenched in terror sweat. I didn't know how I managed to get myself into bed but realized my mother must have coaxed me into my bed during the crying and screaming fits earlier. I couldn't remember how to function without crying or having a hissy fit, and I needed to kick that shit to the curb damn quick. For the sake of my parents, especially my mom throughout the grieving process, but also for the sake of my own disintegrating sanity.

My throat felt raw and I knew my voice would be gone for the next several hours. The screaming never stopped some nights, keeping my parents awake and in the sitting room beside my bedroom should I need an intervention from the persistent nightmares. There was no use in trying to sleep again as I peered over at my phone, the bright light of my screen showing 5:30 am. I knew I needed to pack before the flight, which would be leaving with or without me, heading back to Boston.

Classes would start back up tomorrow, and even though my professors gave me an extension to finish up my finals, I wouldn't be emotionally prepared to face any of my work for the Gods only knew how long. My mother told me time and time again that all would be well, and time alone would heal the pains I'd gone through. I tried my best to believe my mother's words that everything would be okay, but it didn't look like it to me.

Negative. Fucking. Nancy.

I groaned, eliciting a hiss of pain that came from my raw throat and crawled from my bed, peeling off the day-old clothes. I slowly poked through my dresser next to my bed for a pair of leggings and an oversized sweater to fight off the lingering chill in the air. After slipping them on, I groggily roamed around the room collecting the things that I needed to pack in my suitcase. It took me much longer than usual to pack as I began to fold clothes, cried, ripped them out when they didn't fit in my suitcase, cried some more, rubbed my eyes raw, and then started the process over again.

***

8 Months Ago

"Oh, darling, you look absolutely precious," Jamie chirped from where she sat perched on the edge of my bed and looked through a photo album of my childhood. Another album like hers lay across my lap and my eyes glanced up at her to take in every inch of her frame.

The black knee-high socks she wore swung back and forth a few inches above the ground. Her laugh was soft and breathy and urged me to take her here and now on my bed with my parents in the adjacent room.

But I didn't care.

I didn't care about anything in the cosmos as my gaze landed on the beautiful blonde I'd sworn my heart to since the moment my eyes landed on her. The over-sized *Breaking Benjamin* hoodie that adorned her petite body covered just enough to shield my sight from the lacy undergarments I knew she was wearing. From the angle where I sat on my bedroom floor, I could almost make out the black lace spiderweb design, but her leg crossed over at the knee when she realized where my gaze was focused.

"And you look delicious," I murmured, and slowly brought my heated gaze from the direction of her panties up to Jamie's eyes. Jamie rolled her eyes dramatically.

"You've ravished my entire body twice today already, there's no possible way you're still hungry."

Oh, I beg to fucking differ.

I tossed the photo album from my lap onto the rug in the middle of the floor before I crawled over to kneel in front of Jamie. My body wedged itself toward her center which forced her legs to part to allow my entrance. Her smirk grew as she watched me climb in between her legs and my hands coiled around her hips.

"As much as I love you in this hoodie, I'm gonna have to rip it off of you," I whispered in her ear and she trembled beneath my fingertips as they slipped under the hoodie to lock around the waistband of her panties, "Where'd you get this anyway?"

Jamie shrugged in response, "I stole it from a friend, so you can't rip it off. But you can take it off."

Before she could speak again, I obliged her non-explicit request and stripped the hoodie from her with ease. Being knelt before Jamie was one of the most incredible places I would ever be in my entire life. All thoughts of life and matters outside of this bedroom flew from my mind as Jamie's lips collided with mine.

***

But that was past. I'm plagued with the harsh reality that Jamie isn't in front of me with her soft, plush lips crashing against mine. Her delicate, graceful hands ran through my hair. Her curves send my body ablaze as it aligns with mine.

Instead, I'm alone.

I'm alone in a cold bedroom in which her presence has been long since gone. As I kneel in front of my destroyed suitcase and the array of clothes surrounding me, I bury my face and curse the world for taking Jamie from me. The stream of tears and cries breaks loose from my body as I cradle her *Breaking Benjamin* hoodie in my arms.

Around Noon, the suitcase was finally packed, and my father took my bags and put them into the trunk of his car. Being an only child had its downfalls; the coddling, the babying, the constant incessant worrying by my mother every minute of the day that I wasn't within an arm's length of the woman. However, their love and support were astounding and were more than a daughter could ever ask for in a lifetime.

When the time came for me to head to the airport, my mother embraced me tightly. She had cried as most mothers would, and I cried along with her. My mother and I shared such a strong bond since birth.

"You have your ticket?"

"Yes, momma."

"Your phone and wallet?"

"Of course, momma."

"And your-"

I finally had to cut off my mother by placing my hands on my mother's shoulders, "Momma, I've got everything I need. Trust me."

My mother's eyes began to gloss over again, and I tried with every fiber of my being to hold back the waterworks. She reached up to brush a stray lock of my glossy black hair, the same dark hair I inherited from my mother, back behind my ear and caressed my cheek.

"Call me as soon as you land, sweetheart. If you need me to come to get you and bring you home, I'll be there in a flash."

I was grateful for such accepting parents, and right now more than ever, I regretted moving so far away for college. But there were things I needed to sort out in my life, and being on my own might help me focus on sorting out my priorities and issues.

"I'll be okay. I promise." I waved my mother goodbye and my father drove me to the airport. Once we reached the airport, my father decided to bid me goodbye at the departure gate of the airport. When I faced my father, he just gave his daughter a tight hug. Not being a man of many words, his embrace and the tap of his index finger on my forehead, the action vocalized everything he wished to say.

"I love you, and I'll always be right here."

I would always be a daddy's girl, and it broke my heart even more to say goodbye to him, but knew he'd be in the car on his way to Boston at the drop of a hat should I need him. After I said my goodbyes, I took my bags and headed toward my terminal which would take me on the longest flight of my life. The flight that would take me back to the home of my fears and looming dread. If I managed to survive the following weeks, I would be astounded.

6

The Recovery

To say the road to recovery over the following six months has been a hard journey for me would be the understatement of the century. My first worry was having to return to my dorm and live with the looming shadows of Jamie. The next concern was falling into ruts of contemplating whether or not to exist, but regardless, most nights I found myself at the bottom of a whiskey bottle instead. After the first few weeks of moving dorm rooms, and adjusting to my new life without her beside me, things began to fall into place.

Thankfully the school granted me a new dorm selection and roommate to carry out the rest of my college career. Clara Brookhaven, a fellow studio art major, quickly became my new best friend and greatest support system, minus my parents. With the help of Clara, I managed to finish my finals in December before the end of the semester with passing grades all around. I couldn't have asked for anything more as I still coped with the trauma and all that happened.

Finding your lover lifeless in your bedroom isn't a great way to start the holiday season. I didn't believe that a love like that would come around again, and in all honesty, I'd be okay with it. The amount of love and abundance of beauty shown to me in that year I spent with Jamie would be something I would take to my grave. Therefore accepting I wouldn't have that again, and it was enough to last me a lifetime.

May had come around a lot quicker than expected, and finals were finished for the year. The plan was to go home for the summer, do some painting, and get a side job for a few months before classes started back up in September. However, those plans were swiftly thrown in the trash.

As I pack away my clothes into my large suitcase, I hear the familiar 'click' as our dorm room door opens. Clara skips into the room being her usual chipper self and smiles as she bolts over to me. In turn, I brace myself for impact as Clara boulders into my torso and wraps her slender arms around me.

"Bell, Bell, Bell!" Clara shrieks as the two of us topple over onto my bed. We laugh together, and I can't help but shake my head at her.

"Damn girl, where's the fire?"

Clara rolls her eyes at me and looks over toward my half-packed suitcase.

"That better be a bunch of bikinis and the sluttiest dresses you own." The comment has me sitting up, looking over my shoulder and down at Clara with an eyebrow raised.

"Uh-what? What are you talking about?" Clara scooches off of my bed and rummages through the suitcase.

"We're going to Florida, baby!" My eyes widen to the size of saucers at my best friend's reply and my jaw nearly falls to the floor.

"Clara I-I don't have the money for that."

"Don't worry about anything, consider it a gift from my parents." If my jaw hadn't hit the floor yet, it officially did at that moment.

"You're joking, right? That's so much money." The words stumble out of my mouth, sheepishly brushing my hair back from out of my face. My eyes lock with Clara's and my deviously clever roommate gives me a winning smile.

"I want you to enjoy your summer break, babe." Clara walks over and wraps her arms around me in a tight loving embrace as my best friend always does. I willingly return the hug, nearly brought to tears by the gesture from Clara's parents. I'd only met them once before, and they seemed like lovely people, but this is nearly too extreme of a gift to accept.

"And before you even think about saying 'no' like I know you're contemplating right now, don't bother. Your ticket is already booked and we're flying out tonight." Clara beams at me and the surprise plastered across my face must have been purely comical from the laugh that echoes through the dorm from Clara. The idea of saying no to a trip that I knew would grant me a distraction and a new start to my life wasn't possible.

"Re-pack your bags, Bell. The best summer of your fucking life begins today!"

***

Clara was right, as usual. Those next three months would be some of the best months of my life. Drinking margaritas until my heart was content, fucking everything and anything that breathed, and getting enough tan lines to make my mother pray to the Gods I didn't get skin cancer.

But I didn't give a single fuck.

I embraced my newfound freedom and lightness in my soul and decided to spread those wings and take a chance on a once-in-a-lifetime adventure. Clara, as well as a few friends from my art sculpting class who joined us in the Florida vacation of a lifetime, drank, partied, and danced until none of us could remember our names.

This is my time to be alive and embrace it. So I did. I embraced every second of it. This would be a fresh start to a new year and a new life for myself. By the grace of the Gods themselves, one night at a bonfire down on the beach watching a game of drunken volleyball, I found myself in the lap of Tobias Sheppard—a fellow Boston College student who was also in Florida for the summer. Tobias was studying finance but happened to be staying in Upper Campus in the art dorms due to his previous roommate graduating and a student in the art dorms needing a new roommate.

"Hey hot stuff, where do you think you're going?" The slightly slurred words of Tobias came as his fingers embedded themselves harder into my bare hips. I'd been sitting on his lap at the beach for an hour and my legs were falling asleep, so I decided to go out to the main strip for some drinks. However, my plans were halted by the vice-like grip Tobias held on me. I smirked, leaned in, and nipped his bottom lip with my teeth.

"I'm losing my buzz, so I'm getting us another round. Unless you'd care to find a quiet spot along the water with me to occupy our time." My fingers danced through his light copper-colored hair and pulled him toward me for a chaste kiss. In his drunken state, Tobias welcomed the kiss and continued straight down from my lips, across my neck, and down to my collarbone, nipping and sucking along the way down.

"Get a room!" A couple of their friends called out, and the two laughed. I artfully flipped them off before standing and pulled Tobias with me to find us a 'room' for the time being.

***

We spent the rest of the summer finding every private corner imaginable and exploring the nightlife together—nothing serious, of course, as I knew better than to tie myself down like that. Besides, I wasn't in the head space for it, but I needed fun like this to break myself from the old memories. Those 12 weeks came and went like the breeze off the waves, ebbing back into the ocean from whence it came.

Clara, Tobias, and our group of friends all headed back to Boston a few days before classes commenced to re-acclimate ourselves to the frigid New England weather. Which, unfortunately, meant ditching our bikinis and swim trunks for wool sweaters and long johns. The days became surprisingly easier being back in the dorms. I assumed I'd be begging for Clara to take me back to the beach and forget this place existed, but it was instead the contrary. Watching the colors change on the trees in the courtyards around campus from greens to oranges and reds during this time of the year was something I never realized how much I would miss during our time in Florida.

Once classes began again, the grind started, and I focused my time on studying. However, I made sure to prioritize quality time with my friends who truly got me through everything. Along with studying and my friends, I made sure to call my mom every Sunday to check in and to tell my parents that I love them. It was a scheduled event that I never missed no matter what. This year would begin a year of taking time for myself enjoying every second of life I was granted, and never saying no to a new adventure.

And so, my new journey of life began again.

7

The Accountant

I wish just once he'd go down on me for a fucking change. My tongue is drier than the Sahara and my jaw begins to click now and again. I should probably go get that checked out. The farthest reaches of my mind swore he was so much better at sex in Florida.

What changed between there and here?

More booze was in order, to say the least.

Tobias is good company…well, sort of good company. However, he focuses more on his classes and banging the next girl who takes even the slightest interest in him. I didn't care he slept around; it's not like the two of us are exclusive, even though Tobias eluded to me as his and only his. That simply wasn't true. The truth hit me that I really didn't care to sleep around because I had Tobias to share my bed with, and whenever I wasn't with him, my focus was on my classes and excelling beautifully. I am as happily content as I have ever been.

Tobias plays the role of fuck buddy, kind-of-boyfriend-ish very nicely. The boy comes from old money and doesn't mind dishing out a hearty amount of money to take me out to a nice dinner in the heart of Boston. The dates are mostly to play dress-up and look his best for any pair of twinkling eyes and easily-opened legs, but I consistently scored on the deal. I've never paid for a single meal, even upon my insistence, it doesn't work. Tobias dutifully plays the doting boyfriend, and in turn, I happily play along.

I've never cared that Tobias is a fuck boy through and through since by the end of the day, it's my bed that Tobias crawls into -almost- every night. The security he brings to me helps keep the nightmares at bay, well, some of the time. They never indeed went away, but remembering I'm not alone when he shifts around or snores loud enough to jolt me awake, brings a bit of peace to not be alone in the darkness.

"Fuck, Bellamy, yes."

I've been listening to those three words for 10 minutes and I'm about to call it quits if he doesn't switch shit up, or he comes in the next 15 seconds. Finally, as if the Gods answered my prayers, he guides my mouth up off of him and onto my back. Well, at least it's a new position, not a very exciting one, but it's something. My eyes glance up at Tobias as he plants himself over me, teasing my entrance with his cock in his hand. I wait...and wait some more...

What the fuck is taking so long? Is he...oh my Gods.

He pumps his cock for a few seconds in his fist before finishing across my lower stomach, and then he slumps to the bed at my side.

"Did I do something wrong?" I ask, still a little dumbfounded, staring up at the beige ceiling. A faint noise starts to play, and before I can pick up on what it is, he starts laughing. My arms lift to quickly prop myself up on my elbows to death glare at him at my side. He's watching comedy videos on his phone.

Un-fucking-believable.

His boxers are already back on and I shake my head in disbelief since I didn't even feel him wriggle around to slip them on.

"Tobi. Earth to Tobias." My voice raises loud enough for him to hear over his phone, raising an eyebrow at him. He looks over at me heavily annoyed for disrupting him, shrugging his shoulders.

"What? It's your room, you should know where your towels are by now. Go shower."

I scoff, gesturing to my stomach, "What the fuck was this about? You'd been begging me since lunch to hurry up and get back to the dorm. So I threw out half my lunch for *this*?"

Tobias now scoffs in response, returning his attention to the video on his phone.

"I didn't feel like putting a condom on. Besides, I was doing you a favor. If you finished the other half of your sandwich at lunch, your jacket wouldn't have zipped up. So, you're welcome."

I'm officially fucking done with today.

My patience is well more than spent and as I let the scalding hot water pound into my shoulders and back, I wrap my arms around myself in the middle of the shower. I keep reminding myself that I didn't care how good, or terrible, the sex was because it didn't matter. My classes are the most important right now in my life and I shouldn't be caring so much about shitty sex. Tobias isn't the man I would spend forever with by any means, and he will be expendable to me sometime in the future. But there is still something in my chest that wants to keep him near me for some strange reason I can't quite place. I chalk it up to not wanting to be alone, as lame as that sounds.

I shake my head, tilting it back to let the water rain down on my head, over my face, and down my dark raven hair that reaches down nearly to my ass. I take a few moments to draw in a few deep breaths. Inhale…1, 2, 3, 4, 5. Exhale…5, 4, 3, 2, 1. And the motions repeated for several more minutes, clearing my mind into a positive head space.

Just as I turn off the water to the shower, I hear a knock at my dorm room door. There was muffled speaking from the front door for a moment, but I couldn't place the other voice outside of Tobias, but it wasn't female. I snatch my nearby towel and wrap the towel around my torso, trying to dry off to see what is going on outside. Tobias calls out, "I'm going out. I'll be back tonight. Don't call me."

And that was that.

My dorm room door slams shut before I can fully wrap the towel around me and open the en-suite bathroom door. Stepping out of the bathroom, I sigh at the ceiling before walking over to my bed and falling onto it with the grace of an elephant.

Clara went to stay with a friend for a few days off campus, so Tobias has been crashing in our dorm room over the past few nights. He also never wants me in his dorm while his roommate is home for some reason. I don't even know who his roommate is, let alone why Tobias would want to keep me away from him. Unless it hurt his fragile ego too much that his roommate is possibly more attractive than himself, but I didn't care either way. As long as I didn't have to spend the night trying to get through the nightmarish shadows lingering in the dark corners of the room by myself, I'd be content. Even with him there on occasion, I still awoke screaming bloody murder, gripping the sides of my head and telling the demons at the gates to not-so-politely fuck off from whence they came. It pissed him off to be woken up so abruptly, and I apologized for it each time, but I would usually be back on his good side after a makeup blowjob.

Contrary to his statement earlier that day, Tobias didn't come back to the dorm that night. I check my phone and see videos on my social media from friends going out to a party that night and I see Tobias all over the pages. Girls under both of his arms, tonguing one of them so hard it looked painful, and a beer in both hands. It should have stabbed into my heart seeing the person I slept with earlier that day looking the way he did, but the jealousy that should have been there refused to exist. I knew our relationship is strictly fuck buddies and the occasional date, and that is completely okay with me. The only thing I despised was the silence. I hated the silence that followed with Clara being away and Tobias not returning like he said he would. My efforts to stay awake have me attempting my best to exhaust myself for as long as I can stay awake. I sent a quick prayer to the Gods to allow me to fall asleep quickly and hopefully stay asleep, but my requests are usually sent to voicemail.

8

The Birthday Drink

Lights flash around the bar and the music blares so loudly that I can hear my heart beating out through my ears. Entirely confident I'd be at least half deaf by the end of the night. Well, considering it's already the next day, I'd be deaf sometime today. The time on my phone shines up at me reading 1:15 am and no one in the entire bar shows any signs of stopping. It's my birthday, after all. Technically my birthday was yesterday considering the time is well on its way into the early morning, but fuck it. I'd drink until my heart was content and dance until my legs could no longer hold my drunken weight.

The big Two-Two and I couldn't have asked for a better night. Clara and some of my friends from our art class set up a surprise party for me at my favorite pub in the heart of downtown Boston. Of course, Tobias jumped in on the planning by paying for it to be an open bar for party goers throughout the night. A very generous bill it would be, but I doubt he cares in the slightest.

Tobias left me at one end of the bar for a petite blonde down at the other end of the bar a few hours ago and I'm certain they'd gone out to find a coat closet or backseat to fuck in. I thought it would bother me by now, but in honesty, I genuinely didn't care. There's an itching feeling that nags at my senses telling me that what Tobias is doing is wrong, but there's also something telling me to not give a fuck. So Tobias can go and fuck whoever he wants, but I know he'd be at my dorm later tonight because he couldn't stay away for too long without crawling back. Crawling because most nights when he came to my dorm past lights out, he was utterly trashed, and crawling ensured he wouldn't break his neck.

Pushing away the thoughts of Tobias fucking some chick in the bathroom, I'm about to order a drink when Clara orders one for me. I sit perched at the bar top, clad in my favorite red bodycon strapless dress, signature black leather jacket, and black Doc Martens with embroidered roses which in hindsight probably wasn't the best choice considering the blistering October weather. My legs swing at the bar stool as I happily sip my vodka cranberry from Clara and chat with a few friends who approach me throughout the night, buying me a few drinks, and laughing the night away.

Within a few minutes, my glass is drained and I push it over to the end of the bar for the bartender to pick up. A moment after I slide the glass over, a fresh glass of gin and tonic replaces the place of the empty glass. My eyebrow raises with a hint of confusion, eyeing the glass.

"I think this is for someone else, Jack."

I've had a few drinks already and was happily buzzed but still sober enough to compute that I hadn't ordered the drink that was placed in front of me.

Jack, the dirty-blonde bartender with eyes that could have

panties dropping in seconds, gives me a soft smile and nods, "That's yours, Bell. The gentleman across the bar bought it for you. He says 'Happy Birthday'."

I can't help as my lips turn up into a light smirk, glancing at the drink before spinning around toward the direction Jack gestures to. Then I see him.

He sits at a single-seated high-top counter nursing a beer. The only thing I can't place is why he dares to wear a black cotton mask and conceal that beautiful olive-tanned face peaking from the top of his mask. With the attempt of a discreet glance over a shoulder toward him, I catch sight of those icy blue eyes meeting my own. I attempt to keep my jaw from unhinging itself at the sight of his soul-shattering gaze alone; it bores into my soul and strips me bare.

I lift my glass with a devilish smirk toward the mysterious handsome man across the bar, and slowly his beer rises in reply. The butterflies rippling through my stomach and floating up into my chest have me nearly passing out. There's something about him, about that gaze, that pulls me in and tells me that I need to find out who he is and what's hiding behind that mask. Trying to hide my blush, I look down into my glass and take a generous sip from the glass before setting it back down on the bar top.

Grabbing the white square napkin and placing it over the top of the glass, I motion to Jack that I would be right back. I not-so-gracefully stand, pulling down my dress that rises up mid-thigh, and take a quick steadying breath. My boots echo across the tile floor as I make my way toward the table where the mystery man sits. Something in me screams to reach out to him, but my feet scream no, yanking me into a sharp right turn to head in the direction of the women's bathroom.

Moments later, I splash my face with cold water and blot the water away with a paper towel. Sighing, I shake my head and gaze up to meet my reflection looking back at me in the mirror.

What the hell was that about?!

"Bellamy?" My best friend calls into the bathroom and a second later I see Clara round the corner. A sigh of relief releases quickly from my lungs and I turn to hug my friend, Clara returning the embrace.

"Is everything okay?"

Grateful is a word I would use every single day for the rest of my life to describe my gratitude to Clara. The sweetest person I could ever have in my life right now caresses my cheek assessingly. I nod in response, smiling at Clara.

"This guy bought me a drink and I wanted to go talk to him…" Clara's eyes light up and her jaw gapes open.

"Oh my god, Bell! Did you go talk to him?" I shake my head and cover my embarrassed blush with my hands.

"No, I chickened out and practically ran here from across the bar." My words are muffled as I speak into my palms and pray to the Gods that my mystery man hadn't seen me attempt to talk to him. Clara pulls my hands from my red-hot face and looks me dead in the eyes.

"Who is he? Do you know him? Is he hot?" My cheeks flush even further at Clara's onslaught of questions.

"His eyes are so…blue."

Clara glares at me as if to say *'Are you fucking kidding? His eyes, really?'* so I quickly continue.

"He wore a mask, so I couldn't see his face, but there's something about him that I couldn't look away from him. He's…" I want to say *gorgeous*, but I don't know if that is the right word to describe the magnetic attraction I felt in just a few moments of his presence.

"Wait, mask? Black hair, bright blue eyes carved from Icelandic glaciers?"

Now it's my turn to gape, but I nod nonetheless. Glaciers. That was the perfect word to describe those eyes I'd fallen hundreds of years into in a matter of seconds.

"So…do you know him?"

"That's Cyr Maddox. Not many people have seen his face. Some say he got into a car accident or something and messed up his face so now he lives in that mask. No one gets to see him without his mask anymore." Clara explains, a look of pity crossing over her features for a brief moment, "The fact he bought you a drink is huge! I don't think he's dated anyone since being on campus. You should go talk to him!" Clara's the ultimate pep girl and my appreciation for her has grown so much more for it, but with the alcohol in my system, I can't quite say I'm ready to face him yet.

After a few more minutes of pep talks, Clara and I walk out of the bathroom and back over to the bar where Jack has been studiously watching my drink to make sure no one came close to it. I inhale deeply with a calming exhale before taking another sip of my G&T, and when I look back to where Cyr had been sitting, it is now an empty table.

He'd left. *Fuck.*

My cheeks flushed a dark crimson, hoping he didn't leave because he thought I wasn't interested. Well, after buying someone a drink and then rushing off out of sight is a pretty clear neon sign saying *'fuck off I'm not interested'*, but that was so incredibly far from the truth.

Around 3:30 am, I cling for dear life to my best friend for support in my drunken state. Surprisingly there are little to no catcalls sent our way as most of the foot traffic was gone for the night. Not to mention it being twenty degrees outside probably helped that case as well. I have never been the most egotistical person, but at this moment with my dress hugging all of my luxurious curves, I feel like hot shit and wanted every fucking person we passed to know it.

I send up a silent prayer, thanking the Gods for bringing Clara into my life to get my drunken ass a cab back to the campus. The two of us make good time back to the campus, considering the heavy traffic that still lingers throughout the Boston streets on an early Sunday morning. Clara, being the more sober of the two of us, manages to haul me back to our dorm room which is no small feat. She assists in a full strip down and I stumble into some PJ's before ungracefully collapsing into my bed.

I'd had an incredible night, even though I probably wouldn't remember a lot of it in the morning. One thing specifically comes to mind that I know for certain I'd already forgotten. The boy with the mask, that shaggy black hair, and those ice blue eyes that gaze straight through to your soul. Oh, Gods…What the fuck was his name?

Dammit, Bellamy. He was hot, too. Way to go and blow it.
I wished I could have blown him.
Whoa, where the hell did that come from?
That's the alcohol. Definitely, the alcohol talking.
Go to sleep, Bellamy. Maybe you'll remember him in the morning.
Sending that silent prayer to remember the name that rolled off my tongue like a curse and a promise, I drift fast asleep.

9

The Remembrance

The day grows colder, which is physically visible by the way my breath puffs out in plumes in front of me. I pull my leather jacket tighter around me while staring out across the Boston harbor. Thanksgiving is a few days away and I will be flying home tonight to spend the holidays with my family. Tobias already left for home this morning, not bothering to say goodbye before beginning his quick drive home. He would probably text me later tonight or within the next few days for a picture of my tits instead. I've grown used to no 'good morning beautiful' or 'goodnight sexy' texts from him, so it's no surprise to me that he'd left unannounced. But there was one person who would tell me that I was beautiful, who told me how sexy I was, but she wasn't here anymore.

Jamie left this world one year ago today.

In my soul I knew that I couldn't think of a better place to spend the day than at our favorite place to spend time alone together; the Waterfront Park on the edge of downtown Boston. The grassy hills overlooking the bay, the tunnel of love as Jamie would call it, and the numerous buskers who blessed the surrounding area with beautiful music were feats we both adored.

I haven't been to this park in the year since losing her and standing in the tunnel where the two of us shared our first kiss brings all the emotions tumbling back into me. My heart cracks, then mends itself from fond memories we shared. I knew that my heart wouldn't remain broken, but a piece of it went into the ground alongside the woman I loved. Jamie would always carry a piece of me with her for the rest of my existence, and forever after.

My feet aimlessly lead me along as I meander through the tunnel down to the end of the park. Numerous couples sit on the grassy hills snuggled up close together to warm each other against the bitter wind. There were days the two of us would do the same thing, bringing our blankets so we could sit and watch the world pass by in a hustle as we simply enjoyed each other's company.

By the time I reach the other end of the park where rows of benches face each other along the pathway, I could almost see the two of us curled up against each other. I remember sitting on one end of the bench with my favorite book in my hand, my arm being propped up by the bench armrest. The stunning blonde would lay longways across the bench with her head in my lap, one earbud in her ear listening to her latest murder mystery podcast.

A tear slips from my eye, falling down my wind-kissed cheek, and plummets to the ground at my feet. I brush the tear trail away from my cheek harshly with the sleeve of my jacket, quickly looking away from the bench, the memory fading away as Jamie did in front of my eyes.

Parts of me wish Jamie never existed so I wouldn't have to live with the constant pain of losing her. But then again, I wouldn't be who I am today without her coming into my life when she did. The moment when I was stressed beyond belief and couldn't find the right way to cope was when Jamie taught me to inhale and exhale, counting as I went. The times when I couldn't sleep, I could still feel Jamie's feather-soft fingers grazing through my hair, coaxing me to sleep as she would always do for me.

Even this morning as I showered and finished dressing for the day when I glanced into the mirror, I could see Jamie standing next to me with her head leaning on my shoulder. Always standing beside me for support, even in the afterlife, if there even was an afterlife. It could be me losing my mind and seeing figures walking around meant another medication for me to start. My antidepressants are doing the trick for the most part, but the day I start going all *Sixth Sense* and start seeing dead people…well, I'd cross that bridge when I come to it.

My walk is leisurely as I continue my stroll around the park, stopping at the brick wall that separates me from the icy waters of the bay below.

"Talk to me, Jamie. Help me to go on."

The bitter wind answers in reply and sweeps my dark hair back from my face to expose my features to the harsh weather surrounding me. My dark chocolate eyes stare out across the bay as the wind bites into my cheeks and turns them a shade of rose. The sound of the waves as they crash against each other fills the void in my head, and the rhythm of the waves calls to me. My eyes drift closed, and I inhale shakily before taking a step up onto the cement barrier of the water below.

"Join me."

The voice of Jamie fills each of my senses and a soft sob spills from my chapped lips, "Show me how, Jamie. Please. Help me."

When I open my eyes, the opaque figure of the woman I love stands in front of me with an outstretched hand.

"Just take a step, Bell. I'll be here to catch you."

The wind whips around me once again, causing me to sway on the barrier for a brief moment. The waves below grow harsher and splash up to coat my black boots in the bitter salt water.

"You promise?"

"I promise, darling. When have I ever lied to you?"

With a final deep breath, I lift my boot to hover in the open air. The icy, brutal water below would shock my system within seconds and I would be with my love once again in a matter of minutes.

"I'm coming, Jamie."

The words leave my lips in a whisper, and I tip my body forward. Only for a brief moment did I feel like I was falling, but instead, I fall backward. A yank on my leather jacket from behind me sends my body tumbling toward the sidewalk behind me. The blow is not the hard concrete I expected, but a soft body below me instead. My bloodshot eyes flutter open, tears falling down my cheeks as I attempt to come back to reality.

"What the fuck were you thinking?!"

The panic-stricken voice coming from my best friend sends me into hysteria. Clara rolls out from underneath my body to face me and grips my cheeks in her hands. The tears stream down Clara's rosy wind-bit cheeks as our eyes lock. My mouth opens, but no words release, my sobs overtaking each of my senses. Clara reaches out and pulls me to her as we sob together. She holds me tightly as I fight through my tears and emotions rupturing through my body.

"I just wanted it to be over." My throat manages to croak out through ragged breaths. My best friend runs a hand down my wind-tangled hair and attempts to coax me into relaxation, "I don't know what to do anymore." Clara picks me up by the shoulders and helps me to stand. I finally face her, my body weighing a thousand pounds and the pressure crushes my chest like an elephant, "I'm just so fucking tired, Clara."

"You're going to stand up straight, for starters." Clara stares me down, her voice calm but stern. I try my best to oblige, and Clara nods in encouragement. "Good. Then, you're going to take a deep breath."

The two of us pause, and deeply inhale together, holding for a moment, and exhale completely.

"Now, you're going to take life by the Gods damned balls, and make it your bitch." The statement has me shaking my head and I slump my shoulders, but Clara shakes me by the shoulders. "Listen to me!"

The bite in Clara's tone takes me by surprise, my body straightens back up once again.

"You can grieve as long as you need, but you need to see that this can't last forever. It will kill you, Bellamy, and I can't have that." Clara pulls me into her and holds me tight, "I will always be here for you, but I can't be there for you fully unless you talk to me, babe." Clara's voice cracks, and I try my hardest to keep from crying again. I embrace my friend and hold her close to me.

"I thought I could beat it. The need to be with her again, but she never leaves my head." I fight to get the words out, my throat closing up impossibly tight and Clara pulls away after a moment to wipe the tears from my cheeks.

"You're allowed to be sad but you can't fight every battle alone."

I nod knowing the truth in her words and Clara takes my

hands to hold them together in front of us.

"Promise me you'll come to me if you're feeling any doubts. The next time I come into this park, I don't want to be pulling you from the water as a corpse." I release a final tear and brush it off my cheek with my shoulder.

"I promise."

Clara releases my hands and wraps her arm around my back as the two of us walk side by side. My head rests on Clara's shoulder for support as we walk away from the raging water behind me and the ghost of Jamie who I knew was still reaching out for me.

***

Upon returning to our dorm, Clara and I sit on her bed with pints of ice cream and set up a movie on my laptop. We watch the movie in silence for some time, grieving the possible loss that could have happened today. We cry some more, finishing off our entire pints of ice cream, and then tell each other embarrassing stories of our childhoods.

"Don't tell Tobias, please. I don't want him to worry about me during his break." I meet the gaze of my best friend, to which Clara nods in reply.

"It's not my place to speak on it. He won't hear anything from me. Besides, if I don't have to ever talk to him, I'll be happy." My mouth gapes in surprise at my friend's comment and Clara cuts me off before I can speak, "You deserve so much better, Bell. He treats you like shit and you know it."

I sigh, standing up from Clara's bed to take our empty ice cream cartons over to toss them into the trash bin, "He treats me the way I should be treated."

The audible groan that comes from Clara behind me makes me spin around with a raised eyebrow.

"If that's what you believe then you're in even more denial than I thought." My eye roll is much more dramatic than anticipated as I walk over to my suitcase on my bed which lays open half-packed.

"I enjoy being around him, and I never pay for anything, so I can't complain. We can't all be Clara's and have every human falling at your feet, begging for you." I retort and flash Clara a smirk to which Clara shakes her head upon seeing.

"How about we all be Bellamy's who refuses to see her worth and denies herself a chance at enjoying life and some halfway-decent sex!" The two laugh and I pick up a shirt to fold before placing it neatly into my suitcase. I know Tobias will never be an endgame for me, but with my conflicted feelings about myself, and my life, he offers me the escape I need.

"I just want you to be happy, Bell. That's all I've ever wanted since the day I met you." Clara stands up from her bed and walks over to me. I turn and embrace my best friend, hugging her tightly.

"I love you, Clara."

"I love you too, Bell. Promise me you'll be safe during the break. I can't think about getting that phone call from your mom," Clara says softly, and I nod before pulling back from Clara to look at her.

"You saved my life, Clara. In more ways than one. You're stuck with me for eternity now." We laugh in unison and Clara helps me pack up the rest of my suitcase for my upcoming voyage back home.

Later that night, Clara drove me to Logan Airport to board my flight back home to Santa Fe. My best friend kisses me on the cheek and reminds me for the sixtieth time to call her as soon as I land to let her know that I made it home safe. I agreed, for the sixtieth time, and made my way into the airport terminal.

An hour later I was aboard my flight; destination: home. I only wished that this flight was made with my partner in crime by my side, just as I should have been with Jamie this time last year heading home to see my parents.

Some things simply aren't meant to be. Maybe some things aren't written in the stars after all.

10

The Mask

My first day of Spring Semester classes rolled around before I knew it. Christmas break came and went in a flash and now January signals the start of a new year. To heighten my excitement for the new semester, my first class is a new course in film photography. I'm more excited about this than any of my other courses for this semester since photography is the only course I haven't dabbled into before.

After gazing around the room I find a seat in the corner of the room by the professor's desk, setting my backpack on the floor by my feet. I reach into my backpack and pull out my notebook and a pen to jot down the professor's information she wrote on the whiteboard at the front of the room. After a few minutes of organizing my notes, I set down my pen and a tingling feeling in my stomach has my gaze looking up.

My stomach feels as if it's about to shoot up into my throat and the sensation of passing out hits me square in the chest. At that exact moment, I find myself face to face with glacier-blue eyes and a black cotton mask. Those glistening icy blue eyes track my every move and seem to call out my name when I'm certain he doesn't even know my name.

It's been three months since I first laid eyes on the mysterious man I came to find out is named Cyr Maddox. I didn't know if he even remembered who I was since it was a brief moment in time the two of us shared glances. In a very packed pub, with extremely loud music, and a girl who was too chicken to thank this man for buying me a drink. The only thing keeping my words at bay is that same black mask shielding his face from my view. The other thing halting my words is the simple fact that I have no idea what the hell to say to him.

Does he even remember me? Probably not. Just play stupid. Don't embarrass yourself by reminding him that you ran away from him to hide in the bathroom.

A soft smile slides across my cheeks as a way of greeting instead of words that I know I would without a doubt stumble over. I quickly avert my eyes back to my notebook until the professor begins to speak to the class. The woman at the front of the room who would be the Professor for the semester begins the class off with basic rules regarding the class and how the semester will go. I diligently take notes as the professor continues her regular introductory spiel, but every once in a while, I feel a familiar pair of eyes on me. I take a brief moment to glance up, locking eyes with Cyr across the table. In an attempt to hide the blush creeping up my cheeks, I return my focus to the notes on the table.

After about thirty minutes of introductions and instructions, all the students are released into the wild to start the day by taking pictures of the wildlife around campus. All the students are instructed to rent cameras from the campus bookstore if they do not have their own, so most students head to retrieve the required items from the campus bookstore. I, however, purchased my materials in advance, which meant I could get a head start roaming around campus in search of my next muse.

Due to unfortunate planning, I should have taken the class next semester. That way I could have saved myself from having to wander the campus when it was cold enough to turn Hell into a tundra. The trees lining the campus which were beautiful greens and oranges in the fall are now all leafless, and frozen, topped with icicles. I did, however, find a squirrel with a mouthful of nuts hopping along the pathways. I try my damnedest to stay quiet and concealed to snap a few photos of the critter along its journey. As the little squirrel finds its way to a tree nearby, I crouch down to snap a photo, aiming up my shot.

"Guess you're not a huge fan of G&T's?"

A velvety soft voice rings out in the quiet air next to me and the sound nearly sends me to the ground. The squirrel, hearing the commotion, takes off scurrying up the tree, and out of sight from the camera's shot. My groan is audible, watching my muse scamper away from me; gone like the wind. As I make my way back to standing, I growl into the open air. I shove my camera back into my bag as I glance over to see who stands beside me.

"I've been chasing that damn squirrel with his nuts in his mouth for forty-five minutes."

And at that moment, every thought that ever came into my head eddies away. I meet the hauntingly beautiful blue eyes belonging to Cyr Maddox, and blink slowly, bringing myself back to Earth.

"I-I'm sorry. What's G&T-" My heart stops cold in my chest. *Oh, Gods...gin and tonic. He did remember.*

A nervous laugh spills from my lips, glancing down at my shoes, "Oh, I actually love gin and tonics." I make a small circle with my boots in the remnants of snow in front of me on the ground. A light laugh that didn't quite seem humorous left those hidden lips.

"From the way you practically ran to the ladies' room would suggest otherwise." I close my eyes, sighing, and at that moment I want nothing more than to find the nearest hole and climb into it headfirst.

"I'd drank a lot that night and that last drink had already sent me over the edge. I'm surprised you noticed since you'd already left by the time I'd gotten back." I retort, glancing back up to meet his gaze. My knees almost buckle, but I recover before landing on my ass in the snow in front of the most gorgeous man I've ever seen. Never mind the fact I haven't seen the lower half of his face, the tanned skin I could glimpse, regardless of the blistering winter, and his voice alone could make me do things I'd thought I would never want to do again with anyone.

"I didn't plan on staying long. I just thought a pretty girl deserved a nice drink on her birthday," Cyr replies, eyeing me briefly with a quick up and down glance. I have never felt more naked in my entire life under his glacier blue gaze. My brain can't discern if his words are meant in a genuine tone, or if he's trying to be a creep. But those damn butterflies fluttering around in my stomach quickly turn into a full-on swarm that threatens to send my insides, outside onto the ground. There's no way in Hell Cyr is talking about me when he said 'pretty'. I refuse to believe that the man standing before me would even deign to glance at me for longer than necessary.

But I can't seem to take my eyes off of him. That is until I realize how intently I was staring at him that he bends down to me at eye level.

Gods, he's at least a foot taller than me. How the hell do people get to be that tall?!

"I should bend down to this height more often. That way you won't have to crane your neck to stare at me."

There is an underlayer to his tone that contains more of a bite than I was expecting. In that instant, I snap myself from my gawking stupor to see him as he seems to bore into my soul. I'm not here to play games and get distracted by a boy with pretty eyes and a shitty attitude.

"If you'll excuse me, I don't know about you, but I have work to do."

I reciprocate the bite in his tone from moments ago, shrugging past him in search of another animal to chase around the campus. As I walk by, I feel those eyes on me again. Instead of looking back at him, I put a little extra swing in my hips as I leave Cyr to himself in the middle of the frozen courtyard.

***

The rest of the day flies by me in a whirlwind of classes, instructions, and the first day of class homework to complete. This semester I decided to kick myself in the ass and work as hard as I physically can to make the Dean's List. It's not overly important, but it does look great on a transcript.

After my classes are completed for the day, I find myself sitting at a table in the mess hall with my computer. Clara asked to have the dorm to herself for the afternoon, and I obliged my best friend knowing it would give me some quiet time to get a head start on my assignments. As I munch on my potato chips, I feel the table shift and creak as someone sits down across from me. Without bothering to look up I groan audibly.

"This mess hall has one hundred empty tables. Care to acquire another?"

"Well, I sure as Hell can't annoy you from across the room

now can I?"

That God's damned voice.

I nearly choke on my chips as Cyr glances over to me from across the table. I take a quick sip from my water bottle to recover from the mishap. Taking a deep breath after barely avoiding choking to death, I bring my eyes up to meet Cyr's breathtaking gaze.

Quite literally, breath-taking.

"And to what do I owe the honor of this visit?"

I bring my attention back to my laptop in an attempt to look disinterested in anything he has to say. When in reality, he's the most intriguing man I've ever met. I can feel his eyes blazing into me even though I can't see those beautiful blue eyes directly. That velvet-soft voice pierces my ears and sends goosebumps across my skin which is, thankfully, concealed by my thick wool sweater.

"Am I not allowed to make small talk with a classmate?"

His voice is low with a hint of amusement. I can't help but let out a light laugh which is voidless of any humor.

"Oh, yeah. After you snuck up behind me and scared away my object of obsession from the past hour? I'll pass."

I type away on my laptop even though I have no clue what I'm writing about. My mind is completely blank of the topic on hand other than egging Cyr on as much as I can. The idea of trying to push his buttons to see when this guarded man will pop is my current topic of interest. Albeit a little cruel, but after his belittlement earlier this is quite enjoyable for me.

The table shifts under his weight as he adjusts somewhat uncomfortably, "Did I say something to upset you?"

My body feels cold as ice as the words leave his lips. I sigh and shut my laptop with a bit more frustration than I should have. As soon as the *slap* sounds of the laptop closing, a slight flinch comes from Cyr. My eyes widen and before I can react to the flinch, it's gone as if it never happened.

"Look, I think we got off on the wrong foot."

"Yeah, you could say that."

I cock an eyebrow and scoff, shaking my head, "Do you have an issue with me or something? Why did you come over to talk to me if you're just gonna act like a dick?"

As soon as the words leave my lips I regret the tone in which they come out. I attempt to speak and amend my words when Cyr cuts me off.

"I bought you a drink that night because I wanted to talk to you." His voice is soft, barely audible to anyone except me, "You can probably tell that talking is not my forte, but I wanted to try."

My mouth gapes ever so slightly as he speaks, "So why didn't you?"

Cyr shakes his head, refusing to meet my gaze, "I saw you run off and-" He sighs, trailing off and my heart breaks.

Fuck. He took my panicked scurry to the bathroom as disinterest after all.

Those glacier eyes flick up to meet mine, "I waited for you to come back."

"But you weren't there when-"

"I ran," he interjects. At that moment, I swear my heart stops entirely. "I wanted to say something, but when I saw you come back, I lost it. So I ran."

"Why? Am I really that scary?" I speak softly to not startle him from his thoughts. He glances up at me and I flash him a little smile to break the tension. A light chuckle leaves his chest and I can only hope it brings a smile to those olive-tanned cheeks concealed beneath his mask.

"Let's just say I haven't had the balls to buy a girl a drink in a long time."

His voice sounds sad and it strikes a cord in my heart that aches for him, and I barely even know him. I only hope that fact will change sooner rather than later.

"Hey…" I say softly, "Regardless of how the night turned out, you still bought me a drink, and it was a damn good gin and tonic."

"You sound like I made you the damn drink."

"No, but I'd never had one before. You gave me a new experience and I'm grateful for that because it's now my favorite drink. I never would have figured that out if it weren't for you."

My phone begins to vibrate in my pocket again, which I've been openly ignoring since Cyr sat down across from me. After several minutes of vibrating, I quickly pull out my phone to see a series of spam texts from Clara and I roll my eyes with a sigh.

"Sorry, I know you're busy." Cyr stands from the table and begins to turn away.

My eyes instantly shoot up, "No, no! I'm sorry, my roommate is just having one of her daily episodes." I sigh, cursing Clara for ruining this moment I didn't think I would have enjoyed so much.

He glances back in my direction over his shoulder, "Maybe I can buy you another one of those gin and tonics sometime?"

My heart feels like it's going to burst from my chest at the tender way his request floats across my mind. But then it's all ruined as Tobias crosses my mind. I couldn't turn Cyr down, every fiber of my being told me not to fuck this up.

"Maybe," is the only word I can think of. Not a direct yes, but not a definite no.

"I can work with maybe."
And as silently as he appeared, he was gone.

11

The Roommate

Throughout the following few weeks, I rise before the sun even crests the horizon pouring every ounce of knowledge into my art history notes. The librarian most likely believes I'm insane, although the frail old woman would never speak that thought aloud, and she doesn't have to. Even I would call myself insane in someone else's shoes. I've been preparing myself for this midterm exam which would be one of my largest hurdles of the semester and need to be on top of it to pass the course.

I also made an obligation to Clara for the number of times Clara found somewhere else to stay so Tobias could stay over in our dorm. In this case, Clara has a lovely girl over and I know it was only fair to make myself scarce for the time being. I'd be sure to text Clara later to check to make sure the coast was clear before heading back up to our dorm.

I'd spent the night in Tobias' dorm, much to his incessant whining objections since his roommate was home, but I hadn't even seen his roommate at all during the night. By the time I left this morning for the library, it was silent in the dorm, other than Tobias' snoring which was loud enough to wake the dead. I asked him last night who his roommate was and his response was '*Some weird fucking art kid*'. Which was a great help since we lived in the dorm building dedicated to art students. The topic was dropped knowing it would be a fruitless discussion, which would inevitably turn into a full-blown argument for no reason.

The argument would hypothetically begin with Tobias yelling about how he was once again stuck in the art dorms because the building with the finance students was full. Tobias's current roommate needed a new roommate, therefore, Tobias was pulled into the art dormitories to fill the vacancies. Rather than that particular argument, another ensued in its stead.

After an entire day spent slaving over assignments in the library, Clara sends me a text asking for one more night alone with her lady friend, to which I reply with a quick '*of course*', and give them their privacy. So I now find myself in the common area of Tobias's dorm room, toe to toe with him in a screaming match.

"I told you already that last night was an exception. You can't stay over again."

I'm officially up to my wit's end with his bullshit.

"Because you've already got another girl lined up for the night?" I taunt, placing my hands on my hips. His growl of warning has me inching my face closer to his in resistance.

"That's not fucking true," He snaps back in response. "I have a roommate and I don't want him seeing you."

An incredulous scoff leaves my lips as I shake my head, "Why? Am I so fucking ugly you can't let anyone know you're being seen with me?"

Tobias opens his mouth to speak, but the words that fill the air do not belong to him. Instead, they belong to the velvety, sinful voice that I'd found myself attempting to find a way to hear by any means necessary.

No. Fucking. Way.

Cyr Maddox stands not even ten feet away, leaning against the door frame, arms crossed with that same black mask concealing the beautiful tanned skin underneath. The way his black-inked arms flex makes me swear he's going to rip a seam on his black tee shirt from how tight his biceps are being restrained by the fabric. Every time I've seen him in class, he'd been wearing a jacket, but now, wearing a t-shirt my eyes widen at the massive tattoos scaling both arms. The black ink swirls into intricate patterns from the tops of his hands up to where it becomes hidden due to the sleeves of Cyr's tee shirt. My wandering eyes wonder how much of him is truly covered in those swirling patterns, but I force my eyes off of Cyr and back to Tobias.

How had I not noticed he was that tattooed before? Oh right, too focused on those eyes that pin me to the ground every time they're on me.

"What in the fuck is going on?"

Cyr's voice comes out low, yet piercing. The sound sends shivers up my spine and I'm not sure if that's a good thing or a very bad thing.

Tobias groans, rolling his eyes, "This isn't your concern." He turns his attention back to me and speaks low, just enough for me to hear. "I don't understand why you can't seem to get into your thick head that I just don't want you here when another man is here."

At that, my last thread of calmness fully snaps.

"Oh, okay. So I can't even let another man *look* at me, but you're allowed to fuck any creature with big tits and loose lips?

That makes perfect sense." I throw my arms up in the air in a dramatic, exasperated wave. I take another step toward him, my voice a mocking tone, "Is your Gods damned self-esteem that easily broken?"

The movement hadn't registered within me at what happens next until I'm stumbling backward, colliding hard with the front door. My head reverberates against the wooden door when it flies back, sending my vision spinning for a brief moment. Before I can even blink, I hear Tobias squeal as he's sent flying across the room toward the opposite wall. My gaze shoots to where he lands, watching as he uses the wall to catch his fall, his face a mask of pure anger. However, his mask fades quickly as he knows it's no match to the ice blue gaze of rage brewing in Cyr's eyes who stands blocking the path from Tobias to me.

"Don't. Fucking. Touch. Her."

My jaw gapes at Cyr's words, standing upright once again, keeping close behind his shoulder, but off to the side enough to watch Tobias' face contort.

"This is *our* relationship-" Tobias begins, but I interrupt with a scoff and a humorless laugh.

I couldn't believe what I was hearing.

"Relationship?! You're joking, right? Do you call *this* a relationship? You fucking everything with a pulse and I'm confined to you, and you alone?"

"You are *mine*," Tobias growls, turning his direction to Cyr, pointing a finger at him, "And you...stay the fuck out of this." Cyr begins to take a step toward Tobias, but before he can reach him, I extend my hand forward and grab a hold of Cyr's upper arm to halt him. My fingers barely graze his biceps before Cyr yanks his arm away so fast it startles me, quickly bringing my hands back toward my chest. I watch Cyr carefully, feeling the rage pouring off of him and encircling me like an embrace.

Was it because of Tobias?

Was it because of me?

Oh, Gods. Does he not like being touched?

Note to self: he doesn't like being touched or being looked at for too long.

Fuck. That day in the courtyard. He flipped out because I was staring at him.

"I am nothing to you. We fuck around and that's it. If you want to get all aggressive and controlling, you can take that shit somewhere else." I take a step around Cyr to face Tobias who is still reeling at Cyr as he stands a step behind me. I feel his body heat very close to my back, and his voice sends a shiver through my body.

"If you need a place to crash, my room is open." The invitation is thrilling but terrifying in the same breath. Tobias' eyes widen as Cyr's comment hits him, then his eyes flash and narrow on me.

"I swear, Bellamy, go back to your dorm or we'll have issues."

My heart begins racing impossibly fast, knowing the option is clear. I should tell Clara that I couldn't find a place to crash for the night. *But where was the fun in that?* With my mind made up, my gaze locks with Tobias's.

"Fuck yourself, Tobias."

With that, I turn on my heels and B-line for Cyr's bedroom.

***

Cyr's bedroom models all of the other doubled-room dorms in Upper Campus. Blank beige walls, a desk in the corner of the room which didn't hold any books, but instead a record player and a foot-tall stack of vinyl records. The room is immaculate, and it looks even better than my dorm I have to, painfully, admit. To my surprise, there isn't even a random sock lying on the carpet, or a shoe out of place in the row by his closet door.

I hear muffled sounds from Tobias and Cyr in the main hall as I continue roaming around the small room. My fingers flip through the records on his desk, picking up the album *Phobia* by *Breaking Benjamin*, flipping it over, and looking over the songs listed on the back. It's one of my all-time favorite albums, and seeing it on vinyl brings a smile to my lips.

"Are you hurt?"

His voice nearly sends me to my ass, jumping slightly, but clutching the vinyl to not send it tumbling to the floor. I turn toward his voice, seeing Cyr has shut his door, and he leans back against it. My mouth dries up and I can't bring myself to find the right words, so I opt to shake my head in response. Cyr nods, his arms crossed over his chest, making his biceps expand beneath his tee shirt once again.

"I didn't take you for the alternative rock type."

He gestures with a nod to the album in my hands which has me glancing down, remembering I was still holding the vinyl. I completely forget about the vinyl the moment Cyr's voice catches my attention, causing me to bite the corner of my lip to keep my mouth from falling open at the way his gaze takes me in. I can't get over that shade of blue in his eyes. A sight I hope that I will never forget.

"Take a picture, it'll last longer," Cyr grumbles, dropping his arms, and walking over to his nightstand.

Gods dammit. I was staring again.

Good to see his attitude from a few weeks ago still hasn't changed anything. However, to say I have been avoiding him wasn't a complete lie. Yes, we made very minor small talk in class from time to time, but couldn't resist hearing that voice when I got the chance. He makes me feel things I haven't felt in a long time and in full honesty, it scares the shit out of me. I also couldn't help to think about Tobias, so my cause for avoidance has been slightly based on Cyr's request to take me out for a drink. Even though I wanted to so damn badly. But I couldn't help it; to say he was 'hot' is a fucking understatement. A sigh falls from my lips as I place the vinyl back within the others in the stack, before turning back to Cyr.

"Why did you help me?"

My question is blunt, but I need an answer considering it's nothing Cyr needs to involve himself in. Even after our discussion in the mess hall, it didn't require him to jump into my cesspool of bullshit when it comes to Tobias. I couldn't even be sure if his offer of drinks still stood after these few weeks of near-silence. It wouldn't be any surprise if it wasn't, but to say I wouldn't be upset is an absolute and utter lie.

Cyr rummages through the nightstand drawer, picking up a notebook, "A man shouldn't place his hands on a woman like that. Ever." The way his body seems to tense as he speaks strikes a cord in my soul that I can't quite place the reasoning behind.

"It's nothing out of the ordinary. It's just how he is." The soft words barely leave my lips before Cyr snaps.

"And that's what makes him a boy, and not a fucking man."

His words stop me cold, mouth gaping. Cyr glances at me over his shoulder for a brief moment, but shakes his head and returns his attention to his nightstand.

"I know it isn't my place, so I'll keep the rest of my thoughts about the prick to myself." Cyr picks up a pack of pencils and the notebook, walks over toward me, and sets them both down on top of his desk. He stands only mere inches in front of me as I gaze up at him, seeing how tall he truly is being this close to him. My eyeline reaches up to his heart, leaving him a solid foot taller, and I wish at that moment to place my ear against his chest to hear the steady rhythm of his heart. His body grows tense, taking a step back after a moment, and releasing a shaky breath.

Do I make him uncomfortable?

The mysteries that lay beneath his hard exterior beg me to crack it open and learn his secrets.

Fuck. How was I ever going to figure him out?

"The bed is yours. I have a sketch to take care of before tomorrow." Cyr's voice is low, looking over to his perfectly made bed, then back to me. I hesitantly glance at the bed, gently shaking my head.

"I don't want to kick you out of your bed, Cyr." I realize by the way his breath hitches and his chest slightly heaves that it's the first time I'd ever said his name.

"Don't worry about me. Get some sleep."

I accept the defeat and sigh, aiming my body toward the far side of the bed, and toe off my shoes. My body slowly lowers down to climb under the black cotton comforter, concealing my bottom half before undoing the zipper of my jeans and slipping them off. Attempting to sleep in my skinny jeans would be a disaster, but if Cyr didn't notice I'd taken them off, what he didn't know wouldn't kill him, right?

The sleep pushing into my mind tells me to accept the consequences later and to lie down. I couldn't believe whose bed I was lying in. My jeans land on the ground by my shoes with a soft *thud* and I lay my head down on the plush pillow. I curl onto my side, tracking my eyes around Cyr.

Oh, my Gods, Bell. What in the fuck are you doing sleeping in Cyr Maddox's bed?!

My brown eyes gaze over the black-haired man who is sitting at his desk across the room. Cyr sits with his body hunching over the desk, pulling out a few pencils from the pack next to him. I couldn't believe the events of today and how my day began in the library and is now ending in the bed of the man I swore hated me and my entire existence.

I couldn't help but admire him from afar, listening to the sounds of his pencils scribbling away into his notebook. The sounds of Cyr's sketching and the heaviness weighing on my eyelids bring me down to the cusp of sleep which I didn't attempt to fight. The day exhausted me fully; the feeling of the soft fabric under my head and the weighted duvet molding to my body brought me swiftly into a deep state of sleep.

***

My body wanders through the blackness ahead of me, a faint glow encircling my every move. The world is gloomy around me, nothing is alive except for the shadows inside of my mind. I don't know where I'm going, but I know for certain that I'm not alone. In the distance, my certainty becomes true at the sight of glowing white eyes. I venture closer with each step, until the blonde hair that plagues my nightmares, while awake and asleep, steps into the glow around me. Milky eyes stare back at me in the dreary darkness of my mind, digging into my soul, and reaching for me with bony outstretched fingers.

You did this to me.

I couldn't breathe.

I didn't mean to, Jamie...I-I don't know what I did. Tell me what I did wrong.

The blonde didn't deign to answer my pleas.

Why would you hurt me like this? I loved you, Bellamy.

My heart splinters and cracks into a thousand tiny shards,

falling to my knees in front of the woman I loved.

Jamie, I'm sorry. I'm so, so sorry.

Join me, Bellamy. Come with me.

My gaze shoots up to Jamie's. I shake my head, tears glossing over my brown eyes.

I...I can't, Jamie. I-

Jamie scoffs, turning on her heels away from me and back toward where she emerged from.

You are the reason I'm dead. You should be suffering, not me.

All of the words swirl in my mind and I can't stop the tears from welling in my eyes and spilling down my cheeks in cascading droplets.

I am! I am! Please come back. I'm sorry! Come back to me!

Bellamy.

I can't shake the feeling of someone calling my name. I want to wake up, but as Jamie drifts farther away, I only want to run after her.

Bellamy, wake up!

The tears fly faster and I stumble, trying to make it back up to my feet.

BELLAMY!

The scream that tears from my lungs brings me back to the land of the living, sending me upright in a mess of panic, sweat, tears, and...black cotton sheets.

My breathing is jagged while I frantically look around the room for something familiar to pull me back to reality. My eyes land on the one thing I can find to be my anchor; those glacier blue eyes staring right back at me.

"Bellamy. Fucking breathe."

Gods above.

That was the first time he's ever said my name and the sound of my name on his lips makes me completely forget I was having a nightmare in the first place. I steady my breathing, closing my eyes for a brief moment to rein back in the emotions flooding my senses. My breath hitches in the back of my throat at the feeling of soft skin grazing the outside of my thighs and warm breaths close to my face. My eyes fly open, readying my fight or flight response when I lock eyes with Cyr once again. He is mere inches in front of my face, wondering what his motive is since I doubt he plans on kissing me with his mask still on. I glance around us, seeing him leaning halfway over me from the other side of the bed, his hands fisting the sheets next to my hips.

"You kicked the blankets off."

His voice is low, and it fills my blood with every and all things primal, but then I compute what he said. My eyes quickly flick down, noting that his hands next to my hips hold the duvet up over my bare legs and past my waist. A crimson red blush flushes my cheeks as I look back at Cyr, realizing that he has been keeping eye contact with me to not look me over while I was exposed. He had pulled the blankets back up over me to keep me covered and decent in front of him.

"Oh. I…" I pause, doing a double take as my gaze drifts over toward the bedroom door, noting the pillow and blanket in front of it, "Were you sleeping on the floor?" I ask, voice hoarse from my fitful screaming, quickly looking back to Cyr for confirmation. Guilt rips through me for kicking him out of his bed.

"Are you alright?" Cyr asks in question to my question, to which I cross my arms, leaning in closer to him.

"I asked you first."

The movement makes Cyr quickly shift his body up and away

onto his knees beside me on his bed. He sighs, brushing his loose black locks away from his eyes.

"I don't sleep great anyway, so it's not a problem. Now, are you alright?" Cyr's voice grew stern, more concerned about me than his sleeping arrangements, but I couldn't stomach that either.

"I'll be fine once you bring your pillow up here." His bright blue eyes flash to meet my own.

"What are you-"

Brushing the tear stains from my cheeks, and with a huff, I push myself off of his bed. I don't care in the slightest I wasn't covered from the waist down, minus my panties, and I presume Cyr won't mind the sight either. I couldn't lie and say I wasn't indeed blessed with curves like a goddess, after all.

Crouching down as to not show off my entire ass by bending over, I grab the pillow from off the floor, and before I could blink, Cyr is in front of me to block my path to his bed.

"Give it to me."

I raise my eyes upward to meet his own, taking me a moment to crane my head up far enough to meet his gaze. As I'd picked up earlier that day, he won't stand too close to me so I take the opportunity to hold the pillow behind my back and out of his reach.

"It's not fair for you to sleep on the floor. So you sleep in your bed, or I'm sleeping on the floor too." I keep my voice as strong as I can manage even though my throat screams in protest to the pain. Cyr's jaw shifts from under his mask, most likely clenching his jaw at my defiance.

"I don't want Tobias losing his shit if he finds out. So I'll take the floor." Cyr replies, trying to reach for his pillow, but he's a few steps too far away as I angle his pillow away from him. He groans and I shake my head.

"He won't know. It's fine. It's not that we're sleeping together, just sharing the same space." Cyr backs a few steps away and begins to walk toward his desk, and I impatiently huff, "What's the problem? Am I *that* repulsive that you won't-" I'm cut off as Cyr spins on his heels to look back at me.

"Don't pull that shit like what you said to Tobias. I'm not him," He growls, "Anyone on this god's forsaken planet would kill to have you in their bed at night. You are fucking beautiful and should be told nothing less than that."

I swear on the Gods my heart stops beating entirely, and the widening of Cyr's eyes tell me that he wasn't expecting to say any of those words either. I bring the pillow back in front of me and hug it to my chest. I try my best to pull it together as I stare down at the pillow clutched to my chest.

"I wanted to talk to you that night at the bar I just..." The words slip away into the ether, unsure if I'm ready to reveal all of my secrets to him. I take a steadying breath and exhale slowly, "I want to start fresh. A clean slate. What do you say?"

As I bring my gaze back up to meet his, I find his eyes already locked on me and there's something soft in his eyes. His answer is written clear as day inside them, and his nod in reply is more than enough. I slowly walk back over to where I was previously lying down and take a seat, pulling the covers back over my hips to cover myself up. I reach over and set his pillow on the opposite side of the bed, gently patting the pillow twice.

"Here. I'll stay way over on this side. I know you don't like to be touched, and I don't want to force you into my proximity. I just-" I sigh softly, "I just hate that I'm getting a peaceful night's rest in *your* bed and you're sacrificing your sleep. You won't even know I'm here."

Cyr's attention goes from the pillow, quickly back over to me as I say the word 'touched', beginning to shake his head, but I speak first.

"Earlier, in the foyer, you pulled away from me when I went to grab your arm. And when you walked over to your desk with your notebook, you barely lasted 5 seconds standing that close to me." The words escape my lips slowly to not alarm him from my observations, but every fiber of my being calls to explore him, to learn all I can grasp about Cyr Maddox. The beautiful man behind the mask.

Cyr's chest expands then shakily deflates a few beats later, taking a step to walk over toward his bed. He slowly sits, his back facing me and his head drops into his awaiting hands. I want to comfort him, to reach out and graze my fingers across his shoulder blades, through his hair, but I bite back the urge and bide my time, "Do I make you uncomfortable? If I do-"

"No, Bellamy." I couldn't finish my sentence before Cyr cut me off, "It's not you, so don't think for a second that you're the problem. We all have our issues. This just so happens to be mine."

I would be content to take any answers I can get from him, and right now, this is a promising start. My body gently reclines back to lay down on my side, facing Cyr's back, and pull the covers up to my chest. After a few moments of silence and heavy breathing, Cyr lays down on his back on the edge of the bed, facing the ceiling. I watch as his breathing turns from jagged, to slightly uneven, then smooths out after a few moments.

"You never answered my question earlier." Cyr's voice quietly sounds from the other side of the bed, concealed in the darkness of the room. I take a moment to recall when he'd asked me a question.

What had he asked? Then it clicked.

"Oh. I'm fine. It's not a big deal, just a nightmare." I tuck my hands beneath my cheek while lying on my side to face Cyr. In the dimness of the room, I can see his cheekbones shift under his mask as if he opens his mouth to speak. I brace myself for him to ask what the nightmare was about, and even though the two of us are having somewhat of a bonding moment, I wasn't ready to share that side of my nightmares yet. If I ever would be ready.

"How often does he hurt you?" The question leaving Cyr's lips brings my attention immediately to him.

"What? Tobias? He never-" I freeze. Earlier today when he shoved me into the door, Cyr had seen it, "He just had a temper today." Cyr shakes his head, the bed slightly shifting with the movement.

"Why are you defending him?" My body shoots upright at the question, looking down at Cyr who lies still with his arms across his abdomen.

"Why do you care so much about what Tobias does?"

Cyr's head turns the slightest to meet my heated stare and he tilts his head to one side to face me, "Because if I see him lay another hand on you like that, without your consent, I'll have zero hesitation to kill him."

His words send a shiver throughout my entire body, and I release a shaky breath as I lay back down on my side. All thoughts leave me and I don't even know what to say to that.

"He is how he is. No one can change that except for himself." I speak softly, tucking my arms back up to my chest, and glance over to Cyr whose head is still tilted to the side to meet my gaze.

"Then why stay and put up with his shit?" I sigh, knowing

full well that Cyr has a point, but I have my reasons.

"He puts up with mine, so we're even." It's then Cyr's turn to sit up a bit, propping himself on an elbow to gaze down at me from where I lay across the bed from him. I keep my body still to let Cyr determine how close he wants to get to me.

"What in the hell are you talking about? You're the least likely person on this entire campus to have any shit to put up with." I laugh softly, humorlessly, but still laugh as I shake my head at Cyr.

"I'm no saint."

"You're no sinner either, Bellamy." His voice, sultry as sin, sends butterflies swarming low in my belly. I avert my eyes from Cyr's, looking down at the pillow next to me. "Can you promise me something?"

His question brings my eyes back up to him for a brief moment, noting the seriousness of his tone, and nods gently. "If he touches you in any way you don't want to be touched, you come here if you have nowhere to go." My eyes widen in surprise. We've both met on a few different occasions, but the fact Cyr is being so open with me is astounding.

"You don't need to-"

"Promise me, Bellamy. I want you to know this is a safe space for you should you need it." I curl my knees up toward my chest and nod nonetheless.

"I promise."

A moment later I cover my mouth with a hand to hide a yawn. I can see Cyr's outline in the dimmness of the room and watch as his head turns toward me.

"Get some sleep, you've had a long night."

I try to protest, wanting to tell him that he doesn't need to muddle himself in my bullshit. My eyelids droop with each blink, noticing Cyr shift his body to lay on his side with his back to me. Consciousness eddies away, slowly succumbing to exhaustion, and I say to Cyr with the last of my waking strength.

"You're a good guy, Cyr."

Before sleep pulls me under once again into its embrace.

12

The Studio

The day blooms bright, bringing another beautiful late-winter day to Boston. Spring days began to appear, although to New England standards, Spring won't be here until at least April and it was still only March. With the weather warming up for a few odd days, the snow from the previous storm is mostly gone and melted away. A few snow piles remain on a few corners around campus, mostly black from kicked-up dirt and street debris.

I count my blessings and send up a silent prayer to the Gods to grant me a peaceful day to paint after the past few weeks I've had. Between fighting with Tobias every night, studying until I couldn't tell what day it was anymore, and trying my damnedest to get close to Cyr without scaring him away, it's been a struggle, to say the least. The latter has been the hardest to complete, but that was no surprise to me. As Cyr had made me promise, however, I kept to my word.

One night last week, Tobias was well past drunk and decided to get handsy with me, even during my protests for him to stop. Tobias had managed to pop off all the buttons to my flannel, exposing my bare chest while pinning me to the wall of his dorm room. It was after that I'd finally been able to shove him off of me and made a break for the door. I wouldn't dare to attempt to run down the hallway of the dorms completely topless, so I ran over to Cyr's bedroom, slamming the door, and locking it shut. At the same moment, I was upset that Cyr wasn't in his room, but all the same, relieved he wasn't home. He'd left his phone number for me on a note on his desk should I need him. The gesture melted a bit of my heart, and I still couldn't process why he chose to dedicate his kindness to me of all people. Nonetheless, I was grateful for him.

The day wouldn't stay perfect for long as a new storm is on the horizon and I know I need to get to the studio before the storm begins. After three semesters of art classes with Professor Reyes and becoming her teaching assistant, I earned myself a set of keys to the painting studio for my personal use.

After I graduated high school, I was offered an internship as an assistant art teacher at the middle school I attended a few years prior. I gladly accepted, joining the school the following year, and agreeing to take a gap year to add the internship to my resume. My love for art and the internship helped me gain my Professor's favor to become her assistant.

For the past two years, my days off when studying or lectures didn't occupy my time, I found myself in the studio painting away until my heart was content. Some of my students would join me for a therapy painting session, or for anyone who needed some extra practice outside of classroom hours.

I dedicated myself to taking every art class I could outside of my requirements for graduation and took them all in my stride. I adored all things art and wished to be a high school art teacher one day. The arts got me through high school, college, and life for that matter, and wished for my students to be able to have that same sort of escape as I had during school. Some of the hardest years of my life were in high school, and my solace was painting. If I have paints and an easel at my disposal, the rest of my problems and the world they resided in fade away.

Days like today call for a solo painting session. I had another long night with Tobias and left before he'd woken up this morning. Cyr hadn't been in the dorm a lot of the time over the past few weeks, giving Tobias reason to let me stay over with him. However, this morning after I'd woken up, I found myself walking over to Cyr's room. As usual, he was gone, and it made me wonder if he'd been sharing someone else's bed while I'd been sleeping in his bed all alone. I shouldn't be caring about what he does, or who he fucks for that matter. Cyr is nothing to me, other than a…*what the hell was he? A friend? Hell if I knew.*

As I open the classroom door, my mind still thinks back to Cyr's bedroom, a part of me hopes he'd be in here this morning when I enter the studio. Oh, the things I would do to see the sculpted tattooed muscles I know are hiding beneath his shirt.

I close the classroom door behind me and begin to set up my equipment in front of the glass panel windows that line the eastern wall of the room. My gaze travels up through the windows to see the gray clouds rolling in which soon enough will block out the remnants of the beautiful rays of sunlight. If I can set up quickly and beat out the upcoming snow, there might still be some time to capture the image of the sunny day onto a canvas.

I was very wrong, unfortunately. The snow came a lot sooner than expected. After about an hour, which consisted of setting up my paints, easel, and brushes by the floor-to-ceiling windows of the studio, the snow had commenced in full force. I set up my Bluetooth speaker in the corner of the room, sending a random playlist to life all around me as it booms through the studio.

Taking a seat on a bar stool in front of the easel, I position myself in front of the easel and pick up my paint palette to hold in my left hand. The brush being gently held in my right hand begins to move across the canvas in leisurely strokes. The vivid oranges and reds I've laid out to use will now be for nothing when it comes to capturing the snowstorm ensuing before me. My brush takes the lead, and my hand is guided by the strokes the brush wishes to make on the canvas. I am nothing without my brushes, and they are nothing without me. My sole vice is art. It helps to keep me alive when my life crashes down in front of me and gives me a reason to keep going when I no longer want to anymore.

***

Seconds, minutes, and hours pass by. I wasn't exactly sure how long, but I didn't have a care in the world. This is my haven to sweep me away from all of my troubles and doubts. The sound of a creaking door pulls me up and out of my painting daze, blinking my eyes a few times. I swear I'd locked the door, internally punching myself in the face for not being on the ball today. I didn't have the heart to send any of my students away, so I'd put on a happy face and be there for any of my students.

"Hey sweetie, grab an easel and pull up a seat. Need help with an assignment or just free painting this morning?" I call out, putting on my classroom voice for the prospective student behind me.

"I'm not one for painting. I'm better with skin and ink."

My head shoots straight up at the voice that greets me. The voice I haven't heard in weeks, hearing only in my dreams. His voice floats over my skin, the feeling like euphoria as it leaves goosebumps rippling across my body.

I spin in my chair to face the voice as dark as sin, prepping to stand on wobbly legs to glance over at Cyr. My oversized knit sweater fell over one shoulder to reveal the top of a rose tattoo on my left shoulder. The lilac sweater falls to mid-thigh over black leggings and is partnered with my black Doc Martens. My mouth slowly gapes open at the sight of him standing before me with a new haircut. Cyr's hair is shaved in a fade on the sides and the hair at the top is a bit longer and curls over his forehead.

Stop staring. Holy shit, Bell, stop.

"Well, I'm free to give you a few lessons, should you ever want some."

Although I can't see his face below his eyes, the way his cheekbones shift gives me the impression that he's hiding a smirk underneath that mask. The song blaring in the classroom feels fitting to play in the presence of Cyr Maddox. *Dance with the Devil* by *Breaking Benjamin* plays in the background, and I can't help but smirk at the lyrics, glancing back up to meet the icy blue eyes in front of me. I am indeed dancing with the devil, and I wouldn't have it any other way.

"I'm sure there's not much you'd be able to teach me that I'm not already proficient in, but I'll offer the same."

Holy fucking shit.

Cyr slowly begins to approach me and my eyes widen slightly from the closeness between us. Standing a foot in front of me, Cyr takes his time in looking me over and I swear he is gazing at me like I'm naked in front of him. His eyes trail down my entire body, then back up, and locks eyes with mine. The weight of his stare nearly pulls me down to my knees. As if on my knees is exactly where he wants me, and I would happily oblige that particular request.

Gods, I need some good sex. It has been too damn long.

A blush creeps up my cheeks at the promiscuous thoughts, attempting to mask the rosy tint in my cheeks from him. I steel myself, inhaling and calming my racing mind of all its ideas of intertwining myself with Cyr.

"What are you doing here?"

I pause after the words fall from my lips and shake my head.

"I didn't mean-" I stumble on my words, taking a few steps toward him while nervously running a hand through my hair, "Not that I don't mind seeing you, I just- " I immediately stop when I see Cyr take a quick step backward. I didn't realize how close I'd stepped toward him, and I swear softly under my breath.

"Space. I'm sorry I didn't mean to get in your space."

It grows too quiet in the room and my gaze falls to my shoes, crossing my arms across my chest. Footsteps echo and I close my eyes with a sigh. The footsteps I assume are Cyr's as he leaves the room.

Why the hell couldn't I keep my calm around him?

There's something about his presence that makes me crazy for him, and I can't control my feelings toward him…for him.

My eyes fly open in a flash at the feeling of soft skin caressing beneath my chin, gripping it gently. Cyr hasn't even dared to come this close to me before, let alone touch me, standing only a few inches in front of me. If he wasn't wearing his mask, I'd be tempted to kiss him and that frightens a part of me deep down. He gently lifts my head upward to meet his gaze and I swear my heart briefly stops. The feeling of his hand so close to my throat, his eyes burning a hole into my soul, it was too much and not enough all at once.

"I wanted to see you."

Those five words from Cyr have my knees trembling and my damn mouth watering, "I saw that my bed wasn't made when I got back to my room this morning. I needed to make sure you were okay." The stern lilt in his tone makes my heart ache since I know the unsaid question that comes with his comment.

Did he hurt you?

The fact that someone who barely knows me cares for me so much as to seek me out to check up on me melts every fiber in my bones. Surprise fills me as I didn't know that Cyr even knew where the studio is as I'm sure as shit Tobias doesn't have a clue.

"I'm fine."

Words evade me entirely and I can feel myself falling deeper into his touch, and not caring how much I shouldn't be enjoying it. I would never fall in love again. My person had left me, and I would live the rest of my life with shitty fuck buddies from now on. But there's something about Cyr that pulls me out of my head for a few moments and I can't imagine a time when I didn't have him around in any capacity.

"You know what I mean, Bellamy."

Cyr's grip tightens ever so slightly on my chin and my pupils dilate when my eyes connect with his. His voice commands a response from within me, forcing me to pull out of his grasp and take a step back. Slowly, I uncross my arms and raise one of the sleeves of my sweater. Bruises, fresh and fading litter my arm, and from one second to the next I see the rage turn his ice-blue eyes nearly black. Cyr spins on his heels and makes his way to the classroom door.

"Please…" I croak, my eyes turning glossy, and water threatens to fall down my cheeks. I reach out to him but instantly pull my arm back to hug my chest so as to not touch him. Cyr immediately spins back to face me, the anger in his eyes fading ever so slightly back to normal. "Please, Cyr. Don't… he's not worth it."

My voice is on the verge of breaking once again, holding myself tightly, wishing Cyr could hold me for just a single moment. To feel his tight embrace around me and tell me that everything would be okay. But I know that dream will never come true. Not with Cyr.

"But you're worth it, Bellamy." His words echo around me and bring a few tears escaping from my eyes to trail down my cheeks. Cyr begins to reach his hand out toward me, but he pulls it back before it fully extends to me.

"It's okay. I know you can't touch me again. Once was probably already too much." His eyes widen as he connects the dots that I understand. "What did she do to you?" I wipe the tears from my cheeks as I look up at Cyr, not expecting an answer from him. Cyr's gaze falls to the floor, running a hand through his dark waves, and shakes his head.

"You don't have to answer that." I quickly chime in to not scare him off by making him divulge such a personal part of himself.

"Things not worth reliving, we'll leave it at that." A part of my heart broke at the reply. I bring a sleeve up and brush the last remaining tear streaks off my cheeks.

"Where have you been?" The question leaves my lips before I can question the integrity of what those words mean. I have been sleeping in his bed on a handful of occasions and he's been nowhere to be found on those nights. It's absolutely none of my business by far, but I couldn't help but pry.

"Why do you ask? You prefer to share a bed with me than your boy toy?"

Gods, I'd give anything for even 60 seconds in bed with him.

I turn back to my easel, then gaze out of the window ahead of me. Beyond the window, I watch as the snowstorm continues to rage on, much akin to how my heart feels beating inside my chest.

"I can't quite say I'd be against that." I know those words will cost me, but I need Cyr to hear them as much as my mind needs to accept the truth in those words.

"You don't want that, trust me."

I sigh, shaking my head at his response. I pick up the painting palette and the brush from the easel before walking over to the basin across the room.

"Why not? Indulge me."

I can hear his breathing quicken as if he's only a step behind me, and that is confirmed by his deep voice as he coos straight into my ear.

"Don't play with fire, Bellamy. You'll only get burned."

My mouth has never dropped open so fast in my life. It takes me a few moments to fully process the warning, which is also hopefully a promise. I can feel the butterflies in my stomach doing back flips and it sends heat straight down between my legs. The thought of him on top of me, behind me, *or both*, drives my mind head-first into the gutter and I have zero intention of climbing out of it.

"What if I enjoy arson?"

I taunt, my voice breathy and more confident than I expect it to be. After a moment without a reply, I set down the palette into the basin and turn back to face Cyr. Before I can even open my mouth, Cyr is in front of me, bracing both hands on either side of me to pin me between the basin and his solid body mere inches in front of me. All of the breath in my lungs leaves my body in a matter of seconds. It feels like drowning standing this close to him. Cyr's presence is suffocating and I'm quickly learning to love what drowning in him feels like.

"What do you want from me, Bellamy?"

You.

Is what I want to say, but the thought of uttering that word stalls all other words I can possibly say. My shoulders lift innocently in response. His low chuckle sends goosebumps shooting across my entire body.

Gods above I want him. No, Bell. Snap out of it. You don't deserve anyone... especially him.

I've never been one to back away from a confrontation but with his closeness, I feel my body and soul shrink down to the size of a snail.

"Not so ballsy now, are we?" Cyr croons with another low, wicked chuckle, slowly backing away. The soft gasp I inhale, after he creates some distance between us, feels like the first breath I've taken in hours. Without his arms caging me in, his warmth instantly leaves the room and it's suddenly akin to the feeling of stepping into a meat locker. Cyr takes a few steps back and eyes me over like prey at his mercy, and a part of me locked away deep down in my soul didn't mind that. He begins to turn and head for the door and my mind is reeling. I want to reach out and grab hold of his hand and beg him to stay with me.

"You're not going to stick around and show me a few things?" The words come out slightly hoarse from my severe state of cottonmouth. It catches his attention, stopping him in his tracks as he flicks his eyes over his shoulder to meet my gaze, "I could use a few tips…"

Gods, stop me from talking, please.

The shift of Cyr's mask screams clear as day that a damn smirk is plastered on those lips even though I can't see it.

Damn, this gorgeous man.

His eyes narrow ever so slightly as if attempting to assess the legitimacy of my question, "Come find me when you ditch that boy toy of yours. Hell, you spend more time in my bed than his. Guess I should stay home more often."

His words send my body flaring with heat, a blush sliding up my cheeks that I don't bother trying to hide as I'm well aware it's a shade of bright crimson. Cyr turns once again to head for the door and the words escape my lips before I can think twice about them.

"Tomorrow…in the library."

Cyr spins to face me entirely while slowly walking backward toward the front door, "I didn't take you for a voyeur, Bellamy."

My eyes widen to the size of dinner plates and I stutter over my words as my brain unravels like a slinky falling down the stairs.

"I, uh. Well…"

My pause while I attempt to recover my initial thought causes Cyr to raise an incredulous eyebrow. My hands fly up to cover my face as my whole body goes up in flames.

"Fucks sake, Cyr," I grumble and the belly laugh that echoes throughout the room has my eyes instantly flying up to him. That sound stops my heart entirely and once it begins to beat again, it feels like a lightning bolt kickstarted it back to life.

"Use your words, Bellamy."

Those words can be taken as mocking after my series of stutters but the way his voice dips down and skitters over my skin leaves my mouth agape. His eyes darken a few shades as he scans every single inch of my body. Those primal instincts scream inside of me and Cyr knows exactly what the fuck he's doing. I don't appreciate the way he already knows how to climb under my skin and strip me bare with his words alone.

My inhale is shaky as I attempt to collect my thoughts before it all comes out in one quick ramble, "I'm having a study session in the library with Clara tomorrow and I want you to join me-I mean us…" I exhale my words at the speed of lightning and I'm not entirely sure if any of it was audible.

"Tempting."

Is the last thing he says before the soft *click* of the studio door closes behind him. I slump back against the basin as the butterflies doing somersaults in my stomach relentlessly batter against my insides.

Please, Gods, let Clara not murder me for the sins I'm committing.

13

The Library

The eerie quiet that surrounds me makes the hair on my arms stand up on end. Well, it is a library after all, and any sound over half a decibel would earn anyone a 'shh' in return. Friday's are easy days for me with only one morning lecture in my Art History class, then the rest of the day is mine. More times than not, Clara will meet me in the library after her class to bullshit about anything and everything rather than studying which is the actual point of our study sessions.

"And then while Mr. Essler wasn't looking, Chad ran over to the still life display and rearranged the apples and banana into quite a provocative display," Clara whispers across the small table as she attempts to not burst out laughing.

The table in the corner of the room furthest from the librarian's desk, and any other desks, is our usual dwelling. The floor-to-ceiling windows line the entire wall beside the desk illuminating the room in beautiful rays of sunlight.

"It took Mr. Essler at least an hour into the class before he realized and I've never seen a man blush that red before in my life." I can hear Clara speaking as if she's miles away, but in reality, it's indeed my mind which is a million miles away.

My dark brown eyes gaze out through the wall of windows that overlook the courtyard in the center of the campus. The weather is turning bright and sunny, extinguishing the rest of the snow that was grasping onto the ground for dear life. After yesterday's storm, a few light showers washed it away in a firm sweep and the sun came out to play, lighting the courtyard in blissful sunshine with a beautiful early spring breeze.

"Bell? Hellooooo? Earth to Bellamy Adelaide Tyler."

Clara's voice snaps me out of my thoughts and my gaze lulls back to the girl sitting across the table from me, blinking a few times in the process.

"And she's returned. Did you have a fun trip? There's no way you got weed without me." My eyes direct a dramatic roll at my friend and shake my head. I exhale a long breath and glance back outside for a moment. "What going on? You okay, babe?" The concern in Clara's voice instantly brings my attention back to my best friend. I nod and bring a small smile to my lips.

"Do you remember that guy I practically ran away from in the bar back on my birthday?" The words leave my lips softly in question and Clara raises an eyebrow in reply.

"You mean the Adonis that is Cyr Maddox?"

"Adonis, huh? I must say that's a first, but appreciated nonetheless."

The voice as sinful as the Devil himself echoes softly around the table and my eyes quickly flash to meet his which is already on me. The sight of him makes my heart skip a beat but also warms something in my chest that he decided to take up my offer from yesterday. Clara's jaw drops then proceeds to snap it shut just as quickly with an audible *click*. My friend's eyes blaze into my own, causing a smirk to creep up my lips.

"No need to feed his ego, Clara, it's already too big for his head to handle."

"Which head are we talking about?"

My eyes roll as a soft laugh escapes my lips, glancing back over to Cyr, "Definitely both."

Cyr's mask shifts a bit, presumably into a smirk that I'd kill to see. He points over to the chair beside the two of us and I glance to Clara for permission.

"Mind if he crashes our not-really-studying session?"

Clara's eyes are wide enough that I believe my friend's eyes are damn near about to pop out of her skull. She recovers her shocked-beyond-belief expression and looks over to Cyr with a devilish grin.

"Join the party, Maddox."

Cyr slips the chair out from its place against the table, unslinging his bag, and takes a seat. Clara's gaze seeps into the seventh ring of hell inside my soul until our eyes lock and Clara mouths in my direction.

"WHAT. THE. FUCK. BELL."

I try my hardest to contain my laughter and only shrug in reply with a sly grin. Clara gives me a death glare that promises she will rip me a new ass later for not telling her everything that has transpired between Cyr and I.

"I'm glad to see my offer was tempting after all," I quietly say to Cyr and a low rumble of his chest is his only reply, but it's enough to have Clara's eyes back on me in an instant. Her silent stare was enough to telepathically transmit the message:

"What the fuck have you not been telling me?!"

Stifling a laugh, my gaze slides over to my left to watch Cyr pull out his sketchpad and a pack of several different sorts of pencils. He carefully unrolls the collection of pencils and flips to a page in his sketchbook revealing a half-finished sketch of a black and gray dragon. I can't help but gawk at the image regardless if it was completed or not.

"I guess there really isn't anything that I could teach you, after all." The words leave my lips quietly, but enough to catch Cyr's attention. Cyr's ice-blue gaze meets mine and there's a hint of appreciation in those glacier depths that has my heart swooning. At the same time, there's also a hidden statement beneath that gaze which sends a blush soaring across my cheeks.

"But there are some things I could teach you."

After a few moments of deafening silence and heavy eye-fucking, Clara's voice softly rings out into the air between us, "Is that a new client piece?"

The question strikes me stupid for a moment. My gaze flicks from Clara back to Cyr with a raise of my eyebrow, "Client?"

Clara looks at me as if I were a six-headed Hydra eating a peanut butter and jelly sandwich, "Cyr's a tattoo artist. Could you not tell from all the ink he's got? My friend got a piece done by him a few weeks ago."

In all honesty, it never dawned on me. Any time I've seen his sketchbook I assumed his drawings were for a class, not his profession. I focus back on the sketch and slide my hand over to attempt to flatten out the page to see it better. However, my action causes Cyr to flinch his hand back and clench it into a tight fist. My eyes instantly dart up to see him looking down at the hand that he is pulling close to his chest.

The sight of him makes my heart shatter into a thousand tiny pieces. I glance at Clara but she's staring intently at an assignment on her laptop and I'm thankful she didn't catch the interaction. When my eyes trail back to Cyr, his eyes are already on me. I mouth a silent *"I'm sorry"* to him and his reply is a subtle shake of his head.

He's okay. He's not upset.

"It looks amazing. I might even let you tattoo me one day," I say softly with a gentle smile gracing my lips. His eyes dip to my lips to track the movement and I unconsciously bite my lip. Cyr cocks an eyebrow at me and my gaze darts back to my Art History textbook in an attempt to hide the rest of the smile that slides up my cheeks.

"Don't tempt me with a good time, Bell." His voice, low and every ounce dripping with temptation, has me melting into a puddle of goo in my seat.

The use of my nickname, however, did not go unnoticed by Clara whose head perks up from her laptop to eye me down. Her gaze flicks over to Cyr with a smile, "Well shit if you're offering tattoos count me in."

Cyr's mask shifts, denoting a bit of a smile from underneath his mask. Seeing my best friend get along so well with my…well, whatever Cyr is at this point, a friend I guess, makes a piece of my heart swell with happiness.

"It'd be my pleasure, Clara. Stop by anytime."

I bite my bottom lip to suppress a laugh as I watch Clara immediately return her gaze to her laptop as a hint of rose flushes her cheeks. With the fairest of skin and the light freckles dusting her cheeks, it was impossible to hide a blush, but I silently commend her for her efforts.

The next few hours fly by in a flash of studying and writing more notes than I physically know what to deal with to the point where my hand is severely cramping. Clara drifts off to seek out snacks to sneak into the library to fuel our brains into working further. Ultimately the sugary snacks only lead my brain to crash after a thirty-minute sugar high.

During the moments when Clara sneaks off for snacks, I can't help but watch Cyr's hand glide across the pages of his sketchbook in precise motions. If I could, I'd watch him for hours while he sketches, the act oddly mesmerizing and calming. On a few occasions, he catches me staring at his hand as I wish I could wear it like a necklace, blushing furiously, and quickly averting my gaze back to my notes. But each time he catches me gazing, from my peripheral, I can see his mask shift inch by inch from smiles or hidden smirks which makes me look over to him more often.

"BB, I can't do this anymore. My brain is literally coming out of my eyeballs at this point," Clara whines softly from across the table, causing me to drag my eyes up from my textbook.

"You should probably get that checked out," Cyr says pointedly at Clara in response to which she just rolls her eyes, ever the drama queen. I laugh softly which I notice catches Cyr's attention and his gaze meets mine for a brief moment. The calmness of the blue waves in his eyes has me transfixed for a moment until Clara clears her throat.

"I feel like I'm third-wheeling so I'm gonna head back to the dorm and I'll let you two eye-fuck for a while. Sound good?" Clara chirps with that sarcasm I've grown to love about her. Although my skin flares from mortification as I glare at her with a silent curse.

"Alright Clara, we're even now."

"I have an appointment in a few hours so as much as I've had a ball with you ladies, I better head out," Cyr replies, rolling up his pencils and placing them in his backpack along with his sketchbook. As Clara and Cyr pack up, I do the same with my note cards and textbook placing them carefully in my backpack.

Clara says her near-silent goodbyes to Cyr after being

shushed for her chair sliding along the tile floor too loud, "See ya around, Maddox." She says before heading toward the library exit. I sling my backpack over my shoulder and face Cyr as he stands from his chair.

"I'll see you in Photography on Monday?" I ask softly with a smile, hopeful to see him again even though the prospect of waiting another 48 hours is heartbreaking. He nods in reply without a word and I nod back before quickly making my way out after Clara.

***

"I don't know how to explain it, Cee!"

My exasperated voice calls out to my best friend who is currently sitting on my bed attempting to connect our newest Google device to the WiFi network. Struggling, I may add. "There's just something about him that makes me never want to be away from him."

Thoughts of him engulf my senses and make me weak in the knees. I strip out of my clothes and set them on the edge of the sink counter before turning toward the shower and turning the dial on.

"Sounds like a crush to me, babes," Clara replies, albeit somewhat angrily, presumably taking her anger out on the poor Google device. I can't help but laugh at her occasional yelp of frustration. As the water begins to warm up and wafts of steam pour into the bathroom, I step under the head of the shower and douse myself, basking in the heat.

"Cyr Maddox is the most emotionally unavailable man I've ever met. I doubt he's one to date, anyway." The words leave my lips and a wave of sadness rushes over me. Those stolen glances and the way his eyes scream my name throughout the handful of times we've spent together recently, the doubt keeps creeping back into my mind. I squeeze the bottle of shampoo into my palm to collect a small pile before lathering it into my hair.

"Ha! Gotcha, bitch!"

The cry of triumph coming from the bedroom startles me, opening my eyes too soon to assess the situation which leads to the shampoo falling into my eyes, "Mother fu-"

"It's working! I think…"

Clara excitedly yells to me and I shake my head as I rinse my eyes under the shower head to rinse the tear-inducing shampoo from my face. As I submit myself to the near-burning water pouring down from above me, the pounding of the water consumes me. I push the shampoo back from my hair and rid it from my body in a few waves of water.

My eyes close, calming myself into utter serenity from the silence. I allow myself a moment to decompress from the day and the man, as sinful and enticing as the Devil, who clouds every aspect of my mind. Just as the water begins to run cold, the song *"It's Raining Men"* by The Weather Girls plays at an ear-splitting level through the Google device in our bathroom.

"God dammit, that's not what I told it to do!" Clara groans from the bedroom, and my hands quickly rise to cover my ears to muffle the noise.

"Google! Fucking stop!" I scream from the shower and a moment later, silence returns to the bathroom. My hands fall from my ears and a sigh escapes.

"Sorry babes! I told the stupid thing to give me the weather forecast," She grumbles, defeat lacing her tone. I shake my head, laughing for a moment and then the water officially turns to ice against my back. I squeal as I attempt to flick the dial off with my foot for a moment and the water finally shuts off, eliminating the bone-chilling water. A groan leaves my lips, realizing I didn't get to condition my hair before the water turned cold.

I step out of the shower, grab my towel, and briefly dry myself off. My body is still mostly covered with scattered water droplets as I wrap the towel around my body. I open the bathroom door, opening my mouth to rip Clara a new one for shattering my ear drums when I see him.

He's here....Sitting on my bed. Where the fuck is Clara?! I'm going to kill her later.

I tuck my body behind the bathroom door, looking over at him from the crack in the doorway.

"Cyr, uh, hi. Where's-"

Cyr's low, velvety voice easily fills the space between us, "She went to the mess hall. She'll be back in a minute."

His voice has my body from head to toe filling with heat all over again. I attempt a small smile to keep myself as neutral as possible even though every second that passes when his eyes are on me is as if I would melt into a puddle on the floor at any moment.

"What're you doing here? You could have just shot me a text." As soon as the words leave my lips, I realize how insensitive they sound, "That's not what I-"

"You left this at the library," He interrupts while reaching behind him to pull something out of his pocket. Cyr holds a brown twine-bound notebook in his hand in front of him.

Oh, Gods. No fucking way. My diary. How did it get out of my backpack?!

"Did you...read it?" I question while my hands shake in front of me. He raises an eyebrow and shakes his head.

"No, but from your reaction, I imagine I should," Cyr reaches to unbind the twine and my feet spring into motion. Before I can think twice, I'm bolting toward him, holding the towel tightly at my chest as I reach out to snatch the book from his hand. Just as I reach him, his hand shoots straight up to hold the book far above my head out of my grasp. I attempt to jump a few times while using my free hand to grab the book from him. A soft muffled chuckle leaves him and it pauses my act of utter stupidity in trying to obtain my notebook.

"Alright, dick, give it back," I growl, completely not in the mood for his antics. As I meet his gaze, his mask shifts upward as if he's smiling down at me.

How is this man so insufferable yet makes me constantly feel like a ball of Play-Doh?

"And if I don't?"

"I'll-!"

"You'll…what?" His voice is purely sinful as he leans down toward me, only a few inches separating his mask from my lips.

I huff out a whine and stomp my foot, placing my hand face up in front of him to place the book in my hand. A belly laugh instantly leaves his lips and the sound nearly has my jaw dropping to the floor.

"What's so funny?!"

"That was the cutest fucking thing I've ever seen."

Full. Swoon. I'm absolutely and utterly swooning. Is the world spinning or am I?

He shakes his head, laughing once again, "What's the magic word?"

"Fuck yourself."

"It's much more fun with someone else, but I'll accept it," Cyr begins lowering the book toward my hand and a sigh of relief comes up to my lips but halts in my throat when he stops a few inches from my hand, "Under one condition."

I groan, throwing my head back to take a deep breath and I look back at him as I exhale, "Which is what?"

"Come hang out with me."

My eyes go wide, and I raise an eyebrow, "Is this you finally asking to take me out for that drink?"

"Can't say I wouldn't mind. I just want your company."

"I thought you said you had an appointment with a client?" I reply quickly, not necessarily avoiding the statement but also intrigued by what his plan was.

"Canceled on me. Besides, your company would be much more entertaining than some frat boy wanting to get his dick tattooed."

My gag is barely held back at the thought of having to tattoo some random dudes...*I don't even want to think about that.*

Nonetheless, the gears in my head begin turning and my heart warms at the mention of him wanting to spend time with me. He's voluntarily choosing to spend time out of his day...with me. I bite my lip to ponder where to go, and then it hits me. My gaze meets his once again and I smile with a nod.

"Sure."

I hold my hand out once again for him to return the book to me. Cyr's hesitant for a moment as he most likely can see a plan brewing behind my eyes, but nonetheless places the book into my palm.

"What's the plan?"

"Oh, I have an idea."

He raises an eyebrow, "Alright, Bellamy, out with it."

"Let's just say I have a proposal for you."

14

The Club

I have no idea how I did it, but I did. The text from Cyr came in about an hour ago that he'd agreed to my bargain. If he came out to the club with me, then I'd let Cyr tattoo anything he wanted on me. The idea of losing the bet didn't make me afraid and getting a tattoo as I've already gotten a few before, but what did terrify me was the fact I have no control over the subject matter. From what I know of the cruel bastard, he wouldn't show me what the tattoo looked like until it was done. The foreseeable future will entail me attempting to mentally prepare myself for a veiny dick across my arm.

After receiving his text, I quickly jumped back into the shower to condition my hair and shave every single inch of my body. Not that I'm expecting anything to happen between the two of us, but it doesn't hurt to be prepared.

"Do you need a chaperone?" Clara's mocking words earn her a glare and then the two of us share a laugh. I don't know how this night will play out. Whether or not he will freak out in the throngs of people, or he'll melt into the crowd unnoticed, either way, I'll be there to support him. The feeling of wanting him to feel human and not hide consumes me, probably to an unhealthy level. But even for just a few minutes, if that is indeed how long it lasts, I wouldn't care. He agreed to go, and that was more than I could ask of him, so if he wanted to stay for five minutes or five hours, I would happily oblige his request.

A knock on the door of our dorm echoes throughout the room and I run over to open it a moment later. I take a deep breath as I reach for the handle, and pull it open. Those baby blues I've become so accustomed to instantly met mine like they need the sight of me to survive. My mouth gapes slightly as I look him over, taking in Cyr's attire for the night. His signature black and white Chuck Taylor's, black jeans that hugged every muscle from his ankles to his ass, and a black short sleeve button-up shirt with a white skull pattern across it. The top few buttons are undone leaving them open to reveal the top of a chest tattoo I couldn't quite discern, but would instantly examine personally if given the chance.

"You look stunning."

The breathless words leave Cyr's mouth as if he had just run a marathon to reach me. My cheeks brighten into a light shade of rose as I glance down over my outfit. I had shimmied my way into my favorite navy blue bodycon dress that clung to each of my curves along my breasts and down past my hips, ending mid-thigh to show off how true the statement 'thick thighs save lives' is. By the time my eyes travel back up to meet Cyr's, I find his gaze everywhere except for my eyes.

"Why don't you take a picture? It'll last longer." I say, mocking Cyr as he'd said the same thing to me when we'd first met in our photography class.

The panic in Cyr's eyes flashes as he realizes he'd been caught and he instantly looks bashful, rubbing the back of his neck nervously. His loose short black waves fall in front of his eyes with the motion.

Did I still make him nervous? Was this too much for him?

I thought after all this time with the playful comments and the banter that he would have adjusted a bit more to me by now.

"I just haven't-" He pauses, shaking his head, and sighs as he drops his hands back down to his sides. "I don't remember the last time I went…out. Like this."

I cross my arms across my chest, "What, in something other than head-to-toe black?"

Cyr throws me a *'fuck you'* glance and I smirk, taking in his glare with a laugh and returning it with a look of *'I wish you would'*.

"I know I'm just chopped liver over here, but I think you look quite dapper," Clara chirps from where she sits in her gray sweats and black tank top on the corner of her bed. Cyr looks down, the tiniest bit of red staining the tops of his cheeks from what I can see peeking out from the top of his mask.

"Appreciate it, Clara."

His voice comes out softer than I expect coming from Cyr, delicate even. I glance over my shoulder to throw a thankful smile in my best friend's direction, which Clara returns gleefully. I walk back over to my bed, grabbing my black leather jacket off the edge of my bed.

"Shall we?" My questioning glance at Cyr sent to convey he still has a chance to take it back. His nod of confirmation is enough for me. I turn back to my best friend to hug Clara.

"Text me when you get there, and call me if you need anything. I'll be there in a heartbeat." Clara's voice is soft but is laced with sternness, a trait I love most about her.

"Okay, mom."

Clara's glare is accompanied by a poke to my nose which I attempt to quickly bat my friend's hand away from my face. My focus lands back to Cyr and even through his mask, I can feel him smiling at the two of us. My body shifts to Clara for a moment as Cyr and I head toward the front door, "Love you, loser."

Clara laughs with a shake of her head, "Love you too, babe."

I pull the dorm room door shut behind me and with Cyr beside me, the two of us walk side by side out of Upper Campus.

***

As the Uber pulls up in front of the club in Downtown Boston, Cyr exits the vehicle and extends a hand toward me. I hesitate for a single moment before reaching out to gently take hold of Cyr's hand to assist me out of the car. His grip on my hand is soft, and I take every moment I can to memorize the feeling of his hand against my skin. As I step out and stand beside Cyr, his hold on my hand remains for a few lingering seconds before he pulls away. He attempts his best to conceal his shaking hands in his pockets, but I give him a knowing look. Cyr's body relaxes the slightest bit at my understanding gaze as I lead the two of us toward the front doors of the club.

Blinding neon lights flash around the large space illuminating every person in bright-colored clothes under the black lights. The white leather high-top Converse shoes adorning my feet shine brightly under the lights, and I hop around the floor in excitement. My gaze flicks over to Cyr who stands as still as a statue taking in the environment. His wandering gaze makes me question whether or not this was a good idea after all. I turn to walk back toward Cyr whose gaze instantly latches onto mine for any sign of familiarity. The music blaring around the club forces me to carefully move my body closer to Cyr than he probably could handle.

"Just say the word and we'll go."

My voice raises deliberately to holler over the music, standing up on my tiptoes to lean in close to his ear. Cyr turns his head to meet my eyes, simply nodding in reply. I want to reach out and place a comforting hand on his arm, but I know he needs time on his own to acclimate himself to the foreign surroundings.

"For now just let loose, have a drink, and enjoy yourself," I call to him, flashing him an encouraging smile. He nods once again in response, but that same look clouds his eyes and doubt creeps into my mind.

This was not the place to bring him.

I sigh softly before walking over to the bar on the far end of the club, and ordering a gin and tonic for myself. When I look back to where Cyr was previously standing, he was nowhere to be seen.

Relax, Bell. He may have found someone to dance with.

I wish it was me that he would dance with but I wasn't holding my breath on that happening. Every fiber of my being hopes he hasn't bolted from the club, but if he needs some fresh air, I wouldn't blame him. The packed club makes the air in the room feel sparse, and it's difficult to navigate anywhere without rubbing bodies with everyone in the path.

After scouting the area, I find a spot at the bar that isn't completely crowded and sip my G&T while letting the music around me flood my senses. I didn't plan on drinking myself stupid, but I'd allow myself a drink or two throughout the night. In the case that Cyr needs to get out quickly, I don't want to be too far intoxicated that I would be of no use in helping him escape the crowded club.

Several men approach me at the bar top throughout the night, asking for dances nicely and not-so-nicely, and I politely turn all of them down. I've never been one to find the pleasures of grinding my ass against drunk, horny men, but the one thing I do love is to people-watch. Women clad in dazzling dresses that sparkle against the neon lights spanning the room. Men dressed to impress in expensive button-down shirts and ties all fitted with trousers and shoes costing more than my entire college tuition. And of course, all of those in between who give zero fucks about what others think about what they wear, or whose eyes they attract, and dance the night away as if it were their last.

I finish off my drink and cash out with the bartender. Slowly, I stand from the bar stool and saunter my way down the several steps toward the dance floor. A group of girls all dance together toward the center of the floor, one of them in particular catching my eye and waving, beckoning me over to join them. The girl who called me over was Danielle, one of the students I helped teach last semester in my studio art class. Danielle makes quick work by way of introductions, although some of the girls are too far drunk to comprehend the information, most just smile and wave to me. I smile and return the waves as we all begin dancing.

The music consumes my senses and I fall into the rhythms, swirling my hips, and sing aloud until my lungs protest. A few more men approach the group asking for dances, but the girls collectively push them out of the circle and send them all packing. I spin around within the small group, swinging around with Danielle, and laughing harder than I ever have before. My stresses and worries over the past few weeks float away as quickly as they enter my mind.

"What the hell are you doing here?" The voice protruding

from behind my back startles me, forcing me to quickly spin to face the redhead directly behind me.

Tobias. Red-faced, and furious.

What the fuck is his problem?

Danielle swiftly makes her way over to me for backup in pushing him out of our area, but I halt her, telling her it's okay. Once I face Tobias again, I shrug in confusion, "What's the big deal? It's a club," I shout to him over the music.

"You said you were studying. This doesn't look like studying to me." His voice is like gravel, grating against my skin. I roll my eyes at him in response.

"Clara and I finished early in the library and I wanted to enjoy my night. Have you been following me?" My voice grows louder as the music in the club becomes ravenous to my eardrums, but the undeniable anger in my words is plenty clear.

He shakes his head impatiently, "You tell me when you go out from now on. Clara told me you-" I scoff, giving Tobias a light shove to his chest.

"So you *are* fucking following me! You don't own me, Tobias. I can go wherever the hell I want with or without your Gods damned permission." The anger in his eyes shreds through my body like a tornado.

"That's it. You've clearly drank too much. I'm taking you back to the dorm." His grip on my wrist tightens, and I already know it will bruise by the morning. Tobias hauls me from the circle and toward the front door of the club.

"Get the fuck off me!"

The scream tears from my lungs but not nearly loud enough for others to stop and help me within the swarming crowd and blaring music. I claw at Tobias' arm hard enough to draw blood, eliciting a hiss, and a glare that promises a painful night ahead of me. There are zero regrets in my actions, and I especially don't regret looking up at the exact moment a fist flies through the air, clocking Tobias square in the nose.

A gasp lodges in my throat as I watch the scene unfold. Tobias's grip leaves my arm and I instantly pull it back to my chest, quickly taking a few steps away from him. He stumbles back and brings a hand up to cover his now bloody, and most likely broken, nose. I feel a strong arm wrap itself gently around my waist and I have a split-second fight or flight sensation to punch or run. But that sinful voice as soft as velvet enters my mind, calming me down to my core.

"Are you alright?"

I exhale and melt into his touch, nodding as I keep my eyes on Tobias. As Tobias brings his gaze back up to me, his eyes widen at the sight of Cyr standing behind me. He shakes his head in disgust.

"So you're fucking *him* now, too? I didn't take you for a slut." Cyr's grip on me begins to slip away as he starts toward Tobias, but I bring a hand up to cover his own that holds my waist. His body turns rigid beneath my touch and grips harder on my waist to keep himself steady. Gods, the strength he has in only one of his arms makes me question what he was capable of doing with both arms.

Tobias scoffs, shaking his head once again when I don't deign to reply to him, "You're coming home with me. Right now."

His tone is not kindhearted or welcoming but rather laced with brute force that makes me begin to shake. I've been a victim of his verbal assaults and occasionally being pushed around, but never once have I truly been afraid for my physical safety. Tonight is a first for me. I glance back over my shoulder, spinning around within Cyr's grasp. His ice-blue eyes are already on me, surveying every inch of me from head to toe.

"I'm sorry…I have to go. If I don't he'll hurt you, and I couldn't live with myself if he did."

The pain in my eyes shines brightly as they begin to gloss over while holding the tears at bay for as long as I can. At this moment, the last thing I want is for Cyr to see me cry. Cyr's hand tightens against my hip as his eyes dive directly into my soul. I couldn't believe Cyr hadn't pulled away from me yet as it'd been a few minutes since his vice-like grip on me began. I can't deny that I wish I could live in his embrace forever, but even this minor level of intimacy with Cyr frightens me.

"Considering who has the broken nose, I need to be the last thing on your priority list." He drops his hand from around my waist and leans in close to my ear, "It's your choice, Bellamy. Everything in this life is *your* choice. Don't let your feelings cloud your safety." I close my eyes and take a deep, steadying breath. My body turns back to Tobias who is eyeing me with a gaze of fury.

"You'll always be safe with me, Bell."

Rather than the nickname coming from Tobias, it echoes through my head from behind me coming from Cyr's lips. The sound of his voice coaxes all of my senses into submission. I would put myself at risk to protect Cyr, but what he said before rang true in my head. Tobias is the one who should be worried about Cyr breaking him instead of the other way around.

"Go home, Tobias. I'll find you after I've *thoroughly* enjoyed the rest of my night." The words coming out with newfound confidence startles me and I even feel my body stand up taller in front of Tobias. His face is plastered with stunned silence. The warmth against my back as Cyr steps closer brings me more peace than I thought possible, "Someone's a bit cranky tonight, and I think it's past your bedtime."

Tobias's glare in my direction sends shivers down my spine, "We'll talk about this later. Make sure to shower after you fuck him before you climb into my bed tonight."

He spins on his heels and is out of the club in an instant, still holding his broken, bloody nose. Once the club doors shut behind him, I exhale the breath I've been holding tight in my lungs. I feel my body sway with the high coursing through my limbs, but before I can hit the ground that same strong arm coils around my waist to hold me upright.

"Breathe, Bellamy."

His voice nearly sends me tumbling to the ground once again. I slowly turn in his embrace and look up at Cyr, "I'm sorry... I'm so sorry." I frantically glance around, seeing multiple sets of eyes on us. "Everyone's-"

"Don't. Just sway with me."

Cyr's voice is soft as he keeps one arm at the small of my back, gently guiding my hips from side to side. I look down to see there is still some space between the two of us and tears sting the back of my eyes.

There's no way he's okay with this.

Being this close to him before sent him practically running to the opposite side of his bedroom. He must be screaming inside to step back from me. As if I'd said it aloud, Cyr shakes his head in acknowledgment.

He was okay. Somehow.

As I bring my gaze up to meet his own, I know this isn't for me. The swaying and the blissful distraction. It makes my whirring emotions manageable, but this...this was for him. His hand lightly trembles against my lower back, nearly breaking my heart in two. I want to rush him out of the club and apologize since this was too much for him, and I damn well knew it. I was selfish and wanted to show him off to the whole world and let them all know who he showed up with, but he wasn't mine. And I wasn't his. I had no right, and it went too far out of hand. No apology could replace the guilt crawling inside my body.

The way his eyes track my every move to push out the feeling of wandering eyes from the crowds surrounding us makes my heart ache even further. I swear the feeling of his gaze strips me entirely bare from how his eyes scan me from top to bottom and devastatingly slowly back up to my eyes. I suck my bottom lip between my teeth, and his grip on my hip tightens slightly as he intently watches me.

The incessant need to say something makes me want to open my mouth to speak, to say anything, but what could I say? I *chose* to stay with Cyr, here in the club, over my…Gods only knew what Tobias is to me other than a fuck buddy. To Tobias, I'm his, but I'm nothing to anyone except myself, and I intend to keep it that way. But did I?

What was this, then? Between Cyr and I?

I don't even know what to call us, but I know that this sudden relationship has been more life-saving than I realized. Cyr hadn't pulled away from me and didn't seem interested in leaving me yet. I think long and hard about each of the interactions the two of us have shared. From our meeting in the courtyard for class, his bedroom in the dorm, his arms pinning me to the sink in the studio, the position we are currently in. Then it all begins to make sense.

He needs to be the one in control.

In Cyr's bedroom, I approached him, along with in the courtyard. Cyr had no control over how close my proximity would be. But the studio…He had every ounce of control and

I was at his mercy. As the two of us sway to the music, I keep my hands down by my sides in complete submission, and let Cyr take the reins. He leads us both in our silent, sensual dance, and I will follow him willingly.

I take a deep breath, letting myself go, and fade into the music consuming me. My favorite French EDM remix blares around the club and I can't help but smile. My gaze meets Cyr's which is already on me, and my smile creeps up into a smirk as I dare a glance down and back up Cyr's body. When my eyes flick up to meet his once again, I could read in them as if to say:

"I'll let you look me over, just this once."

I continue to keep my hands down at my sides and sway my hips with a bit more flare as Cyr holds tight. As the bass grows, pounding into my head from every direction, I bide my time until the impending drop of the bass hit. Before deciding to make sure Cyr is ready, I slowly dip myself backward and raise one leg alongside his hip. As I expect, his grip only further tightens since I know he'd never let me fall.

"You'll always be safe with me, Bell."

His voice rings out in my head in the mix of the music and I feel like this moment is truly meant to be.

I'm meant to be here. With him.

I couldn't ask for anything more than the pure bliss I feel being around him, especially within his grasp. A slight gasp leaves my lips as I feel his opposite hand gently glide up my raised leg from knee to thigh and then firmly grip my leg to ensure I don't fall. The feeling of his hand against my skin sends goosebumps rippling across my entire body. After several moments of basking in his strong touch, the hand along my back begins pulling me back into reality. My eyes meet his once again, my face completely flush, and I have no intention of attempting to hide it. I'm well aware at this point he knows the effect he has on me, and I want him to witness it firsthand. Cyr's hand remains holding my thigh for a few long moments before slowly releasing my leg back to the ground to stand on my own.

My breath hitches in my throat as Cyr's face closes in toward my ear, "So full of surprises, Raven."

I quickly pull my head back and cock an eyebrow in confusion.

Raven? Did he get his girls mixed up?

A shock wave of hurt flashes across my eyes, and as I meet his eyes they are laced with humor. The slight bouncing of his chest implies that he's laughing, although the music is much too loud to hear. Cyr shakes his head, leaning back in toward my ear even though I'm more than skeptical now that he indeed called me by another girl's name.

"Everyone's allowed to have a nickname, right?"

The sigh that escapes from my lungs feels like a weight is lifted off my chest. His head pulls back to scan my features, and before I can open my mouth to question it, Cyr lifts his free hand to weave his fingers around a strand of raven-black hair that falls over my shoulder. I glance down to watch his hand, and the realization sets in.

Of course. My hair.

I laugh softly under my breath as I bring my dark brown gaze up to meet those glistening blue eyes. I never noticed the depths within his eyes, and I only wish to discover all that resides in them one day. After realizing how long I've fallen lost in his eyes, I sheepishly look away and glance around the crowded room.

"What do you say we get out of here?" I gesture with my head toward the main doors. He raises an eyebrow in question.

"Not enjoying yourself?"

I feel the blush creep back up my cheeks but don't bother hiding it from him. Cyr's hand begins to rise toward my cheek slowly, but the contemplation in his eyes is painted clear as day, letting me know why he brings his hand back down to his side.

"I've had the greatest time I've had in a…well, a long time. But I want to take you somewhere." I tug on my bottom lip with my teeth, shrugging toward the doors once again, "I promise it won't have nearly this many people there."

The hand that has been on my lower back for several minutes drops down from off of me. The lack of warmth there is like a bucket of ice splashing down over me and sending a shiver across my body.

I inhale a sharp breath as he leans close to my ear, "I'd follow you to the end of the world, Raven." He pulls back and gestures toward the front door, "Lead the way."

***

"An ice cream parlor?"

The judgmental gaze in Cyr's eyes as he side-eyes me makes my eyes widen and my mouth slightly gape. Before I can think about the action, I lightly shove him in the shoulder with a hand. My head whips over to Cyr in time to watch him take a staggering step back away from me.

His tattooed hands shake at his sides, clenching his fists and opening them to clench them again. Tears well in my eyes at the sight of it. What I'd just done to him so carelessly. I want to step toward him and comfort him but know that would only worsen it.

"Oh Gods, Cyr. I'm so-"

"What's your favorite flavor?" His eyes close, concealing those beautiful, soul-consuming blue eyes. The soft-spoken question startles me more than the expectant snap I more than deserve. I raise an eyebrow and open my mouth to question him, but Cyr's deathly quiet voice continues before I can, "We're at an ice cream parlor, Bellamy, you know what I mean." His eyes remain shut, and the pain that rips through my heart at the crack in his voice is damn near unbearable.

"Mint chocolate chip. What's yours?" My voice shakes as I reply, and I realize once again that this is a distraction. He needs something to focus on and take away from the war raging on inside his body. The laugh that escapes his lips is void of all humor, but to see him taken aback by my answer makes my heart swell just the slightest.

"Rocky road," His reply comes on an exhale, and my lips tug up at one corner.

"I didn't take you for the type of guy to like white, sticky stuff in his mouth," I reply softly with a light laugh. Cyr's eyes open, glossed over, and upon meeting his gaze with tears daring to fall from my eyes, he shakes his head.

"Those tears better not be for me, or you're buying." The normal velvet-soft lilt to his voice returns as if the last sixty seconds never happened.

A slight scoff leaves my lips, the shade of them nearly beat-red after how hard I've been biting my bottom lip. A single tear slips down my cheek, and I quickly brush it away with the back of my hand. Cyr takes a step toward me, and I retreat a step while shaking my head, "I'm buying, either way, dummy," I sniffle softly, "It's the least I can do after the shit show I put you through with what happened with Tobias and now with-"

Cyr steps forward again, quickly eating up the distance between us, and claims my cheeks with his hands before I can attempt to flee from him again. He forces my head upward to meet his insatiable ice-blue gaze, no longer glossy and now void of all pain.

"Do not blame yourself for Tobias's actions. Ever. He chose to be a prick, and the bastard got what he deserved." His thumb grazes along the side of my cheekbone over the trail of my tears, "And don't you ever feel sorry for the way I am. My own mistakes got me here. One day I might be able to explain it all to you, but right now you just have to trust that nothing you do could ever drive me away from you."

My lungs are exhausted of all air and I feel it hard to breathe with the weight of his gaze and his words. Again, I wonder how it was so easy for him to touch me, but not the other way around. I don't dare to question it, especially since the way his fingers caress my skin is barely more than I can stand without melting into a puddle on the ground. My eyes close for a brief moment and gently nuzzle my head against Cyr's hand as I attempt to compose my thoughts into coherent words.

"I never expected you to tell me what she did to you, but I'm going to try with all that I am to gain that trust one day."

As my eyes open and meet Cyr's gaze, I can see that glossiness in his eyes return for just a moment. He sighs with a nod and takes a deep inhale.

"I-" He stops himself as if contemplating speaking the words he intends. Cyr steps back while releasing his grasp on my cheeks, and he drops them back to his sides. I want to step toward him and force him to say the words I beg to hear from him, but I stand planted where he left me. Stunned, and too far gone from my soul-consuming emotions to attempt to figure out something to say.

"I think the parlor is closing soon. We should get our ice

cream while we can." His words hit me like a ton of bricks.

What was he going to say?

What did he want *to say?*

I know it wasn't about the damn ice cream.

"I never want to see you again"?

"I hate you"?

All the words he could have possibly wanted to say repeated over and over in my head to the point of near madness.

I return to reality and bring my gaze back to Cyr, my knees nearly buckling at the sight of him. The moonlight above us pours down and washes over him in a pale glow illuminating his beautiful features even further. From the light above, it shines down on his hair turning it a shade of midnight blue. He is utterly breathtaking, and it takes everything I am to not walk over to him and entangle my fingers in his hair. To bring him close to me as we had been in the club.

Through the swelling and cracking of my heart, I nod and turn toward the front counter underneath the pale green awning without another word.

15

The Admission

Cyr and I eat our ice cream cones in tangible silence for what feels like a small eternity. We ordered our ice cream, and Cyr dared to attempt to pay, but I was quicker to the action. I pulled out a twenty-dollar bill from my purse and handed it to the woman behind the counter. I withdrew the twenty from the ATM earlier to use to pay for the cover charge at the club, but Cyr beat me to it and paid for my entrance fee. There was no way, especially after all that happened during our night out that Cyr was buying *me* ice cream. It's the absolute least I could do for him to show an ounce of my gratitude for all he's done for me.

I receive an appreciative 'thank you' from Cyr upon receiving our desserts, and we find a park bench not too far from the parlor to sit and enjoy our ice cream. The bench is in a darker part of the street next to the park where most people are vacant. I sit back to back with him so he can finish his dessert without exposing himself. The realization that he's maskless merely a foot away from me has my mind reeling to take a peek over my shoulder.

The time will come, Bell. Hopefully. Just not right now.

Shortly after we finish our sweet treats, the two of us take an Uber back to the campus, and it's mayhem navigating through downtown Boston on a packed Friday night. Which in turn causes the twenty-minute ride to take us nearly an hour. The two of us walk side by side through the dorms of Upper Campus toward my dorm when I slowly come to a stop in the middle of the hallway.

"I'm not going back to my room," I say quietly as it's well past midnight and the last thing I want is to wake anyone in the dormitory.

"Were you planning on staying at another friend's dorm?" His voice echoes softly in the hall, raising an eyebrow in question.

Yes dummy, yours, is what I wish I could tell him. I sigh, glancing down the hall toward the direction of the dorm Cyr and Tobias share.

"I need to talk to Tobias."

My body turns to begin to walk past Cyr, but as Cyr takes hold of my wrist he quickly spins me back around to face him. I glance down to where he gently holds onto my arm and, slowly, I bring my gaze back up to face him when he shakes his head in protestation.

"I strongly advise against that." His voice is firm, but still low to not alert any other students in the surrounding dorms, "After what happened at the club, I doubt he'll be anything akin to a gentleman tonight."

A fact I already know, but I can't run away from Tobias forever. I need to talk to him and explain what happened between Cyr and me tonight. Why I was out with Cyr, and that we weren't fucking like he so rudely assumed of me. Although I can't say I wouldn't mind if we indeed were...

Gods above, Bell, stop it. Wrong time for that.

"I know, Cyr," I say on an exhale, and take a deep breath with my eyes fixed on Cyr's. "But if he's going to take it out on someone, it sure as hell isn't going to be you."

The steel-eyed focus in my gaze elicits a sigh from Cyr, and he drops his hand from my wrist.

"I'm not going to stand here and tell you what you can and cannot do." His voice is like pure velvet floating across my skin, but it's laced with worry, "But do not base your judgments on me. Make your choices because they're your own, not because your mind is clouded with emotion, Bellamy."

I shake my head, trying my damnedest to rein in the storm brewing inside my body. I don't want to fight with him, but if I went to see Tobias tonight, I couldn't guarantee that I would come out of that dorm unscathed. So I do the only thing I believe will be safe for us both. My body turns back toward the direction of my dorm room and I make my way to the front door.

"For all that it's worth, Cyr, I couldn't have asked for a more perfect night," I say softly as I pull out my room key from my wallet clipped to the back of my phone. I glance back to Cyr, and I can see it written clear as day in his eyes.

"Me too."

He nods his agreement, and I push my shoulder into the door, nodding to him in a silent 'goodnight'. Every fiber of my being knows that Cyr waits to make sure my door shuts and locks tightly before leaving. His presence wraps around me like a cloak and brings a shiver down my spine. I keep my ear to the door to listen as soft footsteps sound down the hall and soon fade as Cyr walks back toward his dorm.

***

Over the next hour, I tell Clara all about our night, including Tobias barging into the club. Clara apologizes profusely for telling him where the two of us had gone, not thinking he would have followed me. I didn't care about Tobias, he was nothing to me anymore. I wasn't entirely sure when I stopped caring about Tobias, but I assumed it was the moment I locked eyes with Cyr at the pub on my birthday 5 months ago. The very day I ran off to the bathroom and began hyperventilating because someone other than Tobias showed me any kind of interest.

Even though the two of us had a bumpy start, I found out quickly that there was a lot to Cyr that he hid under the surface. Things I want to discover piece by piece of all that he holds captive in his mind, and heart. Starting with that beautiful bronze skin beneath his mask.

Clara falls asleep soon after I enter the shower in our en-suite bedroom. I take off the light makeup I applied earlier that night and let the events of the night fill my mind. The feeling of Cyr's arm wrapping around my waist, watching his hand knock straight into Tobias' face, the graze of his thumbs against my cheeks.

Gods I want him. Just *him*.

In any aspect that he will grant me. If I have to spend the rest of my life only spending it in his presence and nothing more, it would be enough.

What the hell has gotten into you, Bell? You'll never be what he needs.

But Cyr is the only thing that *I* need. The draw I feel being around him is unlike anything I've ever experienced. The adrenaline that fills my veins, the pure bliss of standing by his side, the feeling of euphoria as his soft skin brushes against mine. I can't understand the attraction that causes my body to be near him for as long as he can bear, but it's real and incredibly tangible.

After drying off and braiding my long raven hair back away from my face, I throw on a pair of sweatpants and a tank top that may have been mine, or possibly Clara's. The two of us share clothes all the time, so it doesn't matter either way who ends up with whose clothes as long as they get washed. Which more times than not comes down to my responsibility.

I lay in bed for an hour staring up at the ceiling. Tobias's name pops up across my phone screen about a dozen times, but I'm in no mindset to talk to him. I don't feel like getting berated and told off over the phone. Tomorrow I'll go over and talk to him when he is, hopefully, in a better mood. My mind won't stop racing and replaying all that happened over the past few hours. Only when I finally roll over to attempt to sleep does my phone buzz beside me on my bed. I reach over to pick it up and see a text from Cyr pop across my screen. The light that shines from my phone illuminates the dark room.

Cyr: *"My room. Now."*

I raise an eyebrow in worry at the blunt text. I pull up the keypad to ask what the hell is going on when another message pops up a moment later.

Cyr: *"Don't knock on the door. Text me when you're outside."*

What in the actual fuck is going on? It's almost 3 am. I don't want to keep him waiting, and I need answers. With my heart racing, I quietly grab my cardigan to not wake up Clara and slip on my flip-flops. Picking up my phone and room key from my nightstand, I silently slip out of the dorm room.

My feet carry me swiftly and silently through the dorm room halls, practically running to Cyr and Tobias' dorm down the hall and taking the steps up to the next floor two at a time. Once

I reach the dorm, I nearly bang on the door but remember Cyr's text. I quickly pull out my phone from my pocket and shoot Cyr a text.

Me: "I'm outside."

And so I wait. One minute. Two minutes. I keep my text messages with Cyr open to not miss a text from him. My head jolts up at the sound of glass shattering beyond the door and I involuntarily jump when I hear Tobias's muffled yell. If he keeps that up the campus police will be here in seconds. I lean in and place my ear to the door to listen.

Silence.

Then the door quickly opens, nearly sending me flying to the ground on my face. The bracing feeling of Cyr's hand on my shoulder steadies my feet to stand upright. He quickly ushers me inside with his hand against the small of my back. Cyr leans in close to my ear, whispering, "My room. Don't make a sound."

My eyes dart around the room, taking note of the glass bottles in shards across the tiled floor. I quietly step over them and glance to see the bar stool chairs by the kitchenette counter overturned on their sides.

What the hell happened?!

I know exactly what happened. All those phone calls I ignored…this is all my fault. I shake my head and bolt for Cyr's bedroom. A moment later he's inside the room, silently shutting the door, and locking it behind him.

"What in the name of fuck is going on?" I whisper-yell to Cyr as he approaches me. He places a finger to his masked lips and shakes his head. Another bottle smashes, causing me to flinch at the sound. He takes a few quick steps toward me and places a hand on my cheek.

"You're okay. You're safe now." He barely speaks louder than a whisper as he caresses my cheekbone with his thumb.

I try my hardest to not melt into his touch, but I can't help it. I gently lean my head into his hand and use it for support. The events of the night are heavily weighing down on me and even the slightest of reprieve from Cyr makes them float away. My eyes open, not realizing I'd closed them, surprised even more to see Cyr hadn't moved. His hand just holds me there in the center of his bedroom while I quietly breathe, losing myself for just a moment in bliss.

"I-I'm sorry," I whisper, standing back upright, and stepping away from him to sit on the corner of his bed. "I thought you said I shouldn't be here," I speak just as quietly as he had moments before. His sigh is audible, and his shoulders drop.

"He's gone ballistic, Raven."

Gods above, that nickname gives me butterflies, and my stomach does a few somersaults as the sound of his voice envelops me.

"I knew I couldn't protect you from your dorm if he'd decided to barge over and find you in the middle of the night." My eyes flash up to meet his where he stands a few feet in front of me.

"Protect me? Do you find me that weak I couldn't tell that prick to fuck off on my own?" There's a bit of hurt that courses through my body, even though the sentimental thoughts of him wanting to help keep me safe warm me to my core. At this moment, I truly meant nothing to him, so the thought of him reaching out to help me began to melt my heart.

Cyr's eyes narrow on me ever so slightly, "If you were able to protect yourself then why did you find yourself in my bed all those nights?"

The question stumps me stupid. I look down at my hands in my lap, intertwining them distractedly. His question isn't patronizing, but rather a question to make me think back at myself and my actions. I could've left Tobias and gone back to my dorm all those nights, but I didn't want to. I wanted the comfort that Cyr brings me. Even a few months back when we didn't know each other all that well yet, he still brought me more peace than Tobias ever has.

"Because I wasn't looking for safety all those nights," My voice is soft, yet filled with more confidence than my body has possessed in a long time. I stand from his bed and take a few short steps toward Cyr. He stands with his feet planted on the ground and doesn't attempt in any way to move away from me. I swear he even leans in toward me as I find myself only inches in front of him.

"I just wanted *you.*"

My chocolate brown eyes float up to meet his, and I can see inside them the need for me. The same need and longing for him flashes within my own eyes. I want Cyr to see every ounce of need, and want, that courses through my veins and begs my body to be colliding passionately with his.

After a moment, I concede a step back and look away shaking my head, "But I know that I can't have you, no matter how hard I want you." My words come out no more than a whisper, and tears threaten to spill from my eyes, "You need someone willing to go slow and gentle with you, and I can't promise I can do that."

"What if I don't want to be gentle?"

The reply that leaves his lips renders me speechless. My eyes widen as I bring my gaze back up to meet his. Gods the question nearly has me racing to him to rip every article of clothing off his body. I exhale and shake my head while I attempt to formulate coherent thoughts compared to the madness overwhelming my senses.

"Cyr, I-"

My words are cut off mid-thought when Cyr places his finger in a 'shh' motion over his lips to warn me to speak quietly. Of all times, now is a time when I want to be anything but quiet.

After a moment of frustration, I spin around walking over to his desk in the corner of the room. My fingers quickly comb through the stack of records on his desk and settle on the first album I found the very first time I came into his room a few months ago. I open the record player, pull out the vinyl with nimble fingers from the sleeve, and place 'Phobia' by *Breaking Benjamin* atop the record player. Carefully, I lift the arm to place it at the beginning of the record, watching the record begin to spin before the music erupts into the space. Quickly, I adjust the volume to play at a manageable volume to help mask our conversation. I turn to look back at Cyr who watches me with admiration which nearly sends me crumbling to the floor under buckling knees. Once I return to a closer distance from Cyr with still a bit of space between the two of us, I continue.

"I know there are things you aren't physically capable of, and I understand. In no way is that bash at you, Cyr. I'm just terrified of what's building in my heart, and I don't ever want to hurt you. Even if by accident. I wouldn't be able to forgive myself." My voice remains firm, but not loud enough to be heard by Tobias from over the music.

A humorless laugh spills from my lips, bringing my hands up to my eyes to catch the impending tears I feel welling up, "Hell, even earlier I wasn't even remotely thinking and I saw what it did to you, and it broke my heart." My words falter to a whisper by the time the thought leaves my lips.

The gentle touch of Cyr's hands against my own is the final

straw before the tears fall, and he holds onto my hands as I silently cry.

"Look at me."

His voice is firm, but soft as silk coating my senses from head to toe. It takes me a moment, but through my crying hiccups, I dare a teary-eyed glance up to meet Cyr's gaze. His icy blue eyes pour into my soul, and all I want at this moment is to curl up into his chest and fade into him with the music surrounding us. Against my wishes, I remain planted in front of him with our hands connected between us. Cyr takes a deep breath and looks down at our hands, something brewing in his eyes that I can't seem to place.

"I care for you, Bellamy."

Those five words knock the breath straight from my lungs. I can't stop the tears from flowing down my cheeks once again, but it dawns on me that I can't tell if they are happy tears or tears of worry for what could become of us. The attraction I felt for Cyr since I first laid eyes on him in the pub was confusing, yet the most real feeling I'd experienced since losing Jamie. I attempt to muster the courage to speak, my mouth beginning to open, then closes again. I don't know what to say or even begin to explain how much I truly and deeply care for him.

"You don't have to say anything. I just needed you to know that."

His words are gentle, and when I break away from his hold on my hands, the warmth previously there instantly turns to ice. My body moves to sit down on the edge of his bed, brushing the tears off my cheeks, and I begin toying with the end of my braid. I need a simple distraction to compute my thoughts into coherent words.

I bring my gaze back to Cyr who still stands in the center of his room, looking down at his hands as if mine are still there intertwined with his. I release a long breath and fall back onto his bed to stare at the ceiling above.

"Bellamy? Are you-"

I hold a hand up in the air to pause him before lowering it back down to lie on my stomach. My opposite hand reaches across the space on his bed and double-taps the comforter urging him over to join me. I bring the hand back to place it atop my other hand, holding myself still so Cyr can approach his bed without contact.

After a moment, the bed sinks slightly with the weight as Cyr mimics my movements. My eyes close for a moment to take in the music surrounding me, and the essence of Cyr's cologne filling my senses. I move my hand from off my stomach and place it on the bed between the two of us. A part of my heart aches for Cyr to hold my hand, but that also means diving into a realm I'm not entirely sure I'm capable of falling into again.

I have never met someone like Cyr. A man so selfless, forgiving, and comforting all at once. It's a shock to my core that he's chosen to bestow those qualities upon me rather than another who I feel will be more deserving of him.

But he chose *me*.

And that makes my heart swell even more than the soft caress of his fingers intertwining with mine. My eyes clamp shut even tighter to suppress the tears I feel brewing behind my eyelids. My fingers gently notch themselves into his hand and we stay like this for some length of time unbeknownst to me, and I couldn't have been more at peace.

I fall deep into my mind basking in the bliss of Cyr at my side until the smashing of glass from the other side of the wall sends me jolting upright. My hold on Cyr's hand quickly releases and

I stand up from his bed. Then, I say the hardest thing I ever have before.

"I can't do this," My voice breaking, and I quickly make my way from his bed to march toward his door.

"What do you mean?" Cyr sits up to watch me, cocking an eyebrow in question. I shake my head, keeping my hand on the doorknob of the bedroom door. My other hand shakes at my side but I clench it tight to mask my nerves.

"He'll tear this whole dorm apart. I have to calm him down and to do that I-" I will the tears welling in my eyes to stop and exhale deeply, "I can't see you anymore, Cyr. If I do, he'll never stop with these tantrums, and I can't risk him hurting you. I'll never forgive myself for dragging you into my mess."

Cyr tilts his head slightly as his glacier eyes lock onto mine.

"Or, you could leave him."

He stands from his bed and takes a few steps toward me. The shock of his words stuns me into silence.

"You still want to keep me safe. Regardless of what your feelings are for me, you can't deny there's something there that makes you feel this way." How Cyr can read my feelings entirely is beyond my comprehension, "Stop trying to appease him. The one thing you can do to protect me, and yourself most importantly, is to leave him."

I know he's right, yet my heart still crumples hearing those brutally honest words. I poured my heart into making Tobias as happy as I physically could over the past several months while, in truth, he's only ever used me for his gain. Tobias was the first person I romantically brought into my life after losing Jamie.

I can't say I care for him as much as someone would with a real partner, but he's been a security blanket for me. In a way, I guess I'd used him for my gain as much as he had done to me.

Although on utterly different levels, the guilt rips through me forcing the tears to trail down my cheeks.

"I care for you, Cyr. Truly, I do." My voice is hardly louder than a whisper, and seeing Cyr's eyes widen breaks my heart even further; the crack shattering my heart echoes through my body, "I don't believe that I'm able to be what you need, and you deserve the whole world." Another tear escapes from my eye as I turn the door handle to the bedroom door.

"So do you, Bellamy. Don't forget that for a fucking second."

Steeling my body and letting Cyr's words sink into my mind, I quietly slip out of his room, pulling the door shut behind me.

***

"What the fuck does he have that I don't, Bellamy?! He's a goddamn nobody!" Tobias's words come out utterly slurred as he fists the neck of his beer bottle. I have no clue how many he's consumed already, but I presume the beer in his hand is several past too many.

"Okay, I think you've had enough to drink."

I attempt to take another step toward him, reaching out to take the bottle from his hand. Before I can reach the bottle, my body is thrown back and lands roughly on the bed behind me. The movement is jarring and the look of horror across my features only intensifies as Tobias laughs. He takes a large gulp of his beer before discarding it on the floor along with several other smashed bottles. The dried blood below his slightly offset nose that visibly wasn't set right disgusts me, but I remember who did that to him to protect me. My best interests have always been placed first and foremost by the most unlikely person I could have ever imagined.

My thoughts are ripped from my mind and I'm thrown back into my harsh reality as my flip-flops are ripped off my feet and tossed across the room. I cower back from him, crawling back further onto his bed to create distance between us.

"Tobias, stop," I say firmly, trying to steel my voice into neutrality. He staggers forward and grabs hold of my ankles, dragging me back towards him across his bed. I can't help the yelp that escapes my lips at the sudden movement. I try to kick him away, but my efforts are for naught as Tobias easily flips me over onto my stomach and climbs up my body. He halts his body over my hips, straddling me, and dips his fingers below the waistband of my sweatpants. The feeling of his weight above me, trapping me in, sent my mind reeling off the deep end at breakneck speed.

"Please, Tobias. Please-"

"Shut up, whore!"

Tobias's words stun me and render me silent as I sob into the sheets beneath me. I try to control my breathing, but I lose all sense of who I am and what I'm doing. More like what's being done to me. I want to call for Cyr, but the hum of his music still blares through the wall, and know he would never hear me. A part of me knows this is what he meant about protecting myself. Not from getting mugged in town, but protecting myself against Tobias in any capacity.

"I'm gonna erase him from your mind, and show you what a good time is like. Even if it takes me all night."

His hands begin to drag my sweatpants down over my ass.

It was now, or never.

Without another second to think, I drive my heels up directly into the center of his spine. He groans, halting his pull on my pants, and while he's momentarily distracted I ball my fist and swing up as hard as I can behind me. The audible *crack* in response to my fist colliding with Tobias's nose is the telltale sign I'd hit my mark. If Cyr hadn't truly broken it earlier, it certainly is now. As is one or two of my fingers, but that's entirely an afterthought.

Tobias' cry of pain is my cue, and I force his body over to throw him off of me. The movement sends his body crashing to the floor among the shards of broken glass. I slip my pants back on swiftly, scrambling off his bed, and grabbing a large shard of glass from the floor.

"Shit, Bellamy!" Tobias groans and sits up from the ground clutching his nose, attempting to stand up.

"Sit your ass down, and shut the fuck up."

My voice is nothing but hard steel with a hint of murderous intent. He freezes where he sits on the floor, wide-eyed and delirious.

"Listen close and hard. You will *never* touch me again." I make a point of enunciating every word as my eyes lock straight onto his. "If I so much as see your face I will blast you for every cruel and horrible thing you are to women and the rest of this world." I don't know where the words come from that escape my lips, but this newfound confidence ripping through me brings tears to my eyes. "You know nothing of what it means to be a man. That's what Cyr has that you don't. You should take some notes instead of shoving your cock in anything that breathes," I drop the glass shard from my hand to the floor and turn toward the door.

"Baby, please. I-I'm sorry."

I scoff and open his bedroom door.

"No, you're not, and you never will be."

I slam the door shut behind me, cutting off those past horrors forever without a second glance.

16

The Question

The front door of Cyr and Tobias's dorm slams shut, but I remain inside. I need Tobias to think I've left the dorm completely, but instead, I turn back for Cyr's room. On nimble feet, I scurry toward Cyr's room, quickly opening the door, and shutting it silently behind me.

After locking the door behind me, I glance around the room to find it empty. I reach for my phone to call him when I hear the faint sound of water running from the en-suite bathroom next to me. I contemplate going in but don't want to catch him in a vulnerable position. My next thought is to lie down and wait for him to finish, but after looking down at my feet, I notice little spots of blood along the floor in a trail from the front door to where I now stand by his bed.

Shit.

I must have caught some glass under my feet rushing out of Tobias' room and with the adrenaline blazing in my system I hadn't even noticed the slight tinge of pain. I sigh, the situation increasing my level of frustration and know I have to tell him I'm here. So, keeping my eyes adverted from the inside of the bathroom, I open the bathroom door just a notch to call inside softly.

"Cyr? Uh-I didn't want to-" I begin, and as soon as I do, the water instantly cuts off, "You don't have to stop. I just didn't want to startle you," I quickly continue, guilt ripping through me that I've now disturbed him when all he wants is probably a relaxing shower after a long night out. I start to shut the door when it's yanked open so hard it nearly sends me sprawling to the floor. What quickly catches me is Cyr's hands slipping around my waist, holding me upright in front of him.

Gods above he's gorgeous. As if that wasn't already a statement for the ages.

Cyr stands in front of me, water droplets falling down his tattooed skin with nothing more than a towel tied low around his hips, and his mask. The waft of steam coming from the shower illuminates him like a messenger sent from the Gods. His hair slick with water is pushed back from his face; the black locks falling back behind his head with one unruly strand falling right across his forehead. I can't help but let my eyes rove for a few moments. My eyes take in every inch of his tattooed arms and chest that I hadn't been able to see in their full glory until now. Where a black and gray dragon climbs up his right side from his hip to his collarbone and meets deep black script across the front of his chest. My eyes trail down to the carved lines of his abs, and then to the deep V leading down towards his-

My eyes flash upwards to meet those ice-blue eyes already on me examining for any sign of harm. His gaze drifts off me toward the floor to see the specs of blood by the door, and down to where I'm now standing in front of him. Cyr's eyes fill with worry and something akin to bloodlust.

"Are you alright? What happened? I thought I heard the door slam outside," Cyr prattles on with questions and I shake my head with a sigh.

"I needed him to believe I'd left, so that was the front door. He tried to…"

Words evade me as my tongue dries up and the world floats away around me. I recall the events of the past twenty minutes and it all crashes into me like a monsoon. The tears begin falling before I even realize and bring my hands up to cover my face. The feeling of crumbling to the floor washes over me until I feel strong arms wrap around my body and pull me close toward warm skin.

I've never been this close to Cyr before and the feeling of his hardened muscles enveloping me makes me feel as safe as I'd ever been before. The pounding of his heart beneath my ear keeps me grounded as I let the tears spill and the emotions invade each of my senses. He remains still, tightly holding onto me as if I'd slip from the face of the Earth if he let go of me. Even while this moment is something I've wanted since I met him, I wish it was under different circumstances. The sobs racking my body won't stop and I can't will them away even with Cyr's hums of relaxation and gentle strokes of his hands through my hair.

"Breathe, Raven."

His words begin to halt the crying, and the sniffles and small hiccups come in waves. Cyr pulls back from me and releases a breath. He takes hold of my hands to gently pull them away from my face. I close my eyes and turn my head away so he won't be able to see the puffy-eyed state I'm in. When his hand comes up to grasp my chin and guide my head up to look at him. The action causes me to finally open my reddening eyes.

"What. Did. He. Do."

Those words, dark and promising death, strike a cord in my heart. In a matter of seconds, I watch his calm facade fade from worried to protective and in search of torture. I sigh, then hiccup, and sniffle. His eyes shift from that beautiful glacier blue to nearly black as rage takes over.

"Nothing. Well, he tried to but..." My voice trails off as I shake the lingering feeling of his body pinning me down. I clamp my eyes shut as I take a deep breath in through my nose before continuing, "I think I helped re-break his nose."

My words are slightly hoarse, sniffling once again. Cyr's eyes widen, with shock, I can discern, but there's also a bit of pride that warms my heart.

"Did he hurt you?" Cyr asks softly while gently caressing the side of my cheek with his thumb.

"No. The blood was my fault for leaving my flip-flops behind," I explain, thanking his comforting touch for settling me down. "But he did make me realize that I'm not his fucking property, and also how right you were this whole damn time." My pride comes through in my words as I meet Cyr's gaze, and I shake my head, "I'm sorry I didn't listen to you. You were right."

"In every aspect of my life, this is a moment when I wish I wasn't right. But some of the hardest things in this life to face are the people we hold onto the tightest for all the wrong reasons." The tears come welling back into my eyes and Cyr brushes them away before they can form, "Breathe. No more crying, Raven. He doesn't deserve those tears."

"I'm not crying over him. I'm crying because I let that piece of shit walk all over me and tell me what I could and couldn't do for too damn long." I exhale, backing away from Cyr's grasp on me, and slowly pace the room, "I let him *use* me for all I had because I didn't think I was good enough. For anyone. Not even myself."

My tone grows slightly louder in anger and frustration, thankful Cyr kept the music playing after I'd left for Tobias's room.

"I was too fucking blind to see that the best thing I have in my life was trying to get me to open my own eyes and see that. In a way, I feel like I used you because I was too much of a coward to let my own heart take the lead in what it wants." I throw my hands up in the air and slap them down at my sides for emphasis. I scoff at myself, "I let that douchebag get in the way of us, and-"

"Us?"

Cyr's question stops me in my tracks. I spin to face him, mouth slightly gaping as I realize what he's asking. My cheeks quickly tinge with a blush as I toy with the edge of my disheveled braid.

"I tried to make myself believe that I wouldn't be good enough for you, and in a way, I know I won't ever fully be good enough." I take a deep breath before continuing, "But being around you these past few months and seeing all the trust you've instilled in me…it frightens me."

My body can't deny the physical attraction I feel towards Cyr, like a magnetic pull I couldn't stop from drawing me to him, even if I wanted it to. I carefully take a few slow steps towards him.

"But I can't deny myself the fact that I deeply care for you, and I hate it took me this long to admit it to you, and myself." My exhale is shaky as I wait for his response, attempting my best efforts to not shake with the anticipation.

Cyr meets me halfway and stops a few inches in front of me,

"You continue to amaze me, Bellamy." I raise an eyebrow in question as his comment throws me completely for a loop.

"How so?"

"You believe that you are less than the ground you walk on, but in reality, the entire world should be worshiping that very ground."

I stand there stunned at his words, gazing up at him awestruck. A small smile slips up my cheeks, and I quickly look away as my blush grows impossibly farther across my body.

"I'm nowhere near perfect, Cyr, but I wouldn't be standing here right now if it weren't for you." I muster all of my courage to look back up at him and let him see all the emotions flooding my mind, "I meant what I said earlier, and I hope when you said you cared for me, you meant it as well."

"When have I ever lied to you, Raven?"

Simple answer. Never.

Not a single time from the moment I met Cyr Maddox did I feel he had ever told me a dishonest thought. I nod to him my understanding, and my smile brightens inch by inch.

"I know I can be a lot to handle, but if you'll have me, I truly think there could be an 'us'. You know, after a little while." I shrug my shoulders lightly and bite my lip as he gazes at me for endless minutes. Cyr lifts a hand to my cheek, holding me in place in front of him.

"You said I deserve the world. So let me give that to you. Let me give you my world. It may scare you, but trust me I'm just as frightened."

His words are laced with longing and admiration. I can hardly keep my knees from buckling at the sound of his voice. Those piercing blue eyes stare right into my soul and expose every thought that has ever come into my mind.

"I know this may be a lot to ask of you, Raven, but to do this, I need one thing."

"Anything."

My response is immediate without even a breath to think about it. Cyr nods, though his eyes seem a bit shocked by my quick reply. I watch his inked chest rise as he inhales, and slowly exhales.

"I need you to submit to me."

The brief flash of my eyes has Cyr quickly continuing.

"I don't need an answer from you now. You've gone through Hell tonight. There are certain things I can't do, but with you, I feel like I could get there again one day. But I need your submission to do that, Raven." His voice is nothing but encouraging and calming.

Thoughts race through my mind a mile a minute. I try to inhale and exhale evenly, but with all that has happened within the past few hours, it all barrels into me like a freight train. The feeling of Cyr's hand against my cheek sends my body into uncontainable bliss. Through the months I'd gotten to know Cyr, I trusted him more and more every day. Countless times he's shown me that all he's done for me has been with my best interests in mind. I couldn't name a singular time when anyone had done that for me. Not even…

I can't think about her right now. Not with the most gorgeous man I'd ever laid eyes on standing in front of me and giving himself to me. The idea of laying bare before him and entirely relinquishing control of myself makes my nerves run rampant. However, I know he'd never hurt me. That's not where my nerves lie, but rather in the fact that I would now be able to uncover those pieces of Cyr hidden away that I've been so desperate to unravel. He trusts me, and that makes my decision all that much easier.

My eyes lock onto Cyr's and without a word, I slowly sink onto my knees before him and bow my head. Cyr brings down a hand to lift my head to face him with a gentle grip under my chin, "Do you consent to this?"

My mouth gapes just the slightest at his words, and the strictness, unlike anything I've ever heard from him. I nod, and Cyr's grip tightens just the slightest in return. "I need to hear you say it, Raven."

"Yes. I consent."

The words escape my lips breathlessly as I try to control my breathing against my racing heart.

"Good girl."

Achievement unlocked: Praise Kink.

My eyes flick up to meet his, and I can't compose any coherent thoughts as I take in Cyr's form in front of me. Every inch of him dripping with primal dominance that beckons me to give him everything. The evidence of his arousal is clear from the bulge growing from underneath his towel. A fierce bright red blush stains my cheeks causing me to look down at the floor.

"No, Raven. Look. At. Me."

The sound of his voice lowering as he voices my nickname sends my core turning into absolute molten lava. I slowly bring my gaze back up, trying my hardest to not stare as I bite down hard on my bottom lip.

"I want you to witness what you do to me."

If the two of us are to carry through with this new relationship, I'm not sure I'll even survive the first night.

"God, you're so beautiful. Especially on your knees for me."

My heart swells nearly to the point of combustion as he softly caresses my cheek, and I melt into his touch. I keep my gaze transfixed on him, and the only thing I see within those icy blue depths is pure adoration. The butterflies in my stomach do not cease their somersaults as I remain kneeling at his feet.

Cyr's grip on my chin drops and he extends a hand down toward me, offering a helping hand up. I gently take hold of his soft, callused hand as he helps me up to my feet, and I nod my thanks to him. After a moment of silence, Cyr pulls away and retreats a step.

"Do you need me to walk you back to your dorm?"

I shift my gaze down to my bare and slightly bloody feet, "I was hoping I could stay…" My voice turns quiet as I trail off.

"With me?"

Cyr finishes my train of thought for me, and I nod as my eyes flick back to meet his own. He sighs, and I brace myself for the upcoming rejection. Tonight out of all nights is one I don't want to spend alone, even though Clara will be in our dorm with me, but it won't be the same without Cyr. I need him, more than I would ever admit aloud to him.

"I'm glad we're on the same page." His reply shocks me, and my eyebrow rises in question.

"We…are?" I ask while trying to keep my voice as neutral as possible even though my happiness is nearly bursting at the seams.

Cyr's cheekbones shift under his mask, and I can only hope he's smiling. The things I would do to see that smile. But on the other hand, the thought of seeing his face in its entirety scares me more than anything. For a man so closely guarded, it would more than likely be a long time before we even remotely come close to being on that level of trust. However, this new foundation for us is indeed a promising beginning to achieving that trust one day.

"I didn't want to overwhelm you by asking. I know tonight has been a lot, and I didn't want you to think I was forcing you to stay with me." Cyr's tone is gentle and it soothes my racing thoughts even further.

"This…" He pauses for a moment as if contemplating his words, "Relationship, is going to take time and it's not something I think either of us is ready for tonight." Cyr reaches toward me, taking a step to close the gap, and brushes a loose strand of my dark hair from my braid back behind my ear, "There is so much I want to do with you but remember, even though you agreed to this arrangement, you can end it at any moment. No matter what we're in the middle of at the time…"

Cyr's implication makes my cheeks quickly redden at the thought of all the two of us could get ourselves into, and I can't deny I wasn't at least a little bit excited.

"I know."

"I know you do, but that doesn't change the fact I never want you to feel pressured into doing something you're not comfortable with." Cyr takes a deep breath, steeling himself, "I haven't been intimate with anyone since…" His voice is shaky, but as his eyes meet mine, I convey my understanding. "I can't lie and say I'm not scared, because that's not fair to you. But what I can say is that I never would have asked you to be a part of this if I didn't want you. And I do, Bellamy, so fucking badly."

I couldn't believe it would be possible to fall so hard for someone so quickly, but the amount of trust and admiration I feel emanating from him set all my worries aside. I slowly bring my hand up to gently place it over Cyr's on my cheek.

"I'm nervous, too, but I've never felt safer than when I'm around you." I can't understand how I've let myself become so vulnerable in front of him, but I know it's part of this bonding process; to trust each other wholly and completely, "But I do need time, Cyr. Not a lot, but…" I take a deep breath and Cyr's thumb grazes my cheek in understanding.

"If you're willing to bide your time and work through this with me, I'll give you all the time you need just as long as you'll stay with me."

His heartfelt words send me melting into a puddle on the floor. In response, ever so slowly, I turn my head to softly kiss Cyr's palm before relaxing back into his touch. His chest expands quickly and I panic thinking I've gone too far, but the even exhale that leaves him calms my thoughts.

"Will you be alright on your own for a minute while I change?"

I nod in response to his sentimental question. Even now, his priority is still me, and I subconsciously know it will always be me.

"Sit."

Cyr gestures with his head towards his bed and drops his hand from my cheek. I feel the rush of the command flood my senses, and I oblige. Taking careful steps, I sit down on the edge of his bed and look back up at him.

"Good girl."

I bite down hard on my bottom lip to distract myself from the praise as my entire belly floods with heat. As Cyr turns to walk back toward the bathroom I know the bastard is smirking underneath his mask. He shuts the door just enough to change with some privacy but leaves it open a crack to not shut me out completely.

I gently lift my leg to rest my foot across my opposite knee to inspect the underside of my bloody foot. My eyes search for any glass, only seeing a tiny sliver which I pull out with ease and set on my lap to discard. The rest of the cuts on my feet are from the shards themselves scattered across Tobias's floor, but none thankfully are fully embedded into my feet.

A few minutes later Cyr emerges from the bathroom in a black tank and sweatpants also in black, which is no surprise to me. In his hands is a small first aid kit, and as he approaches me, Cyr extends it to me to hold. After I take hold of the small box, he lowers down onto his knees in front of me.

"Cyr, you don't have to do that."

"I know I don't."

Cyr's reply silences me, and he carefully lifts my foot to examine the little scrapes. I wince slightly with a soft inhale through my teeth upon Cyr's gentle touch against the cuts. His gaze quickly flashes up to meet mine and through the unspoken words in his eyes, I nod for him to continue. Cyr continues tending to me and my heart swells as he takes care of me.

I couldn't imagine where I'd be if Cyr hadn't waltzed into my life exactly when I needed him most. I hadn't realized how much I truly did need him, and if you asked me a year ago I would have said to fuck off. I was hellbent on being as independent as possible, but the feeling of being around someone who shows me so much compassion and devotion makes me realize I don't have to be alone.

I spent years spiraling deep down inside of myself into a place where only my most horrid of demons slept. It wasn't until Cyr came along with his flashlight and pulled me back up to life that I came to see how much I was capable of being cared for. I fell hard and fast for this beautiful man who is currently kneeling in front of me. A part of me didn't want to believe those feelings for so long because I couldn't imagine myself being worthy enough for anyone, let alone Cyr Maddox.

Those stunning blue eyes consume my soul and strip me bare,

exposing each of those emotions flooding my senses. My name on his lips brings me back into the present and out of my daze.

"Bellamy, did I hurt you?"

I raise an eyebrow in confusion as his question sinks into comprehension. It's then I feel my cheeks are damp. I bring my hands up to my cheeks, wiping the tear stains away, and return my gaze to Cyr.

"Why are you crying? Talk to me." Cyr's voice is gentle yet etched with worry. I shake my head, pulling a small smile up my cheeks.

"Words can't explain it, Cyr, but all you need to know is that I'm happy. For the first time in a long time. I'm genuinely happy," My voice, no louder than a whisper, nearly breaks as the words leave my lips. The exhale that leaves Cyr's chest is one of relief.

A few moments later he finishes his bandaging and stands in front of me. His hands extend out towards me to assist me in standing. I hesitantly take his hands to not startle him, using his hands to help push myself upward to stand in front of him. I crane my neck up to look at the gorgeous olive skin blessing his features and every single time I forget how much he towers over me in my petite 5'4" frame.

"Hold onto me."

His words knock me off guard as Cyr places my hands on his shoulders, and his hands travel down to my waist.

"Wait, what? Why?" I quickly ask, glancing down to where his hands slide down toward the waistband of my sweatpants.

"There's blood on your pants. I'll grab you a pair of my shorts."

"No!"

Panic floods my body as I stumble back a step out of his grip. The adrenaline coursing through me earlier has now entirely worn off and the pain with each step shoots up into my legs. Cyr quickly takes a step back and brings his hands up into an 'I surrender' motion in front of me.

"Fuck, Bellamy. I'm sorry. I should have asked before I touched you. Especially after…" Cyr's voice trails off and his eyes shut tightly for a moment to tamp back his temper. Most likely automatically thinking back to what I had told him transpired in Tobias's room.

"Oh, Cyr. No, no, it's not that…" I feel the heat rise straight up into my cheeks turning them a dark crimson. Cyr's eyes open to meet mine and he cocks an eyebrow in question. I sigh and look down timidly, "I'm…not wearing panties."

Cyr's eyes widen as I glance at him, and I bring my hands up to cover my face which displays an unyielding blush.

"Gods, Raven."

The rasp in his voice as he speaks has my eyes instantly back up to meet his and I cross my arms across my chest.

"What?"

Cyr's low chuckle sends a shiver across my entire body at the sound. The heat in my cheeks races straight down to my core, lighting my entire body ablaze. As his eyes lock onto mine, I notice his mask shift either from his laugh or a smile. It melts my body into nothing but pure lust under that glacier-blue gaze.

"You make me want to do things I never thought I'd ever want to do again."

His voice is filled with nothing but dominance and promise. I attempt to mellow my rapid heartbeat as Cyr's words wash over me and stun me into silence. He takes a step toward me and grips my chin, lifting my gaze upward to meet his.

"Rule #1: No panties allowed in this room."

My jaw gapes for a moment before a smirk creeps up one side

of my lips. Cyr's grip tightens enough for me to snap back my focus to him.

Gods above he's going to be the death of me.

"Yes, sir." My words come out breathlessly, and Cyr nods appreciatively.

"Good girl."

My knees nearly buckle as the praise hits every single sensitive part of my body. The wetness building between my legs has me ever so slightly pushing my thighs together. Of course, the action doesn't go unnoticed and the sound of Cyr's light growl makes my eyes go wide. The predator in him wants so badly to come out to play and his prey wants him to do just that.

"If you do that again I won't be able to keep my promise of waiting until you're ready. Or being gentle with you."

What if I don't want you to?

The question goes unsaid even as every part of my body aches for him to touch me, to explore me. I know I need time or it won't be good for either of us, but fuck, I didn't think I would ever be this Gods damned in need of him in any capacity.

"Now," Cyr exhales evenly and releases his grip on my chin before walking over to his dresser. "I can get you a pair of boxers and a tee shirt. Is that okay?" No previous trace of that predator is present anymore and the soft-toned Cyr I've fallen for over these past few months returns.

"If you don't mind, I'd appreciate it," I reply softly as I attempt to steel my voice back to neutrality as quickly as Cyr has.

He returns a moment later with a black tee shirt and red boxers in hand, holding them out toward me, "You'll drown in the shirt, but it should work for tonight."

I bite onto my bottom lip, taking the clothes from him then

bring my eyes back up to meet his.

"Could you help me?" I ask hesitantly but I wouldn't be surprised if Cyr said no. The two of us have both been through a lot and moving too fast isn't something I want to pressure him into.

He raises an eyebrow as if to ask, *"Are you sure?"*

"I'm afraid I'll lose my balance," I add, struggling to even stand on my own with the pain in my feet.

Cyr nods, taking a tentative few steps toward me, and wraps his fingertips around the base of my tank top. He hesitates for a moment, watching me carefully for any signs of wanting him to stop. I only nod my permission, and keep my gaze locked with his as the feeling of his skin slides along my ribs.

His fingers barely graze my skin as my tank top comes up but the light touches from him send the butterflies in my stomach tumbling. Cyr's gentle hands come up along my ribs to brush against the sides of my breasts. Goosebumps rise along my entire body and the sensation causes my nipples to harden at the feeling. I suck in my bottom lip between my teeth to suppress a moan. Cyr notices the motion and his eyes dart to my lips, then back to my eyes. His gaze hasn't once dipped below my lips to allow me that privacy even as intimate as the moment is between us.

The tank top comes up and over my head, as I raise my arms to allow the top to slip off my body. Cyr discards the tank top to the floor and I hand him the shirt he picked out for me. He efficiently unfolds the shirt and reaches out toward me, still keeping his eyes locked with mine, and guides the shirt over my head, pulling it down gently. My head pops through the top opening and with Cyr's assistance, I reach into each of the side openings for my arms to slide through. Cyr's touch is as soft as a feather as he unravels the shirt down over my torso leaving it to hang around my mid-thigh.

"Hold onto my shoulders, Raven."

I oblige his command and gently place my hands on his shoulders. Through his tank, I can feel the strong muscles across his shoulder blades and try my best to not feel my way along the rest of his arms. I've seen the size of them before when he'd rushed out of the shower, but it still makes me want to explore his body even more.

Cyr takes the boxers from my hand before kneeling in front of me. The sight of him kneeling before me again floods my senses with a whole new set of emotions that heat my core almost unbearably. I swear at any moment my body will burst into flames. His hands trail slowly up my thighs and past my hips, taking his time in seeking out all of my curves. A moan nearly slips through my lips, but I feign a slight cough to mask it in hopes Cyr hadn't heard.

His icy gaze lifts to meet mine as his fingers wrap around the waistband of my sweats and begin to slide them down my legs. From the length of his tee shirt on my body, all the parts I wished to keep hidden were concealed. Cyr deliberately changed me into his shirt first to make me as comfortable as possible without revealing anything I didn't want to be seen. I adore the care and thought Cyr puts into each action he takes regarding me feeling safe around him. I couldn't think of a time when Cyr made me feel anything but safe.

His soft, yet callused, hands from years of drawing, carefully slip my sweatpants down past my ass, my thighs, my calves, and down to a pile on the floor. He takes his time as his fingertips trace every new part of my skin from my waist to my feet. I fall deeply into those eyes that had locked on with mine for countless minutes, and not once did his gaze travel elsewhere. Cyr lifts my feet one by one to carefully remove the sweatpants from my legs without disturbing the bandages he'd so diligently wrapped across my feet.

After a moment, the boxers he picked out are in his hands as he holds them open for me to step into. I slowly lift one foot, then the other, to help Cyr before his hands begin their ascent back up my legs. Once he manages to slide his boxers up past my calves, they tangle in the hem of the tee shirt covering my thighs. Cyr's feather-light hands make quick work of lifting the shirt just enough from the tangled waistband of the boxers to not reveal anything to himself. Even though his face is mere inches away from where I want him so badly to be. As the boxers rise to my hips, Cyr stands with the final pull of the boxers past the curve of my ass to its firm position around my waist. He stands in front of me with his hands still placed around my hips as our eyes connect and I softly slide my hands from his shoulders down to stop above his heart.

"Thank you."

The words come out breathier than I expected, shocking myself even at the sound. Cyr's heartbeat quickens underneath my hands, and I know it isn't from touching him. He nods in reply, glancing over my shoulder toward his bed, then back to me.

"Let's get you to bed. It's been a hell of a night."

Cyr steps back and away from my touch, and the sudden loss of his warmth is like jumping into an ice bath. He walks over to the side of his bed to toss the duvet back enough for me to climb in.

"You're not gonna try to sleep on the floor again, are you?" I question him with a slight smirk sliding up my cheek. Cyr rolls his eyes and the soft chuckle that escapes his lips warms my heart all over again.

"You were right. The bed is much more comfortable than the floor." His reply is gentle as he makes his way back over toward me, "May I?"

I'm hesitant but nod with a raised eyebrow. Before I can object, Cyr lifts me from under my thighs and wraps an arm firmly, but carefully, around my back. I squeal at the quick motion, wrapping my arms delicately around his neck and shoulders.

"Cyr, no, I'm-"

"I fucking swear if you're about to say 'I'm heavy', we're going to have issues."

Cyr's words aren't harsh but told me he meant what he said. I'm not necessarily on the petite side as I have plenty of curves to show for my slightly chubby physique. As Cyr carries me over toward my side of the bed, he shows no display of having trouble with my weight; lifting and carrying me with ease.

For just a moment, I allow my head to rest against his shoulder and breathe in the scent of him. The fresh spring body wash consumes my senses from head to toe. After a longer time than I realize it takes to reach his bed, I notice he's stopped by the side of the bed and hasn't made a move to set me down.

"Everything okay?" I ask softly as I lift my head back up to face him, only centimeters separating my lips from his mask.

"Perfect."

"Then why am I still in the air?"

"I just needed another minute to admire how beautiful you are from this close."

I'm absolutely and utterly certain my cheeks are the deepest shade of crimson. As the words leave Cyr's lips, my heart swells three times its size and is on the brink of exploding from my chest. I can't help but bury my head back down into his shoulder in an attempt to hide my reddened cheeks from him. Cyr's laugh sends me into a pile of putty in his arms. A moment later I'm gracefully lowered down onto his bed. I now lay on the side of the bed that I first occupied the night Cyr saved me from Tobias's outrage all those months ago. He releases me from his gentle grip around my legs and reaches over to pull the duvet up over my torso.

"Do you need anything?" Cyr's voice is quiet but holds a tinge of concern. The man never ceases to amaze me with his endless display of compassion and selflessness.

"Yes."

I watch as Cyr's mask shifts, presumably opening his mouth to inquire about what I may need.

"I need you to come lay down." My voice is whisper soft, with possibly an ounce of seduction laced in my tone. Cyr lightly chuckles with a nod.

"As you wish."

Cyr rounds his bed toward his side then sits down, instantly reclining onto his back to face the ceiling. A deep exhale leaves his chest, and his eyes drift shut. I roll over onto my side to look him over.

"Are you okay?"

"Why do you ask?"

"You've done nothing but take care of me. I just need you to know that I'm here when you need someone to take care of you, Cyr."

It's true. He's done nothing but dote on me from head to toe, and I want nothing more than to make him feel as appreciated as he's done for me. It's truly something I wasn't sure I'd be able to appropriately repay him for. Maybe one day.

Cyr's eyes open at my words and his head falls to the side to meet my gaze. He reaches over to place a hand over my cheek.

"Bellamy…" My name leaves his lips like a promise and it takes everything inside of me to keep my composure, "You have no idea what it means to me that you're even here with me right now."

My head lulls to the side into his touch, and my eyes flutter closed for only a moment, but I can't resist gazing into those glacier eyes. They steal my breath and my heart.

"I feel like all I've brought you is trouble."

Cyr's hand tightens slightly on my cheek as he guides my head to face him directly.

"You've brought me back to life, Raven."

My heart stops in my chest. A quick exhale leaves his lips and he caresses my cheek with his thumb.

"I spent so long in the dark that I forgot who I was, but with you…" I notice his cheeks shift under his mask, and I only hope he's smiling, "With you, I feel like I can start to become who I was again. It's gonna take some time, but your willingness to be patient with me means more than I can physically explain."

I couldn't believe it was possible for my heart to feel as tight as it is in my chest as it does at this very moment. My lungs try harder than ever to keep breathing when Cyr makes it so impossibly difficult to breathe every time he speaks.

"You've been through so much and I'll never expect anything more from you than what you're physically able to give." My words are soft as my eyes meet his and I instantly float through thousands of years of galaxies within those glacier swirls, "Healing takes time and that's okay. Even if we never go farther than this, just know I'm grateful for every second I'm able to spend with you."

His exhale is full of relief and Cyr gently grazes his thumb against my cheekbone, "It won't be overnight, Raven, but believe me when I tell you that I've never wanted someone more in my life." The gentleness yet possessiveness in his tone has heat flooding every inch of my body, "I'm not perfect, but I'll try to be everything you deserve to have in your life for as long as you'll bear it."

"I won't have to bear anything, Cyr. I choose you. Just as you have chosen me." A light laugh escapes my lips and Cyr raises an eyebrow in confusion, "I'll be completely honest. I haven't the slightest idea why you would choose *me*, but I'm glad you did."

Cyr shakes his head with a slight rumble of his chest, "You still don't see how much light you emanate in this world of utter darkness, don't you? I crawled from the darkest pit of Hell to find your light, Bellamy."

"I'm not perfect," I mimic the words he said to me a few moments ago.

"You are to me."

The blush rising up my cheeks tells him exactly how he makes me feel and I didn't dare to hide it. Not anymore. I slowly tilt my head in his hand until my lips press gently against his palm. My lips linger against his skin for a few moments before turning back to face the beautiful man lying beside me.

His eyes are glossy and yet full of appreciation which brings a soft smile to my lips, "I told you, I'm not going anywhere unless you tell me to."

"I'm working through my shit, but please..." Cyr's voice is quiet, almost breaking and I grow curious about his plea, "Don't leave, Raven. I'm fucked up and I may snap sometimes, but I need you to put me in my place if I do."

My nod in reply has Cyr easing and exhaling shakily as if he was afraid I would bolt from the room, "Promise me you'll do the same. I have my issues to sort out, but with each other, we can work them out together. Deal?"

Cyr replies with a nod and slowly pulls his hand back to roll over onto his back. Without his presence, the warmth that was previously there felt so cold and empty without it. He exhales deeply as a hand props under his head and his other falls on the bed between us in a fist. My eyes flick down to watch as he clenches his fist, releases, then clenches again. I look over to him and see his eyes shut tightly and the sight makes my heart ache.

"Cyr, if this is too much please tell me. I don't want to pressure you and I don't mind going-"

"Don't."

That was that. His tone pleads with me and I was already past the point of exhaustion to fight him. He was my priority right now and I'll be damned to Hell if I hurt him. But like everything else that's happened, Cyr initiated this moment. He initiated everything to go at his pace, and all I can do now is to help him walk the path he knows he needs to take. No matter what, I'll be here for him as he's been here for me.

With the blackness of the room closing in, my eyes begin to drift shut but I force myself to stay awake. But once I hear Cyr's staggered breathing fade into a soft melody, I allow myself to drift off with the scent of his cologne guiding me into a blissful sleep.

17

The Tattoo

The next morning, I awaken up to an empty bed. A brief moment of panic floods my body, but this isn't just a one-night fling with a random guy from the bar. The blankets had been tucked up over my body with care and a level of gentleness that warms my heart. The chill lingering throughout the room without his warmth enveloping me sends shivers across my body. Regardless of his absence, I can't remember the last time I slept through the night without waking up in a fit of screams. He makes me feel safe, and I still can't believe this is happening. Last night went by in a blur of emotions and hopeful words that I never believed I would be capable of uttering again.

I glance around the dorm and my sleepy eyes land on a note atop the nightstand. My body, quite ungracefully, rolls across the bed toward the note and I blink the sleep haze from my eyes to peer down at it.

Raven,

I have an early appointment at the shop and didn't want to wake you. Your phone is on the charger and I asked Clara to pick out an outfit for you. As much as I love seeing you in my shirt, I don't think you want everyone in the dorm to see you in my boxers.

A little birdie told me you like the breakfast burritos from the mess hall so there's one for you on the desk next to your clothes. My schedule is packed for today but I'm a phone call away if you need me.

Cyr

Warmth explodes throughout my entire body at his written words, so thoughtful and considerate. I glance back to the nightstand seeing my phone on the charger as he said. My eyes flick over to the desk in the corner of his room seeing a small stack of clothes, a neatly rolled up burrito in tin foil, and a box of apple juice.

Gods, what have I gotten myself into? This man is too good for me.

As I sift through the pile of clothes, under the tee shirt on the top of the pile, my eyes widen into saucers. My mouth drops as I see a matching black lace bra and panty set and I instantly throw the shirt down over the set. I quickly glance around the room as if Cyr is standing right over my shoulder looking down at the lingerie. I make a mental note to murder Clara the next time I see her and also pray to the Gods that Cyr didn't think to look between the seemingly innocent lavender tee shirt and ripped black jeans.

After cursing multiple profanities that would have the holiest of popes rolling in their graves, I collect the clothes and slip into them. As my eyes scale the room, I see a small laundry hamper peeking through from the inside of his closet. A part of my conscience says to not look through his closet, but how else am I supposed to find out what bones Cyr has in there? My fingers inch out toward the gap in the closet doors and slowly pull them open as if a skeleton is going to jump out to attack me. As the doors open entirely, my jaw drops. Hanger after hanger of solid black clothes greets me.

Why am I not surprised?

A soft laugh escapes my lips as I see nothing but layers of fabric and a neat line of more shoes on the closet floor. Definitely no bones in here to dig up. Succumbing to the fact that I'll have to dig up those pieces of Cyr that he's hiding behind that armor on my own, I release a sigh of contentment. I grab his boxers and tee shirt I slept in last night and toss them into his clothes hamper. After closing his closet doors, I turn toward his bed and quickly make up his bed to leave it how it had been the previous night. After returning the room to its usual state of pristine, I take a seat at his desk and unroll the burrito Cyr left for me.

For the first time in who knows how long, I have absolutely nothing planned on my calendar for today. So I decided that this is a Saturday I'm going to take entirely for myself. I take my time enjoying my burrito and flipping through a sketchbook Cyr left on the desk. Some pages are filled with small doodles, smaller flash tattoo pieces, and others that are elaborately drawn with care and immense concentration that put me in a state of awe.

After I reach the end of the sketchbook, I discard the tin foil wrapper and juice box into the small trash bin beneath his desk. As I walked out of Cyr's room to return to my dorm, the state of the common area of the dorm was still destroyed from the events of the night before. There's no sound coming from Tobias's room and I assume he's blacked out. Before returning to my dorm, I made an anonymous call to the campus security and complained about loud noises coming from the dorm the previous night. I quickly headed back to my dorm after finishing the call and being ensured that security would look into the issue.

Clara spends the better part of the next two hours asking me every single question that pops into her mind between what happened at the club, what happened with Tobias, and how I ended up staying the night with Cyr. I disclosed a few bits and pieces but left out others that I didn't want Clara to have to hear. She didn't need to know about what Tobias tried to do because, honestly, if I told Clara what he did, he'd be dead in the next ten minutes and his body would never be found.

With the rest of the day at my disposal, I finish up a few assignments to prep for the next week. Clara heads out shortly after a bit of studying for a brunch date with her girlfriend so I'm left to my own devices. After staring at my laptop for an hour with nothing being accomplished, I know I won't get anything done until I talk to Cyr. My fear is rushing things between us until we are both ready, but texting him a simple 'hello' won't break us right?

As I pick up my phone to pull up my text thread with Cyr, my phone chimes with an incoming text.

Cyr: Not still asleep are you?

A soft laugh escapes my lips as I type out a reply.

Me: This is Bellamy's assistant: can I leave a message?

Cyr: Can you tell her she's beautiful even when she snores?

An audible gasp leaves my lips as my fingers fly over my keyboard.

Me: I do not snore!!!!

Cyr: If you say so.

Me: Do I actually?

Cyr: How's your day going?

Me: DON'T AVOID THE QUESTION!

Cyr: Don't you worry that pretty little head of yours about it, Raven. You're still beautiful...

The term of endearment from Cyr causes my heart to skip a few beats. My fingers begin to type a reply when I receive another ding from my messages.

Cyr: ...Even if you do snore.

Me: I. DO. NOT!

The constant banter never fails to brighten my day and bring a smile to my lips. Cyr continues to avoid my question for an extended period of time before he says a client is coming in soon and he needs to prep.

Me: Don't screw it up, no pressure.

Cyr: Just wait until your tattoo is finished, then you'll be counting your blessings.

*****

The day has come and to say I'm nervous is an understatement. It's been almost a week since I've seen Cyr after our night at the club and spoken words that made me feel capable of love again. A lot was spoken that night in Cyr's dorm and it brought me so much peace to finally be around him again after a stressful week of classes.

Between Cyr's schedule at the tattoo shop and his classes combined with mine, we haven't been able to bump into each other at all. It's been a little disheartening to not see him at all especially with all these newfound feelings blooming throughout my body and heart. Sometimes it's how it goes, especially when school is a priority for both of us. So, I'll take the precious moments to see him when I can and be grateful for the late-night texts in the meantime. I'm anxious about the tattoo, but I've seen Cyr's work before and I know it will be incredible. But at the same time, I lost a bet and I now have no control over how these next few hours will go. I only hope Cyr won't make me regret taking him out to the club.

My screen lights up as I glance down at my phone to check the address my map displays to ensure I'm going in the right direction. Cyr texted me a location pin to the tattoo shop he works at, which is where I'm meeting him today. I'd been up all night thinking about today, but also made sure I had enough sleep in my system as well as food and water. The last thing I needed was to pass out in the tattoo chair in front of Cyr. I was certain if I passed out, I would drop out, change my name, and fall off the face of the Earth. Cyr wouldn't think anything of it, I know that for a fact, but the mortification would be my undoing.

As the train comes to a halt, I exit among the rest of the hoard all on their way to work for the morning. The early Friday morning work rush swarms me as they all depart from the platform, and down to the streets below. I pull out my phone from my jacket pocket once again to find the directions to guide me to the tattoo shop. The map signals it's two blocks up the road from the station and the closer that little blue marker gets to the shop, my heart races even faster. I couldn't discern if my heart was racing from the idea of getting a tattoo to which I have no idea what it'll be, or if it's from seeing Cyr again.

The sign above the door at the tattoo shop read *Black Dragon Tattoo Parlor* in a bold, script font. My fingers wrap around the door handle and I exhale a shaky breath before pulling the door open. A small bell chimes above my head as I walk into the shop and close the door behind me.

Beautiful white marbled tiles cover the expanse of the parlor floor with a few black tattoo beds neatly lined up across the space in sections. Pictures of mythical creatures and tattoo design sketches line the black-marbled walls and my jaw gapes slightly as I take it all in. The space is the epitome of Cyr's aesthetic and it feels like a warm embrace from him.

"I apologize, we're closed for walk-ins this morning. I'll open back up at Noon."

Cyr's voice echoes throughout the room and it sends chills scittering across my entire body. My throat dries up as I glance up and see him with his back facing me at the other end of the parlor. I will my feet to move a few steps further into the shop toward him.

"I happen to have an appointment," I speak softly, brushing a loose strand of my braid behind my ear. Cyr spins his body around and once those glacier-blue eyes lock with mine, my heart skips a beat, "I lost a bet, so now it's time to receive my punishment."

As soon as the words leave my lips, they sound more seductive than lighthearted and innocent as they initially sounded in my head. Cyr's eyebrow cocks up in question and I'm certain my cheeks flush a shade of crimson.

"If that's the case, Raven, lock the door behind you." His reply comes out low and sultry, sending heat deep into the core of my stomach.

Gods above spare me from this man. He shall be my undoing.

"I was uh-…not like um-"

"Anyone tell you you're sexy as hell when you get flustered?"

My knees nearly buckle at his words and the weight of what feels like a boulder crashes down on my soul. I attempt to control my rapid heart as it's moments from combusting within my chest. As if my face couldn't get any redder, I'm sure it is. Although I can't hear it from this distance, Cyr's chest and shoulders vibrate and I can tell the bastard is laughing at me.

"So, what have you picked out for me? Any hints?" I ask as I wander over toward his workstation in the back of the parlor. Cyr continues setting up his station; little plastic containers are set up along his work desk in an array of several different vibrant colors of ink, "Let me guess, killer clown?"

When Cyr laughs this time, it invades every one of my senses and my heart melts a little further hearing the sound. The urge to record the sound to play whenever I craved the beautiful sound is so strong, but in hindsight, that's pretty fucking creepy and ultimately decide against it.

"Did you pick a spot where you want it?" Is his only reply and I huff out a dramatic sigh when I'm not given any hint as to what will be tattooed on my skin forever.

"The back of my shoulder."

I relent as I set my small backpack down on the floor beneath the tattoo table. My fingers reach up to begin unbuttoning the small buttons of my sage green and black flannel. As I glance up to Cyr I watch as he turns his head to me, then back to his station for only a brief moment before doing a double-take at me. His hands halt their movements in wrapping up his tattoo gun as his icy blue stare meets mine.

My fingers slowly trail down my shirt undoing each of the buttons as I go and the slow dip of Cyr's eyes as he tracks each of my fingers lights my body ablaze. As I reach the bottom button and unhook it, my fingers glide up over my collarbone, pulling the flannel back to fall down my arms revealing a solid black lace bralette.

Cyr's eyes flick back to mine and the heat filling those blue orbs has my heart nearly stopping. His gaze alone strips me bare in front of him and my body is ready to comply with that very feeling. The way his chest rises and falls in uneven patterns has me begging to be inside his head to know what he's feeling at this very moment. But in reality, I know exactly what he's thinking because the very same thoughts race through my body. The vision of him taking me right here and now on this table shines clear as day in my eyes.

He places the tattoo gun on the table and pulls the black latex gloves off his hands, tossing them into the trash bin next to him while his gaze never leaves mine. He turns and strides over toward me and I can't help but feel every ounce of oxygen around me evaporate as he grows closer. Without a word, he lifts his index finger and twirls it, motioning for me to spin around. A moment later, his warmth closes in behind me and it takes everything in me to not lean back into him, for him to hold me here for just a little while. My eyes flutter closed as his fingers trace the space behind my right shoulder in little circles. His feather-light touch sends goosebumps erupting over my skin and the flames in my core grow unbearably high.

"Right here?"

Cyr's voice, low and full of sin, fills my senses right by my ear and I force myself to believe the chill rising up my spine to be from the cool temperature of the parlor and not from his voice. As my lips part to reply, no words come out, so I nod in reply.

"Do you want a blanket?" He asks and I turn my head over my shoulder to peer up at him with a raised eyebrow, "Your skin feels like ice. I have a few in the lounge, feel free to pick one out. I just need another minute to finish the stencil."

I nod, giving him a gentle smile, "Thank you."

The words come out slightly hoarse, causing a tinge of rose to climb up my cheeks. Cyr's mask shifts into a supposed smirk before he turns back to his station to finish setting up. My gaze follows him for a moment before glancing over to the front of the room where the couches adorn a few different blankets. I walk over, on somewhat wobbly legs, and choose a black fuzzy blanket from off the back of the couch. The blanket caresses my skin like a lover's embrace and I clutch it tightly to my chest as I walk back over to Cyr.

After a few minutes, Cyr has me standing with my back to him once again to apply a cream to the back of my shoulder which will stain the inky stencil to my skin.

"I know you won't give me any hints…" I stare into the mirror in front of me to meticulously watch Cyr place the stencil and his hands pause as his eyes flick up to meet mine in the mirror. He cocks an eyebrow at me and I pull my bottom lip between my teeth, the action causing Cyr to stiffen behind me, "but please tell me it's not a huge dick that's going on my back."

A chuckle escapes his lips, shaking his head ever so slightly as he finishes applying the stencil. He pulls the stencil off my back but out of sight to not allow me to see it.

"Do you trust me?"

His question nearly knocks me on my ass and stuns me stupid. Without thinking, the reply comes easily.

"Always."

I feel his warmth crowd me as his face comes up close to my ear, his eyes never leaving mine in the reflection of the mirror.

"Then trust me, Raven."

Cyr helps me onto the tattooing bed, laying down on my stomach with the fuzzy blanket under my chest and head. I cradle the blanket with my arms bent across the table in a makeshift pillow for my head to face Cyr. He pulls over a stool beside me and takes a seat with his tattoo gun in hand.

"Are you ready?"

"Ready as I'll ever be."

A smile tugs up my lips as I keep my gaze fixed on him. He applies a dot of cream across the stencil and the whirring of the tattoo gun fills the room. As the gun traces the stencil on my skin, I welcome the light pricks of pain across the sensitive flesh. I've always found the process of getting a new tattoo calming. It brings my mind out of the burdens that currently wrack my mind and helps me focus on the present.

After not too long, Cyr asks if I need a break and I shake my head so he continues his tattooing. My eyes drift shut as I let the sound of the machine lull me into relaxation.

"Are you with me, Raven?" Cyr's soft voice floats into my head and my eyes slowly open to see his gaze already on me. A hint of concern flashes within them and a smile graces my lips with a nod.

"I'm with you."

Cyr reaches over with his free hand and brushes a loose strand of my braid back behind my ear with his knuckle. My head gently nuzzles into his hand for a moment.

"Almost done, just a few touch-ups to go."

The next twenty minutes fly by as he finishes filling in a few spots and perfecting the tattoo. As the room turns silent with the lack of the tattoo gun buzzing, Cyr's voice fills the room even as his voice is gentle.

"Damn, I did good."

I can't help the laugh that escapes my lips at his comment, "If you don't say so yourself."

"Care to take a look?"

Cyr applies a solution to a paper towel and the cool towel against my warm flesh is euphoric. I nod in reply, trying to get my arms underneath me to push myself up. He pulls the gloves off his hands to toss them into the trash before gently placing his hands on the sides of my ribs to help me up. The feeling of his skin against my ribs almost has my elbows buckling underneath me. After a moment, he helps me shift onto my knees so I can step off of the table and onto my feet. My eyes flick up to him and I smile appreciatively with a nod. He returns the nod, turning to pick up a hand mirror to pass over to me.

I take hold of the handle of the mirror and walk over toward the large mirror on the wall across the room. As I reach the mirror, I spin around and hold the small mirror in front of me to see the reflection behind me.

My jaw drops and my free hand comes up to cover my mouth in shock.

"Cyr…"

I can't formulate words as I stare at the tattoo now forever adorning my back. Tears gloss over my eyes and a small sob breaks from my lips. As my gaze flashes to Cyr, his eyes hint with worry and I can't help the laugh that releases from my lips in between my sobs.

"Cyr, it's perfect! How did you-" My words stop cold and my eyes widen to the size of saucers, "You did read my diary, you ass!" The shock that stuns my body has a blush creeping up my cheeks. Cyr brings a hand up to nervously rub the back of his neck.

"To be fair, I didn't actually read it…" He replies, a hint of a laugh in his voice as I narrow my eyes at him. I open my mouth to snap at him when he raises his hands in front of him in surrender, "I opened it and saw that drawing on the first page and knew that was it."

My heart officially melts in my chest. I raise the mirror back up to look at the tattoo which means more to me than he will ever know. The small tattooed easel adorned a painting of marigold and narcissus flowers with a painting palette beside it. The intricacies of it all bring more tears falling down my cheeks as my smile widens from ear to ear.

"That picture I drew was of my mother and father's birth month flowers," My voice is slightly hoarse as I bring my attention back to Cyr, eyes full of adoration. Cyr takes a few steps toward me and brings his hands up to cup both of my cheeks, using his thumbs to brush the trails of tears away. My eyes flutter closed under his touch as my head gently leans into his palms, "I'd kiss you now if I could."

His thumbs pause for a moment and I realize that I said those words aloud. My eyes quickly open to meet his gaze, biting down gently on my bottom lip. Cyr deftly trails his thumbs back and forth over my cheekbones, bringing one down to run it across my lip tucked between my teeth.

"One day, Raven."

The words strike a cord in my heart and another tear slips from my eye which is quickly brushed away by his thumb, "One day..." I repeat and Cyr's answering nod solidifies the promise in his eyes. A promise I will hold him to, no matter how long it takes.

18

The Shower

Cyr bandages up my freshly inked tattoo and offers to give me a ride back to campus. I insist on taking the train back after all he's already done for me. There's little I can do in ways to deny him after he picks me, throws me over his shoulder, and walks me over to his motorcycle. The squeal that leaves my lips has people down the street sending weary glances in our direction.

"Gods dammit, Cyr. I have legs!"

"Oh, trust me, you've got more than just legs," That devilish voice says just moments before I feel a pinch on my ass, eliciting yet another squeal. Every fiber of my being wants to smack him for that, but I refrain to not startle him while he's holding me far too high off the ground. Bastard knows I can't retaliate against him, not that I would want to anyway.

My arms fall limply over his back, being diligent to not touch him more than I already am while simultaneously falling halfway down his back. The height of Cyr with me added to his shoulder makes me feel like I'm thousands of miles from the ground. My vision spins for a moment as he brings me back over his shoulder to stand on the ground on my own two feet.

"If you'd have just agreed to let me take you back, all of that could have been avoided. But no, you had to be a brat about it."

The way he punctuated the word *brat* has a chill racing down my spine, and it wasn't from the swift breeze that flies through the city streets.

"I've just never…" I trail off, looking over to his motorcycle parked beside us and I shake my head in disbelief, "Really, you had to get a black one? Do you own anything that isn't black?" My eyes travel up and down his body, dressed head to toe in black and dark gray. His response, rather than words, is a slight shake of his head and his mask shifts upward. I roll my eyes at the smirk that I know is plastered across those hidden lips.

"Let's get this shit over with," I grumble under my breath, walking over to the motorcycle. Cyr's hand wraps gently around my wrist, pulling me back toward him. My eyebrow rises at him in question, tilting my head, "What?"

Cyr only shakes his head again and walks over to the leather saddle bag strapped to the side of the motorcycle and pulls out a black leather jacket. He turns toward me and extends it out to me.

"Put it on. You'll get cold."

"I'll be fine. Campus isn't too far away."

Cyr steps close to me and I'm almost tempted to create some distance between us as his closeness startles me for a brief moment, "If you don't, I'll put it on you myself. Don't make me tell you twice."

My stomach nearly rockets out of my throat as his words sink into my head. He holds up the jacket between us and I lift my hand to take it from him, proceeding to slip it on.

"Good girl."

Gods above spare me.

Cyr walks back over to his motorcycle while I zip up the leather jacket, taking extra precautions to not rub the tattoo on the back of my shoulder, and take a look down at myself. The jacket falls to nearly my mid-thigh and the sleeves down to my fingertips. I shake my head knowing how ridiculous I must look, but I know he's doing this to make sure I'm safe no matter what. The act warms my heart, even though I look like a damn clown. My jaw drops at the sight of Cyr's helmet as he extends it to me.

"Seriously? Oh, I'm definitely looking like a clown now."

Cyr extends out a bright neon green helmet toward me and I take it, glancing back to him in utter confusion. He rolls his eyes, "You asked if I own anything not black. This is it. It glows in the dark and gives me some visibility at night."

His reasoning makes sense so I can't fault him for it. At least he's taking precautions, especially in a city where I'm pretty sure a driver's license isn't even required. I lift up the helmet and slip it down over my head, beginning to fumble with the straps beneath. Cyr reaches over to me, takes hold of the front of my leather jacket, and tugs me over to him. My motor functions all stop and my brain short circuits at the action, easily being the hottest thing I've ever experienced.

His hands reach under the helmet to tighten the straps and secure it snugly beneath my chin. He flips up the visor on the full-face helmet so he can meet my eyes to make sure everything is on properly. After a moment, he looks me over and gives a nod of approval before walking back over and taking a seat on the motorcycle. The engine roars to life and I jump slightly at the invasion of my eardrums even with his helmet on. I don't know how he's handling this without a helmet on...

"Wait...where's your helmet?" My voice calls out to him to make sure he can hear me even though he's only a foot away from me. Cyr's head turns to me and nods toward me.

"You're wearing it."

His response has me wanting to rip off the helmet and give it back to him but I realize after a moment what he means. He isn't answering my question, it's a command. Even if I did pull off the helmet, we wouldn't be leaving until I put it back on. I sigh, not liking the idea of him riding without a jacket or helmet for protection. But, once again, I'm his priority. Just as I always have been.

Cyr extends a hand out to me and I gingerly take it as he guides me to place my foot on the peg and use my weight against his hand to flip my opposite leg over to the other side. My foot finds the peg on the opposite side then release my hand from his while I glance around me.

"Are there any handlebars to hold or something?"

"You've really never been on a motorcycle before have you?"

"Is it that obvious?" I retort, sarcasm lacing in my tone. Cyr's head shakes back and forth in front of me.

Bastard.

"Hold onto me," Cyr replies, glancing at me sidelong over his shoulder.

I hesitate, wondering if the contact will be too much for him. Before I can decide, the loud rev of the engine and my body jolting forward have my arms flying to wrap around his torso. I grip his shirt in my fists, holding on for dear life.

Cyr quickly inhales and his back goes rigid but he releases it a moment later with a belly laugh so loud I can hear it over the rumbling of the engine. That beautiful laugh has me stunned stupid and I promise myself to commit the sound to memory.

"Found you a handlebar to hold onto," Cyr calls over his shoulder to me and I gently pat his chest passive-aggressively as a 'fuck you' for nearly making me jump out of my skin. His chest rumbles under my hands as the bastard laughs at me, "You can hold onto me here or my shoulders, but I need you to hold on tight."

Those are words I never thought I would hear from Cyr.

Hold on tight.

Gods I would hold onto him for as long as he could stand. I never want to let go of him and breathe him in for the rest of my existence, no matter how long that would be.

My mortality slams into me like a brick wall as Cyr sends the motorcycle flying from the parking space onto the main road. My eyes slam shut as we race down the road back toward the campus. The wind swirls around us, sending the braid down my back flying in every single direction. I attempt to not tighten my grip on Cyr any harder than I know it already is on him.

After what feels like an eternity, the motorcycle comes to a slow halt and I release a breath I didn't realize I've been holding. As I exhale, music fills my ears catching me off guard. "You" by *Breaking Benjamin* plays inside of the helmet and my eyes drift shut once again, taking in the words as I breathe steadily once again. Cyr's hand slides over mine, laying flat against his chest, and gives my hand a gentle squeeze. He picked this song for a reason. He's giving me a piece of himself knowing it would calm me down and give me something to focus on.

The rest of the drive back to campus suddenly went by much too quickly. Cyr pulls up to the sidewalk in front of the art building dorms, slowing to a stop, and cutting the engine. I don't make any move to leave our position causing Cyr to glance over his shoulder to look at me.

"Raven?"

"The song isn't over yet. Can you go around the parking lot a few times?" I lift my head up to meet his gaze and his mask shifts up a bit. He chuckles, shaking his head.

"I have to get back to the shop. Maybe tomorrow, alright?" He replies lightheartedly, and I know he means it. If I asked, he'd willingly do it, just as always.

I pout at him, but I realize he can't see it due to the full-face helmet covering the lower half of my face. Nonetheless, I nod in compliance. Cyr offers a hand for me to take to help me off of the motorcycle and I accept it gently. Using his support, I swing my leg off of the motorcycle and step down from the foot pegs onto the ground. He remains sitting as he uses a finger to beckon me over to him and my feet begin moving before my brain can process the action. Cyr calls to me like a moth to a Gods damned flame and if he is the flame, I'll willingly burn for him.

His hand comes up and tilts the chin of the helmet upward to undo the straps tucked beneath my chin. As the straps fall loose I lift the helmet up and off of my head, shaking my loose strands of hair free and away from my face. My gaze meets Cyr's to find his eyes already observing my every move. A soft smile climbs up my cheeks and I extend his helmet over to him. He accepts the helmet and expertly pulls it on, tightening the straps before I can even get his jacket unzipped.

I remove the leather jacket from my arms and hand it over to him, but my motion stops as I see his hand reach up into his helmet from the underside. My lip is pulled in between my teeth as I watch Cyr pull his mask down through the bottom of his helmet. The black piece of cotton is discarded into his pocket as my eyes flick back up to meet his. His face is completely concealed by the helmet but I see the slightest portion of the top of his cheek raise, smirking at me. Cyr shoots me a wink and I roll my eyes, crossing my arms in front of my chest.

"You're a pain in my ass."

"That can be arranged, Raven."

My mouth dries up and I stammer for a response but before my brain can comprehend his words, his motorcycle roars to life and he's gone in a flash. He flies out of the campus parking lot and I'm stood there on the sidewalk with my mouth hanging open like a Gods damned fish on a hook.

***

It's been three days since my tattoo and since the last time I saw Cyr. To say I miss him sounds so incredibly pathetic, but it's true. His schedule this week has been packed and after watching him drive away the other day I've been impatiently waiting to see him again. My body roams around my room until I finally strike up the courage to pick up my phone, pulling up my text thread with Cyr.

Me: Am I allowed to shower?

Cyr: Do you have running water?

Me: Well, yeah. The water's running fine.

Cyr: Then go shower. You don't need my permission for everything. Even though I'm upset I can't join you.

This man is going to be the fucking death of me.

I roll my eyes so hard at my phone I hope he feels the intensity of it on the other end.

Me: I meant can I shower because of my tattoo, asshole. I don't want to fuck up the colors.

Cyr: Don't soak it, but yes, you can shower. Use that soap I bought for you.

At this moment, I think of something really stupid that I know

178

I shouldn't say. But I let the intrusive thoughts win…

Me: It's in a bit of a hard spot to reach. I may need you to join me after all.

Cyr: Don't push it, Raven.

Every single fiber of my being wants to push every single button this man has, and I have zero regrets.

Me: I mean it! My arm doesn't bend back that far.

Cyr: We'll see about that.

My heart stops entirely for a few seconds too long to the point where I gasp after the third time I read his last text. Warmth floods low in my stomach and I beg my body to not want him so badly every consecutive hour of the day.

I force myself to take a deep breath and steady my racing heart. It's nearing 9 pm and everything in my heart wants to run to his dorm and beg him to take me then and there, but he's the one who calls the shots. My body needs to comply until he's physically ready to be with me on that level.

Me: Guess I'll just have to struggle all on my own until then.

Cyr: I'm sure you'll manage without me.

Me: We'll see.

I begin pacing around the dorm after not receiving a message back from him for over 20 minutes. My stomach coils into knots, automatically assuming the worst and that I've pushed him a little too far. It's just so easy to get carried away with Cyr and I've been mentally punching myself in the face since I hit send on that last text. He could have just fallen asleep early, but I couldn't help but think I'd upset him and that was even more heartbreaking.

My bones nearly jump entirely out of my skin as loud pounding sounds against my dorm room door. Clara's out with her girlfriend for the night and has her own key so why would she bang on the door? I quickly pad over to the door and pull the door open to be met with blazing ice-blue eyes. His body leans in toward the door with one hand gripping the top of the door frame, and the other holding his motorcycle helmet.

Was he still working at the tattoo parlor? Did he come all the way over here just because of me? Gods, I feel like an ass.

"Cyr…what are you doing here?" I question, raising an eyebrow and crossing my arms across my chest. His eyes burrow straight into my soul, his gaze giving me absolutely no hints as to what he's feeling.

"I was planning on crashing at the shop tonight, but apparently a little Raven needs my help and who am I to ignore her *needs?*"

My teeth are biting so hard into my bottom lip that I swear I taste iron against my tongue. I can't find the right words to say, so instead I shift to the side and hold the door open further to allow him to enter. Cyr walks past me, taking a glance around to find Clara isn't around. He tosses his helmet on my bed and peels off the leather jacket, following the same direction as the helmet.

I close the door, locking it behind me before turning back to face Cyr. My jaw hits the floor as I watch Cyr cross his arms in front of him to grab the hem of his fitted black tee shirt, pulling it up and over his head. It lands on my bed a moment later, his gaze never leaving mine even as I can't help but let my eyes wander down his torso, taking in every inch of those sculpted muscles.

The tattooed sleeves along his arms concealed corded muscles that I'd been wrapped in several times and still longed to feel around me. My eyes catch on the black-inked dragon climbing up one side of his ribs to the top of his chest below his collarbone. I feel my lips part in awe when Cyr's voice pulls me out of my trance.

"Your turn."

"Wasn't one strip tease enough?" I counter, referring back to the day of my tattoo. My eyes flick back up to those glacier eyes devouring me. Cyr's eyebrow raises and I know instantly I'm treading on thin ice.

"Don't make me rip those buttons open, Raven."

"You wouldn't…"

"Try me."

The most convenient clothing has been my assortment of flannels while the tattoo heals and now I'm regretting wearing tearable clothing in his presence. However, the thought of Cyr tearing my flannel from my body is eating me alive.

My hands make quick work of the buttons, dropping the flannel from my body onto the floor by my feet. Cyr moves to me, his fingers sliding underneath the waistband of my leggings. His eyes meet mine, asking for permission and I nod. His eyebrow raises again as if the action isn't enough for him.

"Yes." The word leaves my lips in a whisper.

Cyr begins sliding my leggings down my hips and his fingers wrap around the band of my lace panties, pulling them down together. As his body lowers to bring them both down, his eyes never leave mine just as he had the first time he undressed me. He slides the pair down my legs until I step out of them entirely and then rises to stand fully in front of me.

His hands glide across my ribs, sending goosebumps shooting across every inch of my skin. His hands travel up my sides to hook underneath the band of my bralette, slowly beginning to pull it up over my head. He pulls the band out wide to not touch my tattoo and frees it from my body. The chill in the air slams into me, causing my nipples to pebble and turn painfully hard. My bralette falls to the ground leaving me absolutely and utterly bare before him, yet his gaze never strays from mine for even a second.

"Shower. Now."

Cyr's low voice invades my senses and it takes a brief moment before my brain can convey the message to get me moving toward the bathroom. I walk into the en-suite bathroom and turn on the water to the shower. After allowing the water to warm up, I step in, letting the water spray down across my face and chest. Over the sound of the running water, I hear the bathroom door close and the shower curtain slide open. Cyr steps into the shower behind me, sliding the curtain closed after him. I keep my body movements slight so as to not startle him as he presses in close to my back.

My breath hitches in my throat as I feel his hard length press against my ass and it takes all of my self-control to not push back into him. Cyr's hands glide up my back and I shiver under his touch as his hand stops at the bandage covering my fresh tattoo. He carefully peels the bandage off and discards it, taking the special soap he bought for me and ever so gently applying a light layer of it against the sensitive flesh on my back. I see his tattooed hand come up in front of me and detach the removable shower head to focus the spray against my back. The warm water soothes my body and his free hand gently massages around the area, removing the soap from the ink.

His movements halt after a few moments and I feel his hot breath against my ear, eliciting a shudder.

"Close your eyes, Raven."

I obey, closing them a moment before his left hand wraps

around my neck and pulls me back, flush against his chest. Cyr nudges my feet apart with his foot and my heart begins to beat out of my chest as I envision the next few moments.

"Cyr, I…" My words trail off as I feel the shower head in his hand begins making circles against my lower stomach with the nozzle against my skin.

"You, what?"

"I just…Here? In the shower?"

His soft chuckle has my knees nearly buckling from the sound alone.

"Trust me, Raven, the first time I fuck you certainly won't be in this shower. You'll be tied to my bed begging for mercy."

My lips part in a soft moan as his grip tightens against my throat and turns my head away from him. His tongue glides up the column of my neck and I gasp, unsure if it was from the sensation or the fact Cyr's mask was off.

"Tell me when."

Cyr's words catch me off guard until I feel the shower head lower down to the apex of my thighs, sending me shaking in his grasp. I hear the *click* of the shower head changing speed to a new setting, and the process continues until the hardest setting hits my core.

"When."

I cry out in a moan, slightly strangled by the grip of Cyr's hand against my throat. He rotates the shower head in slow circles against the incredibly sensitive flesh between my thighs. The pressure hits every nerve, wanting to shift my legs closed, but Cyr's legs hold mine open for him. My legs begin to tremble as the building heat in my core begins to crest.

"God, Raven. You're so fucking beautiful. You don't know how many times I've fisted my cock imagining it was that pretty mouth of yours."

Cyr's voice rumbles against the shell of my ear and I nearly combust from his words. His mouth trails down my neck, sucking on the sensitive flesh between my neck and collarbone.

"F-fuck Cyr…"

The words spill from my lips and it grows harder to breathe with each passing second. Cyr's hand holding the shower head picks up its pace, using the bubbled face of the shower head to brush against my clit. I can't control the shaking that consumes my body as I'm moments away from losing my mind completely.

"Yes, Raven. Come for me."

A second later, I'm shattering in his grip. My vision goes hazy as Cyr helps me ride through my orgasm, nearly sending me to the ground. His hold on my neck releases and I gasp for air, still shaking from the crash of euphoria racing through my veins. Cyr's hand slides down to wrap an arm around my waist to keep me upright until I gain control of the usage of my legs again.

Cyr hooks the shower head back up to its mounted spot above me then bends down to leave soft kisses along my neck and shoulder. The action causes my heart to skip a beat and I can't help the smile that blooms across my cheeks.

"Was that a sufficient amount of help?"

Bastard.

My mouth opens to reply, but no words form as my body continues to recover from the aftershocks. The low rumble releasing from his chest has my stomach flooding with heat all over again.

"I'll take the silence as a yes."

"Y-yes," I manage to stutter out, internally cursing myself for saying anything at all.

Cyr proceeds to assist me in washing my hair to not get any of my fragrant shampoo or conditioner on my tattoo. He damn well knows I would have been able to manage a shower without him, but Cyr showing up unannounced only confirms one thing. He wants me just as badly as I need him.

19

The Blindfold

Cyr spent the night in the dorm with me last night. I didn't want him to leave. Watching him grab his helmet and jacket made me want to cry, so when I gathered the courage, all it took was one word.

Stay.

I couldn't remember the last time I'd slept so peacefully as we lay on our sides facing each other, gazing into the eyes of the other until we'd fallen asleep. Not touching him and suppressing the want building inside me to have him hold me to his chest as we slept was difficult, but I would happily wait forever until that day came.

As the sun came up the next morning, a few stray sun rays peeked in through the blinds covering the window. I quietly stir as I feel poking against my shoulder, opening one eye a crack to see Clara standing next to me wide-eyed and mouth gaped. My eyes roll back into my head, silently shaking my head at her. She smiles ear to ear and holds up her phone.

Clara mouths silently to me, *"Call me later! I want to know everything!"*

I nod, quickly shooing her off with a wave of my hand. Clara grabs a few things and sneaks out of the room as silently as she had entered. As my head returns to the direction of Cyr, his eyes are still closed and breathing steadily. The serenity and peace across all of his visible features stun me stupidly as I drink him in. My eyes take in his form and I glance down to my hand in between us to see his locked around mine. Tears begin to gloss over my eyes at the sight and I'm certain Cyr didn't even notice his hand had gravitated to take hold of mine. Regardless, I'll hold onto this moment as long as I'm able.

I don't remember falling back asleep until I'm awoken by a feather-light graze of Cyr's hand against my cheek. He softly brushes a few loose strands of my damp hair back away from my eyes. My eyes flutter open and I'm met with a beautiful blue gaze staring down at me from where he stands next to me beside my bed.

"Good morning," Cyr says with a hint of sleep still in his tone and my heart warms at the sound. A lazy, sleepy smile graces my cheeks.

"Hi," I reply, glancing over to my phone and seeing 9:30 am flash across my screen, panic setting in. "Oh shit, don't you have class at 9?"

I quickly sit up with a brief groan as I shift my weight to lean back on my palms. Cyr takes a seat on my bed in front of me, shaking his head.

"10. I have to run and change before class, but wanted to tell you goodbye before I left. Sorry, I don't have a breakfast burrito for you this time."

My cheeks begin to redden at the comment, noting from the last time he had to leave for the tattoo shop he brought me breakfast. I shake my head in reply.

"That's alright, I've got quite a bit of eye candy instead."

Cyr lets out a soft chuckle, and I swear a tint of red stains the tops of his cheeks that I can see from over the top of his mask. He runs a hand through his dark waves to brush them back from his face. His hair has always been styled or sleek straight whenever I've seen it. After the shower from last night, his hair has a sleep-mussed, dried waves style and if I said it wasn't the hottest thing I'd ever seen, I'd be lying.

Cyr leans forward and gently grips my chin, running his thumb across my bottom lip. He drags it down slowly and his eyes meet mine, promising to devour me as if I was his last meal.

"Come over to my dorm tonight," His voice rings out low and I suppress the shiver aching to shoot up my spine. I hesitate for a moment and Cyr's hand drops, eyeing me questioningly, "What is it?"

"I heard that Tobias returned to your dorm. Is it true?" The words slip free from my lips barely any louder than a whisper.

Cyr shakes his head, "No. He's been moved to the finance building where he belongs. It's just me."

I exhale a breath of relief and nod, "Just tell me when and I'll be there."

He stands from my bed and reaches into his back pocket, pulling out his wallet. I eye him curiously until I see a gray key card slip free from his wallet, and he extends it to me.

"Whenever you want, Raven. My room is yours."

My eyes widen slightly as I glance up at him, biting the edge of my bottom lip. He stiffens, releasing a low growl, "Cut that shit or I'm gonna fuck you here and now."

I quickly look away, reaching up blindly and taking hold of the key card before meeting his eyes once again. Cyr's glacier stare burns a hole in my soul under that gaze, pinning me where I sit.

"What if I said please?"

Fucking hell did I actually just say that?!

Cyr's chest rises up and down quicker than normal and his fists are planted on my bed on either side of my hips before I could even blink. His face was mere inches in front of mine.

"If only I had the amount of time I plan to take when I ravage you from the inside out."

My face flushes completely and my jaw gapes at him ever so slightly as his words slam into me like a tidal wave. I'm stunned speechless and words evade me as he caresses my cheek one last time. My eyes fall closed as his skin grazes over mine for just a moment before he pulls away to grab his things. By the time my senses come back to me and my eyes open once again, he's gone, as swift as a shadow.

***

The next few nights we spent together in a blissful blur of flirty banter, long nights talking about music and tattoos, and soundly sleeping next to each other. Most nights he'll sleep with his back to me which I've grown accustomed to since I couldn't imagine what it would be like to sleep in that mask constantly. A ripple of guilt flows through me when I wake up in the middle of the night, or early in the morning, and see his mask still on. He wouldn't have to keep it on if I weren't there, but if he cared, he wouldn't have asked me to stay with him. Or give me his room key for that matter.

When classes are done for the day, Cyr's taken me on short day trips around the city on his motorcycle which I've quickly learned to love. The freedom it gives me while riding with him is unlike anything I've ever felt before. I can't get enough of it, just like I can't get enough of him.

Due to hectic class schedules and an overload of appointments at the tattoo shop for Cyr, it'd been almost two weeks since Cyr had me come to his dorm. I have since explained to Clara the happenings of that night in the shower and my eardrums have yet to fully recover from the screams and squeals released from her throat.

I step out of the shower and walk out into the empty dorm as Clara is with her girlfriend, Gwen, for the night. My phone dings from where it's sitting on my bed and I glance over as a text flashes across my screen.

Cyr: I'm bringing dinner home with me from the shop. I'll be there in 30. Come by my dorm when you're ready.

My eyes widen at the text and in seconds I'm bolting over to my dresser to attempt to find something decent to wear. Today is laundry day and Clara is the one on laundry duty, but of course, she prioritized Gwen's tits over laundry. Not that I could blame her.

After countless minutes of rummaging between remnants of Clara's clothes and my own, I slip into a black crop top with skeleton hands acting out holding onto my breasts and a pair of Clara's ripped black jean shorts with frayed ends. The look is finished off with my black and white Chuck Taylor's and a light gray cardigan.

After deciding against trying to style my hair with only minutes before I should be heading out, I grab my bath towel and lazily wring out my damp hair. Once I've drained most of the moisture out, I finger-comb a bit of mousse into my hair to attempt to give my dark, pin-straight hair some much-needed volume. Once I've come to terms that my hair is as good as it's going to get, I grab my phone and room key before heading up to Cyr's dorm.

The *click* of the door unlocking to Cyr's dorm sends my heart racing as I sit on his bed, fiddling with the accent rings on my fingers. I'd left my cardigan on the small table in the shared common room to let him know I was already there. The last thing I wanted to do was startle him and catch him off guard. Yes, he'd given me a room key to his dorm so I could come by whenever I wanted, but this was all still so new to me that I didn't want to feel like I was invading his personal space.

"Raven?"

That soul-damming voice echoes throughout the common room and into his dorm sending my body ablaze. I've never felt so affected by a nickname before, or is it his voice that lights the kerosene in my veins?

"Good, you're finally here. I'm starving!"

"Trust me, I am too."

There's a hint of seduction in that sinful voice and I bite down hard on my bottom lip to keep from saying anything stupid. Even though every part of my body begs me to egg him on. Before I can speak, Cyr enters the room looking every bit disheveled. He pushes through the door holding his helmet, jacket thrown over his shoulder, and carrying two bags of takeout.

"Do you need a hand?" I ask, butchering my attempt at stifling a small laugh as he struggles to balance the items with his arms.

I receive a glare at my small laughing fit and he manages to flip me off. A wicked smile glides across my cheeks at his gesture. He treks over to his desk, slowly but surely managing to lay everything down from his hands across the surface. A bag crinkles as Cyr sifts through it and pulls out a to-go container and a set of chopsticks. He turns toward me with a container in each hand and I raise an eyebrow at him in question.

"What's on the menu for tonight?"

Cyr's mask shifts up as he cocks an eyebrow at me in reply. My skin flushes crimson as I can read the one word that's gone unsaid in those ice-blue orbs.

You.

I take a deep breath, shaking my head and rolling my eyes at him. A quiet laugh comes from Cyr as he places the Chinese food on the bed in front of where I'm currently sitting crisscrossing. My jaw opens in slight shock as I see my favorite dish being placed in front of me. We'd only gotten Chinese takeout once and that was at least a month ago.

"You remembered…" I whisper, glancing down at the chicken and broccoli platter in front of me.

"I remember all of your favorite things, Raven."

As if my skin couldn't get any hotter, my heart began to melt into a puddle inside of my chest.

"Thank you," I say softly, pulling the lid off of the container and breaking apart the pair of chopsticks with a gentle *snap*.

Cyr nods in reply before climbing atop his bed, sitting directly behind me with his back against the headboard. I feel a tap against my shoulder and I peek over to see the TV remote being extended over to me. My free hand reaches over to take the remote and as I look up at the screen I see Cyr's figure behind me in the reflection of the black screen. Just barely I make out Cyr's hand reaching up to undo the strap of his mask from behind his ear. I immediately find an interest in the food placed on my lap as I click on the TV, waiting for the streaming channels to pop up on the screen.

"Thank you," Comes a soft voice from behind me and I sigh softly knowing he saw my quick reaction.

"I just…wanted to give you the privacy you deserve."

Before I can say anything else, I feel Cyr's hands come up around my hips and his fingers hook through the belt loops of my shorts. A brief yelp leaves my lips as I'm pulled back a few feet, holding onto my dinner for dear life. My back meets a mixture of bone and flesh as Cyr pulls me back to lean me against his shins as a makeshift backrest. The action makes me smile as I gently settle against his legs and begin digging into my dinner.

***

Our dinner dishes have long since been discarded as the movie plays on, filling the room with the voice of Ewan McGregor as he sings the title track of *Moulin Rouge*. Cyr insisted on the fact that I chose our entertainment for the night, so he willingly agreed for me to torture him with my love of musicals. Surprisingly though, he never put up a fight and instead gave a small chuckle when the film began. I tried to find a film he'd never seen before and I succeeded, though he knew about the movie, Cyr was willing to give it a shot. Another reason why I constantly feel so much appreciation and adoration for this man.

Shortly after our meals are finished, Cyr summons yet another yelp from my lips as he pulls me back once again to nestle me between his powerful thighs. I keep my arms draped across my torso as he lowers me down to rest my back against his chest. His hands remain on my hips, keeping a slight hold on me as if I was going to slip away from him. A sigh of relaxation leaves my lips as I feel his warmth envelop me like the embrace of a fire on a cold winter's night.

It seems like forever ago when he couldn't even be in my general vicinity for more than a few seconds before he needed space from me. Not because of me, as he'd assured me on several occasions, but the closeness of people to him in general sent his anxiety rampant. But now, even though he still didn't like being touched without his consent, Cyr wanted me in his hold more times than not. He's grown to be able to withstand the contact for longer periods if he is the one to initiate the contact. Cyr wanting me close to him warms my soul down to my core, wishing to never be out of his grasp.

My breath hitches in my throat as I feel Cyr's hands slowly glide up toward my stomach and across my torso. His arms coil around me, hands sliding underneath mine which are folded across my lower stomach. Using his strength, Cyr's arms softly pull me upwards and back to hold me even tighter against his chest. My hands remain still as I let his hands roam my body and position me where he wants me. As I fall back into his chest again, I feel the strain of his length against his jeans pushing into my tailbone.

I'd felt his hardness against my back the first time he sent me crashing into euphoria in my shower a few weeks ago. I couldn't get him out of my mind since that night, but if this is leading to where I think it is, I don't know if I'm ready. If this begins…I don't think I'll ever want to stop, and I'm afraid of being completely okay with that.

Cyr's hand trails down toward the button on my shorts and I feel his heart racing against my back. He's just as anxious as I am which oddly brings me a small amount of comfort.

"Raven?" His question comes out hoarse as if he was holding back a dam and it was seconds from bursting.

"Yes," I reply in a whisper, knowing exactly where his question is leading and I plan on willingly diving headfirst into it.

Cyr proceeds to undo the button of my shorts and brings

both hands to my waist, lifting my hips to slide my shorts down my legs. I gently kick the shorts off the rest of the way, sending them falling to the floor with a gentle *thud*.

"Good girl, Raven, you listen so well."

With a feather-light graze, his fingertips glide up my thighs devastatingly slow toward the slick wetness at the apex of my thighs. After our night at the club, Cyr told me Rule #1: *no panties allowed*. I haven't forgone panties every time I've come over to his dorm, but there was something in my mind that told me I should tonight. My gut feeling paid off.

He pauses, grabbing each of my thighs in his hands and spreading them to fall on either side of his knees to keep them open for him. Cyr growls feeling how wet I already am for him, and I tilt my head to the side to gauge his reaction. His hand instantly comes up to my neck, angling my head back toward the direction of the TV.

"Keep your eyes on the movie."

His low tone sends a shiver across my body, involuntarily jerking against his hand. Cyr groans, grinding himself into my backside causing a moan to slip free. Before I can catch my breath, his hand slips lower finding that sensitive bud that's begging for his touch. I gasp as he begins rubbing in small, tight circles against my core that have me writing against him.

"Patience, Raven. Don't want you getting too excited before I have the chance to taste every inch of you."

Slowly, Cyr slips a finger inside of me, my eyes rolling back with a moan between my lips. He drags that wicked finger all the way out before plunging itself back in. The motion repeats too painfully slow, and his thumb returns to that most sensitive spot, continuing those small circles against me. The building need in my core causes my breathing to quicken against him.

"Cyr…"

"What's your safe word?"

His question throws me off completely as I attempt to control my breathing for a moment to think properly.

"Pomegranate," I reply in a breathless whisper.

Instantly, he withdraws from me entirely and the sudden loss of his touch has me shaking. Cyr's hands are on my hips sliding me all the way forward to the foot of his bed. My legs dangle off the front of the bed, not quite touching the ground, and my hazy lust-filled eyes find him. He stands from his bed and pulls his black tee shirt up and over his head. My jaw drops taking in that beautiful olive skin and sculpted chest, carved by Michelangelo himself. In moments, his shirt is rolled up and tied over my eyes, concealing my vision in darkness. His hands skate over my shoulders, guiding my body to fall backward flat against his bed. Every one of my senses skyrockets into action as my sight becomes void of everything.

I jolt slightly as Cyr's hands glide up my calves and up to my thighs. I gasp as his soft lips graze my inner thigh, licking along the inside up to the apex of my thighs. My heart rate picks up to the point where I may pass out, never having felt anything like this before in my life. The unknown about to occur before me has me wanting this, wanting *him* even more, but terrifying me all at the same time.

Cyr's hands push my thighs out to the side and before I can comprehend any thought, his lips are closing over that bundle of nerves, sucking it into his mouth. A loud moan comes out in a cry from my lips and I fist the bed sheets below me. His tongue and teeth are relentless against my throbbing core as he devours my body. Cyr's tongue works effortlessly against my aching center as he plunges two fingers inside of me, curling his digits against that spot deep inside of me.

Within moments, I don't even have time to warn him before I crash with my release. My thighs tremble against him and he laps me up as he rides out my release with me. I feel like I could fall off of the edge of the world and I would fall straight into his awaiting arms.

Cyr's mouth leaves me and a shaky exhale escapes as I attempt to drag in the air that no longer exists. The bed shifts in front of me as Cyr's hands grip my hips, sliding me a little further back on his bed. His hands are still against my hips, though I grow weary as Cyr's hands begin to shake against my body.

"Cyr?" I whisper and his touch immediately leaves my hips, the weight on his bed shifting away from me.

"I can't…" His voice is low and something else strikes a cord deep in my chest.

Pain.

The sound breaks my heart into a thousand little pieces. He's battling the demons in his head and I know they're winning. I want to comfort him, but I'm terrified to push him further away into the trenches of his mind.

I slowly raise my hands to peek under the edge of the blindfold over my eyes. The sight before me has my body crumbling. Cyr's sitting on the far corner of his bed, farthest away from me, hunched over with his hands interlocked behind his head. Cyr's mask is discarded on the floor beside him and my gaze cautiously flicks back to him, his face buried between his strong arms. His tattooed back flexes and shudders as he caves further into himself and as much as I want to reach out a hand to him, I keep my arms tucked up against my chest.

"It's okay, Cyr. We knew this would take time," My voice is soft to not startle him, and I don't dare to move as I watch his exhale staggeringly leave his body.

"I want you, Raven. Fuck, I want you more than I need air to breathe." The tone of his voice has my eyes widening in shock, "But I have to make sure you can't touch me."

His voice breaks and it's full of pain. He doesn't want it to be this way, but he can't help it. My eyes drift shut as I inhale and exhale calmly. I lift my hands to bring his shirt back over my eyes, plummeting myself back into darkness. My hands clasp together in front of me, slowly extending my hands toward Cyr's direction but not close enough to touch him.

"Then make sure I can't touch you." My voice is full of calm and I feel the bed slightly shift as if he turns to face me, "But if this is too much, too soon, then take the blindfold off of me."

I want to give Cyr the choice. He always told me that if I wanted to stop this at any time, I could, but right now the ball is in his court. He would always have a choice, and I'd wait forever if that's what it takes.

Cyr leaves the bed entirely with a slight squeak of the bed and I bite my lip unsure of his actions. Is he walking around the bed to remove my blindfold? I remain as still as possible with my hands outstretched in front of me, but I shiver when I feel Cyr's hands take hold of mine. A silky soft material wraps around my wrists, binding them together in a knot tight enough to keep my hands together, but not too tightly to cause pain.

Soft skin slips around the back of my neck as Cyr uses his hand to guide my body down gently toward his bed. The bind around my wrists is pulled up and over my head and it tightens a bit more as my hands touch the headboard. Cyr's hands leave my body and I test the binding, not budging an inch from the headboard. My heart races in my chest and I know I'm safe, but the anticipation has my mind reeling as silence fills the space.

The silence is short-lived as I hear a soft *clink* as Cyr's belt comes undone in front of me and the quick rip of a condom wrapper. Knowing what's to come has my thighs rubbing together as lava fills my lower stomach, attempting to calm my need for him.

A gasp rips from my throat when my legs are thrown to the sides and Cyr's hands grip my thighs hard enough to bruise. The dull pain shoots up my spine and I crave the feeling coursing through me. The bed dips and shifts as Cyr kneels between my legs, his fingertips grazing up my thighs and digs a vice-like grip into my legs, pinning them down into the mattress. A whimper rumbles from my lips as Cyr's tongue circles over my nipple, sucking it into his mouth. I strain against the binds, my back bowing a little against his mouth. Cyr's hand slides up to push my stomach down against the bed as his hard length rubs against my entrance.

With the void of my vision, my imagination takes over as the sensations rip through my body. His tongue and teeth taking over my breasts, his hands rendering me immobile under his grasp, his tip gliding against my core. The feeling sends me writhing beneath him. I stiffen as he slowly pushes inside of me and I gasp for air as he stretches me impossibly far.

Cyr releases a ragged breath and a low growl against my breast as he continues in, allowing me a moment to adjust to him. Inch by devastatingly soul-consuming inch he continues pushing in until I almost can't take it. I need more of him, Gods, I need all of him.

"Fuck, Raven," His voice rumbles against my breast, sending goosebumps across my entire body. Cyr's hands begin shaking once again, but this time it's different. It's not from fear or pain, it's his control. He's holding back, biding time for me, but it's quickly slipping.

"Take what you need," I whisper.

Before the words fully leave my lips, he's slamming into me to the hilt and my cry of a mixture of pain and immense pleasure fills the room. His mouth slides up to my throat, biting down hard against the soft flesh as he pulls out and slams back into me. My eyes roll back into my head, moaning out the ecstasy coursing through my veins.

Cyr picks up a wicked pace as he pumps in and out, soothing the spot on my neck with his tongue. He continues to fill every single inch of me until it's almost too much to handle, sliding the hand on my stomach down to the sensitive bud between my legs. His thumb glides over the bundle of nerves and rubs it in tantalizing circles as his pace does not falter.

My heart beats faster with every thrust of his hips and I'm nearly combusting from overwhelming sensations at every point across my body. I pull against the restraint, my fingernails piercing into my palms further adding pain to the pleasure. His name comes out in a moan across my lips as I combust beneath him. Cyr thrusts once…twice…and he's toppling over the edge with me as we ride out our orgasms together. His panting moans in my ear have me nearly on the verge of another release.

Cyr's hands leave my body and my bindings are released within moments, my hands falling to the bed above my bed. He slides his hands underneath my back, lifting me up until we are chest to chest. Cyr wraps my legs around his hips, guiding my head to lay on his shoulder before removing his shirt from my eyes. The light from the room causes me to squint and blink a few times, adjusting to the brightness around me as I curl my arms between my chest and his. He stands from his bed and holds me tight with one hand around my back and another under one of my thighs. I glance down seeing his mask still discarded on the floor.

"Cyr…your mask," I say softly through wobbling breaths, keeping my gaze facing away from him as my head lays gently atop his shoulder.

"I don't need it where we're going," Cyr replies, a bit of gravel in his voice. He shifts me on his hips and the bastard is still rock-hard inside of me. I bite down hard on my bottom lip at the adjustment and can't contain the urge within me to wriggle my ass just a little against him. His grip on my thigh tightens, halting my movements as he growls into my ear, "Don't test me, Raven. Keep that up and you won't be able to walk tomorrow."

Every intrusive thought in my mind is clawing at my mind to keep going and test that theory, but I realize I do have things to do tomorrow and I'll need my ability to walk.

It'd be worth it though.

Cyr carries me to the shower in his en-suite bathroom and gives me the best aftercare I've ever experienced. He cares for my body like it's a temple and he would lay his life on the line to protect his temple. He holds my hair up to keep it out of the water spray as we rinse our sweaty bodies. I keep my gaze averted down toward the ground as he washes his face, but the sight I'm met with has my body reheating all over again. The sight in front of me of how much I just took into my body has me squeezing my thighs together.

First off, how the fuck did I fit all of him inside of me? The man is incredibly blessed, to say the least. Second, how was he still *that* hard?!

At that moment I was quickly coming to terms with how much I truly did affect him, in more ways than one.

"Take a picture, it'll last longer."

My face turns crimson as I spin my body around completely

to stare at the wall, my back to his chest. The bastard dares to chuckle at my flustered state and I mentally give him a flick to the forehead. That is if I was truly mad at him, he's like a God's damned teddy bear and I couldn't hurt him even if I wished to. So, my brain is content with flicking him in the head which makes the blush across my cheeks lessen slightly.

As we finish, Cyr hands me a towel to dry off and grabs one for himself. I exit the shower and make my way back into the bedroom, Cyr exiting a few moments after me. My eyes catch on his mask and I stop, holding the towel up with one hand as I crouch down to retrieve the mask. I feel Cyr come up behind me, his warmth emanating around me as I stand up straight. My hand comes up over my shoulder to hold the mask in front of him while facing away from him. Cyr plants a kiss on the top of my head and my eyes fall closed in a soft sigh at the feeling. His hand briefly skims across mine as he takes the mask from my hand and I continue walking over toward his dresser.

"Do you mind if I borrow a shirt?" I ask softly, keeping my head down and waiting in front of his dresser until I have his permission.

"I prefer you without clothes, but if that's not going to happen, I'd rather you be in mine," Cyr's husky, slightly muffled voice has my head quickly turning to face him.

Those shining blue orbs steal my breath and I smile with a soft blush. My eyes widen as I realize he's dropped his towel to the floor and is prowling over toward me stark naked. I quickly avert my gaze and look back to his dresser with a laugh.

"Gods above, Cyr! Have you no modesty?"

"Not when it comes to you."

His reply has my toes curling as he comes up behind me, hands grazing my shoulders to reach his top dresser drawer.

Cyr's arms pin me on either side between his muscled chest and the dresser in front of us.

I couldn't say I minded, in all honesty.

Cyr pulls out a *Breaking Benjamin* tee shirt that's a few sizes too big for me, but nonetheless, I accept the shirt and hold it to my chest.

"Thank you," I say softly, glancing up at him over my shoulder and flashing him a grin. He nods, hesitating for a moment before dropping his arms to let me pass by him. The need to be close to him, I can see, is just as strong the other way around for him. It makes the butterflies in my stomach perform an Olympics-level gymnastics performance.

I walk over toward where my clothes were discarded on the floor earlier and search for my panties. After locating them, I slip into them while keeping my towel firmly wrapped around my torso. My eyes flick up to Cyr's when I feel his gaze on me, standing a few feet away in just a pair of black boxers. One of his eyebrows is cocked up to his hairline and I halt my motions with my panties halfway up my thighs.

"What?"

"You realize I just stripped you bare in front of me and now you're wanting to hide those beautiful curves from me?"

A flush instantly spreads across my chest and up my neck, staining my body the shade of rose.

"I…uh. Well-"

The words I want to say completely evade me as I stutter out a response. My gaze trails down to the towel wrapped around me as I pull up my panties the rest of the way. All thoughts eddy from my mind and I chew on my bottom lip as I try to think of a way to explain how I feel about my body. I can't process words or anything coherent, so instead, I raise to hands to the top edge where the towel is tied around my chest.

Cyr is in front of me instantly covering my hands with his, "Raven…you don't have to reveal yourself to me on my behalf. If you're uncomfortable being naked in front of me, that's okay. I just hope it's not *because* of me."

I'm quick to shake my head as I glance up to meet his gaze, my eyes turning slightly glossy.

"Please, don't cry." Cyr's hand slides up to caress my cheek, focusing my eyes up to his, "You are the most beautiful woman I've ever met, inside and out. If you don't believe that's true, I'll spend the rest of my life proving it to you. You never have to be ashamed of how you look and feel like you have to hide yourself from me. Every single curve on you I'll worship until you believe it too."

A tear slips from my eye and rolls down my cheek to Cyr's awaiting thumb, and I smile up at him, "I know I'm beautiful, but not all of me can recognize that sometimes. Just…be patient with me. My moments of confidence pull me out of my head, but now, I'm snapped back to my reality and the doubt creeps back in." I speak softly, barely louder than a whisper. Cyr pulls me against his chest and wraps his arms around my back, holding me close.

"It's easier said than done, but you'll never have to feel insecure around me, Raven. I have my doubts plenty of days too, trust me."

His words cause me to pull back and stare up at him in bewilderment, "Cyr Maddox? Insecure? Have you looked at yourself recently? Even Clara calls you Adonis."

Cyr chuckles softly and shakes his head, "Everyone has their flaws that others don't see."

My heart melts in my chest and I can't help but admire him

even more than I already do. This man continues to amaze me through every twist and turn in this life. My body molds against his and I let out a soft moan as Cyr's fingers tangle through my hair. After what seems like endless minutes in each other embrace, Cyr's voice fills the air, soft and calming.

"Are you with me, Raven?"

"I'm with you."

Cyr helps me change into his tee shirt before we crawl back into his bed. The movie had ended at some point unbeknownst to me and he tells me to flip on another movie, pulling me to his side.

"Cyr?"

"Hmm?" He hums in reply, his fingers playing with the ends of my hair. I bite down on my lip, unsure of how to say what I want to say.

"Don't freak out, okay?"

Cyr's fingers are still in my hair and I sigh knowing that probably wasn't the best way to start this conversation off. My mind races and I take a deep breath as I attempt to formulate words that won't make him run away.

"Please, do carry on with the silence. I'm absolutely not holding my breath while you take your time."

The sarcasm laced in his tone has me rolling my eyes as I gently shift from his hold to look up at him. His head tilts down to me with an eyebrow cocked in confusion.

"I'm on birth control."

Cyr blinks several times at me as if I just told him that two plus two equals four.

"Alright, and I would freak out about that because…?"

My fingers entangle themselves together in my lap, twisting and pulling nervously while my mouth remembers how to speak.

"You don't have to use a condom."

His eyes widen to the point where I'm certain if they get any wider, they'll pop out of his head.

"Not unless you want to! I-I don't mind either way…" I quickly stutter out, attempting to remedy the situation, "After…" I pause, taking another deep breath, "After Tobias, I was tested and I'm clean. I just…wanted to give you the option."

Cyr exhales sharply and nods. He's quiet for a few moments and fear races through my veins. Too soon. Way too soon for this kind of conversation.

"I'm sorry, just…forget I said anything."

I wrap my arms around myself and shrink down onto the pillow, fixating my gaze on the movie playing in front of us. After several long moments which feel like a whole eternity later, Cyr's arms wrap around my torso and pull me back into him. He adjusts me to curl into his side with his chest to my back, keeping his arms firmly wrapped around my waist. A sigh of relief slips past my lips as he allows me to settle into him, still keeping my hands around me to keep them from touching him even if accidentally.

"Thank you for telling me," Cyr whispers into my ear and I tilt my head up to gauge his reaction. His eyes are full of appreciation and honesty. I smile with a nod and his hand comes up to brush a damp strand of hair back from my forehead, "Never be afraid to speak what's on your mind. Promise me that."

"I promise," I reply with another nod, the same appreciation for him glistening in my own eyes. His attention returns to the movie and I allow my body to lean back into him as his arms give me a gentle reassuring squeeze against my middle.

I can't remember much else of what happened next as I'm swiftly pulled into a deep sleep with Cyr's arms around me and his cologne lulling me into a world of dreams.

20

The Picnic

Me: Do you ever stop working?
Cyr: I'll have you know I'm closing the shop early today...

I roll my eyes at Cyr's text, setting down my phone into my lap for a moment to breathe in the late Spring breeze whirling around me. The day is bright and the flowers bloom in beautiful swirls of color throughout the campus courtyard. I can't help but do some studying under a large tree in the center of the commons courtyard and soak up the sun's rays. My eyes flit back to my phone when a new text from Cyr pops up in the thread.

Cyr: After my next client.
Me: Cyr Maddox, you're going to work yourself into an early grave!
Cyr: Miss me that much?
Me: What can I say? I'm lost without you.

The bubbles pop up as he begins to reply, but after a moment they disappear. His next client has most likely come in so he'll be away from his phone for the foreseeable future. My head leans back against the tree trunk and my eyes fall closed, inhaling the fresh air around me once more. A moment later, a light *ding* sounds from my phone, causing me to focus my gaze down on my lap.

Cyr: My client rescheduled. I'll see you soon.

A smile slides up my cheeks, biting the corner of my lip.

Me: Did you cancel on your client? I don't want you to lose out on money because of me.

Cyr: I'll be there in 15.

Is the only response I receive from the wicked man, rolling my eyes at the phone and hoping he feels it on the other end.

***

The sound of a roaring motorcycle engine pulls my gaze up from my textbook to see Cyr whip into the parking lot across the way from the courtyard. I know it's him from that damn helmet, but at least I can always pick him out in a crowd. As if the six foot four tattooed wall of muscle wasn't distinguishable enough.

My eyes catch on Cyr as he removes his helmet, flipping those thick black locks back. I couldn't look away from him no matter how hard I tried. There's always something about him that draws me to him even back when I tried to stay away, I couldn't. Remembering back to the time when I thought he would never want to be with a girl like me is laughable now.

Gods, I feel like a creep staring at the back of his head like he's Jesus Christ rising from the dead.

Those glacier-blue eyes meet mine and from across the courtyard and I can see his mask shift upward. The bastard is smirking at me, I fucking know it. I roll my eyes, quickly adverting my gaze back to the textbook in my lap.

"Brought you a present."

My ears perk up at the sound of Cyr's voice echoing across the grassy courtyard and I glance up in his direction. The energy pouring off of him demands attention as he prowls toward me with his leather jacket open and blowing in the breeze. In that moment he looks absolutely ethereal.

"A present? For me?" I question curiously, setting my textbook aside and noticing the dark maroon bag in his hand, "Please tell me you didn't murder Tobias, chop off his head, and stuff it in a bag. Because if you did, I'll be sorely pissed off I didn't get to witness that." A smirk slips up my cheek and Cyr laughs, shaking his head.

"No, it's not, but noted," Cyr replies and extends the bag toward me. I notice it's an odd shape, not quite circular almost semi-oval. The bag is a soft velvety-like cotton and once it's in my hands, my eyes fly to Cyr's.

"You did not…" I mumble, clutching the bag to my chest. Cyr laughs once again and it's indeed the most beautiful sound I've ever heard. He begins slipping off his leather jacket to reveal those strong arms with every inch covered in varying shades of black ink.

"Are you going to open it? Or just hug the bag all day?"

I bite down on my bottom lip for a moment of hesitation before pulling the drawstring loose and opening the top of the bag. My jaw drops and my eyes flash back to Cyr in disbelief, covering my mouth with one hand. Cyr's mask shifts upward on both sides and I wish I could see that smile I know is meant for me.

My hands frantically dig into the bag, pulling out the pastel motorcycle helmet. The top and sides are covered in different splashes of pastel colors to look like paintbrush strokes across the helmet.

"You did this for me?"

"Now that I know how much you enjoy riding, I thought you'd like your own helmet," Cyr replies, sitting down beside me with his back leaning against the tree. His head tilts toward me and gestures with his head to the helmet, "Do you like it? If you don't-"

"It's perfect, Cyr. I don't know how to thank you enough for this."

The words fly from my lips breathlessly as I glance back to him and he nods in reply.

"Lunch would be a nice 'thank you.'"

I smile ear to ear with a soft laugh, and I look back over to him with a nod, "I think I could manage that. Any suggestions?"

"Surprise me."

***

I race down the hall of the dormitory to my dorm on the other side of the building. My heart is pounding and I suddenly realize I need to add cardio to my daily activities. By the time I reach the door to mine and Clara's dorm, completely winded, I have my key card out and unlock the front door.

At that exact moment, I remember the real reason why I was in the courtyard that afternoon. As the door opens I'm met with the sight of Clara and her girlfriend in a full-blown makeout session.

"Fuck I'm so sorry! I'm totally not here don't mind me!" I spew out in a slur of words that I'm not even positive if any of it was coherent.

"Really, Bell?!"

Clara's groan of frustration has my cheeks turning the brightest crimson as I snatch a quilted blanket from off my bed and grab all the food I can manage.

"Aren't those *my* snacks?" Clara questions, glaring at me so hard I can feel it like lasers drilling into the back of my head.

"Yes, I'll pay you back in double!" I quickly reply, grabbing a few drinks from the mini fridge and tossing it all into the center of the blanket. Once all the food and drinks are packed, I scoop everything up to turn the blanket into a rucksack and swing it over my shoulder.

"Sorry Clara, love you! Bye, Gwen!" The words slip from my lips in one string of consciousness before bolting out of the door and pulling it tightly shut behind me.

***

The walk of mortification back to the tree where Cyr is currently leaning up against is one I wish to never have to make again. My face is still heated as I walk up next to Cyr and gently drop the makeshift rucksack to the ground in front of him.

"You look like you just ran through the trenches. What the hell happened?" Cyr asks while attempting, and failing, to stifle a laugh.

I groan in response, "Oh, I'm going to be digging my own trench to sleep in for the next week, at least. I forgot Clara asked for me to keep the premises of our dorm clear of my presence for the foreseeable future."

A huff leaves my lips as I plop to the ground next to Cyr and pull open the blanket, "I really hope I didn't forget anything because I'm officially banned from my own dorm." I grumble under my breath, flattening out the blanket between us and organizing what I managed to grab within fifteen seconds.

"Good thing you've got a bed at your disposal so you won't have to sleep in the trenches," Cyr says reassuringly and I can't help but smile a bit at his reply.

"I think you did this on purpose to lure me into your bed," I accuse Cyr to which he mocks incredulity at me with a hand to his chest.

"Me? I'm inclined to believe you did this to yourself because you enjoy being in my bed."

A tinge of rose stains the tops of my cheeks and I roll my eyes at the accusation, but a part of me can't deny the truth in his statement.

I line up the array of various lunch items on the blanket in front of us and I pick up one grape and one strawberry Uncrustable, holding them up in front of Cyr.

"Are you a grape guy, or more of a strawberry?"

Cyr uses his index finger and thumb to quizzically stroke his masked chin for a moment bringing a laugh to erupt from my lips. His eyes flick to mine and something soft shines in those ice-blue eyes. The image of Cyr completely comfortable out in the open with me lights a flame inside my chest. Cyr Maddox is sitting on an old knit blanket under a tree in the middle of the courtyard with a bag of jelly beans in his lap.

Wait a fucking second.

I scan the blanket and widen my eyes at him, "When did you snatch the jelly beans?! You better share those or we're gonna have some words, Maddox."

It's Cyr's turn to let loose a laugh and I can't even be upset with him after hearing that sound. A moment later, he's taking the grape Uncrustable from my hand and I raise an eyebrow at him.

"I didn't take you for a grape kind of guy."

"There's much to learn about me, Raven."

"Well, start talking then."

I'm met with silence as he cocks an eyebrow at me and I can

read clear as day the words in his eyes, *"It's not going to be that easy. Try again."*

Without a word, I use my palms to lift my body and rotate 90 degrees so my back is to him. I feel his back flatten against mine and we use each other to lean against one another. I couldn't place why, but having that added element of not seeing him while he eats is somewhat calming. It's an odd sensation, that we can just sit and eat and talk without having to gauge the other's reaction. As if you were to sit in front of a curtain with one person on either side and not have to worry about speaking your truth. Not that I've ever once worried about being able to speak freely with him. Quite the opposite in all honesty.

"Do you want a drink? I think I only grabbed a few sodas. Do you drink soda?"

I half mumble to myself as I rummage through the assorted piles of snacks in front of me on the blanket. With a body like his, I doubt he puts any junk in his body, making me slightly question my eating habits. My face reddens at the fact I brought all complete junk food to Cyr for a lunch date. As if I needed another thing for him to judge me for, but I highly doubt he's ever judged me about anything before. Not compared to how hard I judge myself daily.

"Who doesn't drink soda?" He asks, extending a hand back towards me to accept a can of soda.

I scoff, mumbling under my breath, "Someone like you with the physique of a literal God."

"I'm still human, you know. Even if I was blessed with abs like these," Cyr replies, chuckling lightly.

The urge to look over and see if he lifts his shirt for emphasis has my entire body straining against my mind's intrusive thoughts.

Cocky bastard.

Our picnic continues for what seems like hours, and I enjoy every minute of it. Being in his presence calms my racing mind and sends me into a peaceful bliss. I can listen to his voice forever and never grow tired of the sound. After nearly three-quarters of the bag of jelly beans is empty, I manage to wrangle the bag away from him when he forgetfully sets it on the ground beside him. We pass the bag of chips back and forth as Cyr tells me about trails he'll take on motorcycle trips and promises to take me out for a weekend.

The image of being on Cyr's motorcycle with him, riding throughout New England, and seeing the beautiful upcoming summer scenery has me giddy for trips that have yet to even be planned. It might not be the whole trip itself that has me so excited I can practically jump out of my skin, but rather spending time with Cyr. Holding him close to me and taking in the smell of his cologne as the wind whips around us and binds us together.

Over the past few months, I've become so enthralled by this man that it makes it hard to think clearly when he's not around. He's always there, lingering in the back of my mind, and prodding at every one of my senses making it damn near impossible to forget about him.

Cyr crinkles the bag of chips as he rolls it closed and his weight against my back shifts when he sits forward to stand. The loss of him next to me has me hesitantly turning around to gaze up at him. His mask is adorning his face which I could see from my peripheral and I know it's okay to look up at him fully.

"I say it's time to break in that helmet," Cyr says while packing up the trash and remnants of our lunch. I raise an eyebrow at him.

"Now? It's getting a bit late."

"Good, you'll be able to experience the city in the dark. We can make sure your helmet glows."

My jaw drops, "Wait, it glows?!"

Cyr's mask shifts up a little and my gaping jaw closes to turn into a soft smile, "I needed to make sure others would be able to see you."

"Your helmet is neon green, I think that would have been enough for the both of us."

"Not even close. Your safety means more than mine."

My heart flutters and skips a beat at his words, "Your safety is equally important, Cyr. You're not as expendable as you seem to believe you are."

He looks away from me as he folds up the rest of the food inside the blanket and tucks it into his chest. I can see the war battling in his eyes as my words sink into him. It makes my heart ache at the sight.

Cyr nods his head, and an almost indiscernible, "Thank you" leaves his lips. It makes me wonder if anyone has told him that before, or lately at least, his reply furthermore digging a crater into the valves of my heart. I match his nod in reply as I reach over and hold the motorcycle helmet in its soft velvety bag to my chest.

"Let's go take a ride," Cyr says, extending a hand out to me.

A smirk graces my cheeks as I reach up to take his hand.

"Lead the way."

21

The Goodbye

The next few weeks fly by in a flash of motorcycle rides, cramming for finals, and breathless nights spent blissfully writhing beneath the beautiful man who has captured my heart, body, and soul. Summer vacation will be the hardest few months of my life being away from my two best friends in the world. One, who I know I'll go crazy without. His touch, his cologne, his…everything else that causes me to go ballistic in more ways than one. And the other who has ceaselessly driven me into madness for years. I think a sliver of me will miss her most.

"I don't know how you're going to survive the summer without me, Bell."

Clara's voice rings out from the bathroom where she's currently packing up her toiletries. A dramatic sigh escapes my lips and I fall backward, collapsing to my bed. The back of my hand falls over my forehead, ever the theatrics.

"You're right, my dearest friend. The world is so dark and lonely, how ever shall I manage without you to spare me from this forsaken universe?"

My eyes flutter shut during my speech to which I then crack one eye open to peer over toward Clara who is standing in the bathroom doorway with two middle fingers up. The belly laugh that pours from my lungs sends Clara laughing a second later. Before I can prepare for the assault, she's bounding over toward my bed and I squeal as I see Clara flying through the air a moment before her body falls atop mine. All the oxygen in my body leaves me in a fit of coughs as I attempt to withdraw any air I can back into my lungs. All the while still laughing hard enough to bring tears to my eyes.

"Payback's a bitch, babes."

Clara's reply has my hands darting up to poke her ribs on both sides releasing a series of shrieks and copious amounts of laughter from the both of us.

"Mercy, bitch, mercy!" Clara screams mid-laugh and my hands halt their poking to wrap around her torso tightly. She curls up next to me and we stay there in each other's embrace, attempting to catch our breaths.

"I was being genuine, Cee. I'm a hot mess without you." My reply is melancholy.

Not having Clara around is akin to missing a limb; doable, but it makes life a lot more difficult. Clara sighs, nodding and she brushes a strand of hair back over my shoulder to pinch my cheeks.

"Oh, I know you are, but it's not for forever!"

I roll my eyes and bat her hands away, although a smile creeps up my lips. It'll be hell being away from her, but we have a whole year to look forward to before we graduate. If I didn't have Clara to help me through this next year I'd be an absolute wreck without her. She's been my constant in this unpredictable world of variables from the beginning. I can't say Cyr hasn't as well, but I'll never know another love like I have for Clara. She's seen me in all my lowest points in life, and I'd be truly lost without her. Of course, I'm not about to feed her already giant ego even more and admit that to her, but a part of me already knows that she knows it.

"Were you still planning to stop by Gwen's dorm before you drop me off at the airport?" The question comes out soft, not wanting to lose any more time with her, but her girlfriend does have priority over me, unfortunately. Clara nods, glancing at the clock on the wall and then back to me.

"Don't worry, you and I will have time to sneak in a quickie before we leave," Clara winks and pecks a quick kiss on my cheek before sitting up. A small chuckle leaves my lips as Clara stands from my bed and walks over to grab her phone and room key. As I sit up, I stare at the massive pile of clothes I'm wondering how the hell is going to fit into both of my, still empty, suitcases.

"Careful, wouldn't want Gwen getting jealous." A smirk climbs up one side of my lips, and Clara laughs with a shake of her head.

"Oh, Gwen already knows that she's the side chick when it comes to us." Clara rushes out the door moments later to go track down her girlfriend and the smile on my lips doesn't fade for a single moment.

The next several minutes are spent vigorously attacking my poor, innocent suitcases to hold all of my clothes which are haphazardly tossed in. A knock at the door a second later sends me jumping slightly as my gaze tracks over to the door. Clara has only been gone a few minutes so I presume she forgot something, but why would she knock? She has a room key unless it's Gwen coming to find her instead.

I abandon my suitcase on the floor and turn toward the door. I unlock the door and pull it open, prepared to judge Clara for something when all the breath in my lungs swiftly disappears. My eyes widen at the sight of Cyr standing in front of me with an arm propped against the door frame.

"Cyr."

"Raven," Cyr replies in a husky, low tone which has my entire body turning molten.

I open the door further to allow him inside the dorm. He drops his arm, walking inside, and taking a seat at the edge of my bed. Cyr makes himself at home, leaning back to rest his hands on the bed behind him as his eyes take me in from head to toe.

"I was planning to stop by and see you before I left," My voice comes out soft as I drag my teeth over my bottom lip, glancing over at him. The way his eyes gleam with lust and desire sends a chill over my entire body.

"Beat you to it," He replies, beckoning me over to him with a lift of his chin. My feet pull me forward on unsteady legs as I pause before him. His hands slip around my hips, tugging me toward him to align the most sensitive part of me against his already hard length. My eyes widen slightly as I glance at the door and then back to him.

"Clara could come back any moment…"

"She won't."

Cyr's reply comes quickly and I raise an eyebrow at him at how convenient it was for him to show up only minutes after Clara left the room. He tugs at the bottom of my tank top while staring up at me with a heat-filled gaze.

"Off. Now."

As if in a trance, my hands trail down to the bottom of my

tank top and lift to free it from my body. The tank top drops to the floor leaving my breasts on full display before him as I decided against wearing a bra today. His glacier blue orbs take in the sight and the look in his eyes conveys he needs this as much as I do right now.

With the raise of his hand, index finger pointed up as he motions for me to turn around. I oblige, spinning around to turn my back to him. Before any thoughts can leave my lips, soft fabric, presumably the scarf from my suitcase, is binding my hands together behind my back. The gentle graze of his touch floats up my forearms and back down sending my body into a fit of goosebumps. The waistband of my biker shorts begins to slip down my hips and over the curve of my ass until they hit the floor a moment later. My panties are soon to follow as they slide down to the pile of clothes at my feet. Cyr's grip on my hip is tight enough to bruise and a whimper leaves my lips before I can stifle it. Using his grasp on my hip, Cyr spins me around to face him, completely bare in front of him.

"I never believed I'd be sent an angel, and yet here you are."

His voice rumbles low and promises everything I've been craving. Cyr's free hand travels up my stomach, eliciting a shudder as his hand continues up the valley between my breasts, and stopping at my neck. He squeezes my neck enough for me to inhale a gasp. His fingers wrap around the base of my neck and his thumb presses up against the underside of my chin, forcing my gaze up to the ceiling. My head falls back and my breath hitches in my throat as I feel his lips clamp down over one of my breasts. The moan that slips through my teeth is uncontainable and my hands flex, straining against the scarf behind my back. Before my mind can even process feeling those soft lips against my overly sensitive flesh, I bite down hard on my bottom lip as Cyr's other hand slips down and glides a finger through the wetness at the apex of my thighs.

"I love that you're so fucking wet for me, Raven."

Cyr's voice alone has me soaking and he gives me zero warning before plunging a finger inside me. The vice grip my teeth have on my bottom lip grows even tighter to the point I taste copper on my tongue.

"Let me hear you, Raven."

"I-I have n-neighbors…" I stutter out quietly as his finger slides painstakingly slowly in and out of me. My feet shift back at forth for the need for more friction. It's not enough… I need more of it. More of him.

"Let. Me. Hear. You."

That voice as sultry as sin fills my senses. I'm caught completely unaware as his teeth clamp down on my breast and another one of his fingers invades my body in a blissful thrust. The action has my eyes crossing as the pinch of pain and pleasure bleed together in my soul.

"Oh, Gods…"

The moan releases from my lips into the open air, causing Cyr to tighten his grip ever so slightly on my neck. I attempt to intake air, but the pleasure racking my body makes the action impossible.

"Good girl, Raven. Pray to the Gods all you'd like, but by the time I'm done with you, the only thing you'll be praying for is mercy." His husky tone skitters across my skin as his tongue circles the sensitive bud of my breast.

"Cyr…please," The whimper escapes my lips and I attempt to wriggle my hips to take his fingers in deeper. As I shift around, he pulls out of me entirely causing me to whine in frustration.

"Please, what?"

"Please let me come."

As soon as the last word leaves my lips, three fingers dive into me, stretching me painfully. My lips part in a cry, but the sound evaporates from my throat as his thumb begins rolling in circles over my clit. The sensation nearly brings me to my knees as I let the moans freely leave my lips.

"Fuck, Cyr, yes."

"Do you like that, Raven? You like when I stretch you out to get you ready for my cock?"

Those words have my knees and thighs trembling, my release so unbearably close. I give him a slight nod as I try to catch my breath with my heart nearly bursting from my chest.

"Use your words. Tell me how you like it."

"I-I…fuck…I want your cock."

Cyr's responding low chuckle and hard suck on my nipple has me moaning aloud for him, "You can have my cock when you come on my hand, and I want that wet fucking pussy, Raven. So come for me."

Cyr's thumb applies a bit more pressure to that sensitive bud and with another thrust of his fingers, I shatter. A cry bursts from my lips, and I don't give a damn who can hear me at this point. He continues small circles over my clit as I ride through the aftershocks, my eyes drifting closed as I slowly come down from my high.

His grip on my neck forces me to spin to look away from him and I nearly pitch forward, but a strong arm wraps around my waist. Cyr's hold on me is intoxicating, but also comforting as he holds me with my back to his chest. With his one arm around my waist, he lifts me into the air for a few seconds before setting me down across his lap. Cyr uses his free hand to spread my legs wide and drape them over the outside of his knees to keep my legs apart for him. My hands, still bound behind my back, lay flat against my tailbone to make sure my hands didn't touch his chest.

A moan slips from my lips as I feel his mouth leave kisses and small bites along my back and shoulders. Euphoria like I've never known before I've found within this man's embrace. The most unlikely of men, and he chose me.

Me.

Cyr's free hand drifts slowly up my inner thigh reaching dangerously close to the apex of my legs, causing me to tense ever so slightly in anticipation. My thighs shaking from the pressure building in my body.

"Shh, relax."

Cyr coos into my ear and as his breath hits my ear, it sends me shivering at the warmth. His arm around my waist lifts me gently a few inches off his lap. Within a second, I feel the tip of his cock sliding through my slick folds and my eyes roll back, moaning his name.

"Are you gonna take this cock like a good girl?"

Cyr's voice is slightly strained and I can tell his self-control is starting to slip as his tip rubs back and forth against my clit. The longer he continues, the quicker my control is slipping too. I nod vehemently and Cyr's growl has my heart picking up at a rapid pace.

"I need a yes from you, Raven."

Even though he's already invaded my body in all the best kinds of ways, this was his official request for consent and he always gave me the option to say no. I doubt I would ever say no, but the way he makes me vocalize my consent is the sexiest thing a man has ever done for me.

"Yes. Yes, Cyr, please." The words escape my lips like a plea for salvation that I can only find in his body.

Without another word, Cyr lowers my body down and I feel him break through my entrance. I suck in a sharp breath as he stretches and fills me to the point where it's almost more than I can take. He stops, my body hovering off his lap as he keeps me suspended while I adjust to his size. Slowly, he continues lowering me down his cock inch by crucifying inch until I'm seated to the hilt. Every ounce of oxygen in the room has been sucked out, leaving me panting and in search of air as Cyr glides me slowly up and down his shaft.

"Fuck, Raven, you're so tight."

Cyr grinds out in a mixture of moans into my ear. His hands grip both sides of my hips as he rocks me back and forth against him. The feeling of him fully inside me is almost too much to handle. The tinges of pain from being stretched so much mold with the sweet sensations of ecstasy as I ride him and his guiding of my hips pick up. Each thrust hit that sweet spot that sends his name flying from my lips like a curse and a request for more.

Cyr's hand leaves one of my hips and travels across my belly and down to the sensitive spot in between my thighs that begs for him to explore again. With a whisper of a touch, Cyr's middle and ring fingers begin circling my clit, dragging moans from the depths of my lungs into the air. I feel the release building within my core once again and the need for him to go harder and deeper has me quickening my pace. His grip tightens and slams my hips down onto him with enough force to send my eyes rolling into the back of my head.

"Do you need it rougher, Raven? Tell me what you need."

Cyr's words have me melting in his hold, practically combusting as his fingers continue to tease that sensitive spot.

"H-harder…please."

Instantly, he's sliding me off of him and the sudden loss of him sends an electric shock throughout my body. Before I can open my mouth to question him, he's bending me over my bed and throwing one of my legs up over the side of my bed. A second later he's slamming into me fully without a moment to adjust. The cry that bursts from my lips is loud enough to wake the dead. Cyr wraps my hair around his hand, yanking me upright toward his chest.

"Is this hard enough for you?"

His growl elicits a moan from low in my chest and without thinking, the word leaves my lips before I have the chance to think about what I'm telling him.

"No."

"No? Looks like I'll have to fix that."

Cyr's grip tightens on my hair to the point where my eyes begin to gloss over with tears. To distract from the immediate pain, his free hand travels back over the sensitive bud below my belly, and my body trembles under his touch. As I try to catch my breath from the assault from his fingers, he withdraws fully and slams back into me. The motion sends my body forward but his grip on my hair keeps me upright against his chest. Cyr's pace is brutal yet I can't get enough of him. He repeatedly hits that sweet spot inside of me that has my legs shaking on the precipice of release.

"Cyr…I-I'm going to…" My words trail off as he deepens the pressure against my swollen nub. The world around me starts spinning as he goes harder and I try to keep a hold on reality.

"I want to feel you tighten around me as I fuck you. Come on my cock, Raven."

His command sends me tumbling over the edge into a realm

that's not my own. Cyr's thrusts don't falter as I ride the tidal wave crashing through my body, and he rides through them with me. A moment later, his body slams into mine one last time before stilling, my name releasing from his lips with a loud moan. His forehead leans down to rest against the nape of my neck, gently leaving soft kisses along my spine. His chest heaving against my back while he catches his breath.

Cyr's hand leaves my hair to coil around my stomach to hold me upright on wobbly legs. His other hand drifts up from the apex of my thighs and reaches in between us to untie the scarf. It floats to the floor and my hands fall to my sides without the binding holding them in place. Cyr slowly pulls out of me and tucks himself away back into his jeans before lifting my weightless body into his arms. As I lean my head on his shoulder, I glance up, noticing his mask has returned to that olive-tanned face. I didn't even know when he put his mask back on, but I couldn't focus long enough to care as my eyes drifted shut.

"Are you with me, Raven?"

Cyr asks softly into my ear. My reply comes out in a breathy whisper, a smile sliding up my cheeks.

"I'm with you."

***

A squeal tears from my throat as Cyr lifts me up and plops me on top of my suitcase which is laid on top of my bed. He helped me wrangle all the clothes I could into my smaller carry-on suitcase, and now we're attempting to close my larger suitcase. Using my weight atop the suitcase, Cyr slides the zipper, with a few choice curse words as the zipper gets stuck, and he continues his concentration on it. His forehead creases with the focus and a smile grows at the sight, unable to hold back a soft laugh.

"Care to elaborate what the fuck is so funny? Are you enjoying watching me struggle?" Cyr's slight growl has my eyes widening at him.

How am I so turned on already like the past half an hour didn't just happen?! I need to seriously get checked out...

"I can't lie, it is pretty entertaining."

Before my words have fully left my lips, Cyr's hand is wrapping around my throat and pulling my body forward to him. Mere inches separate his masked face from mine and goosebumps shoot across my body within seconds. Warmth instantly floods my skin; my chest and cheeks turning a deep crimson with the action. Lava forms in my core, an undeniable need for him coursing in my veins. I can't control this ache that craves Cyr, and in all honesty, it scares the hell out of me, but another part of me says damn it all. Damn my conscious telling me this isn't right, and that this relationship can't work. This man has fixed and changed me in so many ways I thought would be irrevocably broken and damaged.

"Want to try that again?" Cyr's voice drops and I have to suck my bottom lip between my teeth to suppress a moan as his hand squeezes a little harder against my throat. Not nearly hard enough to cut off oxygen, but his proximity to me makes it impossible to breathe.

A familiar *click* echoes in the air as the dorm room door unlocks and swings open. My eyes dart to the door and collide with Clara's. Her eyes bulge out from her head, jaw dropping to the floor.

"I just remembered I'm really hungry."

Clara spews almost unintelligible with a nervous laugh and bolts from the room, pulling the door shut behind her as if nothing happened. If I didn't think my face could get any redder, I know I've turned to the shade of a tomato.

"Where were we?"

Cyr's voice pulls me back into reality, my gaze returning to his. I attempt to swallow but his grasp on my neck and the lack of oxygen in the room make that task incredibly difficult.

"Me not laughing at you anymore," The words came out in a whisper.

Cyr's mask shifts presumably into a devilish smirk I wish I could witness for myself. His hand releases from my neck and I suck in a deep breath in response. His hand slides into a gentle hold on my chin, keeping our distance only a breath apart.

"Good girl. Now get your pretty ass back up on the suitcase."

After he releases his hold on my chin, his grip shifts to grappling my soul. It's been there for a while, but that particular hold I feel will never falter and a part of myself never wants it to.

Cyr returns to his task of zipping up the suitcase beneath me which is screaming in resistance to the assault of getting the damn thing to zip closed. Another several minutes pass, and the battle is won, barely though as Cyr threatens to throw the suitcase out the window numerous times. Using my hands, I slide myself off the suitcase to stand in front of Cyr. The flood of emotions coursing through my body slam into me all at once. I will the tears to not gloss over my eyes, but a few slip free leaving tear stains down my cheeks.

"Talk to me."

Cyr's voice is gentle, coating my senses like the softest blanket wrapping around me. I slam my eyes shut and look away, hating to cry in front of him for what feels like the thousandth time. Cyr's touch under my chin forces my head to tip up towards him, "Look at me, Raven."

My eyes open, more tears streaming down as I meet those gorgeous blue orbs stealing my soul and the breath from my lungs.

"I don't want to leave you."

Cyr's head tilts slightly to the side, using a thumb to brush the tears from my cheek and my head falls into hand. He holds my head for a moment before pulling me to his chest. My hands stay down at my sides as I lean my head against his chest. I feel his hands run down my arms and don't think much of it except for a loving touch until he raises my arms. In a swift motion, he takes my forearms and wraps them around his back before returning his arms to hold me. The moment my arms wrap around his torso, the sob rips from my throat before I can stop them.

"Shh, Raven. Don't cry. It's only for a little while, not forever. I refuse to spend the rest of our forever apart," He coos into my ear as his hand cradles the back of my neck and the other rubs small circles into my back.

My grip tightens on him, balling the back of his tee shirt into my fists. Cyr stiffens for a flash before easing back into my touch and holding me closer to him. His cologne fills my nose, committing the smell to memory as I drink him in and I don't know if I'll be able to let go. Cyr holds me like this for endless minutes before he pulls back and takes hold of both of my cheeks in his hands. Once our eyes meet, he begins to slowly inhale, then exhale. My body begins to voluntarily mimic his breathing to the point where my sobs cease and I'm now clear-headed as I stare into those ice-blue pools, falling deeper than I ever have before.

"Our forever?" I question softly, dropping my hands from

around him to fall back at my sides.

"Ours," Cyr answers, his voice laced with promise and his head comes toward me to press his masked lips to my forehead. I take another shaky breath to banish the rest of the tears the act of affection risks bringing, "Let's get your things to the car or you might miss your flight."

I didn't give a damn if I missed my flight if it meant I'd be able to spend my eternity right here in this moment with him.

***

Cyr helps me get my luggage down to Clara's car and loads it up into the trunk. My best friend currently sits in the driver's seat of her car messing with her phone's directions even though I know damn well she knows how to get to the airport from here. I silently send her a thank you for giving me one more moment of privacy alone with Cyr. He closes the lid to the trunk and turns back to me, his mask shifting up into a hidden smile. I'm love drunk at the sight, eliciting a smile from me.

"Text me when you land, okay?"

Cyr's hand reaches down to take a gentle hold of my own. My eyes flick down to where our hands are connected before looking back up to meet his warm gaze.

I nod in response, knowing if I speak I'll start to cry again, and the Gods be damned if I start sobbing again in front of this man. He gives my hand one final squeeze before taking a step back and letting his hand slip free from mine.

With an exhale, I turn and slip into the passenger seat of Clara's car. Cyr shuts the door after me and I steal one more moment to memorize those beautiful eyes. The car begins to roll forward and I watch Cyr's form shrink in the sideview mirror until we turn from the campus and he disappears from sight altogether. It wasn't until after we'd left the campus did I allow the tears to fall once again.

22

The Visitor

The first month and a half of Summer vacation flies by in a flash. I spend most of my time painting in the park or running around with my parent's new German Shepherd puppy, Scout. He's only a few months old, and from the way his nose is constantly in the ground searching for some invisible threat, the name is fitting.

As the sun rises from the horizon and the early morning sunbeams shine through my window, I know it's going to be a beautiful day. I've barely sat up from my bed, sleep-mussed hair flying in several different directions when the smell hits me.

Chocolate chip pancakes.

Saturday morning pancakes have been a tradition in the Tyler house ever since I was little. My father would get up earlier than the sun and slave away at the stove to make sure those mouth-watering pancakes would be hot and ready by the time I had woken up. Even though those pancakes are going to be the highlight of my day, my body still takes its time adjusting to waking up. A yawn escapes my lips and I give my head a slight shake to rid the sleep from my head.

My feet slowly descend from my bed and onto the chill wooden floor. New Mexico is never cold in the summer, but my parents always have the A/C running at all times like it is hotter than Death Valley in the house. I welcome the cool touch against my toes as I pad across the bedroom, opening my door to the hallway in search of the delicious smell wafting from the kitchen. The long hallway is a walk of temptation towards the kitchen where I know I'd find the best kind of surprise on an early morning.

I turn the corner to see my dad washing up the dishes from the massacre he'd made in the kitchen. He's always been a brilliant cook, but could never manage to make a meal, even a simple sandwich, without turning the poor kitchen into the aftermath of an atomic bomb. The chocolate chip pancakes and sides of bacon hit my nose and it's enough to make me practically jump into a seat at the dining room table.

"Good morning, kiddo," My father says, glancing over his shoulder at me with a soft smile.

"Morning, Dad. May I?" I ask, pointing to the stack of pancakes on the table, eager to pile them on my plate.

"Eat up," He replies and I don't bother wasting a moment before grabbing a seat and diving into the pancakes. My dad brings over a plate of scrambled eggs with a serving spoon, "Save your mother some, she should be home soon."

I'm so consumed with breakfast that I stop and take a moment to look around the corner into the living room, "Where'd mom run off to?"

"Farmer's market started early today since it's supposed to storm this afternoon. She left with the dawn to get a head start," He says, setting one last pot into the dishwasher. I feel like a terrible child for not noticing my mother wasn't even home. A wet lick slides up my calf and I jump at the sensation before I look under the table to an awaiting Scout who is waiting not-so-patiently for me to drop some of my breakfast. I roll my eyes with a laugh and ruffle the fur on his head before returning to my breakfast.

"Doesn't she normally take the little gremlin with her?" I ask before shoveling a forkful of pancakes into my mouth.

"Don't beg, Scout," Dad scolds and the puppy lays down at my feet, rolling up into a little ball in an attempt to hide, yet still waiting for any dropped morsels. My father's attention reverts to me, "She was in a hurry and didn't want him finding his way into any of the vegetables."

My mother prides herself on her garden and loves taking her produce to our stall at the farmer's market. She'd been growing our own vegetables since before I was born. It's her other child after me, and now, I guess, the dog. My father joins me to dig into our breakfast and not much else is said, as it usually goes with my dad and I. He's not a man of many words, but the quality time spent with him always brings a smile to my cheeks.

After breakfast, I help Dad clear up the dishes and put the remaining elements of breakfast into Tupperware containers for Mom when she comes home. Not before nonchalantly dropping a few stray pieces of egg onto the floor for the little gremlin begging at my feet. I know it doesn't help his training to not beg for food, but how could I resist those mismatched blue and black puppy eyes?

I excuse myself from the kitchen to shower and change for the day. Rummaging through my dresser drawers, I pull out a pair of jean shorts and a white floral tank top to slip on after drying off with my towel. My hair, I decided, will have to go up into a ponytail to dry as I promised Mom yesterday I'd go into the garden to harvest her fresh bell peppers. I pull on my black and white Converse before calling for Scout to run around the garden as I work in the greenhouse.

Sweat runs down my forehead and I brush the droplets away with the back of my hand. I don't mind gardening, but after two hours of this, I have no idea how my mother does this for *fun*. The sound of gravel under tires has my head perking up as I see my mother's SUV come into view across the field.

"Bell, come help your mother, please!" My father calls from the back porch. I lift a thumbs up in his direction before pulling off my gloves and discarding them on the bench next to me in the greenhouse. An exhale escapes my lips as I exit the glass shed and slowly make my way across the expansive garden toward the driveway. My mother exits out of the car and a moment later the passenger door opens.

My feet halt their movement and my heart stops beating in my chest. As a figure stands from the car, the jet black hair that shines blue from the sun's rays far above catches my eyes first. When he turns, if the mask wasn't enough of a sight, those glacier-blue eyes meet mine from across the field stealing my breath. My feet are sprinting into motion and taking over into auto-pilot jumping over the plots of flowers and vegetables across the garden. My eyes turn glossy at the sight of him and the smile across my cheeks doesn't falter for even a moment. As I grow closer to my mother and the masked man who has stolen my heart from the moment I laid eyes on him, my feet skid to a halt across the gravel a foot in front of him.

"Cyr…" His name leaves my lips in a whisper of shock and disbelief. He's here. He's actually *here*.

"Raven," Cyr says as the corner of his mask shifts up on one side into a hidden smirk. He takes a stride toward me eating up the space between us in a flash as his strong arms coil around my waist, lifting me into his arms. My arms fly around his neck and my legs wrap around his waist as I'm lifted off the ground. Cyr tenses for almost an indiscernible second before he eases into our embrace. A sob breaks from my lips and I softly cry into his neck as he holds me to his chest, his hold on me tightening ever so slightly.

I pull back from him, tears staining my cheeks as I smile, shaking my head, "How are you here?" I ask, dumbfounded how Cyr managed to plan this without me knowing.

A hand comes up to brush one side of my cheek clear of the tear stains and those ice-blue eyes melt my heart even more than I imagined possible.

"You can thank your mom for that one. She was the master-mind behind it all."

My jaw drops as Cyr lowers me to stand on my feet and I stare wide-eyed at my mother who moves to stand beside my father. She only smiles, raising a shoulder into a small shrug. I roll my eyes with a laugh, turning my attention back to the man standing in front of me whose hand moves from my back to take hold of my hand. My eyes fall to where our hands connect and the sight of him being so vulnerable around my parents is more than admirable.

Cyr reaches into the car to grab a backpack and he slings it over his opposite shoulder before shutting the car door. We walk over toward the front door where my parents stand with my mother's head resting on my dad's shoulder. I hadn't told my parents that much about Cyr. Not that I didn't want to tell them everything about the beautiful man standing next to me, but having him meet my parents wasn't something I'd imagined so soon. I told them his dislike of physical touch so when I see Cyr's hand extend out to my father, my eyes nearly pop out of my head at the sight.

"Mr. Tyler, it's a pleasure," Cyr says with a nod in my father's direction.

"Jonathan, please, and the pleasure is mine," My father replies, slowly extending his hand to shake Cyr's in greeting. The sight warms my heart inexplicably and I smile, giving Cyr's hand a gentle squeeze which he mimics against mine.

"Shall we head in? I hope you've left some of those pancakes for our guest," My mother says in a sing-song tone with a wink in my direction. I nod in reply, trailing my parents into the house with Cyr and Scout in tow.

***

Cyr's hand wraps around my mouth, muffling my moans of pure ecstasy as he eases into me. The water pouring from the shower head behind Cyr aids in masking the sounds from him I wish to never stop hearing. As he slides fully into me, the warmth of his chest against my back sends a shiver through me. His lips find my shoulder, biting down on the soft flesh to ground himself through his moans.

The feeling of him inside me and encapsulating me is something I truly didn't know how much I needed. Not just the sex, which is absolute bliss with Cyr, but the way he holds me and comforts me makes the world seem empty without him. My life would never be the same without Cyr in it and that thought alone is absolutely terrifying and wonderful all at once.

"Fuck, Raven…" He lowly grounds out against my ear as he pulls out and thrusts up in one mighty push of pain and pleasure. The pain lights a fire in my stomach and the pleasure wishes it to never stop, "I missed you so fucking much."

Cyr's words have me nearly combusting in his hold as the meaning sinks into my heart. The man I once thought was completely and utterly emotionally unavailable *missed* me.

Oh, how I was so wrong about him.

His pace quickens and the vice grip Cyr has on my hip tells me he's done holding back. I push myself back up against him, silently telling him I don't want him to hold back anymore. In seconds, my chest is flat against the shower wall and the cool tile against my breasts turns my nipples painfully hard. My head tilts away from him, and his hand slips beneath one of my thighs to lift it up. Cyr plants his hand against the shower wall with my thigh resting above it and he doesn't waste any time slamming into me to the hilt. My eyes roll back, biting down hard enough on my bottom lip to break skin. His hand wraps around my hair, pulling hard enough to have my moan slip through my lips.

From this angle, all of him hit every single spot inside me that craved to be explored. My hands splay out against the wall of the shower, rocking against his thrust until my body feels like it's pure lava. I clamp my hand across my lips as I shatter in his grip, stars shining in my blurry vision as I ride through the high. I feel myself clamp down around him and he buries his head into my neck as his release soon chases after mine. Our labored breathing becomes one as we calm down from the rush filling our veins.

"For the record," I say softly, "I missed you, too."

A soft chuckle hits my ear followed by a set of shiver-inducing kisses along my shoulder blade.

"Good, because I wasn't planning on keeping my hands off of you for much longer than I had to."

His admission has me ever so gently pushing back against his still-hard cock. Cyr's grip returns to my hip to stop my motion, "If we're in here any longer, they'll get suspicious."

I know he's right, but damn it all to hell, and damn him for being right when all I want is for him to do everything wrong to me.

"Then don't waste time," I whisper, tempting him as hard as I can since I don't want even a precious minute spent not in his embrace.

"Patience, Raven. We'll have plenty of time for that," He growls low into my ear and the sound nearly has me crumbling in his hold.

After both of us calm the beasts within us to yield, I quickly wash off and leave Cyr to finish his shower. I fish out two towels from underneath the sink and leave one for Cyr on the edge of the counter, wrapping the other around myself before exiting the bathroom. I walk across the hall into my bedroom, shutting the door, and rummaging through my dresser to find a new set of clothes.

A few minutes later, I hear the bedroom door open and I know it's Cyr because either of my parents would have knocked first.

"Do you need me to get your backpack or-"

I choke on my words as Cyr stands in the doorway to my bedroom…completely naked. I clutch the towel around my chest with one hand as I shoo him further into my room, slamming the door shut behind me, "Fucking hell, Cyr!" I whisper shout, "Are you insane!?"

Cyr's mask shifts up, "Insane for you."

I roll my eyes at him even with my insides turning molten all over again at his words, "I left you a towel in the bathroom, didn't you see it?"

"I did."

"Why didn't you use it, then?! My-"

Cyr laughs aloud, cutting off my words and my heart melts a bit more at the sound as his sculpted chest rumbles with the motion.

"Your parents aren't home, Raven."

My jaw drops at him, "What do you mean? How do you-"

"Your mom asked if I needed anything from the store before we went into the bathroom. I think she picked up on the message," He replies and I know there's a smirk on his lips I wish I could slap off his face.

"Then why did you keep me quiet?" I ask, shifting my weight to prop my hands on my hips as I attempt to keep my eyes on his face and not below his imaginary belt.

"As much as I love to hear you sing for me, Raven, I just wanted it all to myself," Cyr says, his voice dripping in lust and the sound has my thighs clamping together. His eyes flick down as he catches the action and the heat in his eyes turns my body into Jell-O as his gaze returns to mine.

"Well, if they're not home…" I start and Cyr prowls toward me, his hands coming up to cup both sides of my cheeks. My eyes slowly drift shut at the feeling of his warm skin against mine.

"There will be plenty of time for that. Right now, I want you to show me all the reasons why you call this place home."

I intend to show him all of my favorite places, but the words I wish to say to him, I can't voice aloud. How my heart will always be at home as long as he's with me.

***

As Dad predicted this morning, a storm rolls through like clockwork, ruining my plans of taking Cyr on a series of adventures for the day. Instead, we're secluded in the house as the rain pours, eliciting joy from my mother as the rain assists her in not having to water the vegetables and flowers herself.

Much to my annoyance, my mother pulls out all of the childhood photo albums she can find to show Cyr my life in pictures from even before a time I can recall.

"Oh, Gods, momma. Not that album, please."

I groan audibly as she hands the album over to Cyr. That particular album contains images of every single Halloween outfit from birth until I left for college.

"Oh hush, you look so adorable!" Mother exclaims, more giddy to look over the pictures she's seen a hundred times before and I catch a glance from Cyr. His mask shifts up on one side and I flip him off, earning myself a glare from my mother.

Time passes in slow motion while my mother shows Cyr album after album. I feel my brain turn to mush and my entire body turns beet red from the most embarrassing pictures my mother can find. I swear this woman is doing it on purpose to see how far she can go before I burn the albums myself. Dad spends his time making dinner in the kitchen, leaving me to sit on the floor of the living room attempting to distract myself with Scout while my mother continues.

Cyr closes another album, passing it back to my mother and as she reaches to pick up another, I silently thank my dark angel for the next words that escape from his lips.

"I think I left my wallet in your car, Mrs. Tyler, I'll be right back." He says, standing up from the couch and taking a step toward where I'm sitting in the middle of the floor, "Care to join me?"

His hand extends down to me and I slowly reach up to take hold of his hand, using his strength to assist in pulling me up from the floor. I stand fully and glance at my mother who is sorting through albums she's yet to show Cyr.

"Is the car unlocked, momma?"

"I'm not sure, but the keys are on the hook, sweetheart."

With Cyr's hand still in mine, I guide him out of the living room toward the front door and out onto the porch. He closes the front door behind us and as soon as we're alone on the porch, his hand still in mine spins me back toward him, colliding with his chest. My eyes widen at the action as my free hand catches myself from falling, planting itself on his chest. Cyr's arm instantly wraps around my waist, tightening his grip to hold me close to him.

"Let me guess, you didn't leave your wallet in the car."

"As much as I'm already in love with your family, Raven, I just needed you to myself for a few minutes."

My heart melts in my chest, the sound of the rain tapping against the tin porch roof sending me into the purest state of serenity. Cyr's masked lips plant a kiss on my forehead and my eyes drift closed.

"I still can't believe you're here," I whisper, shaking my head as I'm still in a state of mild disbelief.

"Was our time in the shower not belief-worthy?"

I laugh, pulling my head back to look up at the beautiful man in front of me. My eyes meet his and I take an extra few seconds to remember this moment with him. A moment I never thought would happen, but a moment I would cherish for the rest of my life. My lips part to speak when faint music sounds from inside the house.

"What's that?" Cyr asks, glancing over a shoulder back toward the direction of the living room. After a moment to recognize the song, I exhale with a smile.

"Mom and Dad are dancing," I reply softly, "This song was

their first dance at their wedding. Every once in a while they'll put on this song and just…dance."

Cyr's hand slowly leaves my waist to the hand placed on his chest, sliding it up to the top of his shoulder. My eyes track the motion and his hand moves back to my waist, pulling my body flush with his. I follow the motion of his body as he begins to sway, instantly the two of us falling into step in slow circles. My head slowly tips forward to lay flat against his chest with his heartbeat steadily beating beneath my ear. Cyr gently rests his head atop mine and my gaze falls on our intertwined hands, giving his hand a soft squeeze. He returns the motion before pulling back and guiding my body to take a step back from him.

Confusion stuns me momentarily until his hand still holding mine begins to spin me with our hands connected up above my head. My head tips back in laughter for a moment, a blush staining my cheeks as I spin slowly in front of him. Once I finish my spin, his hold on me pulls me back toward his chest. Cyr captures me in his embrace with a tight hold around my waist and my free hand returns back to his shoulder, a smile ear to ear spreading across my cheeks.

As our eyes lock on each other, those icy-blue orbs entrancing me wholly, falling harder than I ever have before. Harder than I ever believed possible.

"Ever the romantic, Cyr Maddox."

"Only for you, Raven."

I knew the truth in those words and he meant every one of them. My head returns to his chest as we continue swaying once again, listening as the song guides us through our very own first dance.

But this wasn't our first dance.

We'd done this same dance back in the club in Boston after

Cyr broke Tobias's nose. But this was different. There's nothing in between us now as there had been back then. A moment in time that felt like centuries ago. Whereas now, a moment that's truly brought the two of us together even closer than before all on our own terms. The universe has not impacted this moment to happen, but rather two people who know where they're meant to be, and mine is right here wrapped in Cyr's arms for as long as he'll hold me.

So this would be our first dance. A dance for Cyr to claim me as his, and I him, and I never thought I would ever want to belong to someone again until he came along.

Maybe some things truly are written in the stars.

***

"Why can't you just stay here? Momma said you're welcome to stay at the house as long as you like!" I plead as we walk hand in hand through the main entrance of the airport. Cyr chuckles softly, shaking his head.

"If I stay any longer I'm pretty sure my dick is going to fall off," He mutters under his breath and my face flushes crimson. I give his hand a playful squeeze and he returns the motion, "I promised my sister I'd stay with her for a few weeks and help her move into the new house."

I sigh heavily and dramatically, even though it's only to mask the sadness of losing him so soon. The past two weeks had flown past in a blur feeling like he's only just gotten here yesterday.

"Text me when you land, please."

Cyr pauses at the entrance to TSA, turning to face me and his arms wrap around my shoulders. My arms slowly wrap around his back and pull him close to me. He exhales through the touch until I settle myself in front of his chest.

"I'll see you soon, Raven," Cyr says softly into my hair and I take one last deep inhale of his cologne before he pulls away. He adjusts his backpack over a shoulder before turning to head into the security checkpoint lane.

I knew at that moment that watching Cyr walk away would forever be the hardest thing to watch and a part of me hopes to never see it again.

23

The Truth

The next two months dragged by until I was finally back in Cyr's arms and below that body sculpted by the Gods. The incessant need to have Cyr by my side was almost painful throughout the rest of the Summer. After I'd come home from staying with my parents, the entire world fell back into place all over again. Classes resumed with Clara and I up studying till the early hours of the morning the same day as an exam. And on the nights when studying was pushed to the back burner, I spent the night with Cyr tangled up in his sheets and blissfully at peace with my life. Nothing could ever be wrong when it came to the two of us.

As the weeks turned into months, the November holidays were fast approaching which meant more finals and more studying giving me less time to bask in luxury with Cyr. However, after cramming for days on end, I was able to prepare enough to allow myself a few extra days of freedom to spend with him.

A squeal leaves my lips as I emerge from Cyr's bathroom into his bedroom. He's currently sitting at his desk mid-sketch for an upcoming client. As I walk over to him, he's staring at me with an eyebrow cocked up to his hairline in perpetual confusion to my squealing. I bite the edge of my lip to contain my laugh, but a smile still breaks out from the sight of his expression.

"One of my childhood best friends got married yesterday!" I let out a giddy cheer as I turn my phone so Cyr can see the wedding picture splayed across my screen, "Doesn't she look beautiful?!"

"Not as beautiful as you."

I roll my eyes even though I feel the blush creeping up my cheeks.

"Flattery will get you nowhere, but everywhere all at once," I say, flashing him a wink before retreating to his bed. My body plops back flat against the top of the mattress and a moment later I feel the bed shift as Cyr climbs above me. Those piercing blue eyes meet mine, my eyes widening in surprise as the phone is knocked from my hand and my wrists are pinned on the bed above me.

"You have a client soon! This can wait," I say breathlessly, only inches separating his masked lips from mine.

"I've been waiting to take you all fucking day, Raven. *It* can wait," He replies, sliding his free hand up my tank top. The feeling of his skin against mine sends me shivering from the contact, but at this moment, my mind is plagued with thoughts I can't hold back anymore. A word I'd never thought I would have to say falls softly from my lips in a whisper.

"Pomegranate."

Instantly, Cyr's hand releases me and his hands come underneath my back to pull me up to his chest. His arms gently wrap around me, holding me against him. The warmth emanating from his body could boil me alive, but I'd willingly burn in his embrace.

"Talk to me, Raven."

Cyr's voice sounds pained and it breaks my heart to make him feel as if he's pushed me into something I didn't want. That was never the case. I'd stay wrapped up in his arms for the rest of eternity if I could. I slowly pull my head back to look up at him. Those beautiful blue eyes are almost glossy and all I want is to touch his cheek and comfort him, but I can't. I keep my hands tucked in front of me to not touch him.

"I know the thoughts swirling around in your head, Cyr. You did nothing wrong, so kick those thoughts out."

"You've never…" He trails off and I take a deep breath to keep my brewing tears at bay.

"Exactly. I've never said it which means there has never been a time when you've done something to hurt me, Cyr. At this moment, it just means I do not want it right now, and that's okay," I say softly, giving him a small reassuring smile. Once I see his chest begin to rise and fall evenly once again, I continue. "I just wanted to talk to you about something that's been on my mind for a while is all."

Cyr's eyes lock on mine, wordless as he barely nods for me to continue. The look on his face has me moments from crumbling in front of him. His hand slowly slips from my back to gently cradle my cheek in his palm.

"What is it?" Cyr asks, barely louder than a whisper.

"Have you ever thought about the future?"

Cyr's eyebrow lifts in confusion. A sigh escapes my lips as I compose myself.

"You know…marriage, family, children? Have you ever thought about it?" I question, clarifying my thoughts for Cyr.

His hand drops from my cheek and the loss of his touch feels like ice in my veins. Slowly, he backs up from the bed, shaking his head.

"That's not for me."

My eyes widen as he retreats to his desk, taking a seat in his chair, and picking up his pencil to continue his sketch.

I scoff lightly, "What do you mean *'that's not for me'*? Care to give me a little bit more of an explanation?"

"That's not the kind of life I'm made for."

I release a low groan from my throat.

"Gods, it's like pulling teeth with you sometimes. Care to be a little less fucking cryptic?!" I snap, slamming my hands down on my thighs in frustration.

Instinctually, when I hear his hand slam down on his desk, my body shifts into fight or flight, bolting to stand on the far side of Cyr's bed. I've never been afraid of Cyr before, but he's not the only one whose past haunts them.

Cyr's head snaps to face me and I hug my arms around myself as he stands, his head falling to hang between his shoulders. After a few deep inhales, Cyr stands up fully, turning to face me once again, regret written all over his eyes.

"Look at me, Bellamy." Cyr's voice is like gravel as he speaks.

"I am-"

"Look. At. Me." He growls, eyes flaring with a mixture of anger and pain, "Do you really think I could be a good *father*? Or even a good *husband*? Fucking look at me!" Cyr snaps, his calm demeanor finally broke and I'm the one who pushed him to this point.

The pencil he still holds in his hand cracks in half with a quick *snap* as it breaks apart into pieces in his clenched fist. He releases his grip on the broken lead, letting it fall to the floor. All of the words I want to say dry up in my throat as tears threaten to fall from my eyes. Cyr shakes his head at my silence and I know the lack of words isn't what he wants to hear, but I can't find the right words to voice to him how much I desire a future with him.

Only with him.

"You are the one thing I cannot lose or I'll be nothing. But to keep you, I have to deserve you. And I don't fucking deserve you, Bellamy."

As Cyr says my name, his voice cracks, and so does my heart.

"Nothing I say will change your mind, Cyr. I know that, but you're worth everything to me. Every doubt you have, every demon in your head saying you're not good enough. You may not believe it, but you better fucking believe that I do."

I take a few steps toward him around his bed, but I halt when he stumbles back a step. The sight shocks me to my core.

"I don't want to hurt you…" He whispers and I push past the mental barrier, taking another few slow steps toward him. Cyr doesn't retreat but doesn't move closer to me. He allows me to close the distance.

"You won't," I reply with confidence of steel. Cyr's eyes never once leave mine and I know for absolute certainty that he would rather sacrifice himself to the Devil before he ever laid a hand on me in that way. My body stops a step in front of Cyr, maintaining his gaze to make sure he sees me. All of me. "Tell me all of your problems and make them mine, Cyr. You don't have to suffer through them alone. Let me solve them with you."

Cyr releases a shaky exhale.

"Why did you ask?"

"If I said I hadn't thought about a future with you, I'd be lying," I reply, a small hint of a smile tipping up one corner of my lips.

I'd thought about it on several occasions what life would look like having Cyr by my side, and it was the most beautiful thing I'd ever imagined.

"I'm a wreck, Bellamy."

"Have you seen *me* lately?" I ask, receiving an ounce of a chuckle from him which was better than nothing. Anything to pull Cyr out of his head I'd do without a second thought.

"I only want what's best for you, and I'm terrified it won't be me," He says and the words have my eyes widening. The vulnerability in his voice has me holding up my hand for him to take if he wished to. After a moment of hesitation, Cyr's hand engulfs mine.

"I don't want my forever to not have you in it, Cyr. No matter what." I give his hand a gentle squeeze and he returns the action. "I'm going back to my room," I begin and Cyr's eyes widen.

"Don't," He breathes, shaking his head.

"You need to cool off and finish your sketch before you leave for the shop. If you want me to come back tonight after your appointment, I will," I continue and Cyr exhales, nodding. He gives a gentle tug to my hand, slowly pulling me into his chest. A deep exhale leaves both of our chests once we're in each other's embrace.

"I'm sorry that I snapped," He whispers into my hair.

I sigh, shaking my head softly against his chest, "I'm sorry that I pushed it."

"I'll be home around ten," Cyr says as we pull away and I press a finger to my lips before slowly lifting my finger to place against his masked lips.

"I'll see you at ten."

***

I take the steps two at a time to reach the second floor of the dormitory, jogging down the hall towards Cyr's room. Time had flown by and slipped away from me as I was quizzing Clara for her upcoming exam. By the time we'd wrapped up for the night, I checked my phone seeing 10:30 pop up on my screen, and raced from our room. Of course, I hated being away from Cyr longer than necessary, but I also didn't want him to think I bailed on him because I was upset with him. His outburst, and mine, was my fault and I knew the guilt would eat him alive for no reason other than his incessant need to blame himself for my wrong-doings.

My hand reaches into the elastic pocket of my black biker shorts, pulling out the key card to Cyr's room, and waiting for the soft *click* before pushing the door open. I softly pad across the floor of the common area, turning the handle to his bedroom door and knocking a few times. I don't hear any reply and worry he may have decided to stay at the shop tonight, but then I distantly hear water running. An exhale escapes my lips as I push the door open the rest of the way, closing it behind me once I enter the room.

"Hi," I call out, not loud enough to startle him, but enough for him to know I'm here.

"Hey, I'll be out in a minute," I hear in response from behind the bathroom door.

As I turn to walk to his bed, my eyes catch on a sketch sitting on top of his desk and I walk over, picking up his sketchbook. My eyes widen, jaw-dropping as I scan over the charcoal sketch of…me. The moment immortalized on the page is from over the summer when Cyr came to see me at my parent's house. We'd hiked to the mountain so I could show him where I did most of my painting. I had known he was drawing while I painted, but I never knew he was drawing *me* as I worked on capturing the sunset.

My free hand comes up to my lips, concealing my shock at the accuracy of the moment as my heart damn near explodes from my chest. It's short-lived as I hear the water from the shower cut off. I set down the book just as I found it and quickly, but quietly, tiptoe over to his bed, crawling atop it to hide the fact I'm snooping. It isn't technically snooping since it's sitting open on top of his desk, but that would be an internal debate for another day.

The bathroom door opens a few minutes later as Cyr emerges in a black sleeveless top revealing the entrancing black ink coating his arms and those God's damned gray sweatpants. He knows what those sweatpants do to me.

Bastard.

"I thought you decided against coming over," He says and my heart squeezes tightly in my chest.

"I'm sorry, I got carried away helping Clara study," I twist my fingers around each other anxiously in my lap, gnawing on the corner of my lip.

Cyr chuckles with a nod, rubbing his towel against his wet hair to rid the water from it. He walks past me a few steps before halting in his tracks. The room turns deathly quiet and the silence is deafening. Cyr's body slowly turns back to me, staring directly at my chest and I raise an eyebrow at him, presuming he has no shame in staring at where my breasts should be if they were currently exposed. But there's something else that has my nerves spiking as his body tenses and turns as rigid as a statue.

"Cyr, what is it?" I ask, a slight wobble in my voice.

"Where did you get that?" The voice that fills the air is cold and nothing like I'd ever heard from him before. My eyes drop down to look over the *Breaking Benjamin* hoodie for a moment before looking back up to meet Cyr's gaze.

"Someone very close to me let me have it," I reply, attempting to keep my voice neutral as he stares me down.

"Take it off."

My eyes widen, standing up from his bed, "What?"

Cyr closes the distance between us, standing a breath's distance in front of me.

"Take. It. Off."

"Why?" I snap.

"Because it's mine."

As if my eyes couldn't get any wider, they nearly pop out of my head as his words reverberate against my skull. I shake my head, taking a step back to create distance between us again. With him that close it's impossible to breathe.

"Check the tag if you don't believe me."

My hands shake as I slowly pull the hoodie up and over my head, reaching into the hole at the top to pull on the tag.

MADDOX.

His last name stood out in bold letters on the small label that's stapled onto the sizing tab of the hoodie. My mind reels as my gaze snaps back to Cyr.

"This can't be yours. My…" My words trail off as I take a moment to steady my racing heart, "She gave this to me."

"I know exactly who gave it to you and she stole it from me." Cyr's tone is low and the sound makes me shiver, "I thought the bitch took it with her when she left."

My vision goes red, clenching my fists at my sides.

"*Excuse me?*" I growl, the voice of the Devil himself taking over my tone, "What the fuck do you mean '*she left*'?" I ground out the words for emphasis as I grip the hoodie in a balled fist.

"Before she left for England I assumed she took it with her," Cyr says with a scoff. "How the fuck you ended up with it is beyond me. Hopefully, you didn't know her that well for your own sake."

My heart drops into the pit of my stomach at his words. My hands tremble as I bring the hoodie up to clutch against my chest. Tears spring from my eyes and trail down my cheeks, falling atop the hoodie.

"She's dead."

It's Cyr's turn for his eyes to bulge from his head, "What?"

The tears continue to flow as my eyes slowly shift from the hoodie back up to Cyr. My face is a mask of cold hatred, "She's. Fucking. Dead."

Cyr scoffs, shaking his head, "She told me she was going back home."

"I found her fucking body!"

Rage and malice consume me as I snap, throwing the hoodie at Cyr's chest. He flinches back a step as he catches the hoodie in front of him and not an ounce of me regrets the action, "I don't know what you have against her, but I assure you she's dead if that'll help you sleep better at night."

"Want to know what I have against *Jamie*?" He growls and I point my finger at him.

"You don't have the right to say her fucking name!" I snap through trembling lips.

Cyr laughs loudly and humorlessly, taking a step toward me. The sound ripping apart every piece of my heart. He turns toward his desk, throwing the hoodie straight into the trashcan.

"NO!" I scream, lunging for the trashcan when Cyr's arms catch me around the waist, pulling me back to stand in front of him. Without thinking, I slam my fists down against his arms and his hold instantly releases from me. I whirl on him, teeth bared and tears streaming down my cheeks. Cyr retreats a few steps, his own hands shaking, and the icy realization of what I'd just done slams into me. I take a step toward him, but he's quick to move away out of reach and my eyes slam shut to block out the pain coursing through me.

"She's the reason why I can't kiss you no matter how much I desperately wish to."

Cyr's words have my eyes flying open to face him, but his eyes are closed, internally channeling to himself to calm his body from shaking. After an eternity of staring at the man I love, begging him to look at me, his eyes meet mine.

"The reason why I can't handle being touched. The reason why I almost couldn't stand having sex with you no matter how badly I fucking wanted it. It's all because of her that I live in this shell of a body."

Cyr didn't raise his voice even though I wish he would scream at me. To be angry with me for what I just did to him. The words he speaks into the air float around me like a death sentence I can never escape. I shake my head, refusing to believe that the woman I loved so fiercely could inflict such harm.

"Liar," I growl.

Cyr's eyes fill with pain, narrowing ever so slightly at me, "I have been called many true things in my life, but a *liar* is not one of them, Bellamy. Of all people, I thought you'd be the one to see that."

My body caves in on itself under the weight of his words, settling onto my rib cage and crushing everything within it. I shake my head, refusing to listen to any more of what he has to say. He's never once lied to me about anything and I can't imagine he would lie about something like this. But I can't bear it. The weight of his words or the feeling of his tortured gaze boring into my soul.

Without another word, I bolt out of the room, slamming the door behind me. Once I reach the hallway, I bend over at the waist with my hands on my knees as I attempt to take in oxygen as if it were my first breath after nearly drowning. A tormented scream rips through the air from inside the dorm and I take off running down the hall, covering my ears with my hands. The sobs wrack my body as I run for as long as my legs carry me, running from the one person I never imagined would be my downfall.

24

The Phone Call

The unbearable silence over the past two weeks has been more than I can stand. Days turned to hours, and the hours turned to minutes. Time dragged to a halt knowing I wouldn't be sleeping in Cyr's bed, cradled against that chest that rose and fell in sync with mine.

Within the following days after the fight, I'd retrieved my things from his dorm and brought them back to mine and Clara's dorm while Cyr was at the shop. It was one of the hardest things I'd ever done. It was all too much and all I've wanted since that night was for him to hold me and tell me it would all be okay.

But it wasn't okay, and it wouldn't be until I talked to him.

Living a life without him grew unbearable and with each passing day, another piece of my heart cracked. A crater began to grow in my chest and I felt another shard of myself breaking away, leaving me in scraps of the shell I've become.

Clara attempted her best to take me out and cheer me up after the fight, but nothing would soothe the unyielding ache in my chest. I only wanted him. A part of me realized the only thing

I've ever truly wanted was him. Cyr lit that dull ember in my heart and sent it ablaze. So full of life and light, but it would also be him that would extinguish that very ember in a matter of seconds.

"Are you sure you don't want some company?" Clara asks from where she sits crisscrossing on my bed. I know a bit of social interaction will do me some good, so I decided to go out to my favorite hole-in-the-wall bar downtown to lose myself for a while.

"I'll be fine, Cee. Not like I plan on going home with anyone," I reply from where I stand in the bathroom, tying my hair up into a ponytail with a scrunchie.

It's the truth. I wasn't going out tonight to find someone to claim they'll show me a good time. The idea of climbing into anyone else's bed except for Cyr's nearly makes my meager lunch come up my throat and bile coats my tongue.

"I know you'll be fine," Clara says softly, coming up behind me to rest her head on my shoulder, meeting my gaze in the bathroom mirror in front of us. "I'm your best friend, it's my job to worry about you."

A light smile slides up my lips at her statement and I nod, "This is why I can't live without you, but tonight, I need to get out of my head for a while. How about tomorrow night you and I can go out, alright?"

Clara's eyes beam at the hopefulness in my voice, and it makes a small ounce of hurt in my chest lessen at the sight. She wraps her arms around my middle and squeezes my torso.

"It's a date!" Clara squeals and I can't help the laugh that escapes my lips. I drop my arms to cover hers across my stomach and squeeze her arms. "Be careful, okay? Call me if you need anything," She says, giving me a quick peck on the cheek before releasing me to retreat into our bedroom.

***

The Uber ride to my favorite bar in the city took nearly forty-five minutes due to the late Friday night traffic. As I step out of the car, crowds of people flood the cramped side streets making it impossible to walk down the sidewalk without colliding into someone. The walk down to the front door of the bar is treacherous from the amount of people consuming the space and the sheer amount of broken sidewalk that has me watching my foot placements instead of the people around me.

The bar isn't large, but big enough to house a fair amount of people, including a small stage at the front which is currently occupied by a band for live music. I make quick work of taking a seat at the bar just as a couple stands to leave. The sight of the pair taking hold of each other's hand and leaving the bar makes that weight in my chest feel like a freight train parked on it. My body spins on the bar stool, ordering a gin and tonic when the bartender comes over. A few minutes later he returns, placing the drink on the bar top in front of me and I nod my thanks to him.

The night continues and I people-watch as customers enter the bar, enjoy the live music blaring around the space, and then stumble out toward the street not too long after. One of my favorite pastimes is to observe people, attempting to not be creepy when doing it, but seeing what stories I can create. Why they were at the bar that night, who they may be meeting, or what their reason may be for ordering a certain drink. Time floats away from me and it's exactly what I needed.

"Hey there," A deep voice calls out from next to me. My head swivels to the side to meet a set of light brown eyes on mine. I smile politely and nod in acknowledgment before returning my gaze to the band at the front of the bar, "Can I buy you a drink?"

This was the third man to take a seat next to me, offering the same thing and I suppressed the urge to sigh. All I want is for men to leave me the fuck alone at this point. Except for the bartender. He's my new best friend for as long as the drinks keep coming.

"I'm fine, thank you though," I decline with another soft smile as I nonchalantly look over the man beside me. He's handsome, for sure, but it's that pretty boy kind of handsome that signals he's used to getting what he wants when he asks for it. Not like Cyr. That kind of devastatingly handsome that has me crawling on my hands and knees for him.

"My treat!"

He flashes me a pearly white smile that nearly makes me cringe from how perfect those teeth are. I open my mouth to decline once again when he calls the bartender over to order a drink for me. My mouth closes and I set my empty glass on the bar top behind me, turning my head back to face him. Even though I have zero intention of sleeping with this man, I can't say no to a free drink. I'll just let him down gently after I finish the drink. This will definitely be my last drink before heading back to the dorms. My body is riding out a perfect buzz where I can still keep myself in check, but I know my limits. Another drink after this will put me in an unsafe head space while drinking by myself and I'm not about to find myself passed out on the curb after a few too many.

"Thank you," I lean in ever so slightly to not have to yell over the music to him. That blinding smile appears again as he extends out a hand.

"Parker Kensington."

Gods above. With a name like that it just screams, *'fuck me, I have money'*. I give him a small smile, shaking his hand before returning my attention to the music once again. A few minutes later, Parker extends the glass to me and I look down at it, attempting to not wince at the sight.

I fucking hate rum.

He must have mistaken my previous glass of gin and tonic for a Mojito, but I pull a forced smile up my lips. I raise it to him in thanks as I take a sip and force the mouthful down. The burn is welcomed as it distracts me from the rest of the terrible taste coating my tongue.

"What brings you out tonight?" He asks as I take another sip of the vile concoction in my hands. My usual go-to reaction to a stranger coming up to me is to play deaf and that, more times than not, gets them to leave me alone. Due to the way I've fallen into the music that consumes the bar, I know my trick won't do me any good this time. I've found myself stuck in a conversation that would require me to leave the bar entirely to escape.

"Just wanted some alone time, you know?" I reply, hoping to the Gods he'd get the picture and fuck off from whence he came. He laughs, leaning in close to my space, causing me to slightly lean away from him.

"Friday nights are for fun! What are you doing by yourself?"

Fuck. Not the right thing to have said.

"My girlfriend's on her way over. I just got a head start." I attempt to dissuade him, looking back to the band in front of us as I finish off the liquid in my cup.

"Girlfriend? Lucky girl to have you. Does she share?"

The comment has the rum nearly spewing from my lips. I turn back to the bar to set the glass down, nodding to the bartender

I'm done for the night. The motion from turning sends my head whirring and I see two of the bartender for a moment before it clears.

Time to go, Bellamy. The bartender must have gone heavy on the rum that time.

"Thank you for the drink, but it's time for me to go," I say, not bothering to look at him even though I'm hyper-aware that he's too incredibly close to me right now.

"Aw, come on baby girl, the party's just started!"

The feeling of his arm around my waist, pulling me into him has my body turning rigid. My hands shake as I feel his nose brush against my neck, inhaling deeply. I push off from the bar top, stumbling out of the stool, and onto shaky legs. My hands grasp the bar top as the room spins and I blink furiously to will my head into seeing clearly.

"I uh-" I attempt to swallow, my tongue feeling like sandpaper as it dries up in my mouth, "I need to use the restroom…I'll be…right back."

My body stumbles toward the direction of the bathroom, bursting through the door and slamming myself shut in a stall. The white walls of the bathroom are excruciatingly bright against my vision even with the dim lights surrounding me barely working as is. My hand fumbles pulling my phone from my pocket, the screen of my phone turning into multiples as I strain my eyes to find Clara's number in my emergency contacts. I bring the phone to my ear, unsure if it was her I even dialed due to my vision blackening on the edges. The phone connects after two rings.

"Hey babe, what's up?" Clara's singsong voice questions from the other end of the line. The sigh of relief that escapes my chest almost sounds like a sob, "Bellamy? What's wrong?"

My mouth opens and closes a few times as I try to take a few deep breaths. My eyes drift shut and I feel like falling, my shoulder falling into the stall door to hold myself upright as the need to sleep floods my body.

"BELLAMY?!"

"Location. Come get me. Please."

We always have our location shared with each other so I pray she's be able to decipher my words. I'm not sure if the words are even coherent even though they sound clear in my head. The nausea and need for sleep clouding my mind begins to take over.

I didn't drink any more than usual. I'm nowhere near my limit. It must have been- Oh Gods.

Rule number one for women in our society: Never accept a drink from anyone except your bartender. I was too caught up in the band to realize Parker handed me the drink from the bar top. Tears silently spill down my cheeks as my body begins to shake from head to toe. I barely keep a hold of my phone as the stall begins to shrink, suffocating me and stealing my ability to breathe.

Clara's voice rings through the phone but her words don't reach my head. The words sound a million miles away from where the phone is at my ear. Thunderous footsteps echo through the phone and Clara screams to someone which has my head pounding in pain. Muffled voices ring out from the other side of the line along with a jingle of keys, but I can't make out who it is.

Maybe Gwen came over...great. I ruined Clara's night due to my own stupidity.

"We're coming, Bell! Stay there!" Is the only thing I can clearly make out as I inhale deeply, attempting to stay conscious through the lack of oxygen in the bathroom stall.

We? I guess Gwen is there after all.

My body is fighting against the pounding in my head, forcing me out of the stall. I need air. The phone slips from my hand as I use my free hand to keep standing upright. I slowly slide down the bathroom wall for support to reach for my phone. There are five other phones on the floor below me and I wonder how many people had dropped their phones and not noticed?

But there aren't five…there's just one.

Mine. But I can't find it.

My fingernails dig into the tiled floor, attempting to close my fingers around the imaginary phone to find the real one. The pain ebbs in my fingers as my fingernails break with the search for my phone, using a process of elimination to find the real phone.

A sound like gunfire echoes in my head, rattling every single one of my senses, but my head only lulls to the side in ignorance. Finally, after gripping the case of my phone in a tiny victory I'm then able to slide it into the pocket of my jacket.

I feel the sensation of being pulled, but I can't process the fear shocking my system as my body falls to the ground. My head hits the side of the porcelain toilet, rattling my teeth in my skull. The pounding intensifies and my mind claws at the inside of my skull to react, to fight, to fucking do something. My eyes look up to the ceiling of the bathroom as my body slides along the cold tile floor through the gap below the locked stall door.

My vision blurs and blacks out for a moment as I'm yanked up to stand, colliding against a body as I'm held upright. The weight of my body feeling like a thousand pounds has me struggling to keep my knees from buckling. The music of the bar slams into my head at a deafening pitch for a few moments as I'm half-dragged from the bathroom and out toward the street beyond the bar.

Fight, Bellamy! Fight back!

The war being waged in my head can't communicate the signal to my weighted limbs trailing uselessly at my sides. The dark sky above calls to me, beckoning me to sleep, but the slam of my body against the wall behind me has me inhaling sharply. The fleeting moment of realization flashes across my mind, but it's not enough for me to fight against the intruding hands scaling every inch of my body. Crimson liquid falls into my eye, blurring my vision in red, and I attempt to blink it away as my hands can't lift more than an inch from my sides to wipe it away.

"I must have added a bit too much to your drink, baby girl. I wanted you conscious enough to choke on my cock, but this will do," Parker whispers into my ear and a shiver sends my whole body shaking beneath his touch, "Shh, don't cry."

Am I crying? I can't tell if it's the tears or the drugs hazing my vision. Probably both.

Skin brushes along my lower stomach and the soft *clink* of my belt coming undone has my hands trembling. Lips graze my neck, sucking and biting along my skin. The feeling is paralyzing. I feel as if I'm standing beside him watching this happen through eyes that aren't my own. My mouth opens to scream, to call for help, for anyone to see what's happening, but the rest of the world thinks this is just another crazy night out for two people.

But that isn't the case.

This isn't a fun night out for two drunken people in love and unable to contain their passion. This is my own personal nightmare. One I can't escape no matter how hard I try. My eyes close from the fear and pain and acceptance, shrinking back as far as my mind will allow itself.

In a flash of my vision, my body is thrown to the side, falling atop a trashcan face first. My body lays bent over with my glassy eyes facing the ground in front of me. The sudden jerk of my body has my vision spinning and my brain almost shutting down entirely. Hands grip my hips, wrapping around the waistband of my jeans, and I allow my brain to shut down.

Sleep now. I don't want to know what happens. I can't keep going.

"Bet you wished you'd accepted that drink willingly, after all, baby."

Parker's voice is nowhere near me, even though I know he's right behind me. That much I did know. My body is all too aware of every touch he places on my body without my consent, but I can't do a damn thing to stop it from happening. As his hands begin to pull down my jeans, they stop.

The sound of bone cracking has my eyes flying open against the wish of my vision. It's blurry and makes everything I'd drank today nearly come up entirely, but I force my head to look to the side. The sight of Parker on the ground beside me clutching his head confuses me. I can't lift my body to look, but out of the corner of my vision, a neon green motorcycle helmet speckled with blood stops my heart.

"If you touch her again, I'll drag you to the Gates of Hell myself."

That growl of warning fills every inch of my senses, along with the cries of pain echoing down the alley from the broken man on the ground. My body shudders as I feel a pair of hands return my jeans to normal at my hips, and I shiver against the touch.

"Breathe. You're safe."

Cyr's low voice creates goosebumps covering every inch of my skin and soothes the pounding in my head. My body protests against the movements being made without my ability to process them. I feel weightless for the first time in what seems like a century as I'm lifted into a pair of strong arms. My head lulls to the side against his firm chest, but I can't will myself to look up at him, even though my mind screams for me to look at him. To take in the sight of the man whom I would willingly sell my soul to the devil for if it were asked of me.

My beautiful, dark angel.

"Are you with me, Raven?"

I'm with you.

The words I so desperately wish I could say echo in my mind. My lips part to speak, but the words never come out as the darkness finally pulls me under.

***

The past three days have been a blur of visions and nightmares. I woke up the following day in the hospital with Clara asleep in the chair next to me, but there was no sight of my savior. I wouldn't have expected him to wait around, but the fact he was even there last night had tears flooding my eyes. Clara told me what happened and filled me in on what occurred while I'd been under the influence of Parker's drugs. The nurses ran several blood tests to find my body filled with a combination of Rohypnol and GHB. My body still felt the high of the drugs for another day before it finally flushed out of my system. The invasion to my senses would haunt me for the Gods only knew how fucking long.

Once I'd been cleared to be released from the hospital, Clara took me home to campus in…Cyr's Camaro? She explained that Gwen had gone out and borrowed her car when I called for help. When Clara found my location as I'd managed to say to her that night, she ran to Cyr's dorm as her only option. The thought of Clara running to Cyr for help made my heart ache. I'd already inflicted so much damage on him, but the fact Cyr still came to my rescue had the tears falling all over again. He told Clara to take his car while he took his motorcycle to find me as quickly as possible.

After Clara brought me back to our dorm, we stayed in seclusion, ordering food and watching movies from Clara's projector connected to her phone. My phone was cracked from dropping it and struggling to locate it on the bathroom floor, but Clara had gone out while I was napping to replace the screen for me. She never left my side for any longer than she had to between classes, and I would never be able to repay her for her kindness. I'd truly be dead without her. My professors excused my classes for the following few days and gave me extended grace periods to complete my work.

Once my phone was returned, fixed, and good as new again, I opened my text thread with Cyr constantly only to stare at the messages. Messages that varied from playful banter to the filthiest of flirting. A few days passed before I felt comfortable leaving the dorm room and I trudged up the stairs to Cyr's room. I'd finally worked up the courage to knock on his door, but he wasn't home. Over the next few days I'd gone up to his room twice more, but the outcome was the same. For all I knew, he'd probably been staying at the apartment above the tattoo shop to stay as far away from me as possible.

After nearly a week since that damned night, I went back to class to turn in my overdue work for my classes. I was thankful nothing irrevocably soul-damning happened that night, but my skin still felt disgusting. No matter how many times I showered in a day, it never felt clean from where his hands and lips trailed my body. I slam my eyes shut, shaking my head to rid the blurry memories flashing across my mind.

"Bellamy? Are you okay?" Clara asks softly from beside me. My eyes slowly open, inhaling deeply, and exhaling through my nose. I glance at her with a nod before we continue the walk back to our dorm for the day.

We spend the rest of the day lounging in the room, watching movies, and Gwen stops by with dinner for a game night. The blissful distraction is exactly what I need, regardless if I still don't feel perfect yet. If I ever would feel that way again.

"You should go talk to him," Gwen chirps from the other side of my bed, and my eyes widen a bit at her. She raises her hands into a surrendering position, "Come on, Bellamy. The whole world knows you're miserable right now. It's pretty much tattooed on your forehead, and I mean that with all the love in the world."

I slouch into the pillow behind me, my head falling to rest on Clara's shoulder beside me, "Is it really that obvious?" The question fills the air, not necessarily projected to anyone in particular. My gaze trails up to Clara who's eyeing Gwen sadly and they nod in unison. I sigh, grabbing the pillow next to me, and slamming it into my face to dig my grave inside it.

"He fucking hates me. I'm certain he's avoiding me," I mumble into the pillow.

Clara rips the pillow from my face and I pout seconds before she hits me in the face with the pillow, turning my pout into shock.

"He doesn't hate you, Bell! If only you could have seen the terror in his eyes when I ran to him for help that night. Cyr cares about you. If he didn't, he never would've come for you."

My shock doubles at her words, and I slowly take the pillow from her hand and hug it into my chest. The thought of seeing Cyr's face through Clara's muffled but exasperated cries for help. I couldn't hear everything that was said through my hazed memory, but the thought alone had me wanting to race to him. I know damn well I need to talk to him, especially to apologize for everything I said about him, and now to thank him for saving my soul from damnation. The air grows silent and palpable around us for long moments while I process what I know I need to do to amend this.

"I have to study for a test on Monday. I'll see you two later," Gwen says softly with a smile and my stomach plummets. I didn't want to make her feel like she needed to leave, but clearly, while I was in my thoughts, the two of them had a silent conversation. Gwen leans over the bed, giving Clara a quick kiss and reaching over to gently squeeze my hand in encouragement. I look up, giving her an appreciative smile and a wave before she leaves the room, pulling the door shut behind her.

"There's one thing I have to do before I can talk to Cyr, but I need your help," I say barely louder than a whisper and Clara's bright eyes meet mine, nodding.

"Anything."

After I summon the courage, along with Clara to support me, I pull out the cursed note from my nightstand that I tucked away, promising myself to open it one day. That day has finally come when the contents of that very note may help me repair the hurt and damage I've inflicted on the one man who means the most to me.

My Darling Bellamy,

If you've found this, then you know I am already gone. There are so many things I wish I could tell you, but there isn't time. There's no time left for me. I have done unforgivable things and to live with the guilt for the rest of my life is not a life worth living.

This chapter of my life that I've spent with you this past year has been filled with more love and compassion than I believed would be possible for me. However, I've been holding a secret that can no longer be held to myself. While you've held my heart this past year, I've also been sharing my time with a man who I believed would give me the world if I asked for it. I've lied to you time and time again while hoping to keep him a secret, but now the truth must come to light. Because I never knew what would become of us, I never told my parents you were anything more than my roommate, while I did tell them he was my partner. I never wanted to keep you a secret, Bell, but when he came into my life, I couldn't deny my want for him.

I have done something no person should ever do to another, and that is why I'm writing this note. Should you ever find yourself in the company of Cyr Maddox, just know that he would sell his soul to make others happy, and I fear I've broken that irrevocably. To free him from the pain I've brought him, this is my way of repaying him for the wrongs I've done. I only hope one day you can understand.

All my love,
Jamie

Everything Cyr told me came to light in my head in flashes of our fight, the note revealing the guilt of what she'd done and Cyr's living proof that she'd done it. She couldn't bear the pain from the actions she'd made, as well as lying to me about her parents not wanting to meet me. It's not the fact that the two of us were seeing each other and the homophobic nature I'd presumed of her parents, but Jamie never told her parents we were together. All her parents knew was that we were roommates and nothing more. Their meaning behind allowing me to see the autopsy report wasn't out of malice, but rather them believing I would want to know what happened to my roommate, not my lover.

Jamie believed there was only one way out. But that wasn't true at all. There's always a way past the pain and suffering. If only she had talked to me. But those were fruitless thoughts now. The only thought eddying in my head now is how fucking wrong I was about the situation and I should have trusted Cyr. I remember the last thing he said to me before I bolted from his bedroom a few weeks ago.

'I have been called many true things in my life, but a liar is not one of them'.

Regret floods my entire body after I read the note and throw it back into my nightstand drawer to bury forever. I've spent the past year and a half of my life mourning for someone who had inflicted so much pain on a man who deserves the whole fucking world.

And I sided with her.

I didn't believe him.

Images of Cyr float through my mind, reflecting on the days we'd spent together. Picturing Cyr standing in the bathroom combing his hair, or seeing all his discarded sketches as he balled them up and tossed them all across the floor brought me comfort. All the mundane tasks drive me mad for him, and the sudden lack of those little things has my heart squeezing from the loss.

How the hell do I fix this?

I know the two of us are on shaky ground because of

everything we talked about, well, more like screamed about in regards to…Gods. I can't even say her fucking name anymore after what that bitch had done to Cyr. But now isn't the time for remorse. So, I decided, against my best judgment, to go to the one place I knew he'd be. My glossy eyes look to Clara for confirmation that I'm not making a terrible mistake.

Clara's hands cup both sides of my cheeks, her teary-eyed gaze meeting mine as her smile lights up the room.

"Go get your man, babes."

25

The Parlor

Cyr does something to my senses that drives me crazy when he isn't nearby. The scent of his cologne floating down the hall. His music vibrating through the walls of his bedroom. The papers strewn about with scribbles of long-since-forgotten tattoo ideas on every surface. The way his hands graze across my skin. I miss him. I...

Gods, am I actually going to say it?

I love him.

Of course, I can never say that to him, especially now, but I have to make this right. I was so wrong about him, and the things I said make my body reverberate with rage now that I know the truth. I know he just needs time to process all that was said and with everything that happened at the bar last week, but I need him to know that I now know the truth. The truth he told me which was clear as day that I so blatantly ignored due to my own emotions instead of considering his.

Even if he decided to never speak to me again, I needed him to hear my apology so I could live the rest of my life without the burden of breaking his heart on my conscience. That thought alone makes my steps quicken toward the tattoo parlor as I exit from the doors of the train.

As I reach the front door of the parlor, shoving it open, and hearing that familiar bell jingle above the door, it hit me. His cologne. His presence. I always know Cyr is nearby from the way my body seems to ease around him. I can't place what it is about him that screams out my name and beckons me like a moth to a Gods damned flame.

My lips part to speak, to call out his name, to beg for forgiveness for the brash things I said, to thank him for saving my life, but my mouth gapes open wordlessly. The black mask that I have never seen more than a foot away from the face behind it sits alone on the edge of the front counter. Cyr stands by the back of the parlor with his hands bracing against the table, head hanging low, and his back turned to me.

"Cyr, are you…" My words trail off as a low, guttural swear leaves Cyr's lips, telling me clear as day he wasn't expecting anyone, most of all me. And I just burst into his haven unaware and unannounced after all the shit the two of us have gone through.

"I'm sorry. I-" I stumble on my words as I quickly bring my gaze to the white marbled floor tiles, "I'll go. I just wanted to make sure you were okay." I quickly turn on my heels, reaching for the parlor door. Tears well in my eyes as I wrap my hand around the door handle.

"Wait."

That single word halts me in my tracks. The command alone sends a shiver up my spine and scitters over my skin.

"Don't go."

His voice is dark and low, yet almost a plea. The sound of his voice nearly has my knees buckling underneath me.

I slowly turn my head over my shoulder to see Cyr still planted against the table, facing away from me. I take a shaky breath before walking over to the front counter and picking up the black cotton mask from the counter top. My thumb grazes over the material, slowly walking up behind Cyr, keeping my gaze down toward the floor in front of me. He deserves that privacy after I barged into his safe place.

A part of me wants to look up so badly, to see the mysterious man behind the mask, but I can't. We've gone through so much together and to break this trust he's instilled in me at this moment would be the end of me. My heart and soul would be irrevocably broken if Cyr couldn't forgive me.

I stand only a few inches away, staring at his back, still slightly hunched over. Carefully, I reach an arm out, grazing over the side of his ribs, and his body quickly tenses. I pause for a moment, then continue reaching around until my palm is placed on top of his heart. Slowly, ever so slowly, Cyr's muscles relax under my touch. As he eases into my touch, I once again wrap the other arm around him, holding the mask in my hand in front of his body. I feel him shift as his hands leave the table to take the mask from my hand. I place my cheek against his back, shutting my eyes, and taking in the scent of his cologne for just a moment. My eyes shoot open as I feel one of his hands cover my own that's placed over his heart. My heart skips a few beats at the gesture. Over these past nine months to get to this point, I know now that he still trusts me, and it makes my heart ache for him even more.

We stand like this for a few more moments. Our breathing slowly syncs together until our breaths become one. I take in this moment for as long as his body and mind will allow. The smell of his cologne consumes me and a tear spills from my cheek being close to him again. I'll commit this moment to memory until my dying day. Cyr exhales a long breath and I take that as a sign to pull away. That this moment has exceeded his limitations, and I'd forever be content with that.

I slip my hands on his heart away from underneath his hand holding mine. Taking a step back from him, I look down at the polished floor below me and wrap my arms across myself in a tight embrace.

"If you need me to go, just say the word and I'll leave. I wouldn't blame you-"

The rest of the words on my lips and the current breath I breathe escape my body in a *whoosh* as I feel his hands caress my cheeks. Those gentle, loving hands reach up and Cyr's fingers deftly tuck away a loose strand of hair from my face. My eyes drift shut at the feeling of his touch, falling deeper into the feeling of his skin, and falling deeper in love with him. Every single thought in my mind eddies away as the soft skin of his lips brushes over my forehead.

He didn't put on his mask. It's off. He *kept* it off when I'd handed it to him.

Gods all I have to do is look up. Just fucking look up.

I can't. Not right now. Not because I'm that vain to think he's nothing short of breath-taking underneath that mask. I can barely stand the current emotions rattling through my body let alone the sight of him for the first time without his mask. My breathing quickens and I try my damnedest to stand still as his lips caress my forehead.

"Relax, my Raven."

My. Raven. He's claiming me as his. *His* Raven.

I didn't understand the reason for the nickname other than the color of my hair. From what I know, ravens only bring loss and bad omens. Which I didn't fully disagree with, but as to why he began to call me that, I couldn't comprehend. Until last night, I found myself crying in my dorm room and thought to research anything I could on the meaning of ravens. What I found shook me to the core, and it can be blamed for one of the reasons I'm in this parlor right now.

Once you are visited by a raven, it is indicated that you may require guidance in your life.

That one sentence alone would forever shape how I saw Cyr viewed me. When I first laid eyes on Cyr Maddox, I was definitely in need of guidance, just as much as he's shown me that he needed a guide through life alongside me.

"Raven?"

One single word in his slightly concerned tone brings me crashing back down to reality. I release the breath that hitches so tightly in my chest that it sounds like a sob. A tear begins to fall in a gentle trail down my cheek which is swiftly wiped away by Cyr's awaiting thumb. All the oxygen in the room seems to disappear.

"I'm fine…I'm-" I pause, attempting to let Cyr know I'm okay, still clamping my eyelids tightly shut. I can't find the words, but instead, I lean forward and brace my forehead against Cyr's chest. I don't know why I'm crying, but it all leaves my body in a split second.

"I'm so sorry, Cyr."

I release the words so quickly through panted breaths as I shake from the sobs. What I don't expect are the arms that envelop me, and pull my body close as his hands gently run through my hair. This moment feels more real and intimate than any of the nights we've shared.

"For everything I said. For calling you a liar. I-I didn't mean it. I was just-"

"Shhh. Breathe."

Cyr's soft voice coos in my ear, willing my body to release the built-up tension in my muscles, and melt further into his embrace. I keep my arms curled up in front of me even as I huddle as close as Cyr's body will allow me. The two of us have been through so much emotional and physical bonding, I don't know how long he can stand being touched after what I did to him, but I would hold on to this moment as long as possible.

"Bellamy. Why won't you look at me?" He asks quietly, something akin to hurt reflects in his tone and another soft sob leaves my lips. I can't look up, even as he begins to pull away from me, and Cyr's hands return to cup my cheeks. I keep my eyes shut, and let his hands guide my face to look up at him. But my eyes can't open.

"I don't want this to change anything. All I've ever known is your mask," I reply softly, and his fingers graze across my skin.

I tilt my head to cradle it in his hands. A soft sigh leaves his lips before he pulls away and the absence of his touch slams into me like a brick wall. My head falls back down toward the ground as terror fills my head, praying to any of the Gods listening he won't pull away from me forever.

"Better?"

The slight muffle that comes from Cyr's voice has me instantly shooting my gaze back up to meet his. I exhale in relief seeing that black cotton mask adorning his olive-tanned face once again. The feeling of normalcy returns to me and I slowly take a cautious step forward, and to my surprise, he meets me with a step toward me. I reach up, carefully to not startle him, and gently run my hand over his cheek. I feel the soft fabric underneath my palm and just as I'd done moments before, Cyr's head tilts slightly to rest in my hand. I watch in awe as his eyes drift shut, and I take in the feeling of my hand against his clothed cheek.

"I know we need to talk. This time hopefully without the screaming and the crying," I say softly trying my hardest to not cry from the mere thought of our last conversation. "Mostly on my end." I amend which elicits a soft chuckle from within Cyr's chest, and his glacier-blue eyes open to meet mine once again.

His hand lifts to glide atop mine, taking hold of my hand, and grasping it tightly in his own as he brings it down between the two of us. Cyr's gaze falls to our hands joined together, and the realization of how much contact the two of us have made in a matter of minutes dawns clearly in his eyes. He still didn't pull away.

"Are you okay, Raven?" He glances back up at me, raising an eyebrow in question. The concern flooding his gaze nearly brings the tears falling down my cheeks again. Words evade me, but I manage a nod to him. I'm alive in an emotional and mental capacity because of him, a fact that I don't think I'll ever be able to repay him for.

Unfortunately, our reunion is cut short as Cyr's client shows up for their appointment, the bell attached to the front door jingling as confirmation. He releases my hand and reaches into the back pocket of his jeans to retrieve his wallet. My eyes widen as he pulls out the key card to his dorm.

"I think you forgot something."

My jaw hangs open for a moment as I stare at the key then look back up to meet his gaze.

"Are you sure?" I ask hesitantly. The last time I was in his room gathering the last of my things, I'd left the key on his bed presuming it wouldn't be mine to have anymore. Clearly, I was wrong.

"It's always been yours, Raven. I'll be home around nine," Cyr replies, holding the key card up, "That is if you want it."

Home.

The word stuns me stupid. His room was always our shared space, but after everything we've been through I didn't think he would ever want me back in his domain. Cyr calling it *home* brings hope deep in my chest that I haven't destroyed everything we've built. The question in his eyes brings a small smile to my lips as I nod gently, accepting the key from his hand.

"Are you bringing dinner or am I?"

***

Just as Cyr had told me he would be, he was home at nine on the dot. I made sure to come by his room a few minutes early to make sure he wasn't waiting here alone for me to show up. Clara told me the best place for pizza in the city, quickly ordering it online to arrive preciously five minutes before Cyr would be coming back.

I organized the paper plates, napkins, two cans of soda, an extra large pizza, and cheesy bread sticks in a neat array in the center of his bedroom floor. The arrangement is all neatly sitting atop the quilted blanket I'd used from our picnic date back in the Spring. As the front door opens, I hear that beautiful voice I've missed more than anything in the world echo into the room.

"Raven?"

"In here," I call softly, sitting on the edge of his bed as his footsteps close in across the common area floor.

Cyr's head pops into the room and the corners of his mask tilt up into a hidden smile which then causes a smile to form across my lips. His gaze follows down past the bed to the assortment of food I'd acquired for dinner. His full body shifts into view and my mouth gapes at the beautiful bouquet of roses in his hand. I stand from his bed and meet him halfway across the space as he walks into the room.

"If those aren't for me, I might cry," I say softly with a laugh. Cyr chuckles, extending them out to me to hold in between us.

"Bellamy…I'm sorry."

The apology coming from his lips stuns me and I emphatically shake my head as I accept the bouquet from his hand.

"You have absolutely nothing to apologize for, Cyr. I'm the one who owes you every single apology from now until the end of time," I reply, sighing as I gaze into the flowers in front of me, "The things I said. What I did…it's unforgivable in every sense of the word and I'm so incredibly sorry for everything. I know my apology won't even begin to scratch the surface, but I need you to know I mean it."

My voice begins to break and I chew on the inside of my cheek to attempt to keep my tears at bay. Soft skin touches my chin as his hand tilts my head up to face him. That gentle side of Cyr coming through bright as day as those glacier blue eyes capture mine.

"I had no right to speak to you the way I did. I let my past get the best of me and took it out on you. Forgiveness is both of our worst enemies, but know that I hold nothing against you," Cyr says reassuringly, calming my mind from his admission.

I exhale slowly, nodding up at him, "I wanted to give you space to decide if you still wanted me after…everything. But I couldn't stand being away from you anymore."

His hand glides up to my cheek, warming my heart and soul from his touch alone.

"I came to visit you in the hospital."

My eyes widen and my jaw drops at his comment.

"When? I never-"

"I had to make sure you were okay. I told myself I needed to give you time on your own to come to terms with all that happened, but I had to see you." Cyr's hand begins to shake against my cheek and my hand slowly comes up to rest atop his.

"I wouldn't be standing right here as the woman I am today if it wasn't for you. You didn't have to save me, especially after all I did to you, but you did. You've saved my soul in more ways than one."

Cyr shakes his head, still shaking and I know it's not from our contact, but rather the rage building behind those glacier depths.

"Look at me, Cyr, please."

I set the flowers on top of his bed beside me and place my free hand gently against his chest above his heart. The thumping of his heart races beneath my touch, finally capturing his attention. I slowly inhale, holding my breath, and exhaling deeply. After a moment of repeating the actions, Cyr's chest begins to rise and fall in an even rhythm with mine.

"Did you hear he was arrested?" I ask and there's a brief shake of his head in response, "That was because of you. They found his DNA under my fingernails and with the tests done, it was enough to arrest him. That's because of you, Cyr. My dark angel sent from the Gods."

Cyr's eyes close, his hand moving to wrap around my waist and pulling me close to him. His head bows, placing his forehead against mine as we continue to breathe in time, my eyes drifting shut to embrace this moment. For a few blissful moments in time, there's only Cyr and I, and I couldn't ask for anything more for as long as I live.

"You shouldn't be the one having to comfort me, Raven."

His voice comes out like gravel in his throat, a slight shake of his head against mine has me slowly pull away, opening my eyes to find those ice-blue orbs already focusing on me. It's as if he couldn't allow himself to take his eyes off of me or I'd slip away into the ether.

"I think more than ever is when we need each other, Cyr. I'm here, and I'm not going anywhere."

A long exhale leaves his lips and a slight chuckle has Cyr's chest rumbling against my palm.

"I planned to break down your door tonight after I left the shop, so I'm glad you found me first."

"Simply knocking would have done the trick, but I'm glad too."

The hours pass by into the early morning as we devour the pizza and I make a mental note to thank Clara later for the dinner recommendation. After the smiles and laughter become normal once again, I mentally prepare myself for the hardest truths I'd ever speak.

I confessed everything to Cyr and he listened while holding my hand the entire time. The note. Mine and Jamie's relationship while she was simultaneously seeing Cyr throughout our relationship. All of the hard truths to swallow, but truths that needed to be heard. By the end of the night, we'd spent the night wrapped up in each other's arms on the floor of his bedroom, in his bed, and in the shower.

Sometimes the hardest things to accept in life are the things that need to be brought to light. Once Cyr and I poured our hearts out to each other, the night ended in bliss with his arms tucked tightly around me. Cyr's whispered words send me into the best night's sleep I've ever had.

"I'm never letting you go again, Raven. I promise you that."

26

The Family

I scramble to fold my clothes and haphazardly stuff them into my suitcase with far too many clothes than I'll need for the next three days. I'm not sure what to pack for, even though it's a blistering cold New England winter, I want to be prepared for anything.

"Babe, it's negative 5 outside why in the Hell are you packing a bikini? You're going to Rhode Island for Christmas, not Cancun."

Clara's chirp from across the dorm has me rolling my eyes and tossing a freshly packed bikini onto my pillow. I huff as I stare at the mound of clothes piling out of my case, fully aware that I'm stress-packing. I take a deep breath to steady myself before resuming packing in a more orderly fashion.

A few sweaters and hoodies that refuse to fit cause a bead of sweat to roll across my forehead as I body slam my entire weight into the poor suitcase in all attempts to zip it closed. After my championship match in the tenth round, I finally claim my victory against the damn case.

"Game, set, match."

My body slumps to the ground with my back against the bed only to meet the sight of Clara clapping her hands with mock enthusiasm, "Close match, babe. Didn't know if you'd be able to survive to the next round."

I bring my middle finger up to Clara in reply which earns a laugh from my best friend. My phone chimes next to me with a soft *ding* signaling a text notification. The sound causes me to groan as I make my way up to stand beside my bed. I pick up my phone seeing a text from Cyr pop up on the screen.

Cyr: I'll be there in 10.

"Shit, shit, shit!"

I glance down at myself to see the sweater and shorts I'd slept in and can only imagine the state of my hair after the battle with my suitcase. Bolting to my dresser, I frantically search for anything that will look remotely decent enough to meet Cyr's family. His twin sister, Kora, lives just under two hours away in Newport, Rhode Island, and his older brother, Ryker, lives in California but caught a flight over to join them for Christmas.

With the speed of lightning, I pull a dark gray knitted sweater over my head and slip on a pair of burgundy leggings to pair with my signature black Doc Martens. As I hear a knock on the door from where I stand braiding my hair in the en-suite bathroom, my heart begins to tumble around in my chest. I hear Clara greet the man I know is at the door and finish up my braid, pulling on a few sections to attempt to make my hair appear cute and relaxed compared to not-so-sleep-mussed.

"She's just finishing up, make yourself at home."

A beat of silence, and then the door closes as footsteps grow louder in the room. I hear the squeak of my bed with his weight added to it, taking a deep breath as I look myself over in the bathroom mirror. I realize I hadn't put any makeup on, but didn't bother with makeup most of the time since Cyr never really took an interest in it. I hate putting it on, so it's in both of our favor.

"Any plans for the holidays?"

Cyr asks my friend as the two make small talk while I finish up. Their relationship has my heart soaring knowing the two of them hit it off so well even from the beginning. Having my best friend and the man I love in good standing is a change of pace and an occurrence I only dreamed would happen.

"A few of the girls from my studio art class are getting a hotel on Christmas Eve and we're gonna get trashed doing Secret Santa."

"That sounds…eventful."

The two share a laugh and it brings a smile to my red-painted lips. But there it is again. That feeling. The only thing that continues to gnaw at me is making a good impression on his brother and sister.

Cyr told me their parents had passed away a few years ago and the three of them became closer than ever. Today would be a make-or-break point in our relationship. If they don't like me, I don't know if Cyr would stay with me knowing they didn't approve. Tears begin to sting the back of my eyes and I furiously blink them away. The thought of losing Cyr tore me apart harder than anything else and it terrifies me down to my core.

"Anytime before the year ends, Bell, I have to run to the packie before it closes!"

Clara's call for me quickly forces me to take a deep breath, gazing at my reflection in the mirror once more, giving myself a reassuring nod, before exiting the bathroom. I step out to see Cyr's glacier eyes already on me and the sight of him never ceases to send butterflies tumbling in my stomach. His gaze roves my body not sparing a single inch of me in his assessment. My body feels molten under his gaze and it takes every ounce of my willpower to not kick Clara out for the two of us to have a few blissful minutes to ourselves.

Cyr stands from his place on my bed and makes his way to stand in front of me. He wraps a strong arm around my waist and dips down to bring his mouth to my ear.

"If I didn't like that sweater as much as I do, I'd tear it off to see what's beneath it."

My entire body erupts into flames and suddenly my sweater turns suffocatingly warm. The way Cyr speaks to me has my body lighting ablaze with lust and desire and I can't for the life of me explain the power he has over me. The seduction that pours from him like a waterfall has me diving headfirst into it without hesitation. I'm consumed by the overwhelming attraction that pulls me to him like a magnet no matter how hard I fought it, at first, but now I welcome the pull to him as if I rely on it to survive.

My lips tilt up into a small smile as he pulls back and I meet Cyr's gaze, igniting fire within every vein in my body. Without caring that Clara is mere feet away to witness the interaction, I bring my index finger to my lips before gently placing my finger on Cyr's lips over his mask to transfer the silent kiss. Cyr's eyes flutter closed to accept my kiss and once they open, I swear his eyes shine a brighter blue than I'd ever seen before.

Clara's exasperated groan brings my gaze over to my friend to see her roll her eyes, "You guys are disgustingly cute and now I'm going to buy an extra bottle of Crown Royal to forget how lonely I am. Now get out before the storm hits."

A soft laugh leaves me as I pull away from Cyr's grasp to walk over and embrace my best friend, "You'll only be alone for three days. Besides, you have Gwen. I think you'll manage." I say softly to Clara and her returning embrace nearly brings tears to my eyes.

"She's spending the holidays with her family back in Texas. So that extra bottle is calling my name," She says dramatically, giving my torso an extra squeeze. "Be safe, okay? The storm isn't supposed to hit until tonight, but call me if you need me. Please."

Clara's words are gentle as she brushes my hair lovingly with a hand. I know Clara is warning me not just because of the storm, but I had admitted to Clara my worries about meeting Cyr's family. I know that my best friend will drop anything to be there if I need her. Another reason entirely why I feel bad about leaving Clara alone for Christmas. This week is going to be a huge turning point in my life and finally gaining Cyr's trust to allow me to meet his siblings means more than the world to me.

"I will, I promise."

I give my best friend an extra squeeze of assurance before pulling away and looking back over my shoulder to Cyr. He watches the two of us with something akin to love in his eyes. Cyr knows how much Clara means to me and my heart freezes in my chest as Cyr walks over to Clara with his arms outstretched toward her. I told Clara a little of his past with Jamie, but nothing in detail, in short, explaining he doesn't like to be touched.

Clara's eyes widen briefly in my direction before snapping back to Cyr as his arms wrap around her shoulders. She, ever so gently, returns the embrace, and Cyr's back turns rigid for only a moment before settling into the hug.

My eyes turn glossy at the sight, willing the tears back with a light sniffle. I can hear light muffled words coming from Cyr, but can't make out what's said to Clara. After a moment when Cyr pulls back, Clara looks up to him with a nod, attempting to hold back her tears. The sight of the both of them sharing nods makes my heart melt into a puddle on the floor. Clara's watery eyes look back at me with a smile.

"If he gives you any shit, I give you permission to throw a snowball at him."

"Oh don't you worry, he'll be sleeping in his very own igloo if he starts shit."

Cyr rolls his eyes at our conversation and brings his gaze back to me, and I flash him a wink. When his eyes connect with mine, the heat in his lust-filled gaze warms me straight down to my core.

Clara shakes her head at the two of us, "Will you stop eye fucking each other and get a room? Or better yet, go get in your car and find a room elsewhere."

Cyr raises an eyebrow, quickly flicking his eyes down my body then dangerously slowly back up to my eyes as if silently conveying, *"Oh you're definitely getting it in the car."*

A giggle escapes and I drop my gaze to the floor in an attempt to hide my growing blush. Cyr strolls over to pick up my duffle bag from the top of my bed and slings it over his shoulder, casting his eyes back toward me.

"Ready?"

"As ready as I'll ever be," I reply softly and pick up my jacket from the edge of my bed. The two of us walk toward the front door as I glance back to Clara over my shoulder, "Love you, Cee."

"Love you, babe. Drive safe, Cyr. Text me when you guys get

there!"

"Yes, mom!"

I call to my best friend in mocking, glancing back in time to see Clara flip me off. Our shared laugh echoes through the dorm as Cyr shuts the door behind us.

***

Dark gray storm clouds far above continue to roll in with the wind and snow flurries slam into the sides of Cyr's Camaro from every direction. With the salt on the road and the stains of melted snow coating the black-as-night Camaro, I almost didn't recognize the car as we walked through the campus parking lot to find it.

I offered to drive, but this is the first winter I've experienced driving a vehicle through, and decided Cyr driving would be the better option. As he navigates the both of us through Massachusetts, my eyes drift out the passenger side window and watch each flurry of snow float through the air. As the car flies down the highway kicking up snow, the shimmery flakes spiral around in the air creating an enthralling dance of twinkling ice diamonds.

"Raven?"

The sound of Cyr's voice floats across the car toward me, feeling as if he's a million miles away. After I come back to reality and pull my eyes from the recital of snow outside the window, I meet the glacier-blue eyes that beckon to me.

"What's on your mind? You've been out of it since we started the drive." His tone is gentle yet laced with a hint of worry, "Did I say something wrong earlier?"

"Gods, no, Cyr. It's nothing you did, I just…" My voice falters and I release a sigh, leaning back into the seat.

Cyr's hand reaches across the seat to lay on top of my thigh,

294

squeezing gently. His touch alone sent me into a state of complete serenity. I swear his touch can cure the gravest of illnesses, and in my case, the deepest of worries.

"Talk to me, Raven."

"I'm scared your family won't like me," My voice is barely louder than a whisper as I glance over to Cyr to gauge his reaction. His grip on my thigh tightens just the slightest as he nods his head in understanding.

"I never shut up about you, so they'll be happy to not have to listen to me rant about you and finally learn about you in person." Cyr releases a light laugh from his lips and I didn't think I could ever hear a more beautiful sound, "My brother is an absolute hardass."

"Glad to know that runs in the family."

Cyr shoots me a glare that promises nothing short of a long night of punishment for my comment, and I can't resist flashing him a smirk. His grip on my thigh tightens to the point of pain, yet pleasure rips through me. I bite hard on my bottom lip and even then I can barely keep a moan from escaping.

"Please continue."

I'm not even sure if I meant for Cyr to continue his story, or for his hand to continue distracting me which is inching dangerously close to the apex of my thighs.

His hand halts but still keeps a firm hold on me.

"Ryker takes a while warming up to people, but don't be discouraged if he doesn't say much. He takes his time learning people."

The feeling of his fingers massaging circles into my inner thigh nearly has me telling Cyr to pull the fucking Camaro over to the side of the highway. My eyes drift shut taking in the sensations consuming my body and try to keep a listening ear on the conversation.

"And your sister?"

My eyes slowly open, flicking over to see Cyr's gaze dripping with the same lust that is no doubt in my own eyes. A low groan leaves his lips and sends his chest rumbling as he attempts to regain his focus. Cyr rips his eyes away from mine to watch the road ahead and reluctantly withdraws his hand from my leg. The absence of his touch feels like being doused with ice water as his heat leaves my body.

"Kora is just as stubborn, don't get me wrong, but she's everything good in the world. All she wants to do is help others. I have a feeling you two will get along just fine."

Cyr's voice is neutral as if our last few minutes of eye fucking had ceased to happen. I envy his ability to shut off the lust like a Gods damned light switch while I'm now sat here reeling from the feeling of his touch alone.

"Do you think so?" I ask softly after my lust is tampered down to a manageable level. The worry creeps slowly back into my mind, and my gaze returns out the window in time to see the *"Welcome to Rhode Island"* road sign come into view.

"I know so."

His reassurance is enough to calm me a significant amount and I bring my eyes back to rest on Cyr's profile as he drives. I burn the image of Cyr into my mind in hopes of never forgetting that beautiful face, regardless of what the outcome may be after the next few days. With the image ingrained, I allow the sound of the wind and snow around the car to drift me to sleep.

***

The gentle caress across my cheek and the side of my head brings me back to life from a deep slumber. Soft callused hands brush hair back from my face and my eyes slowly flutter open to meet the ice-blue eyes of Cyr. Mere inches in front of me, he's close enough to kiss if only I could.

"Welcome back to the land of the living."

I raise an eyebrow at Cyr's comment and blink a few times as I adjust to the light outside. The realization hits and I throw my hand out to flip down the visor to see the horror come to light across my face.

"Oh fuck me."

My lipstick is smudged across my bottom lip which is visible from the reddish-purple mark across the back of my hand. Not to mention the slight line of drool along the outside of my mouth.

"That's for later, Raven."

His words, though incredibly enticing, are not what my focus is on at the moment. I shoot him a quick glare before my hands dive into my purse in front of me and grab a small package of travel-size makeup remover wipes. After ripping out one of the wipes, I attempt to clear up the smudge along my lower lip along with the beyond-embarrassing line of drool. I wish to sink into a craterous grave and wallow away knowing Cyr has been witness to my drooling scene. The look in his eyes shines nothing but that same adoration since the beginning which calms me the slightest bit. I remove the lipstick from the back of my hand and reapply the lipstick along my bottom lip, a dark fuchsia to match my leggings.

Once I deem myself presentable enough for introductions, I bring my gaze back to Cyr and nod my head. He nods in reply before exiting the car to retrieve our bags from the trunk. I take a steadying breath before opening the door of the Camaro and am damn near tempted to dive back into the car from the gust of soul-shattering wind that whips around me. The storm is brewing above us, signaling we've reached Kora's house in just the knick of time. A warm hand grasps mine and Cyr gives my hand a reassuring squeeze as we walk toward the front door.

"Oh honey, we're home."

Cyr's sarcastic tone echoes down the long foyer of the beautiful New England home which belongs to his sister. I can't help but gawk at the sight of the interior of the house. The light blue-gray-toned walls adorn several historical blueprints of old Newport and Boston along the foyer.

"I told you to call me when you were almost here! I thought you guys got caught in the storm so I've been rewashing clean dishes for an hour to calm down!"

A melodic female voice calls out from a few rooms over. I'm stunned stupid as the beautiful female rounds the corner and walks toward the two of us. She stands a few inches taller than me and her presence alone demands the attention of anyone around. Standing in front of Kora, I feel like a knock-off drugstore *Barbie* doll that's been run over in the parking lot a few times.

"Sorry Kay, my phone died in the car on the way. Didn't mean to worry you." Cyr's voice is full of sincerity I'd never quite heard from him before. It's a brotherly apology, and it doesn't make me jealous since I understand that his family means everything to him.

Kora's eyes light up and she smiles ear to ear upon seeing Cyr, stopping a foot in front of him and reaching her arms up toward the ceiling. I watch silently as Cyr reaches down to wrap his arms around his sister's torso and then Kora's arms delicately wrap around Cyr's shoulders. The acknowledgment in the action makes my lips gently turn up on one side. After a moment, the two pull apart and Kora's attention turns toward me, then back to her brother.

"Are you planning on introducing us or making the poor girl stand in the doorway all day?"

Her tone is all sarcasm, identical to that of Cyr's. I'm fully able to take in all of Kora then and notice the similarities between the twins. Their olive-tanned skin and striking blue eyes couldn't go unnoticed. The only difference is Cyr's hair, as black as night, while Kora's hair cascades over her shoulders down to her tailbone in a brilliant shade of auburn.

Cyr clears his throat, turning his attention back to me, "Bell, Kora. Kora, meet Bellamy."

"Charming," Kora mutters, rolling her eyes at her brother. I smile at her retort, laughing softly.

"He has that tendency I've found," I reply, taking a step toward Kora. "It's great to finally meet you."

Kora brings her glare from Cyr to smile brightly at me, a set of dimples appearing on the sides of her cheeks, the definition of perfection in one human.

"Cyr's done nothing but rave about you. I'm so glad you could join us!" Kora extends her arms out and brings me in for a tight hug. She brings her lips close to my ear, whispering, "If he pisses you off let me know and Ryker will put him in the doghouse."

A laugh spills from me once again, pulling away as Kora does and as she mentions Ryker, it's as if he appears out of thin air.

I do a double take over Kora's shoulder as a boulder of a man stands leaning against the doorway to the foyer, arms crossed over his massive chest. His muscles seem to nearly burst from the sleeves of his shirt with biceps larger than my head. His dark hair is cropped close to his head in a buzz cut and his eyes a swirling dark chocolate much like my own; a drastic opposite to the glacier blue eyes of his siblings.

"Don't mind him, he just stands there and broods most of the time."

The playful lilt in Kora's voice brings me back out of my thoughts on how Ryker could squash my head like a grape with a single hand if he wished. I smile with a light laugh, glancing back to see Cyr's gaze already on me. He raises an eyebrow, reading the question in his eyes before he has to say anything.

"Raven, are you with me?"

I nod softly to him and reach down to pick up my duffle bag when Kora stops me with a hand on my shoulder.

"Oh absolutely not, that's why we have men in the house. They don't call it *man*ual labor for nothing." Kora wraps an arm around my back and leads me out of the foyer past Ryker. "I thought I told you to lay off the steroids, Ry," Kora drawls, rolling her eyes. She receives nothing but a grunt in return.

The end of the foyer leads into a large living room with even more old blueprints of original buildings in the city and tapestries of mountain ranges and green-hilled valleys. It reminds me of home and it made my heart soar with the lovely images surrounding her. Kora's voice brings me out of her daze.

"Do you like the art? Cyr mentioned you're a painter."

I nod emphatically, glancing around the room at the numerous pieces of art along the walls, "They're beautiful. Where did you find them?"

"My fiancee painted them. Unfortunately, they've been called away for business so they weren't able to make it home for the holidays."

My eyes widen to saucers for the fact that her fiancee is such an incredible painter. I love painting, but never in my wildest dreams can I imagine painting something remotely akin to the beauty of the art lining the walls.

"They're lucky to have you," I say softly with a smile, and Kora's cheeks turn the slightest shade of rose. Kora shakes her head, smiling at one of the paintings.

"No, I'm the lucky one. Delta settled for certain."

The way Kora speaks her partner's name makes my heart swell. I feel the love and adoration pouring from Kora and only wish to possess even a fraction of that much compassion between Cyr and myself.

"Can I get you a drink? I bought a brand new bottle of gin with your name on it."

***

Kora gives me a tour of the house as she asks about my life and my hobbies. The general interest Kora displays in my life makes the conversation easy and I'm upset at myself for stressing so much about meeting her the past few days. She shows me to the room Cyr and I will be staying in for the next few days and does nothing shy of making me feel as welcome as possible.

Afterward, we make our way back downstairs and hear Cyr and Ryker chatting in the living room so we decide to quietly take spots at the dining room table instead. I sip the gin and tonic Kora makes for me before she pours herself a glass of red wine from a bottle on the kitchen counter.

"So you mean to tell me you'd never been to New England and decided to come over here for college?" Kora inquires with a dumbfounded tone as she rounds the counter. I nod, swirling the liquid around in my glass watching the tornado I create within the cup.

"Considering I'd only ever seen snow over a few inches in movies, it was probably a dumb idea, right?"

"An incredibly dumb idea!" Kora proclaims, the two of us sharing a laugh as she takes a seat across from me at the dining

301

room table.

I shake my head, attempting to come up with an excuse as to why I chose New England when in actuality, there is no excuse or true reasoning.

"I wanted somewhere completely foreign to me, and I definitely found just that."

Kora rolls her eyes dramatically, "I'd say so." She sips her wine and then places the glass down on the table in front of her, "You also found the most complicated man on this planet in the process."

The sister of the man I love knows all his inner demons more than I will ever begin to comprehend. Everyone needs a support system and I wasn't there for Cyr's initial downfall with…*her*, but Kora was. Cyr told me how much his sister was there for him when he lost himself. I'm thankful he wasn't alone through all of his past trauma. The thought of Cyr having to struggle through all of it alone makes my stomach churn. I bring the glass up to my lips, taking another sip of my gin.

"He's been everything I need and more. You call him complicated? Then you definitely don't know enough about me, yet."

I glance up to connect with the eyes I've grown so familiar with over the past year. The same striking blue eyes of Cyr that reflect from his female counterpart are still a shock to behold.

"Yet," Kora repeats with a smile, "But I wish to know you more." Her smile turns sad for only a brief moment. "Cyr's been through a lot over the past few years. Losing our parents hurt him almost beyond repair, then the shit with…well, you know."

I did know. I knew all too well.

"I thought I'd lost him a few times. I try to call in and check on him when I can, but there were a few occasions when I couldn't reach him at all and I went days before I heard from him." Kora sounds as if she's a million miles away from the conversation as her eyes drift toward the direction of the living room. "I've always tried to be there for him and annoy him with phone calls because if I continue to pester him, I know he'll answer. Just as he's always been there for me."

The bond between the twins is as clear as day and I'm grateful Cyr has his sister to rely on. There was a time in my life when the world seemed so dark and I had no one to call, and then Clara came along to brighten me back up. Cyr needs a bright light in his life, and in this case, it has always been Kora. I've always known Cyr felt comfortable speaking his truth to me, but there's nothing like that sibling bond. A bond I sometimes envy not having.

"Why weren't we invited to the party?"

The voice of my sinful angel graces our presence and I smile as I feel Cyr's hands gently rub into my shoulders. I melt under his touch and tilt my head upward to look at him from where he towers above me. Cyr's eyes soften as he meets my gaze and I slowly bring my lips down to place a soft kiss on the back of his hand. He gives my shoulder a gentle squeeze before pulling back and taking a seat to my right. Ryker joins the table with a beer in hand and sits at the head of the table to Cyr's right. Kora watches the interaction between the two of us with glossy eyes from across the table.

"Oh, don't you start turning soft now, too," Ryker grumbles from where he sits, rolling his eyes at his sister. Kora flips him the bird before returning her focus to Cyr and me with a smile.

"Unlike meat for brains over here," Kora pointedly glares at Ryker who tips his beer to her in reply before she brings her gaze back to the two of us, "I can see how well you two fit and although I don't know you that well yet, Bellamy, I know Cyr is lucky to have you."

"You said it well earlier, it's me who's the lucky one," I reply softly and take a sip of my drink. Cyr's hand slips beneath the table to place a gentle squeeze on my thigh.

"Are you gonna finger fuck her under the table now?" The grumbled words that leave Ryker have me nearly choking on my drink.

"Ry!" Kora snaps and slaps him on the shoulder. Cyr says nothing but from the corner of my eye, I see the glare he shoots at Ryker that promises death if he keeps speaking.

I clear my throat while standing up from the table, picking up my glass, and walking over to the kitchen sink to dump out the remaining ice cubes. I will the embarrassment to leave my cheeks as I stare into the sink, taking a deep breath.

"Cyr, would you like a drink? I'm sure Kora has straws," I call softly to him in the adjacent dining room. My eyes lift to meet Cyr's, filled with pain and regret. I can read the *'I'm sorry'* in his gaze.

"No, thank you." His voice is quiet as he replies, shaking his head.

"Straws?" Kora raises an eyebrow in confusion and Cyr gestures to his mask in a swift motion. The recognition clicks and she nods although a million questions fly across her features.

"Or you could just take the fucking thing off."

"Ryker, that's enough! What the hell has gotten into you?" Kora snaps at him, her voice the embodiment of a furious mother which I'm certain she'd taken over that role once their parents passed away.

"Apologies if I'm not too keen on Cyr bringing a girl home especially after what that last cunt did to him." Ryker's tone is filled with gravel and as deep as the farthest level of Hell. He turns his attention to Cyr, "How can you stand to have a woman in your bed after that bitch tore up your face? Let me guess. She hasn't even seen your face yet."

"Enough!" Cyr snaps and slams his hands down on the table in front of him. Kora's jaw gapes as she reaches across to attempt to take hold of Cyr's hand.

"Has she not?" His sister inquires, her voice a fraction of a whisper.

My heart shatters in my chest as Ryker's words strike home. My glossy-eyed gaze lifts from the countertop and sinks straight into the eyes that reflect back at me, the same as my own. I stand up straight and walk across the kitchen to the adjoining dining room.

"No, I haven't, and it was my choice." My voice is hard as steel as I glare, as sharp as daggers, at Ryker.

"Why? Because he dicks you down good enough that you don't care to see what happened to him?"

"Because I know what Jamie did to him and it wasn't my place to force Cyr to show me until he was ready." I snap, stopping a few steps away from the table.

Cyr sighs and keeps his gaze down on the table, "I tried to show you, but you wouldn't let me. I was committed."

The stab stings more than I thought it would and I try to force the tears back but it's too late. One slips down my cheek and Cyr glances up at me. He's instantly on his feet and taking a step toward me.

"Raven, I didn't mean it like that."

"It's a mask, not a fucking ring," I whisper through gritted teeth, keeping my red-rimmed eyes locked on Cyr's. "I'm going to take a shower," I mumble into the air, turning, and leaving the dining room without another word.

***

The water pelts my skin to the point of pain and I accept the stings against my body. It drags me from the depths of my mind and away from the war battling on in my head and heart. I know his siblings would be hesitant of me because of what happened in Cyr's past, but the constant blows from Ryker shove me beneath the water, suffocating me, drowning me.

I could hear shouts and slamming but the sounds come into my mind muffled and subdued. The sound of my name being called from thousands of miles away brings my mind slightly into reality but I can't reach it. I don't know from where or who calls for me, and I don't care to try. The water pounds into my ears from where I'm sitting curled up on the floor of the shower. My arms wrap around my knees and my head falls to rest atop them as the icy water douses my body.

"Bellamy?"

The voice sounds closer but the drumming of water against my head forces me to tune the whole world out and shut my senses off. I close my eyes and beg the world to stop spinning, begging the sun to turn cold and consume me wholly. I felt wanted for the first time in my life with Cyr by my side, and my fears of losing him entirely rush back into me like a fucking tidal wave.

"Bell-" The sound of my name being called is next to me now, and it isn't from Cyr. A soft touch to my shoulder brings my head up to find the source of the voice. Kora kneels beside me outside of the bathtub on the floor.

"Bellamy, what are you doing? You'll freeze to death! Your

lips are already blue."

She quickly reaches over to the nozzle and shuts off the spray of the shower. Kora extends her hands out to me to help me out of the bathtub. I bring my puffy-eyed gaze up to Kora for a moment before reluctantly taking hold of her hands. She pulls me up to stand and quickly spins to grab the fluffy white robe from the back of the bathroom door to envelop me in it. Kora helps walk me over to the toilet seat, sitting me down, and plugging in her blow dryer.

"You don't have to talk unless you want to, but if you need to get anything off your chest, I'm here for you, Bellamy."

Kora's words sound muffled as they enter my mind, but the importance of her words brings some warmth back into my heart. I assume Kora knows all of it already, but based on how she reacted at the dinner table tells me otherwise. I inhale sharply as the cold air around me sends a chill through my body. My hands tremble in my lap as I attempt to control my breathing. Although the house is heated, the freezing temperature outside with the ice that spewed over me from the shower causes my body to work overtime to regain warmth.

Kora turns the blow dryer on low and begins aiming the heat down the back of my robe. The sudden shock of heat makes me tremble, but I willingly accept the heat that begins to coax my veins to thaw.

Kora stands behind me and takes a deep breath as she gingerly takes care of me, her voice solemn, "Let me be the first to apologize for Ryker's actions tonight. I knew he was bound to make an ass of himself, but-"

"Did Cyr tell you I was in love with Jamie?"

Kora halts her hands for a brief moment before continuing to slowly send the heat across my body. Her stunned silence is answer enough.

"He probably thought you both would hate me if you knew, so in a way I'm grateful I could be the one to tell you." I say hoarsely, my teeth still chattering in my skull, "She was my best friend and I loved her with everything I had, and then I lost her. I lost myself and I didn't want to be found."

I can't tell how many tears slip down my cheeks, but the salt on my lips makes it evident.

"After she died I met Cyr, and he made me whole again. He taught me to love and feel loved in return." I choke on my words, but the feeling of Kora's hand gently stroking my hair coaxes me into relaxation, allowing me to continue, "Not too long ago we connected the dots. We never knew each other until after she'd died and it nearly broke us. I said so many things to him I wish I could take, but I can't. We both did. It's made us stronger together with our past firmly behind us, but those scars will always remain. His physically, and mine emotionally."

Kora points the dryer down the back of my robe once again, feeling the heat warm up my body back to a semblance of normalcy. My hands stop shaking although a slight chill runs up my spine from time to time.

"Everyone has their demons, Bellamy, we are no saints here. I think in your case, your demons led you exactly where you needed to be." Kora turns off the dryer, setting it on the bathroom counter, and unplugs it. She walks around to crouch down in front of me, taking my hands in her own.

"It means a lot to me that you told me. I know it's never easy digging up those feelings we bury inside of us, but I hope it's brought you a sliver of peace."

My eyes water at her words, and Kora gives me a soft smile. Kora brings a hand up to brush the tears off of my cheeks. I take a deep breath and open my mouth to speak but my throat has gone dry.

Kora shakes her head, "You don't need to say anything else, but know that I meant what I said earlier. You two were brought together for a reason, and I'm so grateful you found each other. I will always be here to support you, and if you need me to, I'll be happy to call and pester you too."

I let out a soft laugh and the last few tears escape my eyelids as I meet Kora's ice blue gaze.

"Same to you. Everyone needs someone to call when they need a friend."

My voice is no louder than a whisper, and from the glossiness that shines in Kora's eyes, I know my words meet their mark. Kora leans in to wrap her arms around me, and I return the embrace with all the strength I can muster.

"Bellamy?" Cyr's voice sounds from the bedroom just outside of the connected bathroom. Kora pulls back and looks over at me.

"Do you want me to send him out for a while?" Her tone is full of concern, but I shake my head.

"I'm okay."

"If that changes, my bedroom is the last one at the end of the hall. Men can be a handful." Kora says softly, brushing a few slightly damp strands of hair back that frame my face, "Especially that one." She gestures with her head toward the direction of the bedroom.

I laugh softly through my nose, "Thank you, Kora. For all of it."

Kora smiles and nods, "And to you, as well."

She stands and makes her way out of the bathroom into the main bedroom. I hear Cyr talk to Kora but only make out a few words from either of them.

"Is she alright?…I know…Kora, stop…"

"Don't you dare…She's special…Sound like Ryker…"

Cyr's growl is one that I know all too well, and even though I can't make out the full conversation, I know Kora is defending me.

"I'm trying, Kora."

The pain in Cyr's voice brings tears to my eyes which I furiously blink away. Kora's parting words to Cyr have me standing from where I sit.

"Go hold your fucking girlfriend and never let her go. She nearly froze the blood inside her body."

The sound of the bedroom door shutting and footsteps quickly walking toward the bathroom have me balancing myself with a hand on the wall as I stand. Cyr stops in the doorway to the bathroom and I don't bother to look up at him.

"Are you okay?"

His voice sounds pained, especially after his conversation with Kora. I push my hand flat out toward him once…twice…to signal him to back away without touching him. His towering figure standing in front of me makes me feel claustrophobic even in the large, luxurious bathroom. I feel so small and need to escape the confines of the icy grave behind me.

Cyr backs away enough to allow me to exit the bathroom and holds out a hand for me to take as I slowly walk toward the bed. I shake my head and continue the trek through the bedroom.

"Raven, please. Don't shut me out."

My bones feel a thousand pounds as I manage to spin and take a seat on the edge of our bed.

"I'm not. I just need a minute."

Cyr sighs, walking over to kneel in front of where I'm sitting.

He reaches his hands around to hold the back of my calves and rests his head on top of my lap.

"I'm sorry for what I said. It wasn't fair of me to bring it up like that."

The action makes my jaw gape and my heart crack at his words. I gently bring a hand up from his line of sight to caress his hair. He doesn't even so much as blink at the contact but rather his eyes close and his body melts into my touch. A tear slips from my cheek and falls into the mass of black waves on my lap. I brush it away and sniffle.

"I'm sorry, too."

Cyr leans up to meet my glossy gaze with his own. I can't bear to see him cry and it breaks my heart.

"You have nothing to apologize for, Bellamy. What I said and how I should have handled Ryker…" He sighs and reaches to brush a tear stain from off my cheek, "For letting him question my feelings for you and the fucking nerve of him to question yours for me. I let you down and didn't defend you when I needed to, and I can't apologize enough."

I shake my head and place my hand over his that held my cheek, "That day in the parlor…" I take a deep breath, throat raw, and exhale, "I told you I didn't want to see behind the mask because I didn't want things to change, but maybe it was because I wasn't ready to see what the woman I used to love did to the man I would lay my life down for."

Cyr's head drops and he rocks back down onto his haunches. His hand leaves my cheek and his body slumps back onto my lap, body and mind defeated by my words.

"I didn't mean to push you into something you weren't ready for. I just thought you would lose you if I didn't show you."

It's now my turn to hang my head in defeat. After all of the trials of the world fighting against us he thought his mask would be the reason I left him. The amount of overwhelming sadness consumes me wholly.

"If you think I'd ever leave you then I've failed you entirely, Cyr."

His head shoots upright to face me just in time to see a single tear fall from his hazy eyes. I reach down and gently take hold of Cyr's hands, running the pads of my thumbs along the back of his knuckles.

"My feelings for you will never falter and never cease. Please, Cyr, please remember that." My voice pleads with him to understand, "And the fact that you think that you have to show me a part of yourself, a piece of you that you weren't ready to reveal, to keep me breaks my heart. The day will come when we are both ready, and it will be a day I will remember forever."

Cyr stands from where he kneels, keeping hold of my hands, and beckons me to stand with him. After a moment, I manage to stand with his help although I'm only on my feet for a moment before Cyr sweeps me up into those familiar strong arms. I gently wrap my arms around his shoulders and bring my head to rest against Cyr's chest, nuzzling myself into the crook of his neck. The feeling of his hands, one rubbing small circles into my side and the other holding tightly under my thighs brings me comfort. Cyr sits on the side of the bed, still holding me tightly against his chest, his shoes thudding against the floor as he kicks them off. He spins us, laying me across his lap while he leans back against the headboard.

"Promise me something," Cyr says softly in my ear.

My head tilts back to look up at him and I nod, telling him silently to carry on.

"Next time I piss you off, don't run off and try to turn yourself into an ice cube."

I clamp my lips shut, but can't keep the laugh at bay as I fall deeply into those glacier-blue eyes, nodding once again.

"Then try not to piss me off."

"Deal."

27

The Piano

As the early morning sun rises, the rays peak in through the blinds of our bedroom illuminating the room in soft shades of amber. Cyr's quiet snores fill the room, soft and peaceful, bringing a smile to my lips. He lays on his side facing me, mask adorning his cheeks, and those beautiful swirls of black ink on display across his bare torso and arms for my eyes and mine alone to drink in. Some days the ability to comprehend that I'm the one he chooses to lay beside at night still has my mind reeling. He is everything I have ever hoped to have in life in a partner, and after all the battles we've fought as individuals, and together, it's managed to withstand all of it.

On nimble feet, I slide from the bed and change out of the fuzzy white robe that Kora wrapped me in last night. By the time Cyr pulled me into his arms and carried me into bed, exhaustion took over, and changing out of the extravagant robe was the least of my worries. All that mattered at that moment was Cyr, and I willingly climbed into his embrace to rock me to sleep.

After pulling out a light red sweater and black leggings from my duffle bag, I change into the clothes as quietly as possible to not wake my dark angel from his slumber. I grab the scrunchie from my nightstand, wrapping my hair up into a messy bun on the top of my head. Tiptoeing over to the door, I slip out into the hall, gently shutting the door closed behind me before venturing downstairs. As I reach the bottom of the stairs, Kora is instantly in front of me wrapping her arms around my shoulders to pull me into a tight embrace.

"How are you feeling, Bellamy?"

The compassion and love shown to me by Kora in the past twenty-four hours is enough to have my heart nearly burst at the seams.

"I'm a lot better now after some much needed sleep. Thank you, Kora."

I return the embrace, holding her close for a few moments before she pulls back to look me over. In that one glance, a part of me feels as if it was Cyr, the two of them both taking on the protective gestures. I chalk it up to the twin intellect in both of them, but nonetheless, it warms my heart to a near-boiling temperature. There was a time in my life when I never believed I could be worthy enough of a partner like Cyr, or a family, other than my own, that would ever care for me this deeply. The sentiment from Kora and her taking care of me to ensure I didn't submit myself to an early icy grave instills in me that I have nothing to worry about as I had the past few days.

"Can I get you a cup of coffee?"

Kora asks before turning to head back toward the direction of the kitchen, picking her coffee mug up from the dining room table.

"That would be lovely, thank you."

I follow behind her until I reach the threshold to the kitchen and my feet cement themselves to the ground. Ryker's eyes are already burrowing holes into my skull from where he stands in front of the stove making breakfast.

"Your omelet is burning, Ry," Kora says monotonously, pouring the coffee from the pot into a mug before topping off her own. Her comment draws his gaze away from me and I release a ragged breath that lodged itself in my throat. "Any creamer, Bellamy?"

"Black is fine, thanks."

Kora rounds the kitchen counter into the adjoining dining room where I stand by the large dining room table. I accept the mug as it's extended out to me and I pull the mug toward my chest, allowing the heat emanating from it to warm my soul.

"I'm watching some cheesy Christmas movies if you'd care to join me?" Kora questions with a wide grin spread across her lips and I laugh softly, nodding.

"Count me in."

Kora loops her arm in mine and the two of us walk down the foyer toward the family room, finding places on the couch to indulge ourselves. We spend more time judging the character's choices of motivating words and certain phrases of professing their love for each other than truly paying attention to the movie. As the movie comes to an end, Kora excuses herself from the room and leaves the television remote in my possession to put on another movie. I sip my coffee, enjoying a few moments of quiet to myself as I peruse through the selection of corny Rom-Com Christmas movies.

"Raven?"

The beautiful voice echoing down the hall has my head shooting toward the doorway of the family room in search of him. My eyes meet those icy blue depths as he rounds the corner, leaning his body into the door frame of the family room. Unfortunately, Cyr had decided to put on clothes, concealing those magnificent tattoos coating his entire body. Regardless if he was completely naked in front of me or had enough layers of clothes on to make an Eskimo sweat, Cyr would continue to be the most breathtaking man I would ever know.

"Good morning, sleepyhead," I mock softly, lifting my mug to take a sip of my coffee. One of Cyr's eyebrows cocks up before approaching me, leaning down to place his hands on either side of my head against the back of the couch.

"Good morning to you too, brat," His voice drops a few octaves, enough to almost have me dropping my mug of coffee, and my panties. My teeth tug on the corner of my bottom lip, but it doesn't stay there for long. Cyr lifts a hand to my chin to tilt my head up and drags his thumb down my lip to release it from my teeth. The action has a smirk gliding up my lips and my lower stomach turning to molten lava under his gaze.

"Want to take this upstairs?"

The words quietly leave my lips with an extra ounce of seduction in my voice. Cyr's mask shifts up a bit and a soft laugh has his chest rumbling.

"As much as I would love nothing else, Kora and I are going out for a little while."

Cyr's words have my smirk fading into a slight frown, "Where are you two going? It's Christmas Eve, Cyr, everywhere is going to be mayhem."

Palpable silence fills the space between us and Cyr stands up straight before me, "We're going to see Mom and Dad."

I'm instantly on my feet in front of him, setting my mug down on the side table next to the couch before returning my full attention to him. I slowly reach out toward Cyr's hand and hold it open for him to take if he chooses. Cyr exhales deeply before bringing his arms up to wrap around my shoulders, pulling me into his chest. I return the embrace, slowly wrapping my arms around his torso, and tears well in my eyes as he doesn't so much as flinch when I touch him. In nearly a year since we officially met in the courtyard during our photography class, Cyr has grown more and more comfortable with me touching him, but he's always been the slightest bit tense to start. After a year of gentle touches and making sure he always sees my actions if I'm to initiate the touch, he only squeezes my body tighter against him. Cyr's come to the realization of the progress we've made just as I have now and I never want to let him go.

"Are they nearby?" I ask softly into Cyr's chest and I feel him nod against the top of my head a moment before his masked lips press a kiss to my temple. My eyes flutter closed at the sensation and inhale deeply, willing my mind to never forget one of the most tender moments we've ever shared. Cyr pulls away, bringing his hands to my cheeks to meet my glassy gaze. My head lulls to the side, melting into his touch and another thought crosses my mind, "Does Ryker not want to go with you two?"

"Mom and Dad always had a tense relationship with Ryker. The three of them had a bit of a falling out before they died and I think that's why he never wants to see them when Kay and I go over there."

My heart cracks in my chest hearing Cyr's words.

"He never got closure," I say, not really a question but more of an open statement that we both know is true. Cyr only nods and although I can't see his facial expressions, his eyes say it all to confirm my words ring true.

"Cyr? You ready?" Kora calls from the foyer a moment before

she turns into the family room, stopping quickly in her tracks. "Oh, I'm sorry. Am I interrupting?" She questions, her tone weary.

My head turns to meet her gaze and I send a smile in her direction with a light shake of my head.

"Not at all," I reply before looking back to Cyr. "Drive safe, okay?"

Cyr's thumb grazes along my cheekbone with a gentleness that warms my heart, "We won't be long."

"Take all the time you both need."

Kora turns to leave the room, walking down the foyer toward the front door, her snow boots thumping softly along the wooden floorboards. Cyr turns to follow her before turning back to face me.

"If Ryker starts bothering you, call me and I'll be on my way back. We had a...chat...last night so he shouldn't have any reason to start shit."

The way Cyr pauses when he says 'chat' makes my heart hurt knowing that I had something to do with causing a rift between the two of them.

"Please, don't worry about me. I'll probably still be right here on this couch when you both get back."

I flash him a reassuring smile to ease his mind before he gives me a final nod in reply, turning back to catch up to Kora. A few moments later, the front door opens and shuts behind them, the sound echoing down the foyer. As the door shuts, I feel infinitely smaller knowing it's only Ryker and I here now, but I know he would never physically hurt me. The flashes of emotional pain from the night before send a shiver through my body, but I shove the feelings away as I take my seat on the couch once more.

After an endless amount of time deciding which movie to watch next, I finally choose one, top off my coffee mug, and settle into the couch with a comfy blanket. Halfway through the movie, from a distance, a faint tune fills the air which I believe for a moment to be coming from the movie, but realize it's from a room down the foyer. I pause the movie, unraveling myself from the confines of the fuzzy blanket, and venture out in search of the music.

My feet pad quietly along the chill wooden floor until I stop in the doorway of a small room, my breath catching in my throat to not startle Ryker. He sits on a piano bench that he dwarfs with his massive frame, his hands floating over the piano keys with such elegance my jaw gapes at the sight. The six-foot-five Goliath playing the piano is a sight I never thought I would ever behold.

The piano's soft melody floats around the space of the music room, completely enveloping me. A mixture of electric and acoustic guitars hang on pegs across one wall and the opposite wall contains floor-to-ceiling bookshelves full of sheet music and practice books. As the music hits my ears fully, my jaw drops further at the song that takes me far too long to recognize as "Dear Agony" by *Breaking Benjamin*. I take in Ryker's profile as his eyes close and his fingers take control of the melody, knowing exactly which keys to press as if his mind and body are on autopilot. My heart warms at the sight, feeling a tinge of regret for taking Ryker at face value as just some mindless brute who is only good at punching things.

"I can see where Cyr gets his impeccable music taste."

The music instantly stops, his fingers halting above the keys, and at that moment I entirely regret speaking, interrupting his beautiful symphony. Ryker doesn't even so much as look in my direction, but a sound I never thought I would ever hear escapes Ryker's lips. A barely audible chuckle floats across the room toward me. My ears almost don't catch the sound at first if the ever so slight rumble of his chest didn't give it away, but it is a laugh nonetheless and I'll take it for what it's worth. Right now, it's worth any progress I can physically make with Ryker. For Cyr's sake.

Without a word, Ryker uses his hands to shift his body over toward the far side of the piano bench. The bench isn't very large considering his massive frame, but the shift in his body leaves enough room for me to sit beside him.

A silent invitation.

I take a deep breath to calm my nerves before walking over and taking a seat next to him. The heat emanating off of Ryker's body is enough to believe his ass is sitting atop a furnace, but I imagine him being as physically cold as his words were last night. So now, it comes as a pleasant surprise to know he isn't as cold-blooded as I believed 12 hours ago.

"They made all of us kids learn something practical growing up," Ryker says, his words leaving his throat like gravel. I can't tell if that's just his voice, or if there's a hint of emotion coming through. He said 'they' and not 'mom and dad' as most children would refer to their parents, but I remember Cyr mentioning things ended on rocky terms when their parents passed away.

"Thank you for clarifying because the last thing I ever imagined on Ryker's hobby list was playing piano," I quip, glancing at Ryker to see his eyes focusing intently on his hands lying atop the keys. A barely discernible smirk flashes for a brief moment across his cheek before it fades.

"You know the kid plays the violin?" Ryker questions and my eyes nearly bulge from their sockets.

"We're both thinking of the same Cyr Maddox, right?"

"I doubt he still plays, but that damn violin almost got smashed a handful of times. Not confirming or denying it was by my hands."

The sarcasm in his tone is enough to momentarily stun me. Attempting to imagine a time when Ryker was a lot smaller than his current frame was semi-startling. Picturing a young Cyr running around with his violin while Ryker chases him in any attempt to break the poor, innocent instrument has me laughing softly at the playfulness as he reflects.

Although the heartfelt moment from their past brings a gentle smile to my lips, it makes me wonder why Ryker is bringing this up. Why is he letting me in? After everything that was said last night and his best efforts to, for the lack of a better phrase, inadvertently tell me to fuck off…why show me this part of their past?

"What instrument does Kora play?" I ask, wondering how far Ryker is willing to take this conversation.

"They wanted her to play the cello, but she preferred dancing," He replies, again using 'they' which makes my heart crack for him. "Kay took ballet for years and she was brilliant, but decided it wasn't for her when she got older."

Out of everything in this world, my initial impression of Kora never would have struck me that she was a dancer. The tidbit of information I tuck into my back pocket should the topic ever arise, I'll be sure to ask if she'll implore me about it someday.

"Thank you," I say softly, bringing my gaze back up to Ryker with a smile. At that moment his dark brown eyes, nearly akin to mine, flash to meet my own almost in a look of shock.

"What the fuck are you thanking me for? I've done nothing to deserve gratitude from you."

The bluntness of his words slams into me like a freight train, and I can only assume his words are coming from a place of remembering last night's altercation. A soft sigh leaves my lips and I bring my gaze back down to the piano keys, my right hand beginning to play the melody of *Mary Had A Little Lamb*.

"My parents wanted me to play piano, but in 23 years, this is the best I could ever retain. I was a lost cause at my mother's wishes for me to become a child prodigy at the piano."

I laugh at my pathetic attempt at the children's lullaby. The laugh fades and a gentle frown falls on my lips.

"I was terrified to meet you and Kora," I admit earnestly, "All Cyr does is talk about you two and all I wished for was to gain your approval. To see that someone would be good enough to ever deserve your brother and I fucking prayed you two would see that in me."

I blink away the glossiness from my eyes and I can feel Ryker's eyes on me but I keep my eyes down at my hand on the piano. Ryker's hand comes into my vision as it gently lands atop mine on the keys. Without a word, his hand guides mine to play a series of notes in a soft, continuous motion. Once I picked up the pattern, his hand leaves mine and his hands move to the other end of the piano. As my hand plays the notes in succession, Ryker's hands continue the series of chords to "Dear Agony" once again. My lips part on a silent gasp hearing the chords come together with the keys he had guided me to play.

"The kid never shuts up about you. Kora's been in love with you since before you even stepped foot inside this house."

Ryker's admission over the music has my heart squeezing at the sentiment. After Kora came to my rescue from my icy grave last night I knew there was nothing I had to worry about in the first place. But when it comes to Ryker, all I've done is worry that I won't be what he believes is best for Cyr.

"And you?" I ask timidly, preparing myself for the worst possible answers that could leave his lips.

The only sound filling the room is our duet for some time, and I assume I have pushed too far. Ryker has already given me so much more than I ever expected I would receive from him and I'm grateful for all of it.

"Kora's always been a great judge of character, so I'm more inclined to trust her from how she's reacted to seeing the two of you together."

Ryker exhales, the look in his eyes showing all the words he's attempting to piece together before continuing, "Cyr has always been the best of all of us. After…" He pauses and I know he doesn't have to say her name for me to understand. Ryker glances in my direction and with a nod of my head, he gives me a nod back before continuing, "He didn't deserve that. Somebody with as good a heart as Cyr's doesn't deserve to live with that. As much as I give him shit, I do it because I love him and I don't want to see him hurt again."

Ryker's words strike a cord in my heart and I know his actions were out of love, no one could deny that for even a second. It doesn't justify the vulgar comments he made last night, but it's evident that Ryker's defensiveness comes from a place of protection for his little brother.

"I know Cyr never would have brought you here to meet us if he didn't care about you. He's never brought a girl home before since…Mom and Dad passed away," Ryker continues and my eyes go slightly wide from him finally addressing them properly other than 'they' but also the realization dawns on me.

Three years and he never brought Jamie back home to meet them?

"I wasn't sure how Cyr would ever trust a woman again, which was also a test for him to see if he'd stand up for you when I said the things I did."

"He seemed to jump on the bandwagon with you when it came to that aspect," I say quietly, continuing to play the notes as Ryker instructed.

"If only you stuck around a little longer…" He says and my eyes flash to him for an explanation, "He sure did rip me a new one for the things I said to you. Which, now that I've come to terms with it, I apologize. It was wrong of me, looking back at it."

My jaw gapes slightly at him before I snap my mouth shut and focus back on the piano keys when I hit a wrong key sending a sour note into the air around us.

"The last thing I want is to come between the two of you. I know how much you care about him, just as much as he does for you. You don't have to apologize, Ryker, but I do appreciate it."

The tension in the room fades and we fall back into pleasant silence as the music fills the space once again. We fall into the melodies from Ryker's masterful playing and my quite mediocre attempt to play the individual notes without knowing what notes I'm even playing. I am indeed a sorry excuse for a piano player, so I allow Ryker to take the reins and perform his heart out. As the song comes to an end and Ryker plays the final set of chords, I finish off the last few notes, holding the final key to ring out in time with the chords. A beautiful sound ebbs and flows from the piano's vibration and a smile slips up my cheeks. The sound of a pair of clapping hands has my head quickly looking to the doorway to see Cyr and Kora applauding our performance.

"Oh, fuck off. Both of you," Ryker grumbles, shaking his head and standing up from the bench.

"Andddd he's back. Well, it was nice while it lasted," Kora chirps with a laugh before retreating down the hall toward the kitchen. I push myself up from the piano bench and walk over to Cyr who holds his arms out to envelope me as soon as I am within arm's reach.

"I didn't know you could play," Cyr says softly in my hair, pressing his masked lips to the top of my head. I smile and pull back an inch to look up at him with a smirk.

"I didn't know you played the violin, so I guess we both have our secrets."

Cyr's eyes are instantly shooting daggers at Ryker who I hear chuckling from behind me. I clamp my lips shut to keep my laugh at bay but it's short-lived before it slips through and those icy dagger eyes are back on me. He rolls those beautiful eyes at me before pulling me back into his chest and I melt into him, inhaling the scent of his cologne, and falling into complete and utter serenity. Ryker walks past us, slipping on his boots and a jacket in the foyer before grabbing the keys to Cyr's Camaro.

"I'm borrowing your car, I'll be back."

Cyr's head whips down the hall to Ryker, dropping his arms from me to run into the foyer.

"Oh hell no, take Kay's car."

I run after the two of them to witness a possible murder occur in Kora's foyer.

"You can't pay me to get back into that Mini Cooper. Seriously, Kora, who lives in New England their entire fucking life and voluntarily buys a Mini Cooper?!" Ryker raises his voice to make sure Kora can hear him down the hall in the kitchen.

"Shut it douche, it's a great car!"

Kora shouts from the kitchen defending her prized possession. Ryker rolls his eyes and holds up Cyr's keys, jangling them for a second before turning toward the front door.

"If there's so much as a single scratch on her, your ass is fucking grass, Ry," Cyr growls, and the tone of his voice promises imminent death if Ryker so much as breathes too hard on Cyr's car.

Ryker turns back to him with a smirk, "Just want to do a few donuts then I'll be back. Nothing too extreme."

And with those words sent into the ether, Ryker hightails it down the foyer and out the front door with Cyr immediately on his heels. As much as my mind screams to make sure the two of them don't kill each other on Christmas Eve, I decide to let the boys battle it out and head up toward the kitchen to meet Kora.

"I swear to the Gods if they get blood on the front steps I'm not letting either of them back in my house," Kora groans and I cover my mouth with my hand to keep from laughing aloud. Her eyes flick up from her task at the kitchen counter with a smirk on her lips which has my laugh releasing from behind my lips.

"How'd it go?" I ask softly with a smile in Kora's direction, taking a seat at the kitchen bar stool to watch Kora pull out a few groceries from a shopping tote. Her answering smile is kind and her nod conveys it was a nice visit which warms my heart. It makes me happy that Cyr was here to go with her and gave time for Ryker and me to, surprisingly, rekindle any brash first impressions.

The front door slams and I spin on the stool to see Cyr cross the threshold into the kitchen. My eyes widen seeing his hand covering the bottom half of his face where his mask previously was a minute ago. I can see a slight tremble in Cyr's hand and I point toward our bedroom above us.

"Bathroom sink. There's an extra in your toiletry bag," I say quickly before turning back to Kora. His footsteps approach from behind me and Cyr's lips press gently against the top of my head. My eyes drift closed at the feeling and a smile slips up my lips.

"Just know, Raven, I'm doing this out of love…"

I don't have any time to process the intent of his words before a snowball mushes itself against my cheek. I squeal, batting the ball of snow off my face as it falls down the front of my sweater and down into my bra. My body freezes in place as the cold snow shocks my breasts and I squeal through the icy pain.

"Cyr Braxton!" Kora shouts as the coward runs up the stairs at warp speed toward our bedroom. My eyes shoot up to her as I'd never heard Cyr's middle name before.

"Braxton?"

"Mom's maiden name," She replies with a smile with her hands firmly planted on her hips like a disappointed mother scolding a child. I scoop the remnants of the snowball from my chest and resculpt it in my hands.

"If you hear screaming, I'm only halfway murdering your brother," I say with a playful smile and Kora laughs.

"Give him Hell, Bellamy."

With Kora's permission, I take off running after Cyr up the stairs and toward our bedroom, snowball in hand.

28

The Eggnog

A booming laugh fills my ears followed by a few *shhh*'s as soft Christmas carols play in the background. My hand glides across the mattress beside me to find…nothing. Slowly, my eyes blink open, adjusting to the light coming in from the blinds to find the bedroom empty. I glance down seeing myself neatly tucked into the blankets like a present under the tree, but Cyr is nowhere to be found. My eyes open fully, tilting my head when I see a set of Christmas pajamas on the corner of the bed. Still groggy, I pull my body upright to sit, pulling the PJ's into my lap to see the little snowmen and gingerbread men holding candy canes in a pattern across the top and matching bottoms.

After slowly crawling my groggy body from the warm, comfy bed, I slip into the PJ's that were laid out for me. I walk out of the bedroom, following the music coming from downstairs and the intermittent bursts of laughter. The sound of the three of them together warms my heart and makes me feel grateful to be invited to witness an event like this.

My feet softly pad down the stairs following the smell of

freshly baked cinnamon rolls, and my eyes nearly roll back into my head at the invasion to my senses. As I enter the dining room, I spot Kora sitting at the table cradling a mug in her hands. When her crystal blue gaze meets mine, her eyes light up. A squeal of excitement bursts from her lips as she bolts from the table to run over to me wearing an identical matching set of pajamas.

"See! I told you she'd wear them!" Kora screams into the air, wrapping her arms around my shoulders, and pulling me in for a tight hug. I laugh, returning the embrace and the comfort the hug brings me is enough to make me damn near cry, "Merry Christmas, Bellamy."

"Merry Christmas, Kora," I reply, our arms wrapping around each other's backs as we walk into the dining room.

"You guys owe me twenty bucks," Kora says proudly and I raise an eyebrow at her in confusion. "The boys said you wouldn't wear the PJ's so I put my unyielding faith in you on a bet. Safe to say my luck has yet to run out."

As much as I'm not sure how to process my being a Christmas Day bet, I'm nonetheless happy to be included. My eyes scan the room and over toward the kitchen where Cyr and Ryker are making breakfast.

"Morning, *Raven*," Ryker says somewhat mocking Cyr's nickname.

The sound of it on Ryker's lips stuns me stupid, but the true stun comes a split second later as I watch Cyr throw an egg toward Ryker's head. A hand comes up to cover my mouth as the egg soars through the air, finding its mark on the side of Ryker's temple. Kora and I wrap our arms around each other to protect us from the inevitable murder that is about to be committed in Kora's kitchen.

"Oh you're gonna fucking pay for that, little brother," Ryker grounds out in a voice possessed by Satan himself. I catch a glimpse of Cyr before he's hauling ass out of the kitchen and around the cut-through entryway into the living room. Kora and I stand clear of the hallway, nearly dying of laughter as Cyr screams for help as the Goliath barrels after him down the hallway.

"How about some eggnog?" Kora asks, flashing me a smile before pulling me into the kitchen.

Once the fight for Cyr's very life is over, the boys clean themselves off from the evidence of their egg battle and join Kora and me in the family room. I gingerly sip my eggnog which Kora neglected to inform me is spiked with enough Fireball to bring down an elephant. Apparently, it's a Maddox family tradition their father had every year and once the kids were old enough to stomach the fiery drink, they joined in with him. Don't get me wrong, it's delicious, but I'm fairly certain Kora poured a double into my mug for good measure.

"Alright, children, settle down," Kora scolds, not bothering to release her grasp on her mug of eggnog as she stares down Ryker and Cyr from across the room. She walks over toward the magnificently large tree decorated in what looks like years of children's ornaments. It must have taken Kora ages to decorate considering the tree is nearly three feet taller than her.

"He started it," Ryker grunts, passive-aggressively kicking Cyr in the shin from where Cyr sits next to him on an ottoman. Cyr flips Ryker off and Kora snaps her fingers, commanding their attention. The poor girl absolutely became their new mother, but the smile that crosses her cheeks makes me feel that she doesn't mind at all taking up the role. Maybe Kora is the one that needs a double shot in her eggnog.

Kora begins handing out a few presents to the boys first. Ryker opens up a new set of boxing gloves from the twins which he accepts appreciatively. Cyr opens his gift from his siblings revealing a sketch pad and a new set of charcoal pencils. I pick up a box from under the tree and pass it to Kora, reading to her that it's from the boys. She wastes no time diving into the box and squealing with delight over the fuzzy pink slippers within. The pure joy from her is laughable, but she explains it was the only thing on her list she truly wanted for the holidays.

After trying on her slippers and reveling in the comfort, Kora reaches under the tree and picks up a haphazardly wrapped present, reading off the label.

"To Bellamy from…Ryker," She says aloud, yet hesitantly before passing it over to me. I glance over to Ryker, catching Cyr staring at him also while he sits stoic during the transaction. I accept the gift from Kora and tear open one end, revealing a set of painting brushes. My jaw drops as I look up to Ryker once again.

"The kid said you liked to paint," Ryker says with a shrug and I can't resist the smile that tugs up my lips.

"I had to leave most of my painting supplies at home when I moved over here. Thank you, Ryker," I say earnestly with a nod.

He shrugs again with a nod in return. My eyes catch Cyr's and I can see within his eyes he wasn't expecting this as much as I was, but my smile ceases to fade. Ryker and I may have gotten off to a bad start, but I can see how protective he is of Cyr because of all that's happened and I don't blame him. The olive branch was extended to me yesterday, and I'll happily accept it.

Kora opens up my gift to her and she gasps at the fine-tip pen and protractor set. To anyone, this would seem quite underwhelming, but to an architect, the joy on her face makes my entire day. She climbs over the discarded wrapping paper to hug me, thanking me profusely.

The day carries on, stopping mid-way to grab a few cinnamon rolls before returning to the family room floor for the last of the gift exchanges. Kora gifts Cyr and me a certificate to a local paint and sip class not too far from campus which earns her a massive hug and gratitude from me and her brother.

Cyr and I are the last ones to trade gifts, Kora passes me a long rectangular box and Cyr nods to me to open mine first. I proceed, pulling at the wrapping paper and opening the lid to the box. My mouth parts with a gasp as the silver chained necklace is revealed to me with a raven wing charm at the end. I meet Cyr's gaze and every part of my body soars with love and admiration. Carefully, I pull the necklace from the box and Kora helps me in clasping it around my neck as Cyr begins to unwrap his gift from me.

After nodding to Cyr to open his, he tears at the end of the paper and stops once the lid of the box is pulled off. He shakes his head in disbelief, looking up at me blinking a few times as he pulls out the brand new tattoo gun from the box. Kora is instantly at his side admiring the white and black dragon coiling around the handle of the tattoo machine.

"Raven…" Cyr whispers, "This must have cost you a fortune."

"No amount of money matters to see the look in your eyes right now," I reply softly, my cheeks tender from the wide smile across my lips. Kora looks as if she's about to cry, and Ryker just groans from the amount of love in the room, causing all of us to laugh in unison.

As the day fades into night, we all spend the time lounging in the family room watching Christmas movies and enjoying each other's company. The three siblings all laugh over stories of past Christmas's gone wrong from their mother's burnt turkey's to their father accidentally lighting the tree on fire one year from a little too much of his special eggnog.

The joy in my heart as I lay in between Cyr's thighs on the couch with Kora and Ryker in the lounges next to us is indescribable. For them to accept me as I am with Cyr by my side truly made this the best Christmas ever.

29

The Kiss

"On. Your. Knees."

At Cyr's tone, I oblige and kneel atop the black satin sheets of his bed. Cyr, whose gaze is entirely fixed on my every movement, sits with his back against the headboard. I'd slipped on my prettiest display of lingerie in his favorite color, black, of course, and knelt in front of him on his bed patiently waiting for further instruction. I feel like a queen in his presence; adored, and admired no matter what I wore or what position he had me in.

"Come here, Raven."

My nickname still sends butterflies tumbling through my stomach even after nearly a year. Cyr pats his gray sweatpants over his lap, a smirk slipping up my lips as I slowly crawl over to him across his bed. I slide up his legs and place myself to straddle over his lap. His hardness pushes up underneath me, filling my core with molten heat. I want him so badly all of the time. It's an attraction that's undeniable and palpable. The love for him that fills my heart, nearly to the point of pain, is a feeling that will stay with me until I no longer breathe.

Cyr's hand comes up to graze my cheek and brushes my hair back from my cheek to sit behind my ear. My dark hair cascades down my back in gentle bouncy waves, per Cyr's request. He never asks much of me except for an occasional outfit of his choice or a hairstyle that piques his interest. I melt into his touch as his fingertips graze down my cheek to my neck, and gently wrap his fingers around my throat.

The moan that escapes my lips makes his grip tighten a bit more against all the sensitive points across my throat. He pulls me closer to him and brings his other hand up to grip my hip, gently grinding me against him. My eyes roll back at the feeling of him underneath me, and I can't get enough of him. I try to grind harder against him, but Cyr stops me with the hand on my hip.

"Patience, Raven." An audible whine leaves my lips at the halting of motion between the two of us. Cyr raises an eyebrow at me, "Be a good girl for me and I'll make certain you receive what you crave. If not…" His voice trails off and a small frown comes to my lips, but I nod in submission.

"Yes, sir."

"Good girl."

Cyr releases his hold on my neck and grips my chin to make me face him. I meet his beautiful blue gaze once again and feel as if I'm falling through oceans to find him. The falling never ceases and it brings me into the arms, and lap, of a man I never thought I would find. My lips curve up into a soft smile and love that Cyr never cares how long I gaze at him now. Almost a year ago when a single moment was too long for him to stand, he now embraces the longing looks I send him constantly. Just as I do now.

"If I only could, I would kiss away all of your scars."

The words float from my lips no louder than a whisper. Cyr's eyes widened for just a moment, presumably not expecting those words to come from me. I lightly shake my head, opening my mouth to apologize when Cyr cuts me off.

"You can."

Cyr's reply has my mouth drying up and all words evading me. I raise an eyebrow in question. The slight rumble that comes from his bare, tattooed chest makes me smile. Even the smallest of laughs that come from Cyr make me the happiest I would ever be.

He releases my chin and brings his hands down to take hold of my own. I continue to eye him curiously, watching intently as he brings my hands up to cup both sides of his cheeks. My touch is gentle as I graze my thumbs across the soft black cotton of his mask. My jaw gapes as he tucks my fingers behind the straps that keep his mask in place by his ears. Cyr drops his hands down into his lap, his breathing completely even, and now, I'm entirely in control.

My eyes meet his, stunned and awe-struck, "Are you sure?"

His cheeks shift under his mask, and I know he's smiling. The silent nod of affirmation from him is all I need. I think back to the day in the parlor a few months ago, and how I didn't want anything to change. I realized that nothing would have changed, and hated myself for even believing that it would change anything between us. The bond we've built together through trust, heartbreak, and love will supersede the test of time as I knew it.

With gentle grace, my fingertips unhook the straps behind both of his ears and slowly bring the mask down from his face.

I'm speechless. Absolutely fucking speechless.

The mask slips from my fingers to fall on my lap. I take in

every single inch of the beauty I've deprived myself of for so long. That olive-tanned skin shines as bright as the sun, and I've never seen anything remotely as brilliant in my whole life.

I reach a hand out to touch his cheek but instantly pull it back to my chest. My eyes quickly dart to him for permission, and a smirk slips up his lips revealing a dimple in the corner of his cheek.

Gods above that dimple.

If my heart hadn't entirely melted yet from the sight of it, it sure as hell is now a puddle on the floor.

"You said you'd kiss them away, right?"

His voice is husky, and every kind of sensual. I can't help but return the smirk as I slowly reach over to run my fingertips along his cheekbone. There, beneath my touch, lay three diagonal claw marks from his cheekbone down to his chin. It breaks my heart into a million pieces knowing that a woman I used to care so deeply for was capable of such a horrible thing. It's still raised on his skin even after two years of healing. Tears well in my eyes as I gaze to the other cheek where a single mark runs from mid-cheek to the corner of his lip. A few tears spill over my cheeks as I take in the pain he must have felt, and the torture she put him through.

"Don't, Raven. There's no need for that."

"I just can't believe she…" I trail off, my words choking me as I quietly sob. Cyr brings his hands up to brush them off my face.

"What happened is in a past life. Right now, I'm here with you. And you are the only thing that matters to me." I smile at his words through my tears, sniffling softly, "I wouldn't have let you see this if I wasn't ready. I trust you, and I know you wouldn't ever do this to me."

I could never physically take any pain or anger out on him to this degree and it makes my heart swell knowing he trusts me so much. I don't know what caused Jamie to do this to him, but it didn't matter. *She* didn't matter. The only good thing she did for me was lead me to Cyr. I wouldn't be the same without him in my life, and can't imagine this life without him.

With a steadying breath to calm my tears, I lean in close to him and start with the set of scars along his cheek. I place a gentle kiss on each one from his cheekbone down to his chin. He takes a deep inhale as my lips meet his scarred skin, but his breathing remains even. I pull back to see Cyr with his eyes closed, and a gentle smile along his lips.

"And the other cheek?"

Cocky bastard.

I laugh softly at his comment and continue my kisses on the other cheek, leaving small kisses down his scar, stopping right before his lips. My eyes flick upward to him and meet his eyes already on me.

"I think you missed a spot."

My lips turn fully up into a smile, laughing at him for a moment. Cyr smiles wide, and Gods above it's the most beautiful sight I have ever seen. Just as I can't physically believe he can be any more perfect, that second dimple makes an appearance on his other cheek.

Without another second of hesitation, my hands lift to cup both of his cheeks, and I lean in to press my lips against his. It's a gentle kiss, his lips gentle against mine. As I pull back, it's only for a second in time to see Cyr smirk, and I combust. I crash my lips back to his, and he meets mine with the same intensity. His hands trail around my hips, and his arms wrap so tightly around my torso as if I was about to float away.

The kiss is deep, real, and filled with so much longing the two of us have pent up over the past year. Cyr's tongue presses against my lips requesting access to my mouth. I willingly open for him, and our tongues clash while exploring every inch of each other. My hands run up the back of his neck and entangle themselves into his hair, tugging lightly. A moan escapes from low in Cyr's throat, echoing into my mouth at the contact between us. I want to close the distance even further causing myself to slide across his lap and grind against him. The pleasure rips through me from his hard length hitting every sensitive spot below me, and the feeling of Cyr's lips against mine send me into a permanent state of euphoria.

Cyr pulls away quickly, chest heaving as he breathlessly speaks, "Are you ready, Raven?"

His words are raspy and sensual. I can feel myself dampening from his words alone. As I attempt to catch up on my breathing rattling my chest, I raise an eyebrow in question.

"Ready for what?"

The sight of those eyes boring into my soul, and those lips I can finally see all puffy and swollen from my teeth.

I feel his hands traveling up my back and one of his hands balls my hair into a fist, tugging my head back. A moan escapes me as his soft lips caress the skin along the side of my neck. Cyr bites down gently causing me to gasp, and my hands tighten their grip on his black locks.

"You're in for a long night ahead of you." His words rumble against my throat, and another moan leaves my lips at the promise. Cyr's tongue trails up my throat, and his hand tugs my hair back to give him further access.

"Gods, yes."

The words escape from my lips in a breathy moan, begging

this moment to never cease.

"Yes, what?"

Cyr's tone is hard steel and pure dominance as his grip loosens, releasing his grip on my hair to allow my head down to face him entirely. I sigh longingly and drop my hands from his hair to rest in my lap, bowing my head.

"Yes, sir."

"Good girl, Raven."

Cyr's touch against my chin brings my eyes back up to meet his. I gaze at him through hooded lashes with a devilish smirk. He leans in and nips at my bottom lip, releasing a squeal from me. Cyr chuckles and leans back against the headboard with his hands placed behind his head.

"Go on, you know what I like."

"Yes, daddy."

The words leave my lips before I can think about what I've just said. I bite down hard on my bottom lip and my eyes widen. A second later a blush quickly rises across my cheeks turning them a bright shade of rose. Cyr's jaw gapes and a smirk creeps up his lips. Apparently, the phrase was the right thing to say as the evidence of his arousal grows.

"Fuck it. Come here."

Cyr's hand wraps around the base of my neck and pulls my lips to him, crashing together in the most beautiful and raw of ways. I never experienced anything like it and knew it would always be Cyr who I ran to. When times grew hard, or I couldn't bear the weight on my shoulders, Cyr would always be there to carry me. With that knowledge, I fall fully and deeply into his kiss, begging it to never stop.

✳✳✳

Time slows to a halt, and I don't even know what year it is

anymore. Cyr praises and worships me over the hours and I'm not even sure what my name is by the end. He takes his time feasting on every place imaginable until I can't bear to stand, literally. Cyr carries me to the en-suite bathroom and takes his time cleaning me off from head to toe. He shampoos and conditions my hair thoroughly before attending to his own body. I cling to him for support as he soaps up a washcloth and attends to my body, then his own. Cyr makes sure all the soap from my hair and body has been rinsed before lifting under my thighs to hook them around his waist and sending me over the edge of ecstasy once again in the shower.

After another quick rinse, Cyr helps dry me off and slips one of his t-shirts over my bosy. The shirt falls mid-thigh on me and I know from the way Cyr can't take his eyes off me that he much rather prefers me in his clothing or nothing at all. Much against my protests that my legs work perfectly fine, Cyr lifts me into his arms to cradle me close to his chest. My head rests gently against his shoulder and I wrap my arms around his neck. Once we reach his bed, he lays me down gently beside him, tucking me into his side.

"Raven, are you alright?"

Cyr's words are gentle as he reaches over to tilt my chin upwards to face him. It's still a shock to see that chiseled jaw and sensuous lips in my line of sight.

"Why would I have any reason not to be?" I reply softly, slowly bringing a hand up to graze my fingertips across his cheek. I only hope the love I feel for him is as clear as day in my eyes as it has been for some time now.

Cyr closes his eyes for a brief time, resting his head against my hand for a moment. When he opens them, they're glossy. The sight stuns me, and I quickly sit upright and pull my hand back to my chest.

"I'm sorry, did I-"

Cyr faces me, shaking his head, "No, Bellamy. You didn't do anything other than show me that I'm capable of being loved again."

Every thought eddies from my head, and my own eyes well with tears. The smile that once graced my features returned, and Cyr's wide smile utterly and completely melts my heart. I lean forward across his chest and place a gentle kiss on his lips.

"I guess since you already know I don't need to say it but…" I say softly against his lips, and Cyr pulls back a little to meet my gaze with a questioning raise of his eyebrow.

"I love you, Cyr Maddox."

A quick exhale leaves his lips as if he'd been holding his breath while he waited for me to finish my thought. Cyr brings my lips back to meet his and with a firm grasp on my hips he lifts me to sit across his lap. He quickly dips me in front of his chest releasing a slight squeal to leave my lips. Cyr's soft chuckle reverberates against my lips as his arm wraps protectively around my torso, while the other supports my head in front of him.

After a breathless kiss, his words are soft against my lips, "I love you too, Bellamy Tyler."

As the campus bell tower chimes midnight and fireworks erupt, I ring out the New Year tangled up in the sheets with the love of my life. A sign that this year will be the start of many beautiful years to come with Cyr at my side.

30

The Graduation

"How long does it take to do your hair, Bell!? We're going to be late!"

Clara whines from outside the bathroom door. I roll my eyes, finishing up by curling the ends of my hair to fall over my shoulders in loose ringlets.

"It's not like it would be the end of the world if we missed it," I tease in response. The bathroom door bursts open to a wide-eyed Clara, eyeing me incredulously.

"I've busted my balls to get this degree so I'm going to be pissed if we miss our *graduation* on account your hair doesn't look perfect."

She props her hands on her hips and a laugh bursts from my lips as I can't remember the last time Clara was this serious about anything. Clara reaches over and pulls on one of my curls to flatten it and I squeal, batting her hand away from my hard work.

"Now it's your fault we're going to be late," I say, returning to my curling.

"You always look perfect, Bell, what makes today the day

you have to try something new for your hair?" Clara asks, leaning in the doorway, still semi-annoyed but her level of sass significantly lessens.

"My parents flew in this morning for this. I'm their only child, not like your parents who had five graduations to attend. I'm doing this for them," I reply, biting the inside of my cheek in concentration as the last perfect ringlet falls from my curling iron.

"Trust me, my parents are stoked to not have to do this anymore," Clara retorts, laughing softly at my concentration face and I flip her off before unplugging the curling iron to cool down. I spin to face her and my best friend smiles at me, pulling me in for a hug.

"I ironed your dress for you," She says as we hold each other tightly.

Not having Clara in my life twenty-four-seven is going to be a drastic shift in my life's tectonic plates. She's been a driving force for me for years and to say it's going to be an emotional day would be an understatement. I hear Clara sniffle and I pull back, scolding her.

"Don't you dare fucking cry. Not now. You can cry when all this shit is over with. If you have to redo your makeup we won't make it to the ceremony until tomorrow."

Clara shoos my hand away and we share a laugh, returning to the bedroom to change for our long-awaited big day.

***

Clara and I depart from our dorm to join the hundreds of other students cramming the hallways as we all head towards the football field for the ceremony. The halls echo with cries of joy and laughter and a few distinct cries of sadness from departing dorm mates. I know Clara and I will be joining those crying from the separation of dearly beloved friends we've come to cherish over the past few years soon enough.

Today is a day of celebration for the accomplishments we've achieved throughout our college careers, but also a celebration of the friendships and relationships we've made that have pulled us through the rough patches. I know without Clara I would already be in a nameless, shallow grave.

We carry on with the hoard of others heading to the field, arms linked to not lose each other in the chaos. Some people push and shove through the crowded halls toward the exit of the dormitory while others run against the flow of traffic to retrieve forgotten items from their rooms. My cap and gown are tucked into the crook of my arm to not lose them as others who are already dressed in their gowns are tripping over the length as we clobber out of the main building.

The early summer breeze whips around me, giving me the much-needed air I've been deprived of in the stuffy dorm hallway. I inhale deeply, taking in the scent of the flowers blooming around the courtyard, exhaling slowly through my nose. With the newfound space to breathe and walk properly, I help Clara into her gown and she does the same for me. I keep my cap in my hand as we walk hand in hand behind the rest of the graduating crowd.

"Where are your parents?" Clara asks from beside me.

"They're already in the bleachers. Momma said they'd come to find us down here when it's over," I reply, raising my voice to call over the rising sound of chatter. The volume grows as we reach the track surrounding the football field. My eyes scan up the giant set of bleachers next to us, scanning over the hundreds of parents eagerly awaiting to see their children graduate.

"Where's the Adonis?" Clara questions, referring to the

nickname she uses for Cyr, following my gaze in search of her parents and siblings. My eyes start to cross from all the faces which forces my eyes back to Clara and I shrug a shoulder. My eyes begin to scan the crowd around us.

"I'm not sure. He said he'd come to find me once we were down at the track," I say, biting the edge of my lip as I search. He's taller than most so finding him shouldn't be as hard a feat as it's becoming. A pinch of dread fills my stomach that maybe he's still sitting in his dorm room afraid of being in this large of a crowd.

"Oh. My. God," Clara utters barely louder than a whisper.

My head turns to follow her line of sight and my jaw drops at the sight of Cyr off to the side by the bleachers away from the crowd. His black leather shoes are polished to perfection with black dress pants neatly ironed. Cyr's white button-up shirt is rolled up to his elbows showing all the ink swirling around his forearms making him look impossibly more attractive and a black tie neatly pressed down the center of his shirt.

The cause of Clara's statement is evident as my eyes continue up to find Cyr's beautiful face completely void of his mask. My mouth dries up entirely as I gawk at the gorgeous man, observing the passing crowd who paid absolutely no heed to him. For the first time, I'm seeing Cyr completely relaxed and not in a state of constant panic due to his agoraphobia and it warms every inch of my soul.

"Go snatch up your man, babes!" Clara squeals, shoving me from behind over toward Cyr's direction. I snap my head to her, rolling my eyes over dramatically with a laugh, making my way to Cyr as quickly as my heels will allow. Before I make it to him, his eyes meet mine and I can't help the smile that blooms across my cheeks. His lips curl up on one side and the sight of that dimple on his cheek makes my heart melt into a puddle in front of me.

"Raven," He croons, taking a few strides to meet me halfway. I bite down on the corner of my lip as I feel a blush creeping up my cheeks.

"Cyr," I reply and fall into his chest as he opens his arms to accept me. Once I'm within an arm's distance, he wraps his arms around my shoulders and my arms coil around his waist. A feather-light kiss sends a shiver down my spine as his lips meet the top of my head. I melt into his embrace, inhaling the scent of his cologne for a few moments. Cyr pulls away slowly, taking hold of my hand to spin me in a slow circle. His predatory gaze makes me feel as if I'm naked in front of him.

"You look beautiful," Cyr says with a bit of a husky tone that has my panties instantly wet in front of him. I smile through the blush turning my face into the shade of a tomato.

"Thank you, it has pockets!"

My tone comes out more giddy than it probably should be over a dress with pockets. As I swish the baby blue sundress side to side, my free hand finds the pocket to show him for emphasis.

A belly laugh erupts from Cyr and he squeezes my hand before abruptly pulling me into his chest. My free hand flies up to catch myself against his hard chest, flicking my eyes up to meet those shimmering blue eyes that captivate my heart, body, and soul.

"Is it a universal girl code that you have to tell everyone your dress has pockets?" Cyr asks, tightening his hold with both arms around my waist. I shoot him a glare, eyes narrowing, and give him a light poke to the chest in mock anger.

"What? You don't like my dress?"

Cyr leans in close to my ear, his warm breath making the hair on my neck stand up on end.

"I love your dress, Raven, but I'd much rather see it on my bedroom floor."

My head tucks into his chest in all attempts to conceal how heated my body is and the fact I don't want the entire graduating class to see me turn stark red. Cyr nips at my earlobe and I give him another light tap, gently pushing back from him to give me enough space to breathe. Being this close to him sucks all of the oxygen from my lungs, trying my best to calm my racing heart and molten core.

"Keep it up and we're going to miss graduation," I mutter and Cyr has the absolute audacity to raise an eyebrow at me, gesturing his head toward the direction of the dormitory. I roll my eyes, "You're unbelievable, you know that right?"

"I think last night made that pretty evident," He replies, smirking and I damn near smack that wicked smirk from his perfect lips.

Last night we'd spent every waking hour devouring each other and tangled in his sheets until the sun came up. If it wasn't for Clara calling me repeatedly to come back to our dorm to change would I even have made it here on time this morning.

"C'mon lovebirds! Showtime!" Clara calls from behind us before following the crowd toward the lineup of other students preparing to walk to the stage.

My gaze turns to Clara for a moment, giving her a nod when soft skin grazes beneath my chin. With a swift pull of my chin to face him, Cyr's lips capture mine, stealing my heart with one breathless kiss. When he pulls back, my eyes are still hazy from my state of love-drunkenness which has a smile tugging up the ends of his cheeks.

"Are you with me, Raven?"

"I'm with you."

***

Caps erupting into the skies around us has cheers, screams of excitement, and cries of joy echoing across the field. A few different caps bump me in the head as they fall but Clara and I burst into laughter, bringing our hands up to shield ourselves from the bombardment. I hear low chuckling from next to me as Cyr observes us making a spectacle of protecting our hair from ruination. I flip him off as the rest of the caps fall to the ground in piles all around the football field. A smirk crosses his lips which makes me lose every ounce of myself and the urge to climb him like a tree nearly wins in that moment.

Cyr catches me off guard and my eyes widen to the size of dinner plates as he bends down onto one knee. My hands fly to my mouth, covering the absolute shock splaying across my face as Cyr glances up to meet my gaze.

"What? My shoe came untied," Cyr says, that smirk growing even wider across his face. My face turns into the physical embodiment of mortification as I quickly spin, my head falling onto Clara's shoulder.

What the fuck was I thinking?! Gods above spare me. I might actually die and the worst part is that he is NEVER going to let me forget what I happened to mistake such a mundane act of tying his damn shoe for.

Clara is completely oblivious to the situation as she's hooting and hollering with the rest of our graduating class in the celebration. I hear a quick gasp muffled by Clara's hand slapping against her mouth, causing me to lift my beet-red face to see what's happening.

"Raven?" Cyr's voice enters the air from behind me. After

350

seeing Clara's eyes nearly bulge from her head, I quickly spin around to see Cyr still on one knee behind me. Only this time when I look down, a small silver band ring with a shimmering opal in the middle is pinched between his index finger and his thumb. After scolding myself for reacting the first time, I wasn't sure how to filter the shock flooding my body.

"Holy hell. You're serious this time."

"Is that a yes?" He asks with a low laugh.

My eyes widen incredulously, "You didn't even ask the question!"

He cocks an eyebrow at me, "Do I really need to?"

"Yes!" I shout, laughing as the nerves finally hit me, my hands shaking in front of me. Cyr's eyes widen slightly and I roll my eyes, "And no, that was not my answer!"

Cyr reaches out, taking my trembling left hand to hold it with his own.

"Bellamy Adelaide Tyler, let me spend the rest of my life proving to you each and every day how much you've made me a better man. Will you marry me?"

Inexplicable joy floods my body from my head to my toes but I attempt to mask it and take my opposite hand, tapping my lips with my index finger.

"I'll have to think about it."

Cyr rolls his eyes and a laugh bursts from my lips, meeting his gaze as my eyes turn glassy.

"Yes, Cyr. My forever has always been yours."

A smile brighter than the sun spreads across Cyr's lips as he slips the ring onto my finger. The sensation of feeling a physical presence to his claim on me is unlike anything I've ever felt before. My heart bursts with pride as Cyr stands, wrapping his arms around my waist and lifting me into the air. Another burst of cheers rings out around us as he spins me around, laying claim to my lips and kissing me so passionately as if the world around us no longer exists. In this celestial plane, there's only him and I, and no force on Earth will change that.

As the crowds disperse, Cyr and I walk hand in hand toward my parents who wait on the edge of the track with Kora and Ryker. The smile on my mother's face and the tears streaming down her cheeks have me bursting into tears alongside her. She pulls me in for a tight hug, my father joining in on the group hug engulfing us both.

My mother pulls away and looks to Cyr, offering an arm out to include him in the group hug. After a moment he steps forward to wrap an arm around my mother and me. My mind reels and I pull back slightly to look up at Cyr.

"When did you ask them?"

Cyr's gaze meets mine and the smirk climbing up his cheek, I realize, is the only answer I'm going to receive from him. I roll my eyes as he laughs and my mother steps away to wrap her arm around my dad, both of them smiling with glossy eyes. Cyr plants a kiss to my temple and the bliss exploding through my body is unparalleled.

I notice my mother hasn't stopped looking at Cyr and it makes me question why, but then it hits me. My parents have never seen Cyr without his mask as I have these past few months since New Year's.

I'm instantly caught off guard from my thoughts as Kora instantly tackles me into a bear hug.

"I've always wanted a sister."

My heart is already so full, her words nearly send it bursting from my chest.

"Me too," I reply, brushing away tears from Kora's cheeks as she does the same for me. Ryker walks up beside us and wraps an arm around my shoulder to pull me in for a side hug. The Goliath towers over me, but the strength in his hug is gentle, maybe more so a friendly giant than a Goliath after all.

"I didn't want another sister, but I guess this keeps Kora off our asses for a while now. Welcome to the family, sis," Ryker says, and as Cyr sidles up beside me, the four of us share a laugh that truly makes the day shine even brighter on us.

***

"Am I allowed to cry now?" Clara asks as Cyr closes the trunk of her car and I nod, the two of us bursting into tears as we engulf each other in a soul-crushing embrace.

I would never have another love in my heart as I do for Clara. She pulled me out of the lowest points I've ever felt in my life and I couldn't be more grateful for her. As Clara heads off to grad school for her Master's in Maine next fall, this will be the longest we'll be apart in almost three years. We sniffle and cry for as long as we need to when a pair of strong arms falls over both of our shoulders.

"I feel left out," Cyr mumbles pathetically from above our heads which has the tears subsiding and the laughs erupting from all of us.

"I'm still going to be your Maid of Honor, right?" Clara asks, wiping her tears away from her cheeks with the back of her hand.

"You might have to fight Kora for that spot, babe."

I wince inwardly at the look of shock on Clara's face.

"I've known you longer that's not fair!" She fake pouts for a minute before smiling, "Even if your decision is the wrong one, I'll still respect it."

"Oh, how gracious of you," I retort with an eye roll, a soft smile settling on my lips, "Drive safe, okay? Call me when you get home."

Clara laughs incredulously, shaking her head, "I've got an hour's drive home, I'll be fine. You guys drive safe! You've got a hell of a journey ahead of you."

"Ain't that the truth," Cyr says, wrapping an arm around my shoulder and tucking me into his side. I roll my eyes at him before returning my gaze to Clara who is looking at us like we're newborn puppies.

"I told you once before and I'll say it again, Maddox. You hurt her, and no one will find your body," She says with a sickly sweet smile. I reach out pulling her in for a final hug.

"I love you, Clara."

"I love you too, babe."

She pulls away a moment later and blows me a kiss. Clara hops into her car and I wave to her car until it disappears from the campus parking lot. A heavy weight fills my chest as I watch her go and a sigh escapes my lips.

Cyr's fingers pull up my chin to face him and I drink in those beautiful blue eyes that have pulled me out of the darkest depths and into the light. His lips find mine, soft and gentle, and as I believe I couldn't possibly fall even further in love with him.

I do.

"Are you with me, Raven?" Cyr whispers against my lips.

"I'm with you."